LORD ANGUISH

Beastly Lords Book Two

SYDNEY JANE BAILY

cat whisker press
Massachusetts

This book is a work of fiction. Names, characters, places, and incidents either are products of the author's imagination or are used fictitiously. Any resemblance to actual events or locales or persons, living or dead, is entirely coincidental.

Copyright © 2019, 2020 Sydney Jane Baily

All rights reserved under International and Pan-American Copyright Conventions.

No part of this book may be reproduced or transmitted in any form or by any means, electronic or mechanical, including photocopying, recording, or by any information storage and retrieval system without written permission from the publisher, except for the inclusion of brief quotations in a review or article.

ISBN: 978-1-938732-35-5
Published by **cat whisker press**
Imprint of JAMES-YORK PRESS

Cover: **cat whisker studio**
In conjunction with Philip Ré
Book Design: **cat whisker studio**

DEDICATION

To Victoria "Vickie" Piercey

A generous heart, a true friend, a strong woman

OTHER WORKS
by
SYDNEY JANE BAILY

THE RARE CONFECTIONERY
Series

The Duchess of Chocolate
The Toffee Heiress
My Lady Marzipan

THE DEFIANT HEARTS
Series

An Improper Situation
An Irresistible Temptation
An Inescapable Attraction
An Inconceivable Deception
An Intriguing Proposition
An Impassioned Redemption

THE BEASTLY LORDS
Series

Lord Despair
Lord Anguish
Lord Vile
Lord Darkness
Lord Misery
Lord Wrath
Eleanor

PRESENTING LADY GUS

A Georgian-Era Novella

ACKNOWLEDGMENTS

Thanks to my editor, Violetta Rand, who made me rethink and who caught my errors. And, as always, thanks to my beloved mom!

PROLOGUE

1848, Turvey House, Bedfordshire, England

Nothing in his rather pampered existence had prepared him for this. John Angsley, Earl of Cambrey, lay upon his back with his severely broken leg in a plaster cast and raised in a sling. Utterly impossible for him to roll over or even change positions, he cursed loudly. It had been a mere few days since he'd taken his last sip of laudanum, and he'd never imagined how quickly the pain would take over.

Not only pain. Every bloody ailment known to man seemed to be visiting itself upon him. Including nausea.

Sitting up as best he could, he grabbed for the bowl at his side and heaved up the contents of his stomach. Thankfully, because his gut hurt all the time, both when taking the tincture of opium and even more so since stopping, he'd barely eaten. Dry-retching, as it turned out, wasn't any more pleasant than heaving on a full stomach.

It was an hour or more past midnight. Even the servants were probably sound asleep. With that irritating notion, he yelled as loudly as he could and then yanked the bell pull, which was more effective in bringing help but not nearly as satisfying as using his lungs to their full capacity.

Shivering and sweating at the same time, aching from his neck to his buttocks and on down through both his good leg and his injured one, he waited for his valet.

After a few minutes, there was a tap on the door, and Peter entered.

Lucky man, Cam thought, to be walking in on two feet, looking perfectly hearty but for his rumpled hair. In fact, his valet was infuriatingly normal, except for the fact he was wearing no jacket and his waistcoat was inside out.

The last detail was the only thing which made Cam feel any better. He had startled his usually immaculate valet out of bed and into his clothing at such a rate, the man had barely been able to dress himself.

Perhaps he should mention it and dock some of his wages. Punish the healthy bastard!

Sighing, Cam wondered who the hell he was becoming.

"Take the bowl and fetch me something."

Peter bowed and reached for the porcelain containing barely more than bile.

"Fetch you what, my lord?"

Cam wanted to say, "The damned opium, of course," but he didn't. That path led to nothing but more stomach aches, wool-headed thinking, and strange dreams, although the bliss of painless days and nights was worth it. Nearly.

Besides, he'd told Peter not to bring him the bottle of laudanum no matter how he begged. How humiliating!

"Bring me brandy. Warmed, I suppose." Would it help him sleep through the painful, vile symptoms that had resulted since he'd stopped taking opium? He doubted it. More likely, the brandy would either come up or go through him, resulting in the other disgusting outcome.

"Go!" he yelled at Peter who was hesitating, possibly awaiting more orders.

How Cam wished he could shed his mortal coil entirely, but only for a short while. He wanted to live through this hell. He wanted to walk again. And more than anything, he wanted to lay eyes upon Margaret Blackwood once more.

CHAPTER ONE

Six months earlier

The Earl of Cambrey, had a choice—another evening at his club surrounded by good friends and good brandy or a long, potentially boring evening at Lord and Lady Marechal's. He chose the latter. After all, along with the music and the insipid young misses, the burnt champagne and sweetmeats, and the puffed-up dandies came the chance to see Miss Margaret Blackwood.

God, if any of his friends ever knew what a mooncalf he had become over the Blackwood girl, why, he'd be drummed out of the clubs. Yet, there was something about her.

True, that *something* wasn't subtle. Every damn young buck at every event all Season saw what Cam saw—her attractive figure, shining caramel-colored hair, gold-flecked eyes which danced when she laughed, and a smile that absolutely took his breath away. And all of this she used to devastating effect.

Unfortunately, she used it on every man jack who came her way. He would have welcomed her showing him a modicum of favoritism, considering they'd met before the Season even began because Margaret's older sister had married his best friend, Simon Devere, and he was the damn Earl of Cambrey!

Yes, it would be nice to be shown a little partiality.

Perhaps she did have a special interest in him. They had spent considerable time together since her mother and two sisters had come early to London. Not only had he dined at the Devere townhouse, Cam and Margaret had sat next to each other at a cricket match at the newly opened Fenner's Ground and cheered the players together. Another time, they'd laughed—as discreetly as possible, of course—when a particularly untalented soprano failed to hit her notes, or any notes, for that matter, on the Sadler's Wells stage.

Nevertheless, under and over his name on Margaret's dance cards were always many other gentlemen's, including Westing, a man younger than Cam by at least seven years, which stung.

It wasn't like Cam was ancient, but at twenty-eight, he was nearly a decade older than Miss Blackwood.

Maybe she was simply too young.

Too fickle.

He groaned when she entered the ballroom with her mother and her older sister.

Too damnably beautiful!

MAGGIE LOVED THE SEASON and everything about it. As much as her older sister, Jenny, thought it frivolous, impractical, even tedious, Maggie thought it exciting, titillating, and, of course, utterly necessary. Her debut Season the year before had been cut short by the death of her father. In quick order, what was left of her family, namely her mother and two sisters with a few servants, had been forced to move out of London. Maggie had left behind her hopes for a well-matched future.

Selling their lovely townhouse had not been easy. Moving back into their small cottage in Sheffield and being forced to become a French tutor had been excruciating. She'd been cut off from all her friends, including her dearest one, Ada, another baron's daughter with expectations of finding a good husband.

And then, thank her lucky stars, her older sister had caught the eye of the Earl of Lindsey, and before one could dance thrice around the Maypole, they had married.

Thus, here Maggie was, with the full social season ahead of her and new gowns. Life was bliss!

What's more, she'd caught the eye of the worldly Earl of Cambrey, who cut quite a dashing figure. Something about him caused her insides to sizzle in an unfamiliar and dangerous manner. However, she feared looking too eager in his eyes, or anyone's, for that matter. Moreover, she didn't want to settle on the first man to capture her attention.

John, as she privately thought of him, was as old as her sister's new husband. Not that he was too old for her, but she feared he might not share her same sense of fun. Perhaps he would want to sit out each dance or demand she produce babies immediately as Jenny was doing, already with child mere months into her marriage.

No, Maggie wanted to live a little before she experienced such a terrifying adventure, all too aware it might cut her life extremely short indeed. She knew of two ladies in their circle of acquaintances who had died in childbirth this past year.

Shuddering, she forced herself to send happy thoughts toward Jenny who would give birth in the fall. *Please, God, let her have an easy and safe delivery.*

"Why are you looking like that?" her mother asked. "With such an expression of worry, you're making a frown line, and no one will approach you."

Her mother was wrong, of course. No sooner did Maggie set foot on the parquet floor than half a dozen gentlemen jockeyed for position to put their names upon her dance card.

"A moment, if you will, *boys*," she teased, knowing she was being impudent. Obviously, one shouldn't call Lords Fowler and Welkes by such a term. But Maggie did. What's more, she knew she could get away with it. Despite her beauty, she would not have deigned to do so were she still *poor Maggie Blackwood from Sheffield*, whose father, the baron, died penniless.

However, as Miss Margaret Blackwood, sister-in-law to the Earl of Lindsey and residing in the Devere townhouse on Portman Square, she was a coveted eligible. She could get away with teasing, and more.

When the crush of gentlemen dissipated, she spied Lord Cambrey standing casually yet assuredly, drink in one hand, expression of mild amusement upon his handsome face. No, she could not think of *him* as a boy, nor ever call him such without embarrassing herself. He was the only one with whom she got a little tongue-tied, felt the flutter of nerves in her stomach, the only one who caused her a bit of unease.

She liked that about him. Immensely.

Furthermore, her worries he might be stuffy had turned out to be completely unfounded. They'd already had barrels of fun, sharing a similar sense of humor and a passion for cricket. What's more, in his strong arms, on the dance floor, Maggie moved lightly and effortlessly with the earl as a superbly confident lead.

Yes, John was high on her list of bachelors, and apparently, he was waiting his turn to write on her dance card.

Setting his glass down, he greeted all three of them.

"Lady Blackwood," he addressed her mother, taking her hand and bowing over it.

"Lady Lindsey," he greeted Maggie's sister in turn. Unfortunately, Jenny looked, as usual, as if she would rather be elsewhere than at a society event. While not yet showing, at least not to the unaware eye, with her husband away on business, her sister seemed unable to enjoy herself.

Maggie rolled her eyes. Jenny was a countess and her life was set, for goodness sake!

John turned to her next. As their gazes briefly met and held, she felt a frisson of delicious anticipation for the evening ahead. Then he bowed low over her hand and brought it to his lips.

"Miss Blackwood."

"Lord Cambrey," she murmured.

When he raised his head, they held each other's gaze another moment, a deliciously long moment, until she felt her lips turn up in an involuntary smile.

What was it about this man that tickled her fancy?

Was it his appearance? Naturally, she thought him a fine-looking man. His hair, the color of rich coffee, and his hazel eyes were appealing, as well as his infectious grin. She liked the height and breadth of him, too. Beyond all that, his turn of phrase, his oft-unique opinions, and his delightfully wicked laugh were utterly charming.

Oh dear, was she mooning over the man?

Blushing slightly, Maggie realized they were all moving as a group of four, claiming a cloth-covered table on the outskirts of the dance floor. Like soldiers setting up camp, they draped their shawls over the chairs and lay their reticules upon the table, knowing here, inside the sanctioned private ballroom, there was little fear of thieves.

The musicians were still warming up for the long evening ahead. Excitement rippled through the room, or maybe Maggie simply imagined everyone was feeling the way she was. Except Jenny.

Soon enough, Maggie was claimed by the first man on her card, Lord Whitely, a viscount's son whose nose was pointy but whose eyelashes were long, fanning over intelligent eyes. And the waltz began.

CAM FOUND IT EASY to converse with his best friend's wife, especially when they spoke about either her husband, Simon, who was away doing God knew what on the Continent, or her charming sister.

While chatting amiably with Jenny, he kept an eye on Margaret who had positively boundless energy, starting near the lead of the Grand March and not sitting out even a single quadrille. As long as she kept up her lively movements, he wasn't too worried about her or her dance partners. After all, it was not the easiest thing to do—to carry on a conversation while not missing a step. Thus, the dancers mostly danced with little more interaction than a smile or a grimace if they trod on each other's toes.

Stop it, he ordered himself. It wasn't his place to consider whether she was engaging in one of her delightful dialogues with a dance partner. He had no claim to her. *Yet*.

Eventually, after about forty minutes, the musicians needed a break, and everyone surged toward the refreshment tables.

Having already secured drinks for Jenny and her mother, Cam was free to wander into the crowd and see if he could assist Margaret.

He found her easily since he'd never truly taken his attention from her, stunning as she was in the palest shade of blue, which seemed to make her glow like an angel. Luckily, instead of a preening buck with whom he'd have to make inane chatter, she was with another young miss, looking equally excited to be a part of the event.

Sighing at how old they made him feel, Cam approached and nodded to each.

"May I assist you ladies in getting some lemonade?"

"How kind of you," Margaret answered at once. "Dancing does make one thirsty. Lord Cambrey, do you know Miss Ada Ellis?"

He bowed to the flaxen-haired miss, who to him, looked washed out beside Margaret's honey-brown hair and warm eyes.

"I don't believe we've had the pleasure. If you both will stay somewhere close, I will procure you each a glass of refreshingly tart nectar."

Ada giggled behind her fan, and Margaret rolled her eyes at his over-the-top chivalry.

Bowing slightly, he left them, pushing his way through the crowd before being stopped by a wall of black and gray-clad jackets in front of the refreshment tables. Servants were filling glasses as quickly as they could, and still, there was a delay.

Minutes later, he returned to the spot where he'd left the ladies, swearing silently only once when someone jostled him, causing him to spill lemonade on his sleeve.

However, when he reached the place where the ladies had been, there was no lovely Margaret. Scowling, he scanned the room. To his annoyance, he saw her a few yards away. Still in her friend's company, although now chatting with two men. Most likely flirting. And they all four held a glass of the cursed lemonade.

"The deuce take them!" Cam said loudly enough for a passing couple to hear. When they paused with their raised eyebrows, he merely bowed politely.

"May I offer you these refreshments?" he asked.

Their expressions changed to relief, and they took the glasses from him with gratitude.

No doubt he'd made friends for life, saving them from having to wait in the blasted line.

Stalking back to the table, he sat down heavily in the chair next to Jenny, back to the wall, with a good view of the proceedings.

"Don't you have an obligation, my lord?" Simon's wife asked.

Dragging his gaze from the crowd, he smiled at her. "Pardon?"

"To dance. Isn't that why a single man comes to a ball during the Season?"

Cam supposed she was right. What's more, he'd been beyond rude to her.

"Would *you* care to dance, Lady Lindsey? It would be my honor."

"Absolutely not," Jenny declared. "In any case, you're not supposed to waste your bachelorhood by dancing with a married woman. That practically goes against the rules. I am utterly superfluous here. You, however, are not."

He watched her survey the room, and he did the same. Except for Margaret's card, he hadn't bothered to set his name down elsewhere, for he didn't really think he was going to suddenly fall in love and find a wife during an exuberant mazurka.

"I see more than one miss with a downturned mouth who would, I'm sure, be extremely grateful if you asked them. That one there, for instance." Jenny nodded behind his shoulder.

Turning, Cam saw Lady Adelia Smythe tapping her toe and watching the dancers from beside a large fern. He had actually danced with her at a different ball and thought her agreeable enough, although she had a laugh which grated on his ears, braying like a stubborn mule in the hot sun.

Sighing loudly at his own unkind thoughts, he stood up, deciding to ask the lady and fervently hoping someone would do the same for his cousin Beryl when it was her turn to come out into society.

"Bravo, my lord," Jenny said, causing Cam to produce a sheepish smile. He wasn't a war hero like her husband. He was merely going to dance with a wallflower. What's more, he wasn't even doing it very graciously. For in his heart, he acknowledged he would rather be dancing with Margaret and was keeping track of the dances until it was his turn.

If he hadn't miscounted, then he would claim her after three more dances for a polka.

Meanwhile, a simple galop, if Lady Smythe wasn't otherwise occupied, would at least get him onto the floor and within smiling range of Margaret.

MAGGIE WAS GETTING WINDED. However, the musicians were extremely adept, their notes bright and clear, and the dances were so enjoyable, alternating between formations and couples, she didn't want to stop. One dance later, though, her partner twisted his knee doing an improvisational movement, and they had to leave the floor.

As she approached her family's table, her mother was berating her older sister for frowning. Poor Jenny, it was her normal expression now, and Maggie wished with all her heart her brother-in-law would return soon from his business trip to claim his melancholy wife.

"I wish you would dance," she told Jenny. Certainly, no one could frown while dancing.

Instead of agreeing, her sister asked her, "Where is Lord Cambrey?"

Maggie supposed it wasn't such an odd thing for Jenny to ask. Indeed, the earl had spent quite a bit of time at each event hovering nearby. Sometimes she wondered if he did so only out of the duty he felt to watch over his best friend's wife or whether, perhaps, there was another more personal reason. Maggie hoped she had not misinterpreted his glances and his smiles.

In any case, it wouldn't do to appear as if they had already formed an attachment, which they had not. Although she did feel somewhat attached to the man.

"We cannot dance more than two dances in a night without someone crying out the banns," Maggie declared. "We have a dance coming up soon enough."

She nearly blushed when she said it. Truthfully, the idea of her and John Angsley linked together and having their marriage banns publicly proclaimed was not displeasing. It was, in fact, thrilling.

"Who is next on your card?" her mother asked.

Maggie angled the square paper dangling from her wrist by a satin ribbon.

"Oh!" She glanced again at Jenny. "I nearly forgot. Your former fiancé sketched in his name before I even realized who he was, but I will not do him the honor, I assure you."

"Why would Lord Alder seek to dance with you?" Lady Blackwood did not sound pleased. "He can be certain I would never allow an association between him and you, not after his shoddy treatment of our Jenny. I'm sure other parents feel the same way. Why, I can't even imagine why he is here!" she finished vehemently, scanning the room as if she thought she' could stop him with the ferocity of her gaze alone.

Maggie was glad her mother's ire wasn't directed at her. What's more, she hoped the fickle viscount, if he knew what was good for him and didn't want to create a scene, stayed far from their table. Although he had treated Jenny poorly after her family's financial ruin, it was no worse than many of the bachelors of the *ton* would do.

In any case, Maggie thought Lord Alder hadn't meant to pencil his name on her particular card at all. They'd actually nearly collided by the refreshments, and likely, he believed it his duty to offer her a dance. His eyes had widened when he'd truly looked at her face and realized she was Jenny's sister, right about the same moment Maggie realized who he was, as well.

"Mummy, I am more than pleased to miss this next quadrille," Maggie stated. "Probably, Lord Alder was simply being polite." She was sorry to have mentioned him. "Why, I doubt he will even show up to claim his dance?"

Relief washed over her when instead of Lord Alder, Lord Westing appeared. He'd kissed her hand tenderly before Christmas at Lady Atwood's grand holiday celebration. As the only son of the Duke of Westing, with dashing good looks to boot, the marquess was considered *the* catch of the Season.

After bowing to each of the ladies beginning with Lady Blackwood, Lord Westing turned his attention to Maggie.

"You are not dancing, Miss Blackwood, which robs the room of much enjoyment. It is too late to begin this dance, yet perchance, I may have the next?"

Maggie couldn't help drinking in the sight of him. He was definitely easy on the eyes. A strong jaw, cornflower-blue eyes, and curly nut-brown hair, he cut as fine a figure as Lord Cambrey.

Why must she compare each man to John Angsley? she scolded herself. John was an exceedingly nice man, but they definitely had no particular understanding. In fact, a few minutes earlier, he'd been dancing with Adelia Smythe and even now, was paired for the quadrille with Jane Chatley, the daughter of an earl.

That shouldn't irk her except Lady Jane was positively perfect in face, figure, and fortune. What's more, John seemed utterly entranced with her.

Maggie offered Lord Westing the smile she practiced before her looking glass, knowing it was neither too big, nor too small. It didn't show off too many teeth, nor her gums. It didn't pull her mouth too wide, either. It looked genuine and pleasing but not like a grinning fool. In short, it was very becoming without an ounce of coyness.

Then she added a flutter of her eyelashes, like the smallest dash of spicy pepper on an already perfect cut of meat. She watched the man's pupils dilate.

"Why, I believe my next dance is free," she told him, not bothering to consult her card.

She heard her sister sigh and knew what she was thinking—it wasn't done to stand up someone whose name was on your card. Nonetheless, Alder had done it to her, and Maggie was none the worse for it.

Lord Westing glanced toward the crowded dance floor.

"We can go together to the refreshment table before our dance begins. It is less crowded there at present."

"A splendid idea." With that, Maggie let her new admirer take her arm in his.

After he bowed once more to her mother and to her older sister, Lord Westing led her away. She couldn't resist a sideways glance to determine John's whereabouts.

To her astonishment, although in mid-dance with Jane, he happened to be looking directly at her, his eyes blazing as they locked gazes. And then it happened, the strange, tantalizing sizzle raced through her.

What would it feel like to be kissed by the Earl of Cambrey? She had the fanciful notion she would combust upon contact with his lips.

Firmly of the opinion it would be well worth it, Maggie decided to test out her theory at the earliest opportunity.

CHAPTER TWO

Cam settled his dance partner back from whence she came and, with undeniable eagerness, headed toward the ladies Blackwood. When he arrived at their table, only Jenny stood there.

Trying not to frown as he scanned the area for Margaret, yet he knew if they weren't on the floor as the music started, they couldn't join the dance at all.

"Both your mother and sister have vanished." Hoping he didn't sound as peeved as he felt at Margaret's failure to honor their dance commitment, he offered a small smile. Even then, the lively polka started and his chance to hold her in his arms vanished. *Damn it all!*

Jenny nodded at him, looking as if there was something on her mind.

"My lord, will you take a stroll along the gallery?"

Tamping down his surprise at her invitation, he felt curiosity slice through him, blended with hesitation. After all, this was his best friend's wife, and the *ton* could be brutal with rumors and innuendo. However, he'd promised Simon he would protect her. If Lady Lindsey wanted to stroll, better with him than some rogue.

"Certainly, my lady." Offering her his arm, they exited through the double doors at the front of the room.

As soon as they were alone at one end of the long promenade, lined with paintings and statues, she stopped.

"I will be brief. I simply wish to know if you've heard from Simon."

He hated to disappoint her. "I'm sorry. I have heard nothing from him. It is as if Simon has disappeared into the heart of the savage nations of Europe."

Hearing her heavy-hearted sigh, he wished he could console her with some promise of his friend's speedy return. All he really had were empty words.

"I would ask you to trust him and not to worry. Why, he was practically singing *Lady Greensleeves* in your honor the first time he told me about you."

Then he thought of Simon's other duties besides those to his wife.

"In any case, he must return soon."

"Why do you say that, my lord?"

"Parliament officially opens in a few weeks, and he had best be there."

They both knew the ramifications for an absentee representative in the House of Lords were not good, including a possible loss of Simon's privilege.

However, Cam doubted Jenny would see her husband for Christmas. The best he could do in his friend's stead was to invite her and her family to attend functions with his family at their London home.

It would be no hardship as his widowed mother was a gracious hostess. He was confident she would enjoy Jenny and her mother's company. What's more, his cousin Beryl was staying at the Cambrey townhouse, on hand to entertain Eleanor, the youngest Blackwood sister. Then, of course, there was Margaret. Entertaining her would be no hardship at all.

Except, she had not even wanted to dance with him.

As they reappeared in the ballroom, he quickly spied Margaret on the dance floor with Westing. The greenest of green devils danced in Cam's head. *How dare she!* True, they didn't have any kind of understanding, but one didn't publicly cut one partner in favor of another, unless the other had already declared for her. Could such have happened in the short space of time between an earlier event and this one?

"Your sister is dancing with Lord Westing," Cam commented to Jenny, immediately wishing he'd kept his mouth shut. His notice and remark most likely spoke volumes about his interest. But, as long as no one else had read Margaret's dance card, then Cam was not actually in peril of public humiliation.

Jenny's next words unfortunately made him fear otherwise.

"Oh, I am sorry, my lord. I feared it was you she was using so terribly."

Using terribly! What a way to express it. "Whatever can you mean?"

"She shouldn't have dashed off with Lord Westing when she knew she had an upcoming dance with you. That was very wrong of her, and I shall reprimand her most—"

"No." His tone was too sharp, but he had his pride. "Dear Lady Lindsey, your sister is enjoying her Season. I signed her card simply because I saw a gap on it. Only for that reason. As long as Miss Margaret is dancing, nothing else matters."

Though if Westing tripped and fell flat on his too handsome face, Cam would not be bothered at all.

"If everyone did as my sister, then these events would dissolve into chaos. From a practical standpoint, she ought to honor her promise."

Cam admired Jenny Blackwood Devere, Countess of Lindsey, very much and knew from Simon she was a most practical female. However, at that moment, she seemed like a dog with a bone she couldn't set down when he simply wanted her to forget all about his missed dance with Margaret. He didn't want to listen to any more talk of how the entire fabric of society, and balls in particular, would dissolve into absolute mayhem because her sister hadn't danced with him.

"Please, my lady, let it rest. There was no harm done."

She paused in her rambling and gave him a sideways look. "Of course, my lord. I'll say nothing further on the matter."

Why did he now think she was going to have a long talk with Margaret about it later? He wished he'd never come to the blasted ball.

"VERY GLAD YOU COULD come to our home," Lord Cambrey's mother intoned, greeting Lady Blackwood and her daughters in the front hall of the Angsleys' townhouse on Cavendish Square.

Cambrey's gaze went right to Margaret, looking exquisite in a green silk gown with gold trim, seeming to bring the Christmas season to life. He stepped forward to welcome each of them, starting with the mother and working his way down to Eleanor. Then his cousin Beryl offered a tour of the townhouse, which only Eleanor agreed to. The girls scampered off like young colts, while the rest of them entered the drawing room.

"Where are Lady Beryl's parents?" Lady Blackwood asked when they were all seated.

"My husband's younger brother and his wife remain in their home in Bedfordshire. They have five other children, with Beryl being the eldest."

"So blessed," Jenny said.

Cam thought so, too. His own parents had only him to whom they could transfer all their hopes and dreams, as well as to carry on the family line. He knew his mother had lost two others, although they never spoke of them.

"Beryl is a delight to have with me," Lady Cambrey added, "but I believe she is not e ready for the upcoming Season, or even the next."

Everyone nodded in agreement as they had recently heard either Eleanor or Beryl shrieking with childish laughter and then running loudly across the main foyer.

"I agree," Lady Blackwood said. "Our Eleanor is not ready to come out."

At that very instant, Margaret's gaze shot toward Cam. When their eyes met, he felt the attraction to her run through his entire body. Was this how one finally knew one had met the right person? For certainly, he'd never experienced such a visceral draw toward a woman.

Lust? God yes! But bone-deep wanting? Never.

Cam spent the rest of the evening wondering how he could get her alone. They hadn't had a private moment for many weeks, not since sitting beside one another at Sadler's Wells, watching an untalented singer. He very much wanted to change that.

After a savory meal of mutton cutlets, his mother's favorite meat, they retired again to the drawing room. Jenny begged off entertaining, but Margaret was persuaded to play the pianoforte. In fact, she seemed to shine even more brightly when she sat upon the bench with all eyes on her.

His mother had a goodly collection of sheet music for Beryl, and Cam watched Margaret sift through the stack. Just before she played, he noted how she sent a withering glance to Eleanor to quell her giggling.

When all was silent, she began a happy sounding song—"A Life on the Ocean Wave," he guessed, although without anyone singing accompaniment, it sounded similar to many others.

He was pleased she was an accomplished player. There was nothing more embarrassing than a well-heeled young lady who made a great show of taking her place at the piano only to plunk out a tune that offended one's ears.

"Do you not sing, Miss Blackwood?" asked his mother between songs.

Margaret cocked her head charmingly. "I'm afraid my voice is not on a par with those of many who perform in the parlors of London, Lady Cambrey. I, for one, prefer not to do something in public at which I am not proficient. It smacks of desperation and clawing for attention. If there is one here, however, who would like to accompany me, I am more than grateful."

Cam stared, eyes wide, as no one moved. After all, who would dare to sing after such a challenge? Smacking of desperation, indeed! None of the ladies sallied forth, even though Beryl actually had a rather lilting voice, which seemed to be on key at least half the time.

Margaret waited, then turned back to the keys, ready to continue her solo performance.

"I'll give it a go," Cam offered, the words out of his mouth before he thought too much of them.

He heard an audible breath from Margaret. Apparently, he'd surprised her by picking up the gauntlet. Having been on a choir at school, he decided he could muddle through as long as the words were in front of him and it was a song he'd heard before.

From his lounging position on a tufted divan, he rose and approached the piano.

Margaret stared at him.

"Your choice, Lord Cambrey." Then she nodded toward the pile of sheet music.

He pawed through it and then placed some pages in front of her. To his delight, her cheeks went pink as she scanned his selection of a tender love song, best sung by a man to the woman he admired.

When Margaret's eyes flashed up at him, he raised an eyebrow. In return, she sent him a dazzling smile, sending him back a step with its vibrancy. Either she appreciated his choice, or she was about to give him a come down.

Did she consider it a challenge, an invitation, a declaration? He couldn't tell. After he'd nodded his readiness, she began to play, the notes crisp if a trifle too quick for his liking, perhaps done to throw him off balance.

Coming in at what he hoped was the exact proper place, he began to sing "Annabelle Lee," which had not too difficult a range.

Leaning over her slightly to read the words, Cam turned the page as necessary, trying not to be distracted by her nearness nor the divine floral scent of her hair. If he wasn't careful, he'd disgrace himself in front of the ladies, and was very glad he wasn't wearing the tight stovepipe breeches some wore, which would leave nothing to their imaginations.

As he turned the page again, he brushed her shoulder, and she faltered. *Good!* He hoped she had some awareness of him as he did her.

At the closing notes, she looked down at the keys, then stood up by turning away from him, making it impossible for him to see her expression. When her family and his clapped, Cam reached for her hand so they could perform a small bow together.

As his fingers closed over hers, he felt her jump, then relax. She curtsied toward the small audience as he bowed, and then, unable to help himself, he squeezed her hand gently.

Instantly, she glanced up at him. He hoped it was happiness he saw in her eyes, for that was what he felt. Simply happy to be around her, to be touching her, however briefly. By the soft bowing of her lips, he decided she was indeed pleased, at least by their duet.

His mother declared cards were next for the evening's entertainment. With an odd number of people, they decided to play Hearts, which caused a great deal of laughter and good-spirited competition until the two younger girls became bored. When they dashed off to Beryl's room for a private chat before the evening was over, Cam envied their freedom.

Truth be told, he wished he could spirit Margaret away to *his* bedroom for some private time, although chatting was not uppermost on his mind.

Still, the opportunity arose to speak alone with her as she wandered the edge of the parlor, examining his mother's baubles and curios on the cabinets before standing in front of the bookshelves.

"You are a good musician," he offered as she drew out a book from the shelf.

Without looking at him, she remarked, "I note you didn't say 'a great one.'"

"I have never lied to you," he told her, and she laughed.

Thank goodness she was not one of those easily offended.

"Fair enough. I don't like empty flattery anyway. I am a *good* musician, but I could become better if I practiced more."

"I have no doubt," Cam agreed. "I suppose you don't receive much empty flattery in any case, not when there are so many qualities about you which engender true admiration."

Her cheeks went a pleasing pink again.

"And you have a good voice," she offered, returning the book to its place and taking another one.

"I note you didn't say 'a great one,'" he teased.

"I have never lied to you," she repeated.

"No, yet you have stood me up quite magnificently."

Frowning, she looked up at him. "I . . . ? Oh, our dance."

Was that chagrin on her face? Was he a rude host to make her uncomfortable?

"It was nothing, really," he added. "I'm sure you simply muddled the names on your card, so very full to overflowing as it was."

"I don't muddle things," Margaret stated simply.

He waited. When it was clear an apology was not forthcoming, he shrugged. "As I said, it was nothing."

Her glance darted past him toward her sister, and he knew, with a sick feeling, Jenny had had words with her about it. What's more, now he'd brought it up, giving it even more importance.

What an idiot! If Margaret had said she was sorry for the mix-up, it would be finished. Instead, she was behaving mulishly by not acknowledging her error, and he was left hanging out to dry.

"John, come tell the ladies what Palmerston and Russell told you about the French. Their government is collapsing, is it not?"

And with that, his *tête-à-tête* with Margaret was at an uncomfortable end.

He needed to stop obsessing with this one young woman for she was too flawed to become his wife. She would drive him mad with her fickleness and her inability to take responsibility for even the smallest of affronts.

However, it was the holidays and his best friend was away for an indeterminate amount of time, and thus, he would continue to invite the Blackwoods to his home, at least until the main Season started after the year's end. There would be a couple large events his mother customarily held, and undoubtedly, Jenny and her family would enjoy being part of them.

When a week later, Cam spied Margaret riding in Hyde Park with Westing, her maid along as a chaperone, he tamped down his irritation and rode past them with a nod of his head. Westing acknowledged him coolly in return, but Margaret's eyes opened wide, her expression unfathomable.

He hadn't gone but a few yards farther down the path when she called his name.

"Lord Cambrey, please wait."

Halting, surprised at her forwardness, he turned in his saddle to see her riding toward him. Beyond her, Westing and the chaperone waited.

"Miss Blackwood, is something the matter?"

She appeared flustered, very unlike herself.

"I wanted to tell you something. It has troubled me since the lovely evening at your house."

"Oh?" Suddenly he thought he knew what was coming, and he wasn't going to make it easy on her. He could, however, take the opportunity to enjoy her sparkling eyes and pink cheeks, and watch her lovely mouth as she apologized. For he was convinced an apology over leaving him unpartnered was about to be tendered.

"I am sorry if Eleanor was too boisterous. I hope it didn't annoy your mother. My sister can be high-spirited and needs little encouragement to become giggly and loud."

He remained silent a moment as her words settled into his brain. An apology of sorts but entirely for the wrong Blackwood daughter. *How strange!* Perhaps Margaret was utterly oblivious to societal rules at a ball.

"I do not recall my mother saying anything regarding Miss Eleanor."

"Good," Margaret said. "Then I shall tell my mother all is well."

"Of course. Let your mother not be worried for an instant. In fact, I believe *my* mother is issuing invitations for a large party at our home next week. Although there will not be any others so young, I am certain Eleanor will be invited to keep company with Beryl."

"Good," Margaret said again.

It seemed they had exhausted this topic and could not conceivably carry on a discourse any longer regarding her sister or Cam's mother, yet Margaret still held her horse at rest next to his.

"Your companions are waiting," he reminded her, glancing past to see Westing's horse prancing, possibly picking up on the irritation of its rider. An irritated marquess. *How perfectly delightful!*

"Well, I should be off then," Margaret said, starting to turn her horse away. When she was facing in the other direction, she added, "I didn't realize it was *your* name on my card for the next dance at the Marechals' ball. Good day, Lord Cambrey."

With a swift motion of her heels to her horse's flanks, she trotted off before he could respond. He kept watching until the three rode away.

So that was how Miss Margaret apologized for herself. A tad off-handed to be sure, but she left him with the impression if she'd looked at her card and realized the next dance was his, then she would not have missed it.

Uplifted by her words, he rode off feeling better than he had in days.

"You poor besotted dunce," he muttered to himself.

CHAPTER THREE

Breathlessly happy with the coincidence of the morning, Maggie entered their townhouse with her maid, glad to be rid of Lord Westing. There was nothing wrong with him at all. Not a blessed thing. But the only bright spot in the ride had been meeting up with John and finally unburdening herself to him.

In truth, she hadn't cared a fig about Eleanor's behavior at the Cambrey home. No one else had either. It had simply seemed like a good way to start an apology, especially when her own actions, while entirely unintentional, had apparently hurt his feelings.

Yes, she felt quite pleased with herself for finally righting that wrong and letting the man know she had not meant to cut him. She'd simply been careless.

And for her virtuous behavior this morning, she'd found out about another party they would be attending with his mother as hostess. *How wonderful!* She liked the smaller events at people's homes even more than the crowded, ticketed balls. True, there was less vigor and birr, less choice of dancers, and a little less excitement. At the same time, there would be more opportunity for talking, and certainly the food was better.

What's more, she very much liked Lady Cambrey, whose husband had sadly passed away about four years earlier, or so Margaret's mother recalled. Nothing tragic, simply an older man falling ill from influenza. The title passed to John, and everything continued as it should. They had not suffered any of the indignities that had befallen the Blackwood family.

"Are you home, dear?"

"Yes, it's me, Mummy. Am I too late for eggs and toast?"

"I'M THRILLED TO SEE your lovely family again," Lady Cambrey graciously received them.

The Cambreys' receiving line, including Beryl, in the front hall of their townhouse, befitted the formal nature of the event. All the Blackwood ladies had dressed more elegantly than for the previous small dinner they'd attended there.

Seeing the furniture had been cleared out in the spacious front parlor whose double doors stood wide open, Maggie almost clapped her hands with delight and had to ball them into fists to stop herself. The dancing here would be intimate. And no dance cards had been handed out, thus offering far more opportunity to partner with the same person than could ever happen at the large balls with hundreds of eligibles vying for each dance.

She couldn't deny she wanted to dance with John Angsley as many times as possible.

When he bent over her gloved hand and brought it to his lips, she hoped her expression told him she would not have missed their dance on purpose. His smiling eyes indicated they were once again on a good footing.

She moved along the line to allow the press of people behind her to enter. Stepping into the parlor, Maggie found a small group of musicians already warming up in one corner. As happened at most of these events, there would be dancing first, then everyone would move into the dining room for food they could easily eat while standing, since there were far too many to sit at the table. Then they would resume dancing for many hours into the night.

Looking forward to a splendid evening, Maggie took up her place by her family to watch as others entered.

CAM DECIDED TO FOREGO nonchalant aloofness. In fact, as soon as he saw Margaret enter, he thought, *To hell with seeming uninterested.* This was his home, his party, and his bloody parlor. Or at least, it was his and his mother's. And Lady Cambrey wouldn't mind a bit if he played favorites and asked Margaret for the first dance and even the second. They would lead the Grand March, even it if it was actually a miniature march.

When Margaret had approached him in the receiving line, he'd felt himself beaming at her, like a schoolboy looking at sweets. Was it possible her eyes were the sparkliest, her skin, especially at her décolletage, the creamiest, and even her ringlets the ringliest of any he'd ever seen? She seemed to have a shimmer about her causing every other woman to appear muted and dull.

He wished his lips could have touched more than merely her gloved hand. And then she'd disappeared among the revelers.

After the last guests arrived, Cam could finally head into the parlor. Seemingly, everyone invited had turned up, for there was quite a crush around the edges of the great room. Preferring the previous intimate get-together they'd had with the Blackwoods, the only thing that would have made the previous gathering better was if his friend Simon had returned from the Continent to claim his wife. That, and if Cam had been able to touch Margaret with more than a shoulder brushing as he'd turned her music sheets.

Tonight, at least, he would hold her in his arms.

As he'd hoped, she agreed to be his partner for the Grand March, and they led the couples in an intricate dance of circles and turns and even through an arch created by the other dancers' arms.

Frustrating as hell, Cam thought. What he wanted was a waltz in order to hold her closely. To his delight, the very next dance was, indeed, a waltz, and since she was still by his side, it was the most natural thing in the world to partner up.

In the space of a few weeks, from the last time he'd danced with her, something had changed. Not *with* her, for she was still as lovely, as spirited, and as light on her feet—and his—as she had been before. Perhaps it was simply getting to speak with her more at the various social events. Maybe it was even the duet they'd performed.

What had changed? he wondered, looking down at her. *What did he feel?*

Proprietary. It felt as if Miss Margaret Blackwood belonged to him. They fit so well. When she looked up at him with her gold-flecked, tawny eyes and stole his breath away, Cam couldn't imagine feeling the same about anyone else. Indeed, he never had before. He'd been to bed with a beautiful courtesan once whom another friend had insisted would absolutely overturn his apple cart. Truly, she had been magnificent in many ways, mostly with her lips and tongue, but she hadn't left him breathless. And she definitely hadn't made him want her only for himself.

Moreover, this unfamiliar possessiveness for Margaret caused an unwelcome emotion, jealousy! He didn't want her to ride with Westing, or dance with him, or anyone else for that matter.

What a bloody nuisance! Tightening his grip on her waist and hand, he watched her eyes widen as they moved smoothly across the floor. He would like to see her eyes when he pleasured her, to hear her make a sound of delight as he . . .

Nearly tripping over his wayward thoughts—and over his own feet—he swallowed and focused on the present. Possibly this was merely lust after all. He should steer Margaret toward a secluded spot in his back garden and kiss her senseless.

One of them would be senseless at any rate!

And then the waltz came to an end, and Cam led her back to her family. Eleanor and Beryl had disappeared. Since they weren't supposed to dance, they were probably sampling the sweets set upon towering trays in the dining room.

Having no wish to remove himself from Margaret's company nor to dance with another lady, Cam considered his options. Dancing a third dance with her would be considered utterly discourteous to the others at the party.

"Shall we go find my cousin and your young sister? They might be up to mischief."

He watched Margaret's expression change from surprise to agreement.

"I suppose I should help bring my sister to heel. Mummy, I was never like Eleanor, was I?"

Lady Blackwood raised an eyebrow. "No, my dear." Turning to him, she added, "None of my daughters have been anything alike. At Eleanor's age, Jenny would not be at a party but home solving a puzzle, while Maggie would most likely be perusing every page of *Le Follet* while trying out new hairstyles in front of her looking glass."

"Mummy," Margaret blurted. "I'm sure you'll have Lord Cambrey thinking I care about nothing but fashion and appearance."

"Not at all," Cam heard himself saying in her defense. "Clearly, you have put the magazine's lessons to good use and should be commended for studying it. You are easily the most fashionable lady here."

What inanity was he uttering? Plus, he'd insulted the other Blackwood women. "Present company excepted, of course," he added hastily.

Stop talking. Just. Stop. The three ladies were looking at him, no doubt thinking the same thing. Jenny was plainly trying to keep from laughing at him, and Margaret was blushing profusely. All he could do was offer his arm, which she took.

After another bow to the other ladies, he took Margaret away, ostensibly to go *look* for the lost girls.

"That was very smooth," she muttered to him under her breath.

He took that as a good sign. They were familiar enough with each other she could tease him for his *faux pas*. Very good indeed.

"I strive to be smooth," he returned. "After all, I am an eligible bachelor this Season."

It sounded as if she snorted. "You've been an eligible bachelor for more than *one* Season. I'm certain ladies have assumed you were seeking a wife. Or didn't you realize?"

Was she calling him old? Maybe, but she also agreed he was eligible.

"I haven't much cared about that, in truth, until this year."

They were standing in the wide hallway. Alone. Glancing around to be sure, he decided to press his case.

"I wish to call on you in the morning and take you riding."

Truthfully, he wanted to skip the weeks of horse rides and carriage outings, accompanied by her maid, and the stilted visits in her parlor with a companion close by during which they would speak about nearly nothing while mildly flirting. It all seemed for younger people.

Yes, he wanted to take her riding, then get her alone, kiss her, talk about whether she liked to live in Town or in the country, kiss her some more, and decide immediately if they were suited.

He could be romantic and even delay gratification *after* they'd made a decision, but to waste time *before* they knew if they would make a good match seemed silly. Perhaps he was too old for this game.

"I would love to," Margaret said. He wasn't imagining she visibly brightened and moved a little closer. Her eyes twinkled and she licked her lips, moistening them, and all he could do was stare at their plump perfection.

Suddenly, he felt encouraged. *Dammit all*, he was John Angsley, nearly thirty and not a wet-behind-the-ears youth. In a swift move, he propelled her backward into the shadows under the staircase, pulled her body against him, bent low, and claimed her mouth.

Soft lips yielded under his firm ones. Glad to discover she wasn't skittish, Cam rested his hands at her waist, small and curved from what he could feel through the layers. In return, she set her gloved hands upon his chest.

Their kiss continued without protest, so he tilted his head, slanting his mouth to better cover hers. Cam wanted to nibble her full lower lip, but that seemed rash. Nevertheless, he couldn't help touching it with his tongue, licking its plump shape, tasting her.

Almost instantly, she parted her lips, and his tongue slipped inside.

Exploring her sweet mouth, he lost track of time until he heard footsteps coming down the stairs above their heads. Quickly, he broke contact and jumped back before taking hold of her hand and pulling her from the secluded area out into the light of the hall.

Margaret looked delightfully dazed, and her mouth had the slightly swollen appearance of the freshly kissed. A swell of pride arose in him.

Most importantly, he needed to ensure they didn't appear to have been loitering or doing precisely what it looked like they'd been doing.

"Yes," he said, loudly, "I agree it was a shame so many houses had to be demolished for Waterloo Bridge Station, but in the end, I'm sure it will benefit Londoners tremendously."

Margaret looked at him as if he'd gone mad. Then she smiled and began to giggle.

"Of course, my lord," she said, trying to catch her breath, "Waterloo Bridge Station!"

By this time, the footsteps, two pairs in fact, had reached the bottom of the stairs and were chasing behind them into the dining room. The wayward girls had reappeared.

"Is it time to eat?" Beryl asked, moving past them to examine what had already been laid out. Small meat-filled pastries one could pick up with one's fingers, equally small squares of mince tart, and more was being brought from the kitchen on trays. The pudding display had not even been put out.

"No, it is not yet time," Cam said, grateful for the ordinary task of chastising his cousin. "The dancing has barely begun. Anyway, it is a warm enough evening. Why don't you and Eleanor take a stroll in the garden? I think I saw fireflies by the roses."

The girls laughed, and Beryl rolled her eyes. "We don't care about fireflies, Cousin. But we will go outside anyway. Maybe we will spot some couples kissing out there."

They wandered toward the door, but then Beryl paused. "Just the same as we found some kissing in here."

Disappearing in a peal of even louder laughter, the girls left them in silence.

Cam looked at Margaret who stared back at him.

"Oh dear," she said at last, although she didn't look particularly concerned. "Eleanor won't say anything, my lord. Do not worry overmuch about her. What of Beryl?"

"Beryl needs to be locked up until she learns some manners. I'm afraid she is running a little wild here without her mother's supervision."

"I believe she would say it was you and I who were running a little wild."

He grinned at her. "*Touché.*"

Should he mention anything more about the kiss? Any apology would be a lie, and she seemed the type who wouldn't take kindly to him pretending regret any more than she would pretend outrage.

Deciding to leave it as a particularly good memory of this party, Cam gestured to the feast being constructed by the servants who kept hurrying in and out of the room with still more trays laden with food.

"Would you like to taste anything before the herd of hungry dancers storms in?"

"Thank you, no." She gave him a long look that left him wondering, but all she said was, "I had better return to my family."

Taking her arm, Cam led her back into the parlor, feeling a strange sense of accomplishment. He had kissed the prettiest woman at the party.

Hell's bells! He'd kissed the prettiest woman in all of London.

Unfortunately, hovering around her sister and mother were Lords Fowler and Burnley, viscounts both. Cam couldn't find any fault with either of them except they existed and were now going to be close to Margaret.

At that moment, there was nothing much he could do except dance with other guests and keep his eye on her. Luckily, Lady Chatley, who was pleasant if a little bland for someone of her youth, had finished the previous dance and hopefully would welcome the next with him.

In no way could he have imagined in thirty minutes by his pocket watch, he would find Margaret kissing another man.

CHAPTER FOUR

"You looked a likely pair," Lady Blackwood said, after Lord Cambrey was out of hearing.

Maggie smiled. *A likely pair*. She hoped so. But what could she say without gushing like a ninny?

"The earl is a superb dancer."

"But do you *like* him?" Jenny asked.

"Well of course, I like him," Margaret answered. What a silly question her sister had asked. So unlike her. "After all, what is there not to like?"

Sighing, Jenny tapped her toe as the musicians signaled the start of the next dance.

In the absence of Lord Westing, with whom she'd greatly enjoyed a number of discussions and dances but who apparently had not been invited, Maggie took the hand of Lord Burnley, who was an admirable polka dancer. When the musicians played two polkas back to back, it seemed only natural to dance a second with him and then to go in search of refreshments together.

The evening was a grand success, mostly because of John Angsley's incredible kiss. Who knew a kiss could be like that, full of the promise of even more delight?

Thinking of it, recalling the feel of his lips—and his tongue!—and how her body had reacted with heat and fluttering and even dampness, all those thoughts had kept her mind busy through the two dances while she smiled and kept up her steps.

While sipping ginger beer, when the fair-haired viscount suggested they take a stroll in Lord Cambrey's garden, she accepted. After all, what harm could there be when Beryl and Eleanor were, in all probability, swinging from the trees like little monkeys and keeping their beady eyes on everyone?

Oddly, however, the garden was deserted. Maggie felt a queer sensation in her stomach as she realized she was alone with a man for the second time in one evening. What did that say of her character? She had no idea. She didn't feel loose or immoral. She simply wanted to experience a little life. Surely at her age, such a longing was acceptable.

Leaving their glasses on the railing, they stepped down from the terrace and into the well-kept gardens.

"It's quite dark," Maggie said, because it surprised her as the Devere townhouse in which she now resided had lamps burning nearly every night in the yard. Still, she realized the foolishness of her statement. Of course, it was dark! It was nighttime and the exterior of the house had not been set up for guests. They should return indoors at once.

Instead, Lord Burnley tucked her arm under his, and they walked down one narrow path, past a birdbath, and down another until they'd traversed the relatively small garden, ending up at the back wall.

"I know we've only been introduced a few times and danced even fewer, but I have watched you and asked after you, Miss Blackwood."

"Really?" Maggie let him step closer. As Lord Burnley gave off no hint of danger, she allowed him to continue.

"Yes, really. I should very much like to get to know you better. From what I know already, you have a lovely disposition."

She nearly laughed.

"That's kind of you to say, my lord. Perhaps the exchange of a vowel is in order as more might call me *lively* than *lovely* in regards to my disposition, and not always in a complimentary way, either."

He smiled at her.

"Difficult to believe. I've heard only from your admirers."

Her admirers? Such as John Angsley, she hoped.

Suddenly, she wished to get a little closer to the house and to the light, which she could see spilling from inside through the many windows.

"Shall we?" Maggie gestured back the way they'd come.

"Of course," the viscount agreed, and they turned as one toward the house. "May I call on you at your brother-in-law's home?"

Considering the matter for a moment, she didn't feel the rush to say absolutely yes as she had when John asked her to go riding. Yet, neither did she feel a definite no. In the back of her mind always was the thought of what had happened to her older sister. Jenny had accepted on faith and a verbal promise Lord Michael Alder was going to declare for her, and then in the blink of an eye, he broke that faith.

No arrangement was certain, Maggie knew that, not until a contract was signed and a ring was placed on one's finger, even then . . .

"Yes, you may." And she looked at him to bolster her rather cool response with her practiced smile.

Soon they were back at the steps of the veranda, and Lord Burnley's hand stroked her arm by her elbow above her glove.

"Miss Blackwood." He held her still.

"Yes?" Turning to him, she felt a small jolt of excitement.

His blue eyes looked very dark in the dim light and intensely focused on her, his pleasing face was made more interesting by the play of shadows, and his pale hair was catching the light, shining like a halo.

"I know this is terribly forward," Lord Burnley said quietly, "but I should very much like to kiss you. May I?"

Her heart sped up. *Oh dear.* She knew it was wrong to kiss John one minute and then Lord Burnley, whose given name she couldn't recall, the next. However, she did want to kiss him. If only to compare. If only to know without a doubt how special it was with John. How else was she to find out if the sensation coursing through her body when John kissed her was extraordinary or the same as she would feel with every kiss?

There was really only one way.

"Yes."

He didn't hesitate, which she liked about him. Lowering his head, he pressed his mouth against hers, even tilting his head as John had done.

His lips were not unpleasant. They were firm and dry. His breath was clean with a hint of ginger. His clean-shaven face was not abrasive. He didn't nibble her or lick her lower lip. And she felt no inclination to part her lips and touch his tongue.

This kiss felt . . . nothing like John's kiss. Agreeable but not toe-curling. Her heart didn't pound, and she didn't get warm and moist. She didn't even mind when it ended. Everything about it was exactly how a kiss ought to be, except for the man doing the kissing.

Maggie had her answer.

And then she heard a cough, or it might have been a growl.

They broke apart with haste, and she turned to see John standing above them on the raised terrace. Backlit by the lights of his own home, Lord Cambrey's face was in darkness. Even so, Maggie could detect an angry scowl. Her insides quivered at the position in which she'd foolishly let herself be discovered. Not because she worried over her reputation, for John would say nothing to anyone, nor because she wished the kiss could have continued.

No, her only regret was in piling on the offense of missing their dance at the Marechal's ball, she'd now shown herself to be as flighty and shallow as she'd heard some claim. Usually those accusations were whispered by other women blatantly jealous of her appearance, looking for some fault to find.

Although Maggie knew better than to claim credit for her looks, if she hurt John, she certainly would have to accept the blame for her thoughtless actions.

"Miss Blackwood, is that you in the darkness?"

How kind of him to pretend he could barely see them.

"Yes, Lord Cambrey, it is. Are you looking for me?" She moved away from Lord Burnley's side and began to climb the stone steps.

"I told your mother I would seek you out. Your sister is not feeling quite herself and wishes to leave. Since Eleanor has already reappeared, it is only you they are waiting for."

His voice was calm, but she could detect an edge to it she'd never heard before. Censoring, disappointed, perhaps let down.

An unfamiliar emotion, shame, trickled through her, causing her throat to tighten. When John did not touch her, did not even take her arm as they reentered his home, she felt a keen sense of loss. Behind her, she heard Lord Burnley's footfalls on the steps but didn't turn to acknowledge him.

John uttered not another word, and they walked in silence down the hallway to the party. Regret consumed her, making her fervently wish she could undo what she'd done, or at least have done it somewhere more discreetly. If only she could have made her discovery over the uniqueness of her feelings for the earl without having been discovered by him.

Blast it!

What's more, her fall from John's good graces was for nothing because Jenny had recovered her good health with a glass of chilled tonic water and mint leaves. They were staying at the party. Everyone now began to move toward the dining room precisely as Maggie reached her family.

With a silent nod, John disappeared into the throng. When next she saw him, he was holding a plate for Jane Chatley while the lady chose what to stuff into her great smiling gob.

"Maggie, are you listening?" Her mother's voice broke through her unkind thoughts.

"Yes, Mummy. What did you say?"

"If you have to ask, then no, you were not listening."

Hearing Eleanor laugh, Maggie turned to her, a flash of irritation nearly making her order her sister to behave. Seeing her sister's wide eyes and innocent face, however, she stopped. She had no one to blame but herself. She was the one who needed to behave better.

Instead of the nasty remark she nearly made, Maggie asked Eleanor, "What do you fancy eating? I say we try everything. It's important to try new things," she added. "Otherwise, how will one know what one truly likes."

Jenny's questioning eyebrows made Maggie stop talking and pick up a plate. Then she added, "I, for one, am going to eat oysters on toast."

GROANING THE NEXT MORNING, CAM nearly didn't rise at his accustomed early hour for a ride in the park. He had been up late, with the last stragglers leaving in the wee hours, long after the Blackwoods had left, thus long after he gave a damn about being at the party. He'd wanted everyone gone as soon as he'd seen Margaret letting Burnley kiss her.

Or had Margaret been kissing Burnley?

Either way, it made him irate and jealous, two feelings he didn't normally associate with his thoughts of women.

Somehow, despite Margaret's disappointing display, he'd had a passingly entertaining conversation with Lady Chatley, who clearly perused more than the fashion section of the daily rags. Moreover, she'd surprised him with her understanding of current affairs. They'd eaten together, standing in a corner, and then danced a few more dances.

Unfortunately, he'd spent too much time craning his neck to see with whom Margaret was partnered, ruining his enjoyment of dancing.

In fact, all enjoyment had been sucked from the night when he saw Burnley's mouth trespassing where his had been a mere few minutes earlier. It made no sense how he could have misjudged the lady so badly in two regards. One, she seemed nothing like her loyal sister who was unwavering in her devotion to Simon Devere, no matter the length of his absence.

And two, Cam had imagined Margaret found their kiss to be as exceptional as he had. He assumed he'd had more experience—*dammit*, he hoped such was the case, or he'd misjudged her thrice. Even for him, who'd kissed his share of the fairer sex, the kiss had left him feeling intoxicated.

And wanting more.

In no way could he imagine laying claim to another lady's lips a half hour later, so full were his thoughts of Margaret *the-deuce-take-her* Blackwood!

Cam had retired to his private room as the butler closed the doors on the last guests, and then he had drunk more than he ought, all the while knowing his head was going to ache in the morning. Better his head, he supposed, than his heart.

That organ was now utterly barred from being affected by the sparkling-eyed, fickle vixen.

Heaving himself out of bed, Cam ordered his horse saddled and made his way to Hyde Park. There, he gave the spirited gelding its head to run. As he whipped along the mostly empty bridal paths for a few minutes, he began to feel better.

After all, he was yet a virile man in possession of his health, living in London, the wealthiest, loveliest city in the world. Moreover, he was an earl, although he would have far preferred his father lived still and let Cam remain a viscount a few years longer.

However, fate was as it was, and as such, many doors were open to him. He had invested wisely and had good friends. He wanted for nothing except a wife, and he should count himself lucky there were many lovely ladies in Town. Furthermore, while still unmarried, he had many opportunities to visit the demimonde and have relations with a gorgeous and skilled Cyprian or two.

Yes, life was good.

And then he came upon Margaret Blackwood, riding with Burnley. Oh, and joy of joys, Westing, too, was astride a fine horse, along with another debutante and a maid as their companion.

As if the maid could do aught if those young bucks wanted to take advantage of the ladies!

As he passed, offering a nod of greeting, he saw Margaret's face pale, no doubt realizing how incredibly capricious she appeared. Briefly, Cam wondered which lady had been asked by which gentleman? Was Margaret there at the behest of her favorite dance partner, Westing, or was she accompanying the man she'd kissed in Cam's own garden, Burnley?

Then he galloped past, and it mattered not to him. After all, Miss Blackwood was only doing as all ladies did during a Season. So why did it seem almost shocking to him?

Instead of going home, he went to meet with a man who imported madeira. They had a productive conversation about diversity and investments, and how Cam might stand to make a good deal of money if he put some of his own into this man's burgeoning business.

When he arrived home, he saw two things on the table in his hallway, a letter from Simon Devere, posted from the German Empire, and a calling card from Miss Margaret Blackwood.

How unexpected. What could she possibly want?

CHAPTER FIVE

"Lord Cambrey to see you, my lady."

Cam waited politely until he heard Jenny's voice telling the butler to show him in.

When he strode into the room a moment later, he couldn't help the smile that broke out on his face, knowing he was going to bring this sweet lady some good news for a change. Their friendship had grown over the weeks and months. He'd felt badly being the one to tell her of her husband's disappearance onto the Continent, seeking treatment for some personal ailment.

He'd tried to make up for it, though, by watching over her at various social events, when he could tear his gaze from Margaret. He'd even rescued Jenny from an encounter with Viscount Alder, the cad who had broken their verbal marriage agreement. Now, he considered this woman his friend.

Nevertheless, Cam had to acknowledge he didn't want to encounter her sister. There would be an element of awkwardness, and for some reason, he thought he might feel the entirely foreign sensation of humiliation. To have his kiss topped by another's so quickly seemed an insult.

Jenny rose to her feet at his entrance, and he could see tears already glistening in her intelligent eyes.

"You've heard from Simon!"

"Yes, I have." Pulling his best friend's missive from his pocket, he handed it to her without preamble. Indeed, he was a little ashamed Simon had written to him and not to her. What was his friend thinking?

"May I?" she asked, even as she already reached her hand out, and he could see she was trembling. "It is not too personal?"

Dammit, Simon, what a mess you're making of your new marriage!

"He's *your* husband, and since it is all about you, no, there is nothing too personal. Though he might have my hide for boots if he knew I was showing it to you rather than summarizing the message."

After giving him her sweet smile, she read the letter. All the while, he stood silently, hoping Margaret was not going to pop into the room at any moment.

When Jenny gasped, he knew she'd read the ending.

"He's coming back!"

They shared a happy look.

"And greatly improved." At least, that's what Cam took the letter to mean.

She waved the piece of paper around as if to scatter his words.

"He was perfectly fine as he was." As her tears began to flow, he whisked out one of his handkerchiefs from his pocket and offered it to her. Then he gave her a moment to collect herself.

After she dabbed at her eyes, she told him, "I needed no improved Simon. However, if he is happier, then everything we have gone through has been worth it."

"You truly are a rare gem, Lady Lindsey."

A lovely ruddy bloom appeared on her cheeks. Then she surprised him with her next words. "As is my sister."

He felt the pleasant expression freeze on his face. Refusing to comment on Margaret, he concentrated on his friend's return.

"It appears we can expect the wayward Simon within weeks. And the *ton* that has declared him lost, demented, even a fugitive from the reality of the present, they can eat their words with a large helping of crow."

Her countenance went through a myriad of emotions.

"Why are you rolling your eyes and looking suddenly so exasperated?" he asked.

"I am merely impatient to lay eyes on him. And I want to shake him for leaving without telling me anything."

"Understandable."

"My manners have failed me. I should have offered you something when you arrived. Will you stay? Maggie should be home any moment. She went riding with Eleanor."

Perfect. If he hurried, he could avoid an encounter with the mercurial Margaret altogether.

"My apologies, but I must be off. Thank you for your offer. Give my regards to your mother."

Faster than he'd moved since outrunning a vicious dog when trespassing in an orchard as a student at Eton, Cam hightailed it from the townhouse on Portman Square.

No, he was not a coward, he assured himself. But the Miss Blackwood had the power to twist his insides if he let her, and he didn't intend to let her.

MAGGIE TRIED TO SWALLOW the nervousness that kept exhibiting itself as a large, uncomfortable lump in her throat and distracted herself by staring out of the carriage window.

She needn't be nervous, she told herself. She hadn't done anything wrong really. In fact, by kissing Lord Burnley, she'd made such a lovely discovery about how truly special

John's kiss had been, he should actually be grateful she'd done what she'd done.

On her way to John's home, with one of the Devere maids as her companion, Maggie was determined to explain her actions to him satisfactorily so they could return to the familiar footing they'd enjoyed *before* he'd encountered her in his garden.

And from there, they could move on to a deeper relationship, which she found herself thinking about daily. *An association with John Angsley. Perhaps receiving an offer from him by the end of the Season. Being engaged to John. Becoming Mrs. John Angsley. Lady Cambrey. Countess of Cambrey.* They all sounded quite splendid!

What had she expected by leaving a calling card? She'd hoped to catch him at home after he'd seen her riding with Westing and Burnley at Hyde Park. *Goodness, what must he have thought?* She'd felt the need to explain how she had to honor her commitments, if only so her friend Ada wouldn't have to cancel the ride. For certainly, Ada couldn't have gone without her, not with two gentlemen! Moreover, Ada had been the one paired with Burnley for the entire excursion.

However, John hadn't been at home that morning, nor had he responded by way of a note. What's more, Jenny had told her he'd visited their townhouse the very next day with news of her sister's husband. Margaret had missed seeing him by only a few minutes, and for that, she was sorely disappointed.

His lack of response, unfortunately, meant she had to trek over to his home, once again uninvited. A tad humiliating, too. Luckily, last time, his mother and Beryl had also been out, thus no one had witnessed her coming and going from Cavendish Square.

Lifting the large brass door knocker, she let it fall. Maggie repeated this once more, then waited, glancing at her maid who stood dutifully at her side.

In mere seconds, the Cambrey butler opened the door and, upon seeing who was on the step, drew it wide, stepped back, and let them enter.

"Miss Blackwood," he said in his low voice, bowing.

"Is Lord Cambrey at home?"

She had repeated the same scene mere days earlier. This time, however, the answer was far more satisfactory.

"Yes, miss. Is his lordship expecting you?"

Maggie twisted her mouth. The butler would know he was not, for that was his job, to know his master's schedule among other things. She could not lie.

"No. I was passing by and hoped to speak with him."

"Yes, miss. If you will wait in the parlor." He gestured toward the first open door, a room Maggie was all too familiar with. "I shall inform his lordship you are here."

With that, the gray-haired man walked sedately down the hallway, past the stairs under which she had shared such a wonderful kiss with his master.

And it had been exactly that, truly wonderful.

Wandering into the parlor, which now looked very different from the night of the party, Maggie found herself a bit too anxious to sit down. When her maid went discreetly to stand a few feet away, she decided to use the time to gather her thoughts. Also, she ought to put herself in the best light for when he entered. Glancing at the large bay windows, the drapes pulled open, she decided to stand in front of the unlit fireplace, sideways to the sunlight, and thus neither entirely backlit nor entirely cast in shadow.

Then she waited. It seemed as if many minutes had passed, more than would reasonably be expected for the butler to tell John she was there and for him to leave whatever he was doing and come to her.

A few more minutes went by, and Maggie found herself shifting her weight from foot to foot. Maybe she should sit after all. Was it too late to change her position, find the best seat in the right light, and artfully arrange her skirts in a pleasing manner? She didn't want to appear too comfortable, as if she was taking it for granted this might be her home someday. However, the longer she stood, the less she wanted to appear as if she were there like a beggar, hat in hand, hoping for his attention.

Another minute and her nerves had calmed. Instead, her anger had begun to boil.

The Earl of Cambrey was being purposefully rude. There could be no other explanation.

By the time Maggie heard footsteps, she was in high dudgeon. She let John enter the room before she stood slowly, deciding to appear as relaxed as possible when she felt like thumping him. Moreover, she knew instantly by his demeanor he had simply kept her waiting on purpose.

Should she take him to task for his rudeness? There was no question she must.

He sketched her a bow. "Miss Blackwood, I understand you want to see me." And then he folded his arms.

Offering him the barest of curtsies, she took steps toward him, only stopping when she'd invaded the space society would deem polite.

"I *wanted* to see you, but that was many minutes hence. Now, I'm not sure."

His eyes widened and his mouth opened slightly, the mouth that could give such delightful pleasure, which now she wanted to smack.

"Pray tell, Lord Cambrey, what has kept you from attending to your company so long I nearly left?"

By his expression, he hadn't thought she would blatantly question him. It simply wasn't done, and was considered terrible manners to make one's host feel uneasy. Maggie didn't give a damn.

Before he could say anything, she added, "I came to tell you something I thought you might find of interest, but now, I am unsure if you will find it of any interest."

He uncrossed his arms. "I apologize for keeping you waiting. It was rude of me. Will you accept my apology?"

She hesitated, precisely long enough for him to doubt whether she would.

"I will." After all, she knew he was still annoyed at having found her kissing Lord Burnley and then riding with two gentlemen the next day. She would allow him a little pique, but nothing more.

"Will you sit?" he asked, sounding much more like himself. He gestured for her to once more take a place on his pale blue sofa.

Without answer, she did.

"Is your mother or cousin at home?" she asked, suddenly realizing all three Angsleys may have shunned her.

"No. I assure you, if one of the fairer members of the family had been around, they would have come to you at once. Would you like tea?"

"No, thank you. I understand you had a letter from my brother-in-law. That was kind of you to bring it right over."

"Yes. I—"

"However, you failed to leave a calling card or a message back for me. Did you not receive my card?"

Again, he looked surprised at her bluntness. She didn't care if she shocked him with her disregard of the usual polite pretense that one was not offended. For she definitely was offended.

"I believe, Miss Blackwood, one's actions often beget a response in kind."

Maggie nearly frowned but, remembering how she might create wrinkles in her forehead, refrained from doing so.

"I do not take your meaning, my lord."

John hesitated, and in that hesitation, she realized something unpleasant was about to be said to her. Bracing herself, she blinked at him.

"In truth," he said, "I am adjusting my notion of you, and while thus doing, I am afraid I am behaving poorly."

It was her turn to widen her eyes.

"You see," he continued, "I believed we had an understanding, although indubitably, a very slight one. And

I also had a misconception of you, which I am now correcting. Neither of these issues is your fault, though, and therefore, I confess my treatment of you is unkind. While you have the excuse of youth and a general frivolity of nature, I am older and should have known better than to act as I have."

Then he stopped talking. Maggie was flummoxed. She had no idea what to say despite being certain she'd been insulted, called the equivalent of immature and shallow.

"I see." She rose to her feet.

John did the same.

Realizing she hadn't said what she'd intended, Maggie sat again.

Frowning, he sat, too.

However, she'd been insulted. Standing once more, she fully planned to walk out.

Lord Cambrey quickly stood again, as well.

Still she hesitated.

"Miss Blackwood, would you care to tell me why you wished to speak with me?"

Staring hard at him, at his soft hazel eyes, her stomach twinged. Her stomach never did that when she was with any of the other men she knew. Sighing, she sat once more.

As soon as he had done the same, she began. "I felt badly at how you came upon me, or rather, us, in your garden, and I wanted to tell you so."

John held up a hand. "Please, Miss Blackwood, you are ill-advised to speak of a transgression, even with someone who witnessed it."

Maggie nearly laughed. Was he actually pursing his lips, this man who had held her close a mere few feet from a roomful of partygoers?

"You sound like a prude, Lord Cambrey, yet I know firsthand you are not one."

"A prude?" His expression showed he was not pleased.

"Indeed," she told him. "Moreover, I know a little about your reputation. You like to spend time at White's, but you do not frequent the terrible gaming hells, nor are you in danger of losing your family's fortune. I have never seen you in your cups, nor have any in my acquaintance, and therefore, I assume you are not a drunkard."

He looked as if he had no idea how to respond.

Warming to the topic of her personal expertise on his nature, Maggie added, "You have escorted more than one Cyprian to the opera and to the ballet, although it seems you have not had an association with more than one at the same time. Since you are not married, I do not hold such behavior against you, especially as you had none of these ladies at your home, to the best of my knowledge. What's more, you kissed me under the stairs, thus I do not think you a prude. So why can't we speak freely?"

His mouth was open again. In a second, he snapped it closed. Then he ran a hand over his eyes. When he looked at her once more, he seemed almost surprised to see her still sitting there. Or maybe he wished her to have disappeared.

"For one thing, Miss Blackwood, we are *not* alone." He kept his gaze firmly on hers, yet she knew he meant her maid, whom she'd practically forgotten and who was seated in the far corner next to a tall potted palm.

Perhaps Maggie was too trusting, but she'd never had one of their staff betray a family confidence, at least not that she knew.

"Bess," she called to her maid. Silence.

Turning in her seat and looking over the back of the sofa, Maggie tried again. "Bess."

The woman stirred, yawned, stretched, and then at last turned toward her mistress. Her cheeks flushed bright red, truly shocked to see two people staring at her from across the room.

"Bess, would you like to go to the kitchen and tell Lord Cambrey's cook you need a cup of tea. Oh, and if they have any sponge, you must have a slice. I will call you when I'm ready to leave. I won't be long."

Standing slowly, looking from her mistress to the earl, she was evidently unsure if she should leave Maggie alone.

"Go on now, tea and sponge or a biscuit," Maggie ordered. "Whatever Lord Cambrey's cook has for sweets. It will perk you right up."

"Yes, miss." Backing toward the door while keeping her eyes on Maggie and Lord Cambrey, she finally turned and fled.

"I don't believe she heard anything we were discussing. Don't you think it would be the height of boredom to spend your days eavesdropping? I imagine Bess has her own thoughts to keep her occupied."

"Frankly, I think you are naïve as all get-out. You were extremely fortunate your maid had nodded off. If that is your method for keeping things private, remind me never to tell you a secret."

Maggie laughed. They were becoming friends again. She was certain.

"Where were we? Oh, yes, I was telling you how I felt badly you came upon me and Lord—"

"Yes, I know whom you were with." He leaned back and crossed his arms again.

"And I believe you now have the wrong impression of me, which pains me."

"Really? I suppose you are going to shower me with a heartfelt apology as you did for cutting me at the dance. Except, as I recall, you didn't really apologize for that, either."

She felt her ire growing.

"I believe I did offer you an apology in measure with the offense you believe I committed, namely neglecting to look at my dance card."

"Oh, I see," he drew out the end of the word. "A *tempered* apology, moderated and diluted until it is only what you deem I deserve for the small portion of the insult toward me."

Sighing, Maggie was finding this harder than she'd anticipated.

"I thought we were past that supposed but *unintentional* offense. In any case, I am not going to apologize for kissing Lord Burnley. In fact, I wanted to tell you it was a good thing I did. Although in truth, I did not kiss him. Well, not any more than I kissed you. In point of fact, he kissed me."

John looked pained. Such was the only word for his expression.

"You are happy he did so?" he asked, his voice sounding odd.

"Immensely." *Finally, they were getting somewhere*, she thought. Now she could tell him of her great discovery, Lord Burnley's kiss was nothing compared to his.

"And you felt the need to tell me."

"Well, yes, of course, because—"

A soft rap sounded at the door, and John looked relieved at the interruption. "Come in." He invited quickly.

His butler, the same who had shown her in, entered the room.

"Lady Emily Chatley and Lady Jane Chatley to see you, my lord."

The annoyance Maggie felt was equal to a bee sting as had happened to her twice as a child in their country home in Sheffield. She used to get too close to the beautiful flowers in her mother's garden, competing with the bees for the most fragrant blooms until she learned her lesson. Jane Chatley obviously thought John Angsley to be quite the eligible bloom.

What a nuisance, right when they were coming to an understanding, too. What's more, John seemed to be finished with their discussion. He stood quickly and glanced at his pocket watch.

"I hadn't realized the time. Tell them to wait in the drawing room, Henry."

"Yes, my lord." And the butler backed out, closing the door behind him.

"While our conversation has been most enlightening, I have a previous engagement, and I don't want to keep the Ladies Chatley waiting."

No, of course not, not like he kept her waiting! Maggie was practically being thrown out.

"If you stay here a moment, Miss Blackwood, I'll have the vigilant Bess returned to you before you depart. Please give your mother, Lady Lindsey, and Miss Eleanor my best regards."

With a curt nod, he walked out, leaving the door open behind him. If she'd hoped for another kiss, she would be sorely disappointed, and she was. Not even a brush of his lips over her knuckles.

She sniffed. *Was she losing her charm?* She had neglected to give him her dazzling smile. Clearly, that had been a fatal mistake. What's more, she wondered if she would ever get the chance.

The only bright spot—Jane Chatley was not meeting alone with him but had her dear mama playing chaperone. But what if it were an important discussion? What if it were about a very serious matter indeed?

Oh dear!

CHAPTER SIX

Cam tried to focus on the Chatleys. Truly, he tried. After such a bizarre encounter with Margaret, though, all he could do was ruminate upon what she'd said.

How impossibly strange for her to come to his home and tell him directly and in person she'd enjoyed kissing Burnley.

Why on earth would she think that a good idea?

For the upcoming match, the Cambrey family, along with the Chatleys, would host at Lord's Cricket Ground in St. John's Wood. Jane and her mother had a hundred ideas regarding the outdoor banquet before the match, designed to raise money for orphans. He ought to be entirely focused on the important occasion. However, Cam could only hope he'd made all the right responses and nodded at the correct moments, and he was relieved when the ladies rose to leave.

If only Simon were back so they could have a serious talk, man to man. Cam didn't feel close enough to anyone else in London to discuss the infernal woman who seemed to still be filling his head with her strange words. Moreover, Simon knew Margaret through his marriage. If anyone could tell him whether the woman was insane or merely immature, he could.

He knew in his heart he ought to stop thinking about her altogether. If he truly wanted a wife, he could hardly do better than Jane Chatley, with her poised manner, her softly spoken words, and her attractive face. She was shapely in a classic way, and she never puzzled him or caused him to want to throttle her. In a word, she was perfect for him. He could already envision their Christmas parties at his family's home, Turvey House in Bedford, where she would make their guests feel warm and welcome. Never uncomfortable.

Cam knew if he married Jane, at no time would he wonder if she were going to kiss another man. Also, they would have exceedingly well-behaved children.

He would never have to see those wickedly glistening, gold-tinged eyes or her breathtakingly dazzling smile again. Not ever.

It would be heaven.

So why did it seem like a lifetime of deadly dullness?

Fine! Perfect! Brilliant! Lord Westing had left his calling card while Maggie was out having a perfectly terrible time at John Angsley's townhouse.

Good! She would send Lord Westing, whom she would start to think of as his given name, Christopher, a return missive. She would allow him to call on her. She would invite him to go driving. She might even ask him to damn well kiss her, to carry on her experiment. In which case, she would hope for better results than with Lord Burnley, for she wanted to have that same exciting sensation as she'd had with John.

With a man who didn't seem set against her, and surely not one who was falling for the incomparable Jane Chatley.

Over the course of the next few weeks of the Season, Christopher kept her busy, although they didn't form an exclusive attachment. In fact, the closer they became as friends, the less she could picture him as her husband. Lord Burnley was still writing his name on her dance card as well as Lord Fowler, and other gentlemen. Oddly, the subject of kissing did not come up with any of them, nor did the situation arise. Maggie had to face it, she was in a blue huff and didn't feel like kissing anyone.

The other blight on her enjoyment was being forced to see John with Lady Chatley upon more than one occasion. When Maggie did encounter him alone, he did nothing more than politely nod as if they were the most distant of acquaintances. She usually stuck her tongue out at the back of his head if she thought herself unobserved.

It was most tiresome for he filled her thoughts in quiet moments and distracted her when she was otherwise occupied. She seemed to conjure John Angsley at events, nearly always with Jane, until Maggie supposed he must have a formal agreement with her—or was close to having one.

One afternoon, Christopher was dropping her home when he offered her an invitation to something a little different than their usual events.

"Will you accompany me to a sporting event? It's a cricket match with a banquet beforehand. There will be others whom I believe you know, including Baron Ellis's daughter. It will be a jolly group."

"Cricket?" Maggie repeated. Immediately, she recalled a time she'd sat next to John Angsley before the Season started. "Yes, I do enjoy cricket."

AND THEN HER SEASON was interrupted again, as it had been the year before. This time, though, in a happy way by the return of her sister's husband, "Lord Despair" as Maggie had called him along with most of the cruel-tongued *ton*.

However, Simon Devere, Lord Lindsey, seemed despondent no longer. What's more, her sister was once more glowing with happiness and with the babe blossoming inside her. Now, the heir could become public knowledge.

Maggie knew John had come by more than once to sit in the parlor with his best friend and talk. She'd stayed clear, not wishing to end up as the topic of the gentlemen's discussion, should John be reminded of her existence.

And then one morning, quite by accident, she nearly plowed into him as she entered the dining room.

"Oh." Maggie stopped in her tracks at seeing the earl in her path. It was the first time they'd been in such close proximity in weeks. Merely from his gaze locking with hers, appearing more green than brown due to his colorful cravat, she felt her cheeks warm.

Beyond him were her older sister and her husband.

"Miss Margaret," John said, offering her a shallow bow.

"Lord Cambrey," she returned with a deeper curtsey. "Have you just arrived? Are you joining us for breakfast?"

She nearly bit her tongue off. He was plainly at the door and about to leave. Why had she invited him like that, sounding far too desirous of his company?

It didn't matter, for his answer was as expected.

"No, my lady, I was on my way out."

My lady! Was he so used to addressing Lady Jane Chatley he forgot Maggie had no such title?

"Very well," she bit out, keeping her back straight and striding past him to the sideboard to help herself to her morning meal. If John didn't wish to even sit at the table with her, she could dismiss him as easily.

"I'll see you out," she heard her brother-in-law offer.

Keeping her back to the proceedings, she picked up a warm plate and took her time selecting a pastry and some eggs.

"Good day, Lady Lindsey," John said to Jenny.

Maggie placed a sausage smack on top of the eggs.

"And to you, Miss Margaret."

She didn't turn at his voice. She cared not a fig for his good wishes. Yet, she had to be civil or her sister would know something was bothering her. Then Jenny would never leave her alone until she'd worried it out of her.

"Good day to you, Lord Cambrey." Maggie stabbed at a piece of ham and piled it on as well.

And then he was gone, along with her appetite.

She wanted to forget how *he* looked, strikingly handsome even when he wasn't smiling at her, and with eyes that made her catch her breath.

Jenny stared at her for a moment.

"I would have expected you to invite Lord Cambrey to eat with us and not take no for an answer."

Maggie took a seat across from her sister, amazed at how much food she'd put on her plate. *The deuce take John Angsley!* Her heartbeat had returned to normal, and with him gone, she could relax, being neither observed nor judged. Most positively, she didn't want to be compared to the incomparable Jane, who most likely never ate before noon, and then, most likely, nothing but clear broth.

"What has happened?" Jenny asked, pouring herself a cup of tea from the pot on the table.

"About what?" Maggie asked, attempting to sound oblivious.

"With you and Lord Cambrey, of course."

Maggie paused before responding, cutting the end of the thick sausage, spearing it with her fork, and holding it to her mouth.

"I have no idea to what you're referring. What about *me* and Lord Cambrey?"

Then she put the food in her mouth and gazed back at her sister while she chewed.

Jenny frowned. "I thought . . . that is, don't you enjoy his company?"

Maggie shrugged, reached for a piece of toast from the center silver holder, tapped off the crumbs, and buttered it. Then she considered her choices: gooseberry or strawberry jam? Deciding on the gooseberry, she lifted the silver lid from the glass pot and dipped her knife in before spreading a generous layer onto her toast.

"He is nice enough, I suppose. Yet he is certainly no Lord Westing."

There, that should put an end to her big sister's prying.

"I see."

Now, to push it home with a dash of reasonableness with which her pragmatic sister could not possibly argue.

"There is nothing to *see*, really, Jenn. I am meeting many gentlemen I like this Season. There is no reason to set my cap for any single one of them now."

Jenny laughed.

"Now what is it?" Maggie asked.

"I just realized I was fretting over you sounding so practical, when you are saying exactly what I would wish you to say."

Well done, Maggie thought. If only she truly felt that way. She would rather have the whole matter done and dusted, with her heart captured by one man who felt the same in return and was ready to offer for her hand.

If only. Instead, she feared the Season would drag on with her not feeling a particular *tendre* for any of the men who currently pursued her. And suddenly, the long weeks ahead didn't seem entertaining at all.

Even less so when a couple weeks later, Maggie walked into the drawing room to find Eleanor having a spirited discussion with Jenny over the latter's imminent departure for Sheffield. Yes, her sister was in the family way, but this seemed far sooner than expected to lose her to the country.

"I can't believe you're leaving before the Season's end." Maggie tried to keep the dismay from her voice, but Jenny was their rudder. The notion of having to be the responsible one for both her mother and Eleanor was slightly terrifying.

True, it had been two months since Simon's return, and he'd dutifully escorted all of them to many events, and yes, her sister deserved to have the remainder of her lying-in happen exactly how and where she wanted. In fact, Jenny hadn't really wanted to come to London in the first place, even before she'd known she was with child.

"I want to take long walks, and I can't do so here," Jenny explained, sounding patient but determined. Evidently, she would not be swayed.

"Most women only want to lie abed," Eleanor complained. "You can do that here in London."

How on earth did Eleanor know anything about what women wanted when with child? Maggie wondered.

"Or perhaps they are given no choice." Jenny crossed her arms. "Besides, what difference does it make if I'm locked away here in this house or back at Belton?"

Maggie was convinced her expression was as downtrodden as Eleanor's. In truth, though, Jenny had started to stay home with Eleanor more and more, sometimes not staying awake to hear her mother and sister's excited reports of a ball or a dinner party.

Reaching out, she touched Jenny's arm.

"It *does* make a difference. We love you, and your presence is always welcome, even if you are back here at home waiting to hear the details of what's happening with Lady Pomley or Lord Twiggins."

Maggie could feel tears crowding her eyes, but this was the time to consider her sister's well-being above all else.

"However, I completely understand I'm being selfish. You should do what's best for you at this time. If you feel the need for country air and walks in the field, then those are what you should have."

"Thank you." Jenny sounded so relieved at having Maggie's support, she felt positively saint-like.

Eleanor sighed. "I suppose we must get used to being without you, in any case. When we get back to Sheffield, we'll be in our home and you'll be far away in your manor."

They all laughed at Eleanor's flare for drama, and Jenny put her arm around both of them.

"You know you can visit anytime. Besides, it's only a mile from door to door."

MAGGIE WAS GLAD THEY had one more event to attend together, and she laced her arm through Jenny's as they entered the Fortner's residence. A more intimate affair than a coming-out ball, this dinner and dance would have only about sixty people, all friends of the hosts. There were many married couples, supposedly to offer a good example of what awaited the bachelors and single ladies should they accept the handfasting rope.

Playing matchmaker, the hostess had paired up the eligibles for the evening, each person having someone to sit with at dinner and with whom to dance.

Maggie felt a few butterflies, wondering with whom she had been partnered, hoping against hope it could be John Angsley, which meant he would be forced to spend the evening with her. If it happened, she hadn't decided whether she would charm him out of his stockings or be cool as ice.

As Lord and Lady Fortner were good friends of Simon's deceased father, he and Jenny were offered places of honor near the table's head. When they left her side to take their places, Maggie's escort for the evening appeared before her, Lord Christopher Westing.

She could own up to a sliver of disappointment, followed quickly by relief. With Christopher, she could relax. It would be a far easier evening, without any sparring, hurt feelings, or guilt.

When they were all seated, Lord Fortner called for quiet and introduced himself and his wife at the other end of the table. Making special note of his honored guests, Maggie's heart swelled with pride when he introduced Lord and Lady Lindsey. Then the guests were charged with enjoying themselves and "not to bore the others."

Everyone laughed. After a brief exchange with Christopher on her left, Maggie turned to her other side to greet a gentleman whom she'd never met before. In doing so, her gaze swept the far end of the table and she saw him. *John!* He was already deep in conversation with the granddaughter of their hosts, Lady Isabella Fortner.

Hm, at least it wasn't the ever-present Lady Chatley.

Then John leaned back, and lo, there was Jane on his other side.

Which one was he paired with for the evening? Maggie supposed she would find out when the dancing began. Turning her attention back to Christopher, she knew she had better try to forget Lord Cambrey had ever kissed her.

CAM COULDN'T FORGET MARGARET was seated at the end of the table between the infernal Westing and the newcomer, what was his name? Some sort of bird. No matter!

For his part, he had Jane at his side, of whom he had grown increasingly fond. She was steady. Yet, he could occasionally hear Margaret's effervescent laughter cut through the muddied voices of all the other diners. Like a particularly sonorous instrument to his ears, or like fine wine trickling down his throat when everyone else was like well water.

Stop it, Cam. What was Jane saying about the hors d'oeuvres they would serve before the banquet at the cricket match?

He felt himself frowning at his lovely companion. It seemed good ale and crusty bread, perhaps with thick slices of bacon interspersed, ought to be the food of choice. Or pork pies wrapped in waxy paper one could hold easily while watching the match. However, he doubted London's finest would pay a hefty ticket price for such food, even for the orphans.

His mind wandered back to the stairwell in his own home, to the delight of feeling Maggie's lips part beneath his. He could still recall the surge through his body as his yard rose to attention, and how easily he could imagine the pleasure they would give one another in the marital bed. Or in any bed, for that matter.

"Yes, fig glaze on crackers," Jane was saying.

Cam wanted to glaze Maggie's nipples with fig jelly and lick it off of her while she squirmed beneath him.

Christ!

Glancing down the end of the table again, his gaze met his best friend's. Simon offered him a smile, oblivious in his own marital happiness to the torment his friend was undergoing. Simon deserved his newfound joy, and Cam only hoped the forthcoming heir would be delivered easily of Jenny. The two of them had suffered enough.

Speaking of suffering, he couldn't keep his eyes off Margaret another moment, even though it was only the back of her lovely head since she was turned away and in close conversation with Westing.

Westing! Bah! If only there was one thing wrong with the man. That he had no flaws was the solitary trait one could hold against him. What an annoyance, this paragon. This—

"Do you agree?" Jane asked.

"Yes, fondant-iced cakes after the match," Cam repeated the last words he'd heard.

How would Westing feel when Maggie led him on a merry dance and started to kiss Burnley or even the nameless man beside her? Would he give up as Cam had done, or would he dig in his heels and fight for her affections?

Undoubtedly, she was worth fighting for. Like Helen of Troy. As Maggie turned, she flashed her dazzling smile that stole the breath from his lungs. There it was, being wasted on all and sundry. Perhaps he had been too hasty in deciding she was not suited to being a wife, anyone's wife, until she grew up. Possibly, the better course of action would be to offer tutelage as she matured into the spectacular woman she would become.

Reaching for his goblet, Cam drank down the Spanish red, hoping it had come from the business in which he'd invested. Then he signaled for more.

MAGGIE BEGAN TO FIDGET. This interminable meal had far too many courses. She was ready to dance. Westing was not as good at the polka as Burnley, but they made a good couple on the dance floor. She hoped for a quadrille and a few other of the *Anglais* country dances when couples mixed and danced with others.

Why? she asked herself. She knew why. Thus, even indirectly, she could dance with John.

There was no Grand March, but the first dance was indeed a quadrille, followed by another, and yet another, until every couple who wished had had a turn. Then a waltz. Then a comprehensive *Anglais* in which nearly everyone fit onto the dance floor in the Fortner's grand room, which was serving as a ballroom.

Feeling a tremor of anticipation as she worked her way along the line, being twirled and spun by each gentleman, suddenly, she was in John's arms once again.

She would savor it. Looking at him directly instead of off to the side as all the other dancers, Maggie took in his fine-looking face, positively appealing in every regard. And then, as their gazes locked, delicious warmth twisted through her.

She saw in his eyes he, too, felt something, like flame to a wick, stir between them. For a few seconds, they stared at one another. The music faded, as did the noise of the other couples enjoying themselves. She could hardly believe she was still dancing.

Gracious!

And then he spun her into the arms of the next dancer.

TO HELL WITH DECORUM and being restrained by the whim of their hosts, Cam was determined to hold Margaret again. That brief moment during the *Anglais* country dance was torment when he had to give her up. Like passing the single most delectable morsel of sponge cake to the next unworthy diner while Cam was left with a feast of dry, tasteless blocks of wood.

No offense intended to the other ladies, especially Jane, whom many men would find delectable, he was sure, but she wasn't Margaret. No one was. That was the problem.

Thus, as the first notes of a waltz began, when Jane was in the retiring room, Cam looked for Margaret. Westing stood next to her but was too foolish to have taken his partner to the dance floor. Instead, the marquess had turned away to speak with another couple.

Moving quickly, Cam crossed the parquet floor in three strides, grabbed Margaret by the wrist, and yanked her into the middle of the ongoing dance, making room for them among those already waltzing.

Obviously, she was stunned into silence for she hadn't protested. With his hand on her back, Cam guided her around the floor. At last, he could take a moment to simply hold her body close against his and look down into her lovely, upturned face.

He half-expected to see a mask of fury. Any other lady might struggle, pull away, and leave him to be disgraced for poaching someone else's partner and breaching dance-floor etiquette after the waltz had already started.

Instead, Margaret's golden-brown eyes twinkled with excitement. Her gorgeous lips were upturned into a delighted bow. Apparently, he had done something right at last.

"That was very naughty of you, Lord Cambrey," she said without a hint of censure. "Lord Westing might come after you and challenge you to a duel."

"I would win," he said, feeling utterly confident he spoke the truth. "However, we both know this is not exactly a dueling offense. After all, he has not declared for you. Has he?"

Her smile grew bigger. "Even if he had, I could certainly dance with you in a public place without causing an incident."

Cam felt his heart stutter. "Has he?"

"Has he what?"

She was enjoying teasing him. It could be immensely fun in the bedroom, but not in the ballroom, and not about this.

"You *know* what. Has Westing offered for your hand?"

Her hesitation nearly did him in. Then slowly, Margaret shook her head.

"Not yet."

Yet! He twirled her around the edge of the floor and back into the thick of the dancers.

"Are you expecting him to?"

Her catlike expression made him feel like a cornered mouse.

"Anything is possible, my lord. Don't you think? Why, this very evening, Christopher might tell me he plans to speak with my mother. In the same way as you might offer for Lady Chatley."

"Christopher?"

She merely shrugged delicately at her familiar use of Westing's given name. The minx!

Aware by the music the dance was near its end, Cam maneuvered her once again to the far end of the dance floor. Then he guided her off of it altogether. A well-placed door offered him the escape he sought, and soon, they were on the other side in a long hallway. *Alone.*

He wasted no time. Glancing up and down the corridor to confirm their privacy, he backed Margaret Blackwood and all her lusciousness against the robin's-egg blue wall, in between a portrait of an ugly man on her left and an even uglier woman on her right.

Peculiar, he thought, *since the contemporary Fortners seemed like an attractive family.*

Then Cam thought no more of anything as he pressed his advantage and, at the same time, pressed himself against the object of his most fervent desire.

Margaret went along willingly with everything he was doing. Even as he wove one of his thighs between her legs, hampered only by her skirts swirling around them both, she still said nothing, simply clinging to his upper arms.

Then she moaned softly, and he was lost. The sound tugged at his groin, and he lowered his head and claimed her lips. Finally.

Sighing, she opened her mouth under his almost at once, and he took what she willingly offered. Feeling her hands intertwine behind his neck and pull him closer, he pictured what they would look like to anyone who stumbled upon them. Her reputation would be ruined at once, and he would be forced to marry her.

Strangely, that didn't bother him in the least. But she might feel otherwise.

In any case, all Cam could do was deepen their kiss, exploring her mouth with his tongue before sucking on it. When he drew back to nibble on her full lower lip, dragging at it gently with his teeth, Margaret moaned again.

Arching into her lower body, he felt her hips lift toward him in response. He had never shared anything like this with a woman who wasn't paid for the pleasure, making it a heady experience indeed.

Knowing he was pushing his luck, he finally pulled away. Someone, probably Westing, would come looking for her.

Or maybe Simon. He would hate to have to explain to his best friend how he was practically ravishing his sister-in-law in the hallway of Fortner's London home. No, that wouldn't do at all.

CHAPTER SEVEN

"We should return to the party." Cam didn't look down, for he didn't want to draw Margaret's attention to the bulge in the front of his trousers. Instead, he offered her his arm.

Margaret hesitated to take it, staring up at him with flashing eyes. Her chest was heaving delightfully, and she had bright spots of color on her creamy cheeks. Her mouth was reddened to perfection, unfortunately letting everyone who saw her know she'd been thoroughly kissed.

Perhaps they shouldn't go back into the ballroom immediately. Taking her hand, which she'd pressed to her décolletage, the very spot where he wanted to place his lips and taste her, Cam tucked it into the crook of his arm.

"Why don't we stroll the gallery a few minutes until we both return to a calmer state?"

At last she spoke. "That sounds like a good idea."

Thus, when the ballroom doors opened a little while later, they were discovered merely discussing the merits of a Dutch painting with its intricate lacey detail.

"There you are."

Surprisingly, it was Lady Chatley and not Westing who had come seeking. She gave them both a genuine smile, but he felt Margaret's arm stiffen and pull away, taking her out of touching range altogether.

"*John*, it's the most exciting news," Jane began, and Margaret stepped back farther. "Prince Albert is coming to *our* cricket match! He wants to set up a private tent, of course, but he will donate quite a bit to the orphanage. And his attendance will assure us a large turnout. No word so far as to whether the queen will accompany him. She might though." Jane clapped her hands. "Only think of the donations."

She was practically prancing with excitement over this good fortune for the orphans of St. Giles.

"That's wonderful news," Cam said, although he wished he could have heard it later because, right then, even the queen herself wasn't as important to him as Margaret. "Do you know Miss Blackwood?"

Jane stopped fidgeting and focused on Margaret. "Of course, yes! We've met before, haven't we? I'm so sorry for my rudeness. It's just this is absolutely thrilling. Did John tell you about our event?"

Cam cringed as she had twice used his given name. Too familiarly, and in front of the woman he'd recently kissed.

Margaret shook her head, her expression neutral. "No, I hadn't heard."

Before she could say more, Westing appeared in the hallway, followed by another couple of ladies who were, no doubt, heading for the retiring room to fix their ribbons.

"There's my companion for the evening," the marquess said, giving Cam the once over. However, since Jane Chatley was also there, he didn't sound disapproving.

"I was looking at the Vermeer," Margaret said, casually gesturing toward the painting.

"And I was hoping to claim another dance," Westing said. "And your sister is looking for you. May I escort you back inside?" He offered his arm.

When Margaret took it, Cam couldn't help but clench his jaw. They strolled away, the vixen of his dreams not even bestowing him with a backward glance.

At last, he could focus on Jane.

"From whom did you hear this information?"

"About the prince consort's interest? I heard it from Sir Clark while we drank champagne only a few minutes ago."

Good, then he could return to the ballroom and keep an eye on Margaret.

"Come, then, Jane. Introduce me to Sir Clark, and we'll make sure the prince buys two dozen tickets at the least."

With that, Cam took Jane's arm and hurried her back into the dance.

MAGGIE FAIRLY FLOATED THROUGH the rest of the evening. She could barely hear anything Westing or even her sister Jenny said to her. Entirely wool-gathering with a silly happy grin pasted to her face, she didn't mind when the evening ended, and they climbed back into her brother-in-law's carriage.

"Are you well?" Jenny asked.

Was she well? Maggie touched her own lips, still positive she could feel and taste John upon them. It was as if he'd branded her as his own. And the feel of his thigh against her most intimate, womanly parts had made her long for much more.

Never before had she wished to be unclothed with any man. Quite the opposite. Normally, she wanted to show off her figure in a gorgeous gown. Yet, after John's kiss, she wanted to lie with him, with no finery between them at all. Absolutely bare. She wanted to touch him as much as she wanted to be touched.

"Mags?"

"I'm fine. It was a lovely evening, wasn't it?"

Her sister sighed. "Truthfully, I'm glad it's over. I'm ready for Sheffield."

Her words brought Maggie into the present moment. Jenny was leaving shortly. Taking her hand, she squeezed it, looking over at her brother-in-law.

"You must take care of her," she told Simon.

He smiled. "Precisely what I intend to do, for every moment before, during, and after our child is born." He gave Jenny a loving smile.

Maggie sighed. "I'm so happy for you both."

And now, she was happy for herself, too.

ALL OF LONDON'S SOCIETY was talking about the Chatley-Cambrey pre-match banquet. Not having realized it was the event to which Westing had invited her, Maggie would sit at a table with the marquess and his younger brother, as well as her friend, Ada, and two others of their acquaintance. Her sister Eleanor was attending, too, and would probably find Beryl Angsley awaiting her.

They would probably sit with John. Lucky girls!

When Maggie arrived, a crowd of attendees awaited Prince Albert, standing near the edges of his tent hoping to catch a glimpse of him. As far as everyone knew, the fundraising efforts, spurred by the promise of a royal presence, were wildly successful. There would be enough for two orphanages to be built and sustained for at least two years, keeping some of the thousands of "guttersnipes" or "mudlarks," as the unfortunate children were called, off the streets. Even Simon and Jenny had donated a huge sum to the cause before they'd left London.

For her part, Maggie skirted the crowds, more desirous of seeing John than the prince consort, having not been in the earl's company since the Fortner's ball. Having examined what had occurred from every side, Maggie had mulled over any words he'd said, which had been very few. Most of their encounter had been spent kissing. What did it mean, if anything? It was the second time he'd taken tremendous liberties with her person, the second time she'd willingly let him.

What did he think of her for allowing such?

Did he do the same with other debutantes? she had wondered one night, sitting in her room on Portman Square. How could she ever know? He seemed adept at finding a moment alone with her. Perhaps he had a particular talent for doing the same, and often, with other women. There was simply no way to discover if that were the case short of asking each single lady of her acquaintance if they'd been kissed by the Earl of Cambrey.

A disheartening thought. And what of Lady Jane Chatley? It was difficult to believe a man who was as good at kissing and as eager to do it as John Angsley could have spent so much time with the wealthy and attractive Jane and not kissed her.

Westing led her to their table, and Maggie could see for the first time what Jane's skills were as a hostess. There were fresh flowers everywhere, giving the entire tent a sweet aroma. Banners hung from the tent's scaffolds, proclaiming messages of welcome and gratitude for everyone's generosity.

Maggie couldn't help smirking. After all, she knew of very few of the *ton* who cared a fig for the many orphans they studiously tried to avoid in the streets each day. Most held a perfumed handkerchief to their noses to keep out the children's rough odors if encountered. Moreover, if they cared to, the elite of London could donate to orphanages *without* the benefit of attending a high-profile banquet and cricket match, but then they wouldn't get to gawk at Prince Albert.

Jane had done a good thing, along with John, Maggie reminded herself. And with the benefit itself, Maggie could find no fault. It was running smoothly, with servants threading the crowd, offering trays of hors d'oeuvres and glasses of champagne or wine. A band was playing in the corner as if they were indoors in a ballroom.

Eleanor was already seated at a table of honor with John's mother, Lady Cambrey, as well as Lady Beryl Angsley, and Lady Chatley, Jane's mother. There were two others as well as two empty seats, presumably for the host and hostess.

Where were they? And why was it so very irksome to keep thinking of the two of them, the houses of Cambrey and Chatley, linked together?

Maggie knew why. Because John's lips had made her sizzle all over, and she definitely wanted him to kiss her again.

Then suddenly, the music stopped, and all eyes turned in the direction of the band, including Maggie's, and there he was. In a perfect suit of dove gray with a bold cranberry-colored waistcoat, the Earl of Cambrey.

With Jane, looking exquisite in rose silk, by his side. *Drat her!*

"Thank you all for coming," John said, his booming voice filling the tent and silencing any last talkers on the outskirts. "For those of you who don't know me, I'm Lord Angsley, Earl of Cambrey. For those of you who do, I'm happy you came anyway."

A few men cheered. "Go on with you, Cam!"

"We have lovely weather today for the match presently, but you know our country. It may rain at any moment. Even so, the sun will be out again in mere minutes. That's one of the charms of England, isn't it? The fickle weather!"

A few people chuckled.

"And the other charm is our beautiful English ladies. While she needs no introduction, I will offer one anyway. Our delightful and lovely hostess, Lady Jane Chatley. She's going to tell you more about the charity we're supporting today."

Turning to Jane, he took her hand and drew her forward, bowed as he released it, and stepped back. Front and center of attention, Jane's cheeks pinkened until they matched her gown, and then she spoke about the plight of London's orphans and the good all of those present could do.

Maggie's attention drifted to where John had moved away from the band and began skirting along the side of the tent. Helping himself to a glass of champagne off of a passing tray, he then scanned the room, until, to her surprise, his gaze alighted on her.

He smiled with a slow, sexy grin that made her knees become weak and cause a strange fluttering low in her stomach.

Gracious! He could do all that to her with only a look and a smile.

Then he nodded, lifted his glass to her slightly as if toasting, and drank down a long sip.

Feeling all hot and bothered, Maggie grabbed for her own glass and took a healthy swallow, feeling it go immediately to her head. Offering John what she hoped was her best smile and not a lopsided foolish grin, she tried to turn her attention back to Jane, who seemed to be babbling on for longer than she should.

At last, to Maggie's relief, Jane stopped talking, people clapped and cheered, and then Cam yelled out from where he stood, telling everyone to enjoy the feast and then go watch a cracking good game of cricket.

To her delight, he appeared to be making his way through the attendees, weaving his way through the tables, toward her. Patting her chignon below her smartly situated hat, Maggie involuntarily licked her lips to moisten them even though, obviously, they weren't going to kiss right there and then. She nearly giggled at the thought of the chaos that would ensue if they were to touch lips in the middle of a civilized social gathering. No doubt the place would erupt in flames followed by a great hole appearing beneath their feet, and they would all tumble to hell for the absolute immorality of it.

It would be worth it, she decided.

He was nearly at her table, when he was waylaid by a serious-looking man wearing the royal livery, and Maggie knew the prince consort had arrived. This man with his gleaming saber strapped to his side was most likely some type of guard for Prince Albert.

As he turned, she saw he also had a pistol in a holster on his other side, confirming her suspicion. Ever since the attempted assassination of the queen eight years earlier, the royals traveled with heightened security.

Maggie shivered and sent up a prayer the only fighting this day would be between the cricket teams battling on the field. Still, she was sad to see John detour from his path and accompany the royal servant out of the tent toward the prince's private area.

At the last moment, he stopped, and she held her breath. However, instead of looking toward her, he glanced toward the band until he saw Jane and gestured to her.

Although Maggie couldn't hear what he said, Jane hurried to his side, and the two of them left the tent. Then her view was blocked by a veritable troop of servants carrying in platters of food for every table.

Sighing loudly, she sat down and tucked in to a most delicious meal. While she listened to the lively conversation among those at her table, including a particularly heated debate over the merits of the two teams, Maggie kept an eye on the tent opening, but John did not reappear, nor did Jane. It seemed they'd been invited to dine with the prince.

"Don't you think, Miss Blackwood?"

The words floated into her brain belatedly, and Maggie turned to see the entire table was looking at her. She thought it was one of the gentlemen on the other side who'd addressed her, Lord Stanley possibly.

Drat!

Ada, who was seated beside her, touched her hand. "Don't tell us you're rooting for Sussex over Nottinghamshire."

Bless her friend, Maggie thought. "Of course I'm for Mr. Parr and Nottinghamshire. Not only is he a great batsman, he has the dash-fire that is rarely overcome."

Half the table cheered, the others, those for Sussex, booed.

Christopher, on her other side, gave her an approving smile. It did not turn her knees weak or her insides to butterflies but was pleasant all the same.

"Have you picked out our seats, Lord Westing? I hope we have a good view for our victory."

Those at the table booed and cheered again, and then they all arose and left the tent to find where Westing had secured their seats, having sent servants to claim enough for all of them. Unlike most matches, there would be chairs all around the field, with no one needing to stand unless they wanted to. Prince Albert, of course, had taken the entire second-floor balcony of the small pavilion.

As one, the entire crowd looked up at the Lord's pavilion as a bat boy ran up the steps to present the prince consort with a new ball. Maggie thought Prince Albert looked a tad doubtful about the gift. She'd certainly never heard of him playing cricket, and therefore, it wasn't surprising when he simply tucked it under his chair. The crowd cheered nonetheless.

What was surprising, however, was the Earl of Cambrey and Lady Chatley had ostensibly been given the royal boot, for they were not seated upstairs near the prince. Instead, they had seats on the sidelines like everyone else about a quarter of the way around the field from her own small party. Moreover, much to Maggie's dismay, they were seated together, reminding her of when she and John had sat side-by-side many months earlier, enjoying a match. The opportunity for one's shoulder and leg to touch were numerous, as well as intimate conversation with heads bowed together.

Jealousy sat on her lap and refused to move. *Double drat!*

WHEN CAM WAS SETTLED in his chair to watch the match with his family and Jane's around him, he could search for his heart's desire in the crowd. Even with Jane beside him, her friend Isabella Fortner sat on her other side, keeping her occupied.

If only Prince Albert hadn't requested meeting the host and hostess of the banquet, Cam would have pushed his way into a seat at Margaret's table, even if it meant dragging a chair between her and Westing.

Instead, he'd had to sit nearly in silence while the prince consort and Jane discussed social issues, particularly education of the youth of their country. Cam had spent the time stifling yawns and trying to keep his eyelids open. Not that he wasn't interested in educating people. Actually, truth be told, he wasn't. He'd had a good education at Eton, and since he had yet to have children of his own, how was it any business of his how others became educated?

Relief had washed over him like summer rain when the horns blew announcing the start of the match. They'd bowed and curtsied to Albert and left him to his own companions.

Margaret was fairly easy to spot, or maybe he was simply attuned to her now. Her gorgeous caramel-colored hair stood out to him, like gold amongst the dun-colored masses. Even though today, perched atop her head was a striking sapphire-blue hat with feathers dancing this way and that.

There she was, between Miss Ellis and Lord always-present Westing. And then, fortuitously, her glance fell upon him. Gossips-be-damned, he lifted his hand and waved to her. Margaret didn't respond, but she did smile broadly enough so he could see it, even at a distance.

Somehow today, he would find a way to speak alone with her. Thankfully, he would have far more time to devote to his own selfish interests now the banquet was over. All the planning had been successful, and he could go back to his life of pursuing Miss Blackwood, having done well for the orphans while keeping up the grand Cambrey tradition as benefactors to the community at large and England as a whole.

Yes, it had been a triumph all around, and his mother was beyond pleased.

Moreover, despite his own doubts over Margaret's maturity still shadowed his frank admiration of her, he'd decided after their last exhilarating kiss to ignore any shortcomings she might have. He wanted her, plain and simple, for his own.

The game was exciting but torturously long when all Cam wanted to do was speak with her—to create an understanding between them in which she would no longer keep company with other men. He wanted her to forego the rest of the Season's events unless he was accompanying her, which he would happily do.

Hoping to catch her eye again, he spent as much time looking over at her as he did watching cricketer George Barr make mincemeat of the other team.

At last, it seemed Margaret saw and understood what he meant by his violent head movements that made him look as if he were having some sort of apoplectic fit, and which he kept telling Jane were merely the result of a gnat biting his neck. As soon as he saw Margaret rise from her seat, he, too, excused himself and walked back to the tent.

Glad to see there was still champagne, he snagged two glasses and waited by the tent flap. Should he practice a speech or simply shove the glass in her hand and say what was in his heart?

"Margaret Blackwood, you are the jammiest bit of jam and I adore you above any other lady I have ever met or kept company with."

No, he shouldn't mention anyone else at all. It might get her mind thinking of other women with whom he'd been associated. *Think again*, he told himself.

The flap opened behind him, and he spun around, thrusting the glass toward . . . *Jane.*

"There you are," she said, taking the glass from him and sipping. "Is your neck all right?"

"My neck? Oh, yes. Fine." What could he say?

She sighed. "I see we had the same idea, to celebrate a bit in private."

Odsbodikins! Did she have aspirations regarding him? He had never had the least intimation she cared a fig for him.

"This has all been rather exhausting, hasn't it?" Drinking the champagne rather quickly, she gave an unladylike burp and then lurched against him. He was forced to drop his own glass to the grassy ground and grab hold of her before she toppled over.

Looking down, he saw a look in her eyes which hadn't been there previously, not desire but more like desperation. He also suspected she'd had far more glasses of champagne than he had. But when?

"My mother was very impressed," she mumbled. "We've spent a lot of time together, you and I, yet from now on, we won't have reason to do so. Unless . . ."

She let her words trail off.

Unless he offered for her hand. Was that what she meant? He must break it to her he had absolutely no intention of asking her to be his wife. At this juncture, he felt more brotherly toward her than anything else.

"My mother wanted me to tell you how impressed *we* are with you," she continued.

Pressing her face against his chest, he heard her start to sob. *Dear God!* What was wrong with this woman who had, until that moment, seemed the picture of placid, unruffled reasonableness?

Hell!

"Dearest Jane," he started. Yes, d*earest!* Because she was crying, after all, and he had to be tender. "What can I do to help?"

Patting her back, feeling a tad awkward as he'd never touched a woman this way. If his hands were around a lady, it was always in preparation for kissing her or even tupping her soundly. Comforting a woman who was not a member of his family felt entirely too intimate.

"*She* thinks I've been standoffish and off-putting, and other dreadful 'off' words."

"Who?"

"My mother."

Ah. He was beginning to see the picture.

"You haven't been," he assured her. "We've worked well together, and I've had a marvelous time. You're very skilled at organization and planning."

She pulled back to look up at his face.

"I'm sorry, John. I don't know what's wrong with me. I truly value your friendship. I don't want to ruin it."

He stopped rubbing her back and took her face in his hands. "How much champagne have you had?"

All of a sudden, she grinned broadly at him. "I found two glasses on my way in here. I simply wanted a moment alone with you because I feared either you or my mother was going to try to make a monumental decision today, one with which I am presently unable to accept."

"I understand entirely. Not to worry. I have no intention of making any monumental decisions today, and I can handle your mother. Truth be told, I have some experience with eligible young ladies' mamas. You won't be forced to do anything."

With that, he dropped a kiss on her forehead, as he would to Beryl, and released her.

Unsteadily, she stumbled, and he grabbed for her again, both of them laughing.

"One of us had best get out of here, though, before we are discovered alone, or it will be out of my hands. And in your state, I think you should be the one to remain. Please sit. I'll send one of your friends in."

He pressed her down onto the nearest chair.

"Not my mother!"

"No, not your mother."

Patting her shoulder, he left the tent in search of someone Jane could trust. *Lady Isabella Fortner*, he decided. She and Jane had got on very well the other night, enough so Jane had invited her to sit with them for the match.

As he strolled behind the chairs, approaching the area at which his little party had been seated, he glanced toward Margaret's group. Some were still there, but Margaret had disappeared. As had Westing.

An unpleasant knot tied up his insides. Still, he had to locate Lady Fortner first. Luckily, he found Beryl who knew Isabella had headed into the pavilion where a ladies' withdrawing area had been set up.

Spinning about, Cam headed directly under the Prince's balcony and inside the cool wooden structure. It looked to him as if it could do with a slight renovation, at least to keep it up to snuff.

He certainly couldn't follow Lady Fortner into the ladies' room. *Blast it!* He should have brought Beryl with him. He would have to loiter outside awaiting the young woman's exit.

As he paced the pavilion floor, he glanced behind him to the farthest reaches where refreshments would have been set up if this were a normal match day. Instead, he could hardly give credence to what he saw.

Margaret, *his* Margaret, was standing alone with Lord Westing, whose hands were on her upper arms. In turn, her arms seemed to be resting on his chest. She looked emotional, if Cam was reading her expression correctly, as she stared up at the marquess. In the next moment, Westing hunched closer to her and turned slightly, hiding her from Cam's view.

Hell's bells!

Now, he knew what someone meant by their blood boiling, for he felt as if he could see a red haze like a curtain over his eyes. Taking a step in their direction, Cam was unsure what he would do or say, but he couldn't stand idly by while the woman he . . . while Margaret played him for a fool.

CHAPTER EIGHT

"Lord Cambrey, you have pulled off a magnificent event."

Turning, he found himself face-to-face with Isabella Fortner, and suddenly he remembered Jane. Poor Jane, sitting alone in the tent on the site of their great triumph, drinking herself into a stupor over her boorish mother. Lady Emily Chatley obviously wished her daughter to fall for him, and vice versa.

Well, if wishes were horses, then beggars would ride, as they said.

"Lady Fortner, I was actually looking for you. Lady Chatley is in need of your assistance. She is in the large banquet tent. Will you let me take you to her?"

"Of course, my lord."

And with that, this sensible lady let him hurry her to the side of her friend—her mature, stable, sweet, smart, organized, loyal friend Jane, and away from the fickle, flighty, flirty Margaret Blackwood.

"Please, Christopher, take me home!" Maggie knew at any moment she would dissolve into tears. What she'd seen when arriving at the banquet tent had been like a slap in the face, at the same time twisting her heart until it ached.

"Eleanor will be dropped off later, I'm sure, by . . . the Cambreys." She could barely say the name without wanting to cry. What a fool she'd been! An absolute ninny!

She'd seen enough and heard enough to make her finally understand Lord Cambrey and Lady Chatley were headed for an engagement. The way they touched each other and spoke softly and then laughed. Maggie's stomach hurt merely recalling the scene she'd witnessed through the tent flap.

"I'm very sorry you've been sorely used," Lord Westing told her. "I cannot believe what a scoundrel the earl has been. If your father lived, we would go to him at once and have him call Cambrey out. If you and I had an understanding, Margaret, then I would do it in his stead. I will anyway, if you like."

She had blurted out too much, and now regretted it. What she hadn't said, Christopher had guessed. That somehow, John had toyed with her affections, despite how he was plainly attached to another.

"I have been foolish," she muttered, thinking about trying to compete with the wealthy, polished, and titled Lady Chatley.

"No, it isn't your fault." Tucking her hand into his, Christopher walked her from the cool shadowy interior out of the pavilion and toward the waiting line of carriages.

"Believe me, you are not the first to have your head turned by a man who had ill-intentions. Nor will you be the last."

He helped her into his carriage and tapped on the roof.

"Unfortunately, you are alone with me in this carriage, and your reputation is in peril once again. It is a difficult world of rules we live by, even though it is all smoke and mirrors as if we're all in a phantasmagoria show."

Maggie couldn't speak at first, afraid she would cry. She appreciated Christopher's kindness and, for the world, would not cause him any trouble.

"I will get out alone and you shall stay inside. For all anyone knows, the carriage is full of our friends, and we were never alone in it."

He nodded, staring at her with his crystal-clear blue eyes.

"Are you all right? I have no right to ask, but we have kept company enough to be considered friends, don't you think?"

She nodded.

"Are you in trouble, meaning, that is, did he . . . ? Christ almighty! I can't even figure out the polite way to ask if he's ruined you."

His blunt words shook Maggie out of her misery. Suddenly, she was grateful she could answer with a resounding no.

"No, not at all. The mistake was all in my head, I believe, and most likely due to my lack of worldliness. I confess," she added with a self-deprecating shake of her head, "I am not experienced enough to know the nuances of these matters between men and women."

There, she'd said it, admitting to being an inexperienced innocent. She would be mortified if she wasn't already so disgusted with herself.

Christopher Westing stared at her a moment. Then he smiled.

"I think you are too kind. If you felt the gentleman was sending you signals of interest, then you were receiving such. Even if you are green in such matters, I can assure you Lord Cambrey is not. He is to blame in all this, in leading you on, and in whatever else occurred."

The carriage came to a shaky halt. They had only seconds before the coachman opened the door.

"I don't know how to thank you," Maggie told him. "I really don't. For pulling me out of the public eye and into the pavilion when I was in a state fit to be tied, and for whisking me away in your carriage. You've been a stalwart friend."

The door popped open and the coachman's hand reached in.

"Send me word if there is anything more I can do, including going to speak to the bounder himself."

"Thank you." She left the calming presence of Christopher Westing and entered her brother-in-law's empty townhouse, grateful her sister was still at St. John's Wood and her mother was having tea with her friends.

Heading straight for her room, Maggie asked to have a very hot bath drawn. She would soothe herself in fragrant water and emerge a new woman, one who didn't give a tinker's damn for John Angsley.

Two hours later, when her family returned, a note arrived from Simon. The baby seemed to be on its way, and if they wanted to be there for the birth, they must head north at once.

No one would believe how quickly the household of women could decamp, but an hour after they'd read Simon's words, Eleanor, Maggie, and their mother were on the way to Sheffield and to Belton Manor.

CAM FELT SICK. THAT was the only way to describe the sensation in his stomach and in his heart. When he discovered Margaret Blackwood had left London, and he was a mere few hours too late the next morning when he showed up on her doorstep, the disappointment was severe. Yes, he was heartsick.

Determined to ask her if she truly felt nothing for him despite their astonishing kisses, he had rapped on the door in daylight, exposed for all to see when he was turned away by a servant.

Climbing onto the seat of his lightweight tilbury, he could at least be grateful at having been spared what might have been a devastating discussion. Willing to give her the benefit of the doubt that she simply didn't know how positively remarkable was the connection between them, Cam had intended to ask what she felt when she kissed Burnley or Westing, assuming she'd kissed him, too.

Without question, it would have been a painful conversation, and he should be grateful for its avoidance.

Flicking the reins, he started down Orchard Street, away from Portman Square as it no longer held anyone of interest. The maid had the decency to inform him Lord and Lady Lindsey had requested the countess's family return to Sheffield, and Cam guessed it must be to do with the imminent arrival of the Lindsey heir.

Thinking of how far Margaret might have got in merely a few hours, he considered packing up his trunks and chasing her north. After all, he could as easily speak with her in Sheffield with Simon as his second, as wait for who knew how long for the Blackwoods to return to London.

But would she welcome him, or would she consider him a pesky intruder? Perhaps Westing had already been invited to Sheffield.

Turning left at the corner onto busy Oxford Street heading toward his home, Cam heard the carriage before he saw it. Or rather, he heard shouting, particularly folks yelling to "beware" and "watch out."

Whipping his head around, he saw a high-flyer phaeton, a dangerous top-heavy antique, heading directly for him. Instantly, he knew what had happened. Some fool had been racing early in the morning at Hyde Park and had come out onto the main road still going far too fast.

Already rocking and careening on two wheels, the driver jerked the reins to try to avoid Cam.

"No," he yelled, knowing the horses' erratic movement would tip the carriage over. Sure enough, the phaeton overturned just before it reached him, even as he tried to get his horse into faster motion and avoid the collision.

His lower-to-the-ground, sporty tilbury didn't stand a chance. Even though the two horses belonging to the other driver managed to avoid him, they dragged the sliding carriage, now driverless, directly into his rig.

Airborne in seconds and flying headfirst over his horse, Cam kept his eyes open as the cobblestone street rushed up to meet him amidst the shrieks and screams of onlookers. He stretched out his arms to break his fall, and then, everything went silent and dark.

MAGGIE WAS RELIEVED TO have witnessed the event of childbirth and afterbirth. Somehow the whole thing seemed less frightening now her older sister had gone through the ordeal, painfully but without problems. Relieved she would not be one of those to share a story of tragedy in her family, instead, Maggie was now aunt to a little boy with extremely strong lungs.

During the many hours of labor, she'd stayed by her sister's side, along with the midwife, Emily, who conveniently was also the baker's wife. They'd not only been delivered of a delightful bundle of joy, but also a basket of clove buns.

She and Eleanor and their mother had barely made it to Sheffield before her sister's pangs began in earnest. And now thankfully, it was over, and Maggie had only recently sent Emily home driven by the Deveres' butler.

Simon and Jenny's bedroom door was wide open, thus, after knocking once, Maggie entered, hearing her sister say, "I doubt any mid-husband, no matter how competent, would have thought to bring the baker's best goods."

Simon was seated in a chair pulled up next to the bed, close enough to stroke his son's fuzzy head.

Smiling at the tired but happy new mother, Maggie snatched up one of the buns herself, before they were all gone.

"Unlikely an accoucheur would be married to a baker anyway," she said, belatedly putting her hand to her lips after spraying crumbs onto the counterpane. "By the way, the admiral has taken Emily home. She said she would stop by again tomorrow to help you with . . . *um* . . ."

Oh dear! She couldn't possibly discuss nursing with her brother-in-law in the room. Widening her eyes at her sister, she glanced at Simon.

"With what?" he asked.

What an oblivious male!

Looking into Jenny's amused eyes once more, Maggie gestured her head from the baby to her sister's ample bosom.

"With feeding the little one there. Emily said you didn't seem the type to have a wet nurse."

"Of course I won't. Why would I let my own milk go to waste?"

"So practical," remarked Simon, and then the two new parents grinned at each other, sharing some delighted secret. No one was mentioning the fact the wee, new Lord Devere was screaming like a mythical banshee.

Maggie ate the bun and waited to be noticed again.

"Please sit, Mags. Where's Mummy?"

"She'll be back shortly." Sitting a little gingerly on the edge of Simon and Jenny's bed, feeling a tad self-conscious, she added, "Mummy and Eleanor are still settling in."

"I'm glad you made it in time, but sorry you had to cut your Season short again."

Maggie couldn't tell Jenny how extremely thrilled she was to have been called away, but she was. Absolutely ecstatic to be away from the scene of her devastation. The baby's arrival meant she didn't have to face another social event, another smack in the face at seeing John attending with Jane. Consequently, she shrugged.

"No ball is as important as you."

"You can still go back," Simon offered. "The townhouse awaits you."

"I appreciate that. However, I believe I am done for this year."

Maggie noticed her sister glance at her husband. Jenny would worry something was wrong, and then she'd start to ask questions if Maggie didn't put a stop to it right then.

"The Season is ending in a couple short weeks. I see no reason to drag out the agony. There might have been an offer coming, but not one I would have accepted."

As expected, Jenny got one of her hands free by resting the baby's feet on her lap, and then she reached out and touched Maggie's hand.

"No," Maggie told her, rolling her eyes. "Don't get all sympathetic on me. I'm perfectly fine." She simply had to divert her older sister's attention to something else. "What a dear little boy. If only he wasn't bawling quite so loudly. It's hard to hear oneself think."

Jenny laughed. "Perhaps we should call him Lionel, for he roars like a lion." She glanced to Simon for approval.

"I like it," he agreed.

"Here, let me hold him." Maggie reached for the bawling infant and then rose to her feet. Strolling about the immense bedroom, she rocked him in her arms.

The babe continued to yell.

"Hmm." Maggie considered the little boy, Lionel Devere. Recalling what her mother did when Eleanor was a squalling babe, she slipped her smallest finger into the heir's open mouth. She felt him clamp down firmly. Blissful silence ensued.

"Dear God in Heaven," Simon marveled.

"How did you know?" Jenny asked.

"I saw Mummy do it with Eleanor. You were busy at the time doing something useful, I'm sure. My goodness, he's got a good grip."

"Let me try," Jenny said, popping the last of the sticky bun into her mouth and wiping her fingers on the coverlet.

Maggie returned the baby to his eager mother.

"If the finger works this well," Jenny considered, "I imagine the breast will work even better."

"Oh my." Maggie couldn't even look at Simon, not with Jenny discussing breasts in his presence. She had to escape from this close-knit family in the next minute and let them find their own way. As her sister slipped her shift off one shoulder and bared her left breast, Maggie made it to the door.

"Ouch," Jenny exclaimed, and Maggie winced for her while Simon leaped from his chair. Emily most likely wouldn't be needed again, for it seemed the baby knew precisely what to do.

"Well," Maggie said. "I'll see about getting you some tea." She slipped from the room.

Now what?

What was left to her in the upcoming days and weeks and months? Roaming the hallways of Belton Manor felt as aimless as her life. What's more, for the first time, the onset of fall saddened her. Last year, Maggie had thought by this time, she would be engaged. Or at least she imagined she would have found a gentleman with whom she would have an understanding. Maybe they would correspond over the winter and agree to meet at the holidays, conceivably announcing a Christmas engagement.

Sighing loudly at the idea of a third Season, she would encounter not only the same people but all the fresh-faced debutantes as well. Good lord!

She stopped in her tracks. Was it possible she, Margaret Blackwood, would end up firmly on the shelf of spinsterhood? Never to know the joys she'd witnessed back in her sister's room?

It had happened to ladies she actually knew. When her sister first came out three Seasons ago, that same year, one lady who was on her fifth Season simply gave up and walked into the River Thames. Someone actually saw her do it. The weight of her clothing pulled her down nearly at once before the river spat her back up, dead upon its shore.

Ironically, this was usually the fate of the unmarried women who found themselves in the family way. The newspapers were rife with news of bodies washed onto the embankment. Normally, these women were dressed moderately, as shop girls, or in rags, hopeless creatures who had no way to care for an infant.

What had shocked the ton was the intentional drowning by a viscount's daughter.

"She had everything to live for," Maggie murmured out loud. Except apparently, she'd desperately wanted a husband.

Without the prospect of one, what was Maggie's purpose? She had no intention of taking a last swim in the Thames or the local River Don, for that matter. Nor did she want to become a French tutor again, as she'd done in order to help out her family before Jenny married the earl and saved them financially.

No, she hadn't the patience or the humility for such a position again. It seemed like a selfless thing more suited to the faultless Lady Jane Chatley, who would most likely teach the orphans in Coddingtown.

Passing a large gilded mirror, Maggie realized she was sneering at the notion of Jane, not a particularly attractive look. Relaxing her features, she purposefully kept all thoughts of John out of her head. Except in trying to do so, the thoughts and memories flooded back.

"Bother!"

Entering the kitchen as if she owned the place, Maggie ignored the surprised look of the scullery maid and addressed the Devere cook.

"Would you send a pot of tea up to the new parents? I don't think they need biscuits since they have sticky buns, but some apples might be welcome, or if you have no fresh fruit, perhaps some preserves."

"Yes, miss," came the immediate reply.

This woman had purpose. Of course, it was beastly hot in the kitchen, and the cook's job was considered drudgery by nearly everyone. Yet, surely Maggie could find something to do with herself now she no longer had London to look forward to. Why, she could decide to become the very best auntie in the world.

"Do you need anything else, miss?"

Obviously, she was in the way and making the kitchen staff anxious.

"No, thank you. I shall most likely walk back home now while the weather is fine."

With that, she left, realizing the cook and scullery maid and the other girl who had been chopping vegetables until Maggie showed up and interrupted their work, none of them wanted to hear her plans for a stroll in the sunshine.

How thoughtless of her!

As she headed back to their stone cottage a short walk away at Norman's Corner, she tried to push the bleakness from her brain. What did women of a certain upbringing do if they didn't marry?

While she pondered this, a rider galloped past her as if the hounds of Hell were on his heels. He disappeared between the gates to Belton directly behind her.

Her mind was playing tricks on her, but Maggie could have sworn he wore the livery of the Earl of Cambrey.

Nonsense! Despite everything he'd done to play fast and loose with her affections, she was obsessed with John and saw signs of him everywhere, even when utterly unlikely. She ambled onward down the lane.

CHAPTER NINE

An hour after returning home, Maggie opened the door to find a stable boy from Belton Manor on the step. He'd rushed down to the cottage with a missive clutched in his hand. Immediately, as if her obsession haunted her, she saw *his* name:

Dearest Mags,
John Angsley, Simon's greatest friend, has been badly injured in a carriage accident. We just received word from Lady Cambrey, who said it's a wonder he lives at all. But you know how mothers can exaggerate, so we are trying to keep good thoughts. Cam is still at Cavendish Square under the able care of a King's College physician but will be moved to Bedfordshire as soon as they think it's prudent. I thought you would want to know.
Love,
Jenny

Maggie put the letter down on the dining room table, then picked it up again with a trembling hand and reread it. Feeling light-headed, she sat. It was hard to imagine John injured, strapping as he was, powerful and full of vim and vigor.

A wonder he lives at all.

How injured was he? Was he in pain even then? Her heart squeezed tightly, and for a moment, it was hard to breathe.

But the town of Bedford and Turvey House, his family home, were closer than London. Perhaps she could visit him.

In the next moment, she wondered what possible excuse she could use to go to his house. She was nothing to him.

So why was he still everything to her? Resting her head on her arms, she began to cry.

CAM DIDN'T SPEAK THE oath that sprung to his lips each time the coach rocked and dipped. If he did, it would be one long string of swearing for many hours to come. Stretched out in the largest carriage he owned, he was about as comfortable as one could expect to be with his broken bones and tender, bandaged head.

Tired of the constant laudanum-infused dreams, he had not taken a dose that morning when they set out, with his mother and his cousin Beryl in a separate carriage. Presently, he was reconsidering his rash decision and glanced over to make sure the bottle of bitter, reddish-brown liquid was close at hand.

Rather than bear the humiliation of being carried into an inn for the night, Cam had decided to make it hard on all of them and travel straight through by changing horses as necessary. Let the expense be damned! The coachman could get him food when he wanted it and empty his bedpan, too, for the next two days. Or his valet could do it, or whoever else was now seated atop the infernally lumbering growler that carted his broken body up to Bedfordshire.

At least he was alive.

Those were his mother's words, and Cam was trying every bloody day to feel the same way. But he didn't. Three weeks after the fateful morning, he still ached. Every movement of his limbs was painful, and his ribs were wrapped so tightly it was hard to breathe, let alone move. His vision still seemed strange in his right eye, and he hoped to God his eyeball wasn't looking off at a strange angle.

No one would let him look in a mirror, too scraped and scarred as he was, both on his right cheek and forehead. In all likelihood, he now resembled Mrs. Shelley's terrible creature, the very embodiment of Victor Frankenstein's experiments.

Using his left hand because his right arm was trussed up in a heavy plaster cast, with a similar contrivance on the entirety of his right leg, Cam picked up a newspaper from the stack he'd brought with him. He planned to catch up on what had occurred while he'd been heavily sedated and convalescing under the physician's care.

Wincing at the pain, squinting because of his damaged eye, he tried to concentrate on the news of the government of which he was an esteemed member of the House of Lords.

However, his mind drifted to the one person who had occupied his many fitful dreams. Margaret. He doubted she knew of his plight. Moreover, he dreaded the notion she would ever see him in such a state. Bad enough she preferred Westing over him, with all the attractiveness of the younger man's vitality. Now Cam was not only older, he was also disfigured and would most likely limp the rest of his life.

He read the same sentence in *The Times* over again, realizing he didn't give a fig about the Hungarian or the Italian revolutionaries, nor Prime Minister Palmerston's seemingly selfish handling of any of the current uprisings of the day. At that moment, they could all go to the devil.

Flipping over the page, he saw his friend's name and felt his spirits lift. There was the announcement of the heir to the earldom of Lindsey. Simon and Jenny had a baby boy who, God willing, would live to be the 8th earl in the Devere family. Margaret was an aunt and most likely would remain in Sheffield with her family.

At least, he was heading north and in the right direction.

"Fool," he muttered to himself. For what did it matter how close in proximity he was to Miss Blackwood? It would be utter torment ever to meet her again, knowing he had enjoyed their kisses far more than she had. And he couldn't bear to see a look of pity on her lovely features. *No*, that would do him in entirely.

Reaching for the bottle, he decided a small snooze was in order. Maybe for the next few days.

"HAVE A CARE," CAM yelled as the coachman and footman eased him out of the coach and onto a long stretcher as his doctor had called it, which had been carted up from London and stowed somewhere on the roof of the carriage.

"Let's not be clumsy, my good men. I haven't produced an heir yet."

Both men chuckled, which pleased Cam, for he knew he'd been a horse's arse to them the entire journey. At some point, unable to stand the unrelenting hours on the road, his mother had decided to stop at an inn. She would be arriving in Bedford the following day, pausing only to drop Beryl off at her parents' nearby home.

Cam didn't envy them one bit. Relief at being finally at Turvey washed over him like a welcome rain shower on a scorching day. He couldn't wait to lie upon his own down-filled mattress. In fact, he couldn't remember the last time he'd looked forward to going to bed when not anticipating the pleasures of a skilled and luscious female.

Suddenly, he no longer cared about this last humiliating and painful journey of a few yards. Hardly victorious, he was arriving home and being carried by strong men, from the carriage through his own front door and up to his bedroom, which had been his father's up until four years hence.

In any case, the ride on the canvas and wood stretcher felt smoother than the entire excursion from London. Lifting his head, he saw the familiar shock of black hair of his estate manager, Grayson O'Connor, who even then had hold of the front two poles, keeping him steady and smoothly level.

"Gray, have you got me?" Cam was suddenly feeling almost giddy at being home. That, and the generous amount of laudanum which suddenly seemed his best friend.

"I've got you, my lord."

Cam laughed. "None of that 'my lord' stuff for you and me. Remember that or I'll box your ears like when we were lads."

"You mean how you *tried* to box my ears."

Gray had been on the estate almost as long as Cam could remember, being the son of a servant originally from Cam's uncle's house, a few miles away. Cam couldn't recall why his uncle had sent young Gray to Turvey House when they were both boys just out of leading strings, but he'd always been glad of having a close companion. And while much of their upbringing as well as their futures were vastly different, they'd played and even fought like brothers.

Gray would get him upstairs safely. Cam had no doubt, and thus, he closed his eyes again.

The next time he awakened, he was in his own bed. Glancing around, he made sure his laudanum was right next to him, for when the pain returned, it stole his breath.

The way Margaret's smile used to. Yes, exactly so.

He'd learned not to move too much when he awakened. His right leg was propped and elevated in a sling contraption, as it had been on the coach. Dr. Adams thought this was the best angle, but it made it impossible for

Cam to turn on his side. The more he knew he couldn't, the more he wanted to above anything else.

From what he understood, the next inconvenience was going to be the itching. His doctor had warned him his skin would start to tickle inside the bandages under the plaster until it drove him nearly mad.

Glancing again at the laudanum, he hoped he had enough to see him through his recovery. Knowing there were more bottles in his trunk, he focused on his surroundings. His room looked as it always had, dove-gray walls and white wainscoting. Very pleasing.

Shifting his weight and trying to sit up by pushing on the pillows with his good arm, he groaned at the discomfort. Remembering how Jenny Devere mentioned wanting to walk in the fresh air the moment she knew she would spend weeks in confinement, Cam could now fully appreciate that.

He supposed he should be glad a blacksmith or a barber hadn't been called to set his broken bones. Luckily, he'd had Dr. Philip Adams, the best surgeon his family knew, who brought enough able-bodied assistants to help him set the earl's thigh bone, his ankle bone, and his arm, as well as tightly wrap a cracked rib.

It had taken two men following the doctor's instructions to fight the contraction of Cam's strong thigh muscles in order to set the large bone in place and hold it there while Adams applied thin wooden splints and gypsum plaster spread over the woven bandages.

Luckily, Cam had missed most of the ordeal due to laudanum and alcohol, of which he decided to prescribe his own dosage.

Also, luckily for him, as the surgeon explained when Cam awakened in anguish and wanting to die from the pain in his head and body, was the two breaks in his leg and the break in his arm were all "simple and clean."

"Simple and clean?" Cam had asked, barely able to mumble the words.

"Yes, nothing appeared to be shattered. I don't anticipate any gangrene or amputation necessary, but we'll watch your toes for a few days."

Amputation! "My toes?"

"Yes, for telltale signs of infection."

Christ! He'd taken another dose of laudanum right then.

MAGGIE WALKED SLOWLY ALONG the lane toward the manor, passing Jonling Hall and the new mysterious owner whom Jenny and Simon had met but whom Maggie had yet to be introduced. He was a man. A single man. An attractive man of marriageable age, according to her sister, and vaguely related to Simon. A bastard, Maggie had determined, and a wealthy one, too.

Normally, all of those things would have been enough to make her giddy with excitement and eager to receive an introduction as soon as possible. However, she found she couldn't muster even a smidge of interest.

John lay hurt somewhere, and she had no way to get to him, nor any reason to do so that would seem plausible to anyone who thought about it.

It had been a week since she'd learned of his accident. Every day afterward, when she walked to the manor to keep Jenny company and help with her wee nephew, Maggie hoped there was more news. Every day, she was disappointed.

"There you are, Mags." Jenny looked well-rested, still propped up in her bed like Lady Muck-Muck, as Eleanor had teased the day before.

"I'm allowed to be Lady Muck-Muck as long as I want to be. Let me tell you, producing enough milk to feed Lionel is exhausting. I'm always tired, thirsty, or hungry."

"So is he," Eleanor had said, as the baby started to cry again. Jenny told her sisters the sound of his crying made her breasts tingle as soon as he began.

"Isn't it all fascinating?" Eleanor had expressed how much more interesting human breeding was than when she'd seen animals mate, reproduce, and nurse. At that statement, Maggie and Jenny had exchanged a glance and decided to switch topics.

Today, Eleanor was elsewhere.

"Where is Simon?" Maggie asked, since usually his lordship was hovering nearby until one of the Blackwood women arrived to keep the new mother company.

Jenny waved her hand vaguely. "I don't know. Working somewhere, I suppose. He's trying to get a lot done before he leaves for Bedford."

Maggie's ears perked up.

"Bedford? You didn't mention yesterday he was going."

Jenny had been less than her usual focused self since before Lionel was born. However, this seemed like a large thing to have forgotten, especially as her sister knew of her interest in John's health.

"That's right," Jenny said, "because I didn't know yesterday. Simon hasn't wanted to leave my side, or Lionel's, of course. But he's been rather twitchy with concern for Cam. I told him to go see how he's doing. Last night, when we got into bed, and Lionel was sleeping peacefully, Simon said he was considering a journey in a few weeks."

"Weeks?" Maggie repeated, absently. She wanted to leave immediately. On the other hand, she hated to leave Jenny and Lionel.

"Yes. He's decided to wait until the baby is at least one month old, as if it is some magical number."

They exchanged an understanding glance. No age in infancy or even childhood was safe, yet one could only live in fear for so long. Maggie knew of many families who'd lost children. Even John had told her how his parents lost two other babies, leaving him their sole heir.

John, the sole heir, who'd almost died in a ridiculous carriage accident.

"Poor Lady Cambrey," Maggie murmured.

"Yes, indeed. She must have been nearly out of her mind with worry."

"I wonder how he is doing now," Maggie ventured, in case Jenny had learned anything more.

Her sister shrugged. "If we get another letter, I will surely let you know. I believed early on you had developed a *tendre* for him." Jenny watched her carefully. "However, before I left London, I thought I'd been entirely mistaken. Was I?"

Maggie didn't know what to say. If she started to go into detail about what had happened, they would spend hours dissecting it from every angle, trying to decide how Maggie had got it dreadfully wrong. Yet, what if Jenny also had witnessed what Maggie had thought—that John had an interest in her?

Deciding to divulge some of her story, Maggie sat on the bed.

"You are correct. I did for a short time believe he and I might be suited. I simply hadn't had enough experience with men to know my feelings. Or his. Then he became attached to Lady Chatley."

Jenny raised her eyebrows. "Jane Chatley seems a lovely person, but she is nothing like you."

"Well, thank you very much!"

"No, no, Mags." Jenny reached for her hand. "I meant if Cam liked you, it seems strange he would as easily fall for Jane, who is bland in comparison. Plus, she is . . ."

When Jenny hesitated, Maggie supplied a few careful adjectives. "She is intelligent, placid, well-spoken. Most likely organized, capable, dutiful, and loyal, too. And dull as dishwater."

"Mags!" Jenny protested. Then after a pause, she added, "We don't know for sure she is placid."

They both dissolved in laughter.

"Fair enough," Maggie agreed, "but she does seem to be the epitome of womanhood, someone any man would want to have running his household and bearing his children."

"No more than any man would want you to do the same. And you have a sparkle, those eyes, your mouth. Come along, dear sister, you know you have that special something. You've always turned heads."

"Effortlessly," Maggie agreed without hubris. "In face, so easily I don't believe I know how to win someone over by trying. Speaking plainly to him certainly wasn't the answer, nor letting a man kiss me."

"Hold on," Jenny said, before practically squealing. "You didn't mention a kiss. With Cam?"

Maggie felt her cheeks heat up but said nothing.

"That changes everything, don't you think?"

"Why?" Maggie asked. "Changes everything how?"

"Cam is Simon's best friend. He wouldn't play fast and loose with you, not with his best friend's sister-in-law. He must really like you."

"No, I am quite positive he really likes Lady Chatley. I saw them together, and I heard things they said."

Jenny frowned. "Oh."

"But I confess, I do still like him, even though I kept company with other gentlemen."

"And did others kiss you, too?" Jenny asked it jokingly, but when Maggie remained silent, her sister's smile died.

"Oh."

"Stop saying that."

"In any case, I think you should go see Cam for yourself," Jenny decided. "We were all friends before the Season started, before Simon even returned from abroad. Moreover, as a friend, you could go to Turvey House to pay your regards."

Maggie wasn't convinced it was a good idea, but her sister was clearly warming to her own plan.

"No, don't you see. It's perfect. You can go as my proxy. When Simon goes in a few weeks, you shall accompany him since I cannot."

"First of all, no one has a proxy for their wife. That's ridiculous. I cannot show up as the Countess Lindsey substitute."

"True, but you can say I was concerned enough to send you in my stead."

The idea of seeing him again caused Maggie's heartbeat to speed up, although her doubts lingered.

"What if John is not happy to see me, especially if he is gravely injured?"

Jenny grunted in an unladylike fashion. "What man doesn't want the attention of a beautiful woman?"

"One who might rather have Jane Chatley at his bedside."

Lionel, nestled in his crib at the foot of the bed, began to cry.

"Hand him to me, will you?"

As Maggie placed the baby in her sister's arms, Jenny observed, "He kissed you more than once. You don't know he has kissed her at all."

Maggie shook her head. "I cannot leave you and Lionel."

"Could you pour me a glass of water?" Jenny asked as she lowered her shift and let the babe latch on. Immediately, he started to suck noisily.

As soon as Lionel got to his appointed task, Jenny fixed on Maggie again.

"Nonsense. *I* am here to care for Lionel. He is my concern."

"And who will look after you?" Maggie asked, pointedly handing Jenny the glass of water. "You would lie there in an agony of thirst if I wasn't here when your little man starts feeding."

"Mother will be here. You know she comes every day after lunch. She wants to spend lashings of time with her first grandson."

Thus, two weeks later, Maggie, with a Devere maid along as a companion, set out for Turvey House with her brother-in-law. If Simon thought it strange his wife had pushed her sister upon him, he didn't say so. In fact, after they sent the maid into the accompanying carriage with Simon's valet, they relaxed and chatted like old friends.

He was good company for the journey, and Maggie came to appreciate more what her sister saw in the former Lord Despair. What's more, with his stories of Burma and of the Continent, as well as Sheffield village when he was a boy, he managed to distract her from the butterflies that kept swirling in her stomach at the notion of seeing John again.

At one point, she got up the nerve to ask about his days at Eton, knowing Simon had met John there as a youth of only thirteen. Luckily, nearly all his recollections featured the saucy Viscount of Cambrey, who would one day be its earl. They got into fisticuffs in the courtyard, smuggled whisky into the dormitories, and hid hot pies in their pockets to snack on during lectures. In short, they had fun as all boys do.

"And we always had each other's back. Toby, too," Simon mentioned his now deceased cousin who'd died in the Burmese War, a terrible experience from which the earl barely made it back alive.

"Cam probably would have gone to war, too, if his father hadn't recently passed away."

Maggie nodded. "I suppose when one is thrust into the earldom at an early age, and is the sole heir, duty to family must come first."

Simon gave a wry smile. "I believe the order is God first, then queen and country, and then family, but I think Cam did the right thing. His mother needed him, and he's not the kind to let a lady down."

Maggie shot him a glance to see if her brother-in-law meant something extra by his words, somehow referring to John and his treatment of either her or Jane. But no. by his expression, there was no hidden meaning.

"You have had the mantle of an earldom laid upon you as well. How are you holding up?"

"Thank you for asking. It wasn't going well until I met your sister, as you know. Now I have all of you Blackwoods as family, which I have got used to and confess to liking." He shot her another grin. "Your mother has loosened up a tad, enough to start treating me like a son instead of an earl. I like that, too. When Cam gets a wife, I guess he'll get a readymade family as I have. I hope he is as lucky."

From his words, Maggie decided Jenny must have kept her confidence entirely, and Simon knew nothing about any feelings she might have for his friend.

"Eleanor was in a foul mood when she found out she was not coming."

"Why?" Simon looked puzzled.

"*Ah,* you didn't know she became firm friends with Lord Cambrey's cousin Beryl, whom I believe lives nearby."

"I see. Yes, her father is the younger brother of Cam's father. They live a few miles away at most. I can see why Eleanor would be upset. And with her nature, she no doubt let everyone in your cottage know it. Yes?"

"Yes."

Simon looked serious for a moment.

"You were right to refuse her, though. I have no idea how badly he is injured, and it might not be a good thing for a girl of her years to witness."

"That's what my mother thought, too."

He glanced at her sideways. "You might find it a bit upsetting yourself. I think it very brave of you to come, and I appreciate your company."

Brave? What did he expect they would find?

In the early evening the next day, after a night at an inn, as the carriage rocked to a halt in the large courtyard in front of Turvey House, Maggie was about to find out.

CHAPTER TEN

Cam awakened from a long and deep sleep, hating the groggy feeling that greeted him each time he opened his eyes. He knew it was from the laudanum, but he also knew how much everything hurt if he neglected a dose. At some point, he supposed, he would have to face it. But not today.

He'd been home for a week, maybe already two, and nothing ever changed, nor did he see any hope in variance from the monotony of each day. He spent nearly every moment in bed. Dr. Adams had said it was his best hope to recover the full use of his leg, keeping it raised and immobilized. His valet gave him regular sponge baths and his food was brought to his room.

True, his mother had arrived, and her company, while welcome, was occasionally tedious. He did not need to hear about every member of the *ton*, whether behaving or, more likely, misbehaving. He now knew more than he ever thought he would about their constantly changing *affaires de coeur*.

In fact, the only thing constant about high society during the end of the Season was its desperate scrambling and switching of associations. Partners were rearranged as if people's lives were one complex quadrille.

Nor did he care about the latest French fashion, which his mother loved to pore over and relate to him in excruciating detail. After a few days, he felt he knew too much about lacey trim and the correct plunge of a neckline. That, he had to admit, perked his interest, imagining how much décolletage he would see with each variance of the cut.

Every detail regarding the Season and even fashion led to Margaret. After the birth of her sister's child, he imagined she had rushed back down south to London to squeeze excitement out of the last weeks of social events.

"I don't need you to read the dailies to me," Cam told his mother for the umpteenth time when she came in after her late-morning meal armed with stacks of newspapers.

She loved the luxury of receiving the papers when she was away from Town, getting them by courier every other day.

"I know you don't need me to, dear boy, but it is more pleasant for me to share them with you than to read them alone. And I don't want you to tax yourself by reading them to me."

She was undoubtedly still worried about his right eye. Although he thought he had less side vision than before the accident, other than that, it seemed much improved.

"You're simply worried I'll leave out all the juicy bits and bobs," Cam teased her, sipping tea, which he still found awkward to do with his left hand. "Very well, if you insist on reading to me as if I'm still in leading strings, then please read the news of the government."

At the crestfallen expression on his mother's face, he added, "Directly *after* you tell me the new girth of a lady's bustle for the Christmas season."

She laughed, sat upon the end of his bed, and spread out her papers.

Good, he thought. He'd rarely seen her relax since he'd awakened in their home in Cavendish Square in a world of agony and bewilderment. What a capricious accident, and so bloody avoidable. The other chap had died as his carriage turned over, his head being bashed to smithereens on the cobbles.

Not for the first time, Cam thanked God his fate had not been the same, at least for his mother's sake. He might not look as handsome as he used to, but he had lived to carry on the Angsley name and the Cambrey earldom for his family.

As his mother began to read, he squeezed his right hand into a fist, painful but doable. And then he wiggled his toes, or tried to. They weren't gangrenous—of that he was immensely grateful, for he didn't fancy a peg leg. However, they didn't move as they should. Staring hard at the foot protruding from the plaster cast, he tried again to wiggle his toes.

There! Didn't his big toe twitch?

"Mother," he interrupted her reading. "You're closer. Look at my foot and tell me if my toes are moving."

"The right foot, dear?"

"Yes, the right foot, for God's sake. The one at the end of my badly broken leg!"

"No need to shout, dear. At least it's not swollen."

"How could it be? It's devoid of blood, if you ask me. My foot is numb from being raised up in the air so damn long."

"No need to swear either," she admonished, standing up and bending over his foot, peering at it. "Are you wiggling your toes now?"

"Yes," he ground out, feeling irrationally irritated at her. It certainly wasn't her fault.

"*Hmm.* Do it again."

"I am, Mother."

She put her face even closer, and he hoped his foot smelled fresh after his recent wipe down.

Then she straightened and looked at him, her face telling him all he needed to know.

"Give it more time," she said.

That was all he could give anything or anyone, his time. What a useless lump, he felt, unable to even move his own toes properly.

"Keep reading," he said, knowing he sounded imperial and short-tempered.

His mother resumed for the next few hours.

The rest of his day was spent napping, eating, stretching his good limbs, and eyeing his bottle of laudanum until Gray entered. Like clockwork, his mother visited him each morning and Gray, in the late afternoons.

Today, Cam intended on dictating a letter to his business manager in London.

"You could try learning to write with your left hand," Gray said after he pulled up a chair beside the bed and leaned his tablet of paper upon the mattress. "It would probably look as good as my chicken scratch."

Cam barely cracked a smile. "I hope you're joking with me about both. Firstly, I don't want to learn as it implies my right arm might not work correctly when this bloody cast comes off in another month. And my arm is itching, by the way."

Wrinkling his nose, he stared at the offending plaster.

"Secondly, you had better write as clearly as you can. This isn't some frivolous love letter or laundry list. This is business, and if done correctly, it pays for all of us."

"Folks break bones every day. Your arm will be right as rain. Didn't the doctor say the same?"

Did he? Cam couldn't recall.

"Besides," Gray continued, "I haven't had a chance to tell you, but I invested as you suggested." He waggled his eyebrows and offered Cam a smug smile.

"Is that so? How did you do?"

"Rather well. Therefore, if your business dealings don't work out as you hope, I could be the one paying for all of us, as you say."

Cam nodded. "I hope you're erring on the side of caution, just a wee bit."

Gray grinned. "Coming from the man lying immobile in a sling."

Offering him his most sour expression, Cam felt like growling.

"It wasn't my fault. I am a good driver, you know that. The other fellow was a fool." He paused, realizing he knew nothing of the other man except he was dead.

"I hope he didn't leave behind too many loved ones."

"I will look into it if you like," Gray offered.

Cam nodded.

Then, he began to dictate his wishes regarding his investments. Now he was enjoying the healing benefits of laudanum, he wondered if his money was being used to sell Indian opium to China, giving the East India Company enough money to purchase Chinese tea, which now seemed to be in every household in England and Scotland.

When the long shadows of early evening turned Cam's room dusky blue, Gray lit the lamps and went off to see about dinner which they'd taken to eating together with companionable conversation. Cam told Gray about the past year in London, and Gray told him about the ins and outs of the estate, as well as any news of Cam's uncle's estate close by.

"Your mother is in good health?" Cam asked, feeling a little sheepish he hadn't inquired beforehand.

Gray's mother was a housekeeper at his cousin Beryl's home, working for Cam's uncle and aunt. Or maybe she was retired somewhere now. He didn't know.

Gray nodded. "Better than you, I'd warrant."

Cam tried to swing at him with his left hand, feeling like a girl swatting at a wild boar. Ridiculous!

Pretending to duck as if Cam were a real threat, Gray laughed, nearly upsetting his meal on a tray on his lap.

"She's not at the old granary lodge yet."

Cam's aunt and uncle had some servants living in a modified granary, the older folks who had nowhere else to go and who could no longer offer much service.

"Mum's still one of the two sewing maids," Gray continued. "She doesn't mind it. She says, 'What else have I got to do?' And then goes on as how I haven't given her any grandchildren."

"I guess we're both supposed to start thinking about heirs," Cam said.

"You more than me, I'd warrant."

A knock on the door interrupted him.

"Come," Cam said at once for anything out of the ordinary was welcome.

His butler, Cyril, entered and bowed.

"My lord, you have visitors."

"Visitors?" Cam asked, stupefied by the idea anyone had arrived uninvited.

Normally, if he weren't bored beyond belief by the sameness of each of his days, Cam would have been prepared to tell his butler to send them packing at once.

As he hesitated, Cyril added, "Yes, my lord, the Earl of Lindsey has arrived with his—"

"Simon! He's here?" With joy, Cam looked to Gray who merely shrugged good naturedly. Gray knew Simon, of course, from when his friend had visited over the years, but they didn't have the close connection of going to Eton.

"Send him up at once." Cam felt like bouncing right off the bed. "Wonderful!" Then he groaned in pain.

"What is it?"

"Too much enthusiasm," Cam said, reaching for his laudanum. "God almighty. All this resting will be the death of me. My muscles will forget how to work entirely if I'm not careful."

CHAPTER ELEVEN

Maggie, with Simon pacing nearby, waited in the spacious parlor for Cyril, the Turvey House butler, to return. Her maid and his valet were seated discreetly at one end of the room. From the moment Maggie had entered, a veil of shyness had covered her at being in John's home, especially uninvited.

At the sound of footsteps, she tensed. When Lady Cambrey entered, Maggie felt as if her face were frozen in a grimacing smile. In any case, John's mother went straight to Simon whom she'd known for many years.

"So good of you to come, dear boy," Lady Cambrey said, moving toward him to offer and receive a comforting embrace. Then she glanced at Maggie and frowned.

After a deep curtsey, Maggie stammered, "I came to . . . to . . ." *Good Lord! Why had she come?*

"Oh, I'm very glad you've come," Lady Cambrey said. "I merely expected you to be Lady Lindsey. Naturally, you are welcome." And she gave Maggie a brief kiss on each cheek.

"My wife is only lately delivered of our son," Simon explained, "or she would have come, as well. She, too, considers John to be her friend."

"Of course, yes. Congratulations. Nothing like a son," she murmured, and Maggie saw tears well up in the older lady's eyes. However, in a moment, with visible determination, Lady Cambrey steeled herself, taking a deep breath.

"What can I offer you? You must be starving and thirsty."

Before she could say more, the butler returned. Bowing to Simon, he said, "Lord Cambrey asks that you go upstairs to his room. May I show you the way, my lord?"

"No, I know where it is." He glanced at Maggie. "Will you be all right staying here?"

"Of course she will," Lady Cambrey answered for her. "I will get her fed and send food up to John's room for you. It is sent up there regularly anyway as he hasn't been downstairs since he arrived home."

Maggie's heart sunk while at the same time, nervous tension drained from her. On the one hand, she felt badly John was now sequestered in his bedroom. On the other hand, she could postpone seeing him. Perhaps there would be no welcoming expression on his handsome face. At least, Simon could warn him she was there, and John could remain in his room and never have to speak to her if he wished.

"Cyril," Lady Cambrey addressed the butler. "A meal for Lord Lindsey upstairs, and the same for Miss Blackwood in here. And then have two rooms made up."

"Yes, my lady."

With that, both Simon and the butler left, as did their servants they'd brought from Belton who would unpack their things and get them settled.

"I'm sorry for coming along," Maggie blurted when she was alone with Lady Cambrey. "It seemed a good idea to keep my brother-in-law company on the trip when my sister suggested it. I don't want you to go to any trouble, though."

"Nonsense. I was delighted to meet your family in London and just as happy to have you here with me in Bedford."

She crossed to one of two large sofas facing each other before the fireplace. "Please, sit, dear girl."

Maggie did as she was told, relaxing more. After all, even if this woman had her heart set on Lady Jane Chatley being her daughter-in-law, she could hardly begrudge Maggie sitting in the drawing room with no designs at all upon her son.

"How is Lord Cambrey doing?"

The older lady smiled slightly. "I still think of my husband when someone says those words," she confessed. "It's been four years since his passing. I'm out of mourning, of course, but not finished grieving, if you understand my meaning."

Maggie nodded. "I believe it is the same with my mother."

Waiting, she desperately wanted to know how John fared. Simon would tell her later, but after coming this far and now being merely a floor away from him, Maggie longed to learn of his condition.

"My son is much improved from the day of the accident. I have never been as frightened as when I saw him carried into our front hall on a litter by two constables. Beryl saw him first and started screaming. There was blood all over his face," Lady Cambrey added, her words drifting off with her thoughts.

"I was ever so glad we had our crest painted on even the small tilbury carriage. Otherwise, he might've ended up in one of those disease-ridden, filthy hospitals."

Still imagining John's bloody face, Maggie nodded although she had no opinion on the state of London's hospitals, only glad she'd never needed the services of one.

A maid came in with food on a tray and set it upon a clever folding table, which she placed directly in front of Maggie.

"Would you care for a drink, miss?"

Glancing at her hostess, who was not drinking anything, Maggie hesitated.

"A glass of Rhenish wine for each of us," Lady Cambrey told the girl, who curtsied and hurried away.

"Now you eat, and I'll keep talking. I cannot tell you how glad I am to have someone with whom I can converse about my son."

Maggie nodded and began her meal.

"I'm used to having my niece Beryl with me in London, and then there was sweet Lady Chatley who helped John with the cricket banquet. Did you attend? I'm afraid I can't recall."

The food became a hard lump in the back of Maggie's throat at the mention of both Jane and the banquet.

"Yes," she croaked and then coughed. Where was that wine? "I attended. It was very well organized. My younger sister, Eleanor, whom you may remember, also was there. She has become close friends with Beryl."

"Oh yes, Eleanor. Next time you come, you can bring her with you. She could stay with my husband's brother and his wife, who live not too far, and visit with Beryl while you come here."

What a strange yet welcoming invitation. This visit had barely begun, and Lady Cambrey was already thinking of the next one.

"And how is your mother?" the older woman asked, even though all Maggie wanted was to hear more about John.

"She is well, thank you for asking. Currently, she is enthusiastically enjoying being a grandmother for the first time to baby Lionel."

"Lionel? Is that what Simon named his son? Goodness, what a fine, strong name."

Sighing, Lady Cambrey said nothing as their wine was brought in. They each held up the glass to the other in a silent toast. No doubt, they were each wishing for John Angsley's good health.

"I should like to have grandchildren," Lady Cambrey continued. "When I saw my John injured, when I saw his broken bones, I thought I would no longer be a mother, never mind a grandmother."

"What are his injuries?" Maggie asked.

Perhaps she was being too direct, even impolite, but she could simply wait no longer.

CAM DIDN'T MIND WHEN, after visiting politely with Simon for a few minutes, Gray picked up his dinner tray and excused himself. Simon had met Cam's estate manager many times, even before Gray became such, when he was merely a general *jack-of-all*, as the former Earl of Cambrey described young Grayson O'Connor. Never a servant in the way a footman or a valet was, still Gray had always served them in some capacity.

Simon, as with many of Cam's friends, didn't know exactly what to make of Gray's position or status until Cam made him his estate manager, elevating him to the highest position he could have at Turvey House. Then his ambiguity became crystalized.

"I'll check on your meal," Gray told Simon as he reached the door. "*Ah*, no need. Here it is, and our own Tilda is bringing it in."

Opening the door wider, he admitted a maid carrying a tray. After placing it in front of Simon, who sat on a chair beside Cam's bed, she bowed and left with Gray.

When they were alone, Simon gave him a long appraisal. "You look . . .," he trailed off, frowning.

"Like a carriage ran over me?" Cam supplied. "Well, it did, or nearly. My doctor kept reminding me if my leg bone or arm bone had broken through my skin, they would have amputated the limb." He shuddered, still in disbelief.

"Anyway, the blasted cobblestones actually did the most damage. Tell me," he asked, offering Simon his profile, "have I lost my good looks?"

"I didn't know you had any!" With that, Simon grinned and began to eat.

Cam shrugged. "Honestly, am I gruesome? It's hard to see much in a knife blade or a soup spoon."

Simon put down his fork. "You mean you haven't seen yourself? I'm sorry, I thought you were joking."

Looking around, he realized the problem, for any and all mirrors had been removed.

"Is your mother trying to protect you?"

Cam nodded, lifting his hands to feel the scars where the stitches had been removed.

"Do they itch?" Simon asked. "Your skin looks to be healing well."

"Now you mention it, yes, they do." He gingerly rubbed on either side of the healing gashes on his face. "I bled quite a bit apparently. Scared my mother and cousin. Don't think I didn't notice you avoided answering. Come on. How bad am I?"

Simon scrunched up his face considering. "You look a little more *hard-lived* than you did before."

Cam groaned. "I don't want to look like I've been in a knife fight."

"Or two or three." Simon shoveled in another forkful of roast. "Excellent food as always here at Turvey."

Cam shot him a dirty look.

"Besides, your piratical appearance will probably make you even more popular with the ladies. Adds a bit of dash-fire to your reputation."

"I don't want to be a pirate," Cam protested. "And I had plenty of dash-fire before, thank you. No female ever complained."

"Speaking of females, shall I bring up my lovely traveling companion? I know she'd like to see you and will prattle on and keep you company for hours."

Cam's mouth opened in surprise. "You brought Jenny? Why didn't you tell me? And the baby, too?"

But Simon was already shaking his head.

"No. She wouldn't travel yet, and Lionel, as we've named him, is a bit colicky. Basically, a crying, shrieking terror, the opposite of restful, unless he's got a breast shoved in his mouth."

Cam laughed at his friend's honesty. "Well, who can blame him where that's concerned?" Then he had to stop, putting a hand to his healing ribs. "It actually hurts to laugh."

Simon winced. "I shouldn't have said what I said, since my wife is the one feeding our son. I don't want to put any crude imaginings into your brain, and you shouldn't have laughed at my improper statement. Anyway, I've brought Maggie, and I have to confess, I already miss Jenny and the baby somewhat fiercely so you'd better appreciate me while I'm here."

Cam had stopped listening after he heard *her* name. He knew his smile had died off his face, too. *Margaret was here!* In his home? And he was stuck in bed like an invalid. *God damnit!*

"I'll go get Maggie, shall I?"

"No," Cam barked, seeing a look of surprise on his friend's face. "I mean, it's getting late for one thing. She's had a couple days of traveling to get here. Tomorrow, maybe," he added. Then he shook his head. "For God's sake, Simon, look at me. No, on second thought, let *me* take a look at me. Go get a blasted mirror."

Simon stared at him. "It's only Maggie."

"It's only Maggie," Cam mimicked him in a sing-song voice. "I have my pride."

"Pride and vanity, it seems. You know, Jenny came into my room when I was a raving lunatic sitting in the dark, afraid of closing my eyes. And it didn't scare her off."

"Jenny is a rare bird if you ask me. Besides, you still had your looks, what they are, and the use of your limbs. No one is ever going to flinch when they see your face. What's more, you could be a lunatic and still dance with her, couldn't you?"

"A dancing lunatic," Simon considered. "I suppose, but there was a little more to my problems than you know. Now's not the time to go into them, however. I'll find you a mirror." Striding to the door, he looked back and quipped, "Wait here."

"Very amusing."

With such a friend, Cam wasn't sure he needed any foes. Would he let Margaret visit him? In his bedroom? He didn't know. Why had she come? To gawk at him, and take a report back to the drawing rooms and ballrooms of London?

At that moment, he decided he would refuse to see her. He didn't owe her an audience, not after how she'd treated him at the cricket banquet, rushing into Westing's arms the minute she could find a private place to do so.

In a minute, Simon struggled into the room with a large mirror.

"That's from the early-1700s," Cam said, recognizing it as one which had long hung at the top of the stairs. "Mother will kill you if it gets damaged."

"Carrying the bloody thing will kill me," Simon grumbled, staggering slightly with the unwieldy object. "But I couldn't go poking into the other rooms to find another one."

Setting it down on the end of the bed, he held it propped upright, steadying it with both hands.

Cam swallowed, feeling suddenly afraid.

"Come on," Simon urged him. "I promise, it's not that bad."

Puffing out his cheeks and releasing his breath in a big sigh, he struggled to sit up a little higher and then glanced at his reflection.

"Christ!" Cam's eyes widened, barely recognizing the face he saw. "Not that bad?" he whispered. "At least, they've kept me clean shaven, or I'd resemble a beggar from Bedlam."

"Better to resemble one than to be one."

"I would rather do neither." Cam tilted his head, examining the healing slash on his forehead and the matching one on his cheek. Around the right eye and over his cheekbone, he was not surprised to see bruising, for it had been tender so long, but it was no longer swollen. The cut he had felt with his tongue on his lower lip had all but healed. And where the skin had been scraped off his chin and scabbed over, there was now fresh pink skin. Possibly a little scarred, he couldn't be sure.

"Not too bad," Simon repeated. "Don't you think?"

Not taking his gaze off himself, Cam reached up to touch each imperfection he could see clearly for the first time. Even some of his right eyebrow was missing, for God's sake.

"I've got some ointment my valet applies twice a day. Greasy stuff but supposed to help the scars heal. He's been slathering it on me ever since I had the stitches removed. A delightful experience, I must say."

He stared a while longer. Miraculously, his nose hadn't broken, nor had he lost his front teeth. "Somehow, I'm still a bloody attractive fellow."

"With a bit more character," Simon promised. He nodded to the mirror. "Can I take it back now?"

Cam hesitated. Was this the face of a man who could win a beauty like Margaret Blackwood? He hadn't been good enough before. Now, his face had been shredded and sewn. And that was only the half of it. His body still ached. And what of his limbs?

"Take it away," he told his friend gruffly. "In fact, I'm exhausted. You probably are, too."

Simon nodded. "I'll send in your valet, and I'll see you tomorrow."

Cam nodded, wanting his friend to leave quickly, suddenly desperate to be alone. He knew he should offer him thanks for coming, but he didn't feel particularly grateful right then. He shut his eyes until he heard Simon leave.

Then he reached over and grabbed for his laudanum bottle. Everything hurt, and nothing was going to get better as far as he could see. At least the opium tincture relaxed him and took away most of the pain. He deserved that little kindness.

The next thing he knew, some noise awakened him. Opening his eyes, he saw Margaret standing before him, a vision in white silk, low cut at the front and cinched in at her slender waist, flaring over her shapely hips. Her hair was pinned up except for loose tendrils clinging to her shoulders and draping over her barely concealed breasts.

The effect was entirely erotic, and most definitely not the proper look for a debutante. Except they were no longer in a London ballroom before the entranced eyes of the *ton*. No, they were in his bedroom. Simon must have sent her up after all, against Cam's wishes. He couldn't imagine why he hadn't wanted her to visit him.

"You look enchanting." With those words, his rod hardened like a tree trunk.

She said nothing, merely standing there beside the bed, staring at him. *Dammit!* He wasn't an animal on display at the Zoological Society's gardens.

"Say something," Cam demanded.

Maggie's lush lips, painted pink and glistening, curved into a smile. Instead of speaking, she began to undress.

Deciding to enjoy whatever was compelling her to entertain him, he lapsed into silence.

Amazingly, instead of her dealing with a million tiny buttons down her back, she shrugged effortlessly out of her gossamer gown, first one shoulder, then the other. Underneath, she wore no corset and no shift. In a moment, her breasts were exposed to him, firm and high, with pink nipples also seeming to glisten like her lips.

His breath caught in his throat. She was even more magnificent than he'd imagined, and he'd imagined her many times in many ways.

"Keep going," he pleaded.

She nodded and slid the gown over her flared hips, letting it drop to the carpeted floor. Wearing nothing but a garter and stockings, her mound was on display, with nothing but soft brown curls to shield her.

His mouth went utterly dry. He longed to suckle on her breasts and, more than that, he wanted to put his lips on her quim and taste her there. His shaft was throbbing pleasantly, and he hoped she would be willing to do something about it.

"Will you touch me?"

CHAPTER TWELVE

Smiling broadly, her eyes sparkling, she nodded. Stepping closer, Maggie reached toward the part of him most needing her attention. Following her gaze, he realized his blankets were already pushed aside and his yard stood up impressively. *Thank God it hadn't been injured!*

Watching as she closed her fingers around him, he groaned with anticipation, wanting to shut his eyes and enjoy it while also wanting to continue gazing upon her glorious, bare curves. In the end, his lids seemed too heavy to remain open, and he let them sink closed even as she began to stroke him.

Up and down, she worked her magic. Where had she learned to do such a thing? As she squeezed him, it didn't take long for Cam to reach the point of no return and spend into the air.

Hearing his own guttural sound of pleasure, feeling the sticky warmth on his thigh, Cam opened his eyes again. He was alone, his own left hand clasping his now flaccid rod. Still foolishly hopeful, he glanced over the side of the bed, but no gorgeous gown pooled upon his rug.

The most vivid dream he'd ever had—and all because he knew Margaret Blackwood was under the same roof.

THE NEXT MORNING, MAGGIE met Simon in an informal sunny dining room adorned with fresh flowers and the delicious aromas of hot breakfast foods.

Her brother-in-law had already told her his opinion of his friend's condition the night before, and then they'd retired, leaving Maggie to lie in bed and think on how to hide any shock she might feel when first looking upon him. She mustn't let John think she felt revulsion or, worse, pity.

As she ate a hearty breakfast of eggs and bacon, she simply wanted to go see him.

"When can I visit Lord Cambrey?"

Simon chewed thoughtfully. "I believe his mother goes to sit with him in the mornings. When I go see him midday, I'll ask him if I can fetch you in."

How frustrating! Yet, she could hardly barge into his room. She would have to wait until invited. In the meanwhile, she would tour the house and the grounds of the lovely estate as Lady Cambrey had promised.

Thus, after waiting for Cam's mother to read him the papers, Maggie spent the day in her company, along with his estate manager, an affable man introduced to her as Mr. O'Connor. Trying not to sound too nosey, she plied him with questions about his employer's condition, which he answered kindly but a little vaguely, as if protecting John's privacy. *And so he should*, Maggie thought.

Yet when the first day turned into the second day, and still, she had been put off, she began to feel slighted and annoyed. After all, as Simon's sister-in-law, she was practically family.

No, she reasoned, *that didn't make her related to John Angsley at all*.

To have come all this way, though, to be mentally and emotionally prepared to visit with him, only to be denied access, how could she bear it?

This was most definitely not about her, she reminded herself for the tenth time. It was about John, and from what she gathered, he was enjoying his visits with Simon when he was awake and alert. Apparently, with John's terrible pain, his doctor had prescribed a daily dosing of laudanum that could make him sleepy or dazed.

Poor man.

On day three, she met Lady Cambrey at the bottom of the great central staircase under the well-lit dome. Knowing John's mother was going up to her son's room, Maggie had placed herself in a position to intercept her.

"My lady, shall I accompany you and offer my well wishes to Lord Cambrey?"

"Haven't you stopped in and said hello?" His mother seemed surprised. "Why, of course, you must. You needn't stand on ceremony, dear girl. If you're worried about your reputation, I think the fact he is bedridden with his leg in a sling is protection enough."

Maggie felt a little like a fraud. She knew Simon had specifically asked John if she could go in and the injured earl had said no. He wasn't *up to it*. Whatever that meant. However, his mother didn't know of her son's wishes.

"Margaret, why don't *you* take these papers in to him? Cook said there was something wrong with the duck, and I told her I'd consult with her after my visit with John, but I'll do so now. We don't want a delay with our supper, do we?"

Thrusting a stack of newspapers into Maggie's hands, she started back down the main staircase. At the bottom, she turned and offered her an encouraging smile.

"Don't be shy, dear girl. He won't bite, I assure you. You can knock first, but sometimes he's deeply asleep. Therefore, do go in if he doesn't answer. And by all means, awaken him. The doctor said we can't have him sleeping all day and night, or he'll become like a soft pudding."

Gracious! John Angsley becoming a pudding!

Nodding to the retreating figure of Lady Cambrey, Maggie continued her climb. Instantly, the butterflies were back, tickling her insides.

"Well, in for a penny in for a pound," she muttered, wishing she had the buffer of John's mother with her in case he protested her presence. After all, he wouldn't be rude with Lady Cambrey in the room. Or would he?

Tapping on the door as his mother suggested, when there was no answer, Maggie pushed it open, her heart beating a fast tattoo. Even though it was late morning and the sun was streaming through the open draperies and into the pale gray room, the figure in the bed was lying prone and unmoving.

Hmm. Approaching the bed on tiptoe, Maggie realized he was snoring. Flat on his back and, as his mother mentioned, his leg raised up in a sling hanging from a wooden contraption on the bed, John was nearly immobilized.

Letting her gaze move up his body to the plaster cast on his right arm, slowly, she drank in the sight of him, right up until she reached his face.

Gasping, Maggie raised a hand to her mouth, all at once glad he was asleep while she had time to become accustomed to his appearance. *Dear God*, how it must have stung to have one's face split open in two places. And very close to his eye!

His mouth—the one that kissed so divinely—was nearly undamaged except for the very bottom of his lower lip, which appeared to have been cut. From there down across his chin, he was healing from many scrapes.

Still, after a few moments of studying him, she realized nothing she could see detracted from his innate handsomeness, not one bit, not even the strange greenish-yellow tinge of the healing bruises.

The stitches must have been very neat and uniform, indeed, and obviously done by a skilled surgeon. With them removed, they'd left behind pink healing wounds that would most likely end up as thin white lines where each gash had been. Nothing more. And those would fade in time.

Looking at his two injuries though, she hoped he made a full recovery. With what she knew of John Angsley, he wouldn't care for any inconvenience in his usual way of living life.

If only he would awaken naturally, then she wouldn't feel like such an intruder. However, it seemed she had to rouse him somehow. Tossing the papers onto the end of the bed, she made sure they fanned across his good leg. Still, he didn't stir.

Hands on hips, she considered clearing her throat or beginning to hum. Staring at his toes, suddenly, she saw them wiggle.

"Oh," she exclaimed loudly, and that was all it took. He awakened.

Turning his head as he opened his eyes, he smiled slightly, looking utterly unconcerned by her presence, almost as if expecting it.

"I liked you better in the white dress," he said, resting his good arm behind his head and offering her an indolent smile.

Even with his scars and scrapes, both his familiar face and the wicked glint in his eyes caused her stomach to flutter, this time in a pleasant way.

Glancing down, Maggie took in her gown of pale green. She liked it immensely. And to what white dress did her refer? She almost never wore white, as it didn't show her hair to its best advantage.

Shrugging, she opened her mouth to greet him more formally when he sighed.

"You're slow today, Margaret. Go on, take it off. Let me see those luscious breasts and the fine downy curls over your quim."

She felt her mouth drop open. *Her luscious breasts! Her quim!* Speechless, she stared at him.

When he lifted his good arm and reached for her, his fingers fell a little short, brushing the back of her hand. Stepping away, she shook her head. Was he still sleeping perhaps? Yet, he seemed fully awake when he frowned.

"Come along. My yard is already at full mast." As he spoke, John rubbed his hand along the stiff bulge that had blossomed under the blanket, drawing her gaze there in fascinated disbelief.

He petted his member like a cat and then grinned at her again, beginning to pull the blanket to the side, possibly for better access.

"No," she ordered him, jumping forward to hold the cover down.

As soon as she was within reach, John's left hand snaked out and grabbed her wrist.

"You feel entirely real," he said, pulling her even closer until she nearly fell across his chest.

Mindful of his bandaged ribs, which were on display, Maggie held herself up, a hand on either side of him. He took the opportunity to run the back of his knuckles across her breasts.

"And if you would just take off this blasted gown, I already know how real you will appear."

Maggie knew her cheeks must be twin flames of scarlet, especially when her nipples began hardening against the front of her dress. Even through the layers of her clothes, she was certain he could see them.

Struggling, she attempted to push herself off the bed. But even flat on his back and with the use of only one arm, he seemed to be in complete control.

With his hand behind her head, he brought her face close to his.

"There you are," he whispered. "With those eyes that draw a man into their depths to drown. How many men, I don't want to know."

What on earth?

Before she could even form an outraged thought, he pulled her head down, and thus brought her mouth close to meet his. As soon as their lips touched, a flame sparked and raced through her body.

John Angsley, even incapacitated, had such power over her. Relaxing against his chest, Maggie stopped fighting. Hearing his slight gasp, maybe from the weight of her atop his tender ribcage, she remained still so as not to injure him further.

At some point, his kiss stopped being demanding and controlling. Instead, they engaged in mutual exploration. He slanted one way, she, the other, and they were for many minutes joined as one.

"Oh! Oh my!" The shocked sounds reached Maggie's ears about a second before John started to thrust her away from him.

Then she heard a man's cough.

Struggling to stand while John still pushed at her shoulder to help her up, Maggie wished a large bottomless well would open up in the floor and let her fall to her doom.

With her dress in disarray as well as her hair, and her face feeling shamefully hot, Maggie turned and faced Lady Cambrey, and next to her, Mr. O'Connor.

"John!" his mother exclaimed. "What is the meaning of this?"

Glancing back at the man in the bed, Maggie noted his cheeks were a ruddy shade of embarrassed red that must be mirroring her own.

"You can see her?" he asked, staring from his mother to Mr. O'Connor and back to Maggie again. His words entered her ears but made no sense. Perhaps he had hit his head very hard indeed.

"Of course we can *see* her!" Lady Cambrey said, stamping her foot as if tired of some childish game her very adult son were playing.

"She looks like a woman whose been thoroughly kissed," the estate manager added unnecessarily, as if he were enjoying every moment of his boss's predicament.

Lady Cambrey shot Mr. O'Connor an annoyed glance. Then she took a steadying breath.

"She looks like a debutante who is now going to marry my son."

"What?" Maggie said at the same time as John.

The estate manager actually had the gall to chuckle, and Maggie took an instant dislike to him. How dare he find amusement at her humiliation.

"It's entirely my fault," John blurted out. "I grabbed her when she got near the bed."

"Why?" his mother asked him. "Never mind. Miss Blackwood looked as if she were entirely capable of resisting you if she'd wanted. After all, she was on top."

As if realizing she'd strayed into improper territory, the older lady closed her mouth into a firm disapproving line.

"No," John explained, struggling to sit up while his leg was raised in the air.

Since no one else looked to be going to help, Maggie put her shoulder to his back, letting him push against her. At the same time, she reached across the bed and grabbed another pillow which she stuffed behind him.

Nodding his gratitude, he continued, "I pulled her off her feet, and she was trying to regain her balance when—"

"When your lips struck hers?"

John stared daggers at Mr. O'Connor who'd spoken.

Then, as if her mortification couldn't get any worse, Simon arrived.

"Is this a gathering of thieves?" he joked, nodding a greeting to each in turn, until his smile died at their grim countenances. "Whatever has happened?"

Lady Cambrey was the first to speak. "I'm sorry to say my son has put your sister-in-law in a compromising position."

"Oh?" Simon looked more bemused than upset, with an eyebrow raised in query.

"I would think it calls for pistols at dawn," Mr. O'Connor quipped, "except shooting a man in his bed is considered poor sportsmanship."

"That will be all, Grayson," Lady Cambrey told him.

Maggie was surprised by the man's decidedly non-deferential attitude as, still looking entertained by the whole business, the estate manager nodded to the countess and to Simon, saucily saluted John, and left.

"They must marry," Lady Cambrey declared into the silence.

"No." Maggie and John spoke in unison. She turned her head to look at him. He shrugged.

"Let's not be hasty," Simon said to the older lady. "I'm confident it's a simple misunderstanding."

"You have all been speaking as if I'm not here," Maggie said, starting to get her dander up. After all, she was innocent in the entire matter.

"*Harrumph*," Lady Cambrey said, ignoring her words. "In my day, eligible, unengaged people did not kiss in a bedroom unsupervised."

"Mother," John reasoned, "we could hardly have kissed if we had been supervised."

Apparently, he was regaining his good humor. Perhaps due to her nerves, this statement made Maggie giggle until she could control herself.

Simon cleared his throat, and Maggie suspected he was trying not to laugh.

"John," Lady Cambrey warned her only son.

"Sorry, Mother. I suppose you can't simply forget what you saw."

"No." She crossed her arms before her ample bosom.

"What precisely did you see?" Simon asked.

"Miss Blackwood was lying atop my son, and they were kissing. There is no doubt in my mind."

"*Ahh*, yes," Simon said. "I suppose that is difficult to misunderstand."

Finally, Lady Cambrey addressed Margaret. "My dear, I hold you blameless for many reasons. Firstly, my son is a good catch. I acknowledge it. Who could blame you for wanting to become his wife, by hook or by crook?"

"Now, see here," Maggie began. She had never been accused of trying to trap a husband, and she wasn't about to let the countess get away with such, no matter how elevated above Maggie's station the woman was.

However, Simon stopped her with a quelling gesture, leaving her mid-rant, with her mouth open.

"Secondly, I understand how, upon seeing John stretched out helpless, you were compelled to minister to him."

"Compelled to minister to me?" John repeated, sounding outraged. "What hogwash, Mother?"

"Lastly," the countess continued undeterred, "I am frankly touched beyond words you still find my son as becoming as you obviously do despite his current condition. Sickness and health, and all that," she finished.

Sickness and health, as in marriage vows? Maggie wanted to sit, but the bed was the only thing close, and being on it was what got her into trouble in the first place.

Behind her, she heard John mutter, "My current condition, indeed." Then in a louder tone, he said, "It was a mistake. I honestly thought she was a dream."

Maggie didn't think she could blush any more deeply, but she felt it down to her toes.

"Well," his mother admitted, "she *is* a beautiful girl. I'm sure many would claim her to be like a dream. Why, in my youth, I looked rather like her."

Simon was clearing his throat again, and Maggie wanted to clobber him.

"You must marry," Lady Cambrey declared again.

"But why?" John asked.

"I found you on the bed with her. Grayson saw it, too."

"I tell you, Mother, I believed she was a phantom and I was dreaming her very existence. Thus, I grabbed Miss Blackwood, and she stumbled on top of me. You're not going to say anything to ruin her. I know Gray won't. No one need ever know. That's the end of it."

Maggie thought he sounded extremely reasonable. She wished, though, he seemed instead a little more amenable to the idea of marrying her. After all, given his circumstances, it wouldn't be the worst thing to ever happen to him.

Maybe he would think it was, if his heart was set on Lady Jane Chatley. She was definitely no Lady Jane!

His mother proved to be like a dog with a particularly juicy bone, unable to let it go.

"But why don't you want to marry?" As if Lady Cambrey couldn't believe two people of a certain age and status didn't simply desire to enter the bonds of matrimony.

"He doesn't want to."

"She doesn't want to."

Maggie and John spoke simultaneously, a duet of gainsaying.

"That's settled it, then," Simon said, stepping into the fray. "We don't want anyone forced to do something they don't want to do. Besides, my wife would kill me."

Lady Cambrey pursed her lips, then shook her head at him.

"I've known you since you were a green youth!" With such a mystifying statement causing Simon to shrug, she turned on her heel and walked out.

Simon exchanged a wide-eyed glance with John. Sighing, Maggie moved toward the door. What a trying morning it had been. At that moment, she wished they could depart for Belton Manor at once.

"Where are you going?" It was John who asked her.

Where *was* she going? After what had occurred, she could hardly sit with him and read the newspapers.

"I took a ride around the estate with Mr. O'Connor yesterday on a particularly gentle horse named Nell. I think

I should like to do the same again. There is a lot more to see, and I can't bear being cooped up."

As soon as she'd said it, she wished she could take back her thoughtless words. The expression of bleakness that crossed his face tugged at her heart.

"Sorry," she muttered and left quickly without looking back. Best to end the already disastrous visit on a bad note instead of an even worse one.

CHAPTER THIRTEEN

"So, you've had a nice visit with my sister-in-law?"

At Simon's words, Cam couldn't help laughing. He tossed himself back onto the pillows and groaned. Then he reached for the laudanum. After taking a sip, he relaxed instantly, even before the medicine could do its magic.

"Why did you kiss my sister-in-law?"

Because I love her madly. What would Simon say to that?

"Because she is a tempting morsel," Cam said, hoping he sounded like his old self.

"Is she?" Simon pondered.

"Well, not to you," Cam pointed out. "At least, one hopes *not* to you."

Simon bristled. "Of course not to me! Jenny is my world. As soon as I think of my wife, I feel warm."

"Warm or hot?" Cam asked.

Simon grinned. "Warm in my heart because she's extraordinarily special to me. Hot everywhere else." He laughed. "Especially when I've been away from her for a few days."

"Margaret makes me a little warm," Cam ventured. "We spent some time in each other's company during the Season. Well, me and many other men."

His friend's chuckling did not lift his mood.

"What is so funny?"

"Isn't that the whole point and goal of a Season for a young lady?" Simon asked. "Or even for an old bachelor like yourself?"

"Old," Cam repeated, feeling a bit glum, "and now crippled." Even then, Gray was probably out riding with Margaret, seeing the sunlight on her glorious hair. He gripped the sheets.

"Nonsense," Simon scolded. "Being injured is not the same thing. Let me get your valet and we'll have you outside on the veranda, observing your beautiful estate in no time. It will do you good."

Cam considered. "As long as I keep my leg up, I guess it will do no harm."

"Back to Maggie," Simon began.

"Must we?"

"Do you have feelings for my sister-in-law?"

Cam made a face. "I would prefer to discuss the best manufacturer of ale or the best houses of ill repute where one is least likely to catch a disease than to discuss my *feelings*."

"She feels like family to me."

"I don't feel brotherly toward her. Is that enough of a confession?"

"Is there someone you prefer more? Do you find her unsuitable to marry because of her lack of title?"

Cam barked a laugh. "You know I don't give a fig for a woman's title. I have my own and that's enough. Fortune, too, for that matter."

"You skipped my first question," Simon pointed out.

Cam crossed his arms. "It's personal."

"I thought we could discuss anything."

Clenching his jaw, Cam considered. "I believe I haven't determined the answer yet, and thus, I cannot tell you."

Simon nodded. "Fair enough. But no more shenanigans like this morning. Don't hurt her or play with her sentiments. I'd hate to have to add to your pain by punching you in your one good eye. Now, let's get you outside, shall we?"

BEING DRAGGED INTO A kiss she actually enjoyed beyond measure was one thing. Being forced to marry a man who didn't want her was quite another. What would her mother and sisters say if she suddenly wrote to them of an engagement? And only think of society's opinion? If she and John suddenly married, the *ton* would speculate for the next two Seasons as to why.

Preposterous! Thank goodness Simon had intervened.

Facing Mr. O'Connor, painfully aware he had witnessed her splayed atop his employer, was bad enough. She found him in his office on the first floor, as directed by one of the maids.

Knocking, Maggie entered at his behest. He rose to his feet.

"Sorry to bother you, sir, but I was hoping I could go riding again."

"Do you have feelings for John Angsley?"

Gasping before she could stop herself, Maggie felt a surge of annoyance.

"I beg your pardon, but that is none of your business. I shall go find a groom and not trouble you any further. Evidently, you already have much on your mind. Perhaps too much."

She turned to leave.

"Please, Miss Blackwood, stay. That was inexcusable. Won't you sit and I'll explain myself."

Hesitating, finally, she took the seat he offered.

"I only ask because John is like a brother to me. We have known each other since we were very young. Seeing him laid up like this has, I admit, sobered me as to our mortality."

Maggie nodded. "Something can happen accidentally to any one of us. That is certain."

"Exactly. John will recover. I have no doubt. Moreover, I know he was already in search of a wife, if not exactly in a straightforward way. Still, it was on his mind. An heir for the Cambrey earldom and all that."

What could she say? Should she point out Lady Jane Chatley would fill the position perfectly, and John seemed to have already chosen her? Shrugging slightly, she waited.

"If you are interested in becoming his wife because you care for him, then I wish you joy. If you are not interested, then I hope you will leave here soon because I know he will come to care for you since you are pretty and well-spoken. In my opinion, as his friend, I don't think he ought to be injured in any further manner, not even in his heart."

"I appreciate your plain speaking, although I must still tell you it is not any of your business."

"Be that as it may, there is a third scenario I think is my business. If you do not care for Lord Cambrey but think you can now snag a somewhat damaged earl for your husband, then I must warn you, I will do everything I can to stop you. As his estate manager, I consider the earldom under my purview, and I won't take kindly to a female fortune hunter."

"You are thinking of this from every angle." Maggie was actually glad John had such a friend. "However, don't you think you are putting too much power regarding whom Lord Cambrey will marry into *my* hands? Have you forgotten he has a say in it?"

"Not at all. Yet, bedridden as he is, with his self-confidence dented like a tin milking bucket that's been kicked by a particularly heavy hoof, I think he might be more malleable to someone else's whims or machinations. I am keeping my eye out for him. As I said, like a brother."

"Good." Maggie stood, and the estate manager did, too. "Then I believe since I am neither whimsical, nor at this time involved in any machinations toward the earl, we are not at cross purposes. Do you wish to ride or shall I locate a groom?"

"I shall be happy to ride with you, Miss Blackwood."

SEATED ON THE VERANDA with his injured leg propped on the chair in front of him and his arm in a sling, Cam felt the green-eyed monster inhabit his body. Right before him, coming in from a long ride was Margaret on the slightly rotund Nell. Beside her was his own estate manager, laughing at something she had just said. They looked relaxed and happy, the picture of easy camaraderie.

It vexed him he couldn't jump on a horse and take her on a tour himself.

Jealousy warred with envy, and they tied.

Gripping his teacup so hard, Cam feared he would snap its delicate handle. He knew it had been a long ride, as he'd been sitting there for the better part of two hours with Simon by his side. They'd talked about everything, including Simon's reason for going to the Continent earlier in the year. It had been eye-opening, to say the least. Cam was beyond thrilled his friend had found a cure for his violent outbursts while asleep, so disturbing they had nearly ended not only his marriage but his wife's life.

After being sworn to secrecy, especially not to tell Margaret, Cam had moved the conversation to lighter topics of importing wine and of horse breeding.

Simon stood and waved to his sister-in-law as she and Gray entered the paddock. In a few minutes, she rushed across the grass until she reached the paving stones and then the terrace. Finally, she mounted the steps to the veranda, beginning to speak as soon as she was within their hearing.

"What a glorious day," she exclaimed, gesturing to the blue sky and bright sun, "and your estate, Lord Cambrey, is positively lovely. I've seen fields of gorgeous flowers and orchards with every kind of fruit. Cows, sheep, pigs, all well-tended. And Nell never faltered. Grayson was kind to show me around."

Cam felt her words like a knife twisting in him. He should have been the one showing her around. And he noted her use of Gray's first name, while she still called him—after so many kisses—by his title. Even after he'd bloody well had her on top of him a few hours earlier.

"I never noticed before how you babble like a brook, Miss Blackwood," he heard himself say, and his tone was practically a snarl.

"Cam," Simon protested. "Maggie's simply excited by how well you maintain Turvey House. You've lived here all your life and forget how it looks to fresh eyes."

However, Margaret's expression had tensed, and neither of them sat down. That only irritated him more.

"*I* don't maintain it at all, and if I did, I certainly wouldn't be doing so in the near future. And excuse me, Miss Blackwood, for not standing."

God, but he felt irritable. What's more, his entire body ached and his stomach hurt. *Blasted tea!* Pushing it away from him, both cup and saucer, not caring how it sloshed over the side of one and into the other, he scrabbled in his coat pocket.

His fingers found and held the bottle of laudanum he'd remembered to grab as his valet lifted him onto the stretcher to bring him downstairs. Yanking it out, he unstopped it and took a small sip.

"Are you two going to stand there all day like a couple of Greek statues?"

Simon frowned at him. "I'm going to go for a walk and stretch my legs." Then he winced. "Sorry, old chum. I didn't mean to rub salt in your wound. As soon as you have the cast off, you'll be strolling around like you used to."

Cam could think of no response as he still had months before that terrifying event. He said nothing, only glaring at Simon until the man nodded and wandered off in the direction of the stables. He expected Margaret to do the same since he'd offended her. To his surprise, she pulled out a chair and sat down.

As soon as a servant had offered her some refreshments, she turned her attention to him, staring at him.

"Are you in a great deal of pain?"

"At present?" Cam considered. The ache he thought he'd felt had vanished as soon as he'd sipped from the bottle. "No, the opium tincture works almost immediately."

"Good, because I wouldn't want to speak frankly while you were distracted by your injuries."

"I'm always somewhat distracted by them," he confessed, his irritation dwindling. *Because of her nearness.* "The plaster casts are hot, and my skin has started to itch under them."

"Does your mother knit?"

"Rarely," he responded. "What a strange question. Do you wish to speak to me about knitting?"

"No, but if Lady Cambrey has any knitting needles, I believe you could slide one between your skin and the cast and ease some of the itching."

He opened his mouth, then closed it. Actually, he wanted to hug her.

"What a dashed good suggestion. I can already imagine the relief."

"Is the itchy skin why you were so beastly rude when I came back from my ride? Because I do not babble."

He felt his face heat up with embarrassment. "I'm sorry."

"You are forgiven." She sipped her tea. "Also, I've seen pushchairs in the city."

He held up his hand. "I've already got one on the way although mostly, I need to keep my leg up."

"Still, it will offer you a degree of mobility. You can race between the dining room and the front parlor. Or ride it across the grass to the river."

"Yes, if I can convince Cyril to give it a hearty push."

She laughed lightly, and he relaxed. *Why had he been such a boorish cur?* He couldn't even recall.

"Why did you think I was a dream this morning?" she asked him, and he knew their frank discussion had begun.

Remembering how he told her to remove her gown and then, good God, he'd mentioned her female parts, Cam wished he could slide under the table and disappear. Somehow, until that moment, he'd pushed aside his entirely inappropriate behavior, or the laudanum kindly had.

"I had a dream about you. I have many dreams, of course." That was all she needed to know.

"I've heard opium tincture can cause dreams to be vivid."

Nodding, he fiddled with the tea cup in front of him until she reached over and poured him a fresh cup.

"It helps with the pain and with sleeping," he told her.

She nodded. "I'm sure it does. Were you awake when they set your bones? It's terribly painful, isn't it?"

"The surgeon offered me ether or chloroform," he said. "I actually don't really remember this, but Mother told me I said it was too experimental, and I could handle having my bones set without being put to sleep unnaturally. In all likelihood, I was afraid I wouldn't wake up. Who knows?"

"Indeed," she remarked. "I would feel the same way. I've read some success stories in the papers, and also a few tragedies."

"Laudanum and brandy are far safer, in my humble opinion. The worst pain was waking up while someone, I don't know who, carried me off Oxford Street. I was already a bleeding, crumpled heap. I suppose it was imperative I be moved, or I might have been run over any number of times."

Despite how he attempted to make a little jest, Margaret didn't look amused.

"You could have been killed instantly. I heard the driver of the carriage that hit you was."

Cam nodded, recalling why he'd been where he was in the city at that moment. Margaret didn't know he'd gone to speak with her. How he'd left her door feeling despondent after learning she'd departed for Sheffield. How he'd wanted to ask her if she understood their kisses were better than any he'd ever had and demand to know if she felt the same.

Here they were, chatting together in the sunshine, sipping tea. He should count his lucky stars.

"May I?" she asked, pulling the laudanum bottle across the table toward herself. Oddly, he had the impulse to snatch it back but didn't. She lifted the stained cork and sniffed.

"I thought it would smell more bitter," she noted. "What's in it?"

"Sherry, cloves, and cinnamon," he said, irrationally wanting her to return it immediately so he could hold it close. "Dr. Adams said it was the most palatable blend."

Eyeing him over the bottle, she put the stopper back in.

"You don't mind the dreams?"

Holding his hand out, she placed it in his palm, their fingers brushing as she did.

"Not some of them, no."

He watched her cheeks pinken delightfully. For his part, he felt a surge in his loins as he recalled his dreams and the reality of having her atop him, her bounteous breasts crushed to his chest.

Should he do what his mother practically insisted and ask her to marry him?

"When do your plaster casts come off?"

Not soon enough! He wanted to scream it out loud. Such behavior would frighten her.

"I have months to wait still, at least for the leg. I think the one on my arm will be removed sooner."

He'd answered his own question about proposing. Even if he wanted to ask for her hand, he wouldn't do it in his current state, not while standing at the altar to say his vows was an impossibility. They couldn't go on a proper wedding trip. He wasn't fit to be anyone's groom at present.

"It was kind of you to come visit."

"Jenny would have come if she could, but there is Lionel."

Cam couldn't help smiling, thinking of his friend as a father.

"What is it?" Margaret asked, seeing his expression.

"I'm adjusting to Simon as an adult, I suppose. One minute we're green youths, then we're supposed to be responsible enough to raise children."

There was no question he would have children of his own one day. What of Margaret? He hadn't thought of her in any maternal sense before, only as a sensuous, fun-loving creature.

"And do you like being an aunt?"

Her smile spread. "It seems I am good at it. I figured out how to stop Lionel from crying, and that was a blessing. He is easy to love, warm and cuddly. Yes, I confess, I enjoy being an aunt."

As she'd spoken, he'd fallen in love.

He wanted to sigh loudly, his heart was beating fast, and he was making moon-eyes at a woman while she spoke. He couldn't deny it. Hearing her talk about holding a baby, Cam could easily picture her with their own child in her arms. *Yes, this was love.*

"Do you realize since I sat down you've had two swallows of your laudanum mixture?"

Sitting up straight, he stared at her.

"No, you are mistaken." Then he looked around for his bottle, realizing he still clutched it in his good hand. "It's right here."

"Yes, but you've raised it to your lips twice. By the way, how much did your physician advise you to take? Each day, I mean?"

Why was she asking him such personal questions?

"I believe I may take the amount which eases my pain. How would Dr. Adams know if I need a few drops more or less?"

"I suppose a good doctor would have an idea of how much is correct. And safe."

Safe!

"I assure you, after what I've been through, I am proceeding with all due caution."

Even in the matter of love.

"THERE'S A FLOWER IN your garden as big as a dinner plate," Simon commented without preamble when he returned. "I've never seen the like. Not in England, anyway."

Maggie was glad he'd returned. She thought it might be better if her brother-in-law were to make sure John wasn't taking too much of the strong opium tincture. Nearly monthly, she read in the papers about some poor soul who'd become addicted to it. What's more, there was the titillating book from a couple decades earlier, poor Thomas de Quincey and his *Confessions of an Opium Addict*.

Moreover, everyone suspected the recent death of the brother of those clever Bronte sisters was tied to the young man's use of laudanum.

Yes, the more she mused on this, the less she liked it.

"I'm going indoors for a moment. I'll leave you two gentlemen to talk."

Simon stood, of course, whereas John could not. Slowly, she walked around the table until she was behind the earl's chair, and then she widened her eyes at Simon and nodded at the laudanum bottle still grasped in John's fingers.

When Simon frowned at her, and John began to squirm in his seat trying to see behind him, Maggie even mimicked someone drinking.

Finally, her brother-in-law stopped staring at her blankly and smiled down at his friend.

"I'll go find out about our next meal, shall I?"

Simon grabbed her arm as he passed her, hurrying her into the back hall of the manor.

"What was all that about?"

"I am concerned with Lord Cambrey's use of opium tincture."

She watched Simon's thoughts play across his face. He didn't dismiss her worries out of hand, for which she was appreciative.

"You understand he is in considerable pain," Simon pointed out.

"Yes, I know, but perhaps we should keep an eye on how much he is taking. Opium is not without its ill effects. De Quincey, you recall."

Simon nodded. "I've read the *Confessions*."

"Who has not?" she said. "In some ways, it glorified the pleasurable aspects."

He glanced back over his shoulder. "Is there some reason you are concerned. Has he been acting strangely?"

Maggie hesitated. "Well, he kissed me."

Simon shrugged. "I'm not sure that is so strange. Besides, hasn't he kissed you before?"

"Jenny!" Maggie exclaimed, realizing her sister must have disclosed this personal detail of her time in London.

This time her brother-in-law grinned.

"All right, I'll tell you," she said. "Being grabbed off my feet and hauled atop him was not the type of kiss we've exchanged before. And what about his ungentlemanly remark right before you left the table?"

"Hardly the terrible ramblings of an addict."

"No, but completely out of character. What's more, as soon as he had a sip from that bottle, he became his sweet self again."

"I will keep my eye on him."

"Thank you."

Simon gazed at her a moment. "You sound as though I am doing it for you, as if you *care* for him. Do you?"

Maggie shot him her candid smile.

"I don't usually allow people to kiss me unless I care for them." Then she recalled some of the other men she'd kissed during her Seasons. "Actually, I suppose that is not entirely accurate. I—"

Simon held up his hand. "I think I've heard enough. Unless there are men against whom I need to defend your honor, please don't say anymore."

"You are a dear brother-in-law."

"Visitors!" came Lady Cambrey's excited voice, floating down the corridor. "Where is everyone?"

CHAPTER FOURTEEN

Lady Cambrey appeared in a lovely day gown of cream brocade with navy thread. "Where is John?"

"On the veranda," Simon told her. "I was just going back outside."

"I've put our guests in the front parlor. I don't think after a long journey they should be asked to come outside. On the other hand, John will not want to be carried into the room in such a way as they can see him. I know that."

Maggie could see her dilemma. "Simon and your butler could take Lord Cambrey into another receiving room, the drawing room, I suppose. Then in a minute, you could lead your guests in there to visit with him."

"Splendid," Lady Cambrey said. She gave Maggie a long stare. "You have a good head on your shoulders, my girl. Why don't you go greet them in the parlor, and I'll find Cyril. Simon, please prepare John and tell him to be on his best behavior. I've noticed he's had a tendency toward crankiness lately."

Maggie made eye contact with Simon, trying to add that to the list of uncharacteristic behaviors. But her brother-in-law only sighed.

"Yes, Lady Cambrey. Don't worry about a thing."

"Hurry along, Miss Blackwood," the older woman ordered her. "Someone has to see to the guests." Then, she disappeared through a doorway, no doubt in search of her butler.

Simon nodded to her. "Hurry along, Miss Blackwood," and with a parting smile, he left her standing there.

Glancing down, Maggie realized she was still in her riding habit. However, it was not dirty and it was a becoming shade of burgundy. As she walked down the hallway, she paused only to check her reflection in a mirror. No smudges on her face, and her hair was still neatly pinned.

With that, she crossed the domed main hall and thrust open one of the front parlor's double doors, entering the room decorated in pea green and white. There, seated on one of the two sofas was Lady Emily Chatley and her daughter, Jane.

Oh, joy!

The ladies stood, both with equally perplexed expressions at seeing Maggie.

"How lovely to see you both," Maggie exclaimed, moving in for the obligatory cheek kiss.

Neither said anything for a moment, then Jane recovered from her surprise.

"We had no idea you were here, Miss Blackwood. Your family's home is not in Bedfordshire, is it?"

"No, when not in Town, we are in Sheffield. Please, sit down. Lady Cambrey will return shortly. My brother-in-law, Lord Lindsey, is Lord Cambrey's dearest friend. We came as soon as he could tear himself away from his new baby."

"Oh, a baby," the senior Lady Chatley said with a wistful smile Jane did not share.

"Yes," Maggie intoned. "My sister had a boy about a month and a half ago."

"How lovely." Again, it was Jane's mother who spoke, clearly desirous of a grandchild of her own.

Knowing it was simply not done to have any guest feel uncomfortable, Maggie turned the conversation to something that ought to please Jane.

"I wish to offer my congratulations on the success of the benefit for the orphans. The banquet was very smoothly run, and it was glorious weather for cricket."

However, her mention of the banquet did not produce the desired results of bringing a smile to Jane's face. It served only to remove the one from her mother's. Their gloomy countenances were so obvious and pronounced Maggie nearly remarked upon them, catching herself only just in time from rudely questioning them.

Jane merely nodded. "The orphanages will be built, and many children will be removed from the street. They are the only thing of importance," she said as if her mother had said something to the contrary.

Luckily, Lady Cambrey returned at that moment.

"Please, ladies, follow me to the drawing room. Much cozier in there. I have refreshments awaiting you, as well as my son, who was determined to arise from his convalescence to visit with you."

Arise from his convalescence? Maggie barely stopped herself from rolling her eyes. It wasn't as if John were Lazarus, for pity's sake. He hadn't even been in his bed, but simply relaxing on the veranda.

Following the others to the drawing room, Maggie couldn't imagine how any room with eleven-foot ceilings could be considered cozy. Last to enter, she waited for everyone to sort themselves out. The ladies Chatley had to exclaim at John's appearance and offer their sympathies for what had befallen him. Finally, as Cyril moved out of the way, and the ladies took their seats, Maggie found John in a wingchair, with his leg raised upon a matching ottoman stool.

"Excuse me for not standing upon your arrival, ladies," John said, slipping instantly into the polished gentleman she knew him to be. When he wasn't kissing her. Or holding Jane close.

Maggie sat next to Lady Cambrey since the Chatleys were upon the other sofa, and at last, Simon took the other wingchair.

"We were thrilled your mother invited us here," Lady Emily Chatley began, addressing herself to the earl. "Turvey House, for its grounds alone, is worth the trip from London. We didn't realize you would have other guests, like a country party. Are there others coming, too?"

"You'll have to ask my mother, as I wasn't aware anyone at all was coming," John said.

He offered a pleasant smile Maggie took to be false.

"All four of you have been quite a surprise."

"Oh," Emily Chatley exclaimed while John's mother laughed, although no one had said anything remotely funny. "I do hope we are a welcome surprise."

"Indubitably," John said. "Like a dream."

Simon coughed, and Maggie cleared her throat, guessing he was mischievously referring to the morning's escapade.

"No," Lady Cambrey said sharply, as if aware of their thoughts. "No one else is coming. This is enough company for my son while he recovers."

Maggie was grateful John's mother hadn't seen fit to mention she hadn't even been invited. Of all of them, Maggie was the only interloper. Jane was a welcome guest, on the other hand, and it was obvious why Lady Cambrey had wanted her to come. Undoubtedly, she hoped by spending time outside of the pressures of London, Jane and her son might form a solid attachment.

If that were the case, the last thing any of them wanted was Margaret Blackwood in the middle of things.

"When are we leaving, Simon?" It popped out of her mouth before she could rein herself in.

All eyes turned to her and then swiveled over to Simon, who returned her a slightly puzzled look.

"I hadn't decided exactly when. I don't want to be too long away from Jenny and Lionel. Perhaps another few days."

And then the ladies drank tea and pummeled Simon with inquiries about his wife and baby, going over every detail of Lionel's appearance and Jenny's health.

Maggie sat back and hoped, after the tea, a good claret would be brought in or, at the very least, sherry before dinner. Swinging her leg under her gown, she tried to keep interested in the chatter, but she'd heard all the stories before.

Maybe she should go speak with the housekeeper, Mrs. Mackle, about the drink. Or should she ask the butler?

Sighing quietly, she hadn't yet got it straight at Belton Manor and certainly not at Turvey. She supposed it didn't matter. She would be gone before working out the hierarchy of the Cambrey servants. Without question, an earl's daughter such as Jane knew precisely whom to ask about getting a glass of something deliciously relaxing.

At that moment, somehow her glance collided with John's. Instead of either of them politely and intently listening to the conversation in case they were called upon to offer some contribution, they stared at one another. Ever so slightly, his left eyebrow rose. Maggie had the absurd notion he was using his left brow because it was in better shape than his sadly savaged right one.

A small bubble of amusement began to float around inside her. *Oh dear*. She mustn't burst out laughing or these ladies would think her truly mad. But then John was doing something with his lips. Was he? Or was she imagining it?

Jane's mother laughed and the others, including Simon, joined in, giving Maggie the distraction, she needed to lean forward and see if . . . yes, he *was* pursing his lips. Was he pretending to blow her a kiss?

"Do you agree, Miss Blackwood?"

Sitting back quickly, glancing around, at first, she wasn't even sure who had addressed her. One of the two older ladies, she guessed. Usually people only asked if they wanted you to agree or assumed you did, and thus, it was probably safe to do so.

Looking between the women, she decided to tilt her head and speak to the very high ceiling as if pondering her answer, rather than look at the wrong person.

Glancing up, after a brief hesitation, she said, "Yes, I do agree."

"I'm shocked!" came the immediate response from the elder Lady Chatley. "A girl of your breeding and upbringing."

Oh dear! Now what infamy had she brought down upon herself.

Glancing at Simon for clarification, all he did was shrug unhelpfully. A look at John gave her nothing but widened eyes in return. Sighing, she tried again to focus on the conversation. Half an hour later, they were finally released to change for dinner.

Their small party was increased by the addition of Grayson O'Connor. Therefore, they had an equal number of single ladies to bachelors, no matter the status of the gentleman, lord or commoner.

With Cam at one end and his mother at the other, Maggie sat next to Simon on one side of the table, and the ladies Chatley sat across with the estate manager between them.

The elder Lady Chatley spent the evening trying to understand exactly who Mr. O'Connor was, what his place was at Turvey House, and why, if a servant, he was seated at the table with them, especially next to her precious daughter.

Maggie had to admit Jane was a good conversationalist, easily discussing topics from agricultural practices to the revolutions overseas to the latest acts of Parliament. The latter grabbed John's attention, and Maggie watched as the two conversed about the recent public health act.

"But surely they must make it compulsory," Jane was insisting.

"I wish it were the case," John agreed. "I fear only like-minded individuals will voluntarily make improvements."

Maggie thought his to be an overly pessimistic view.

"I believe people are basically decent," she stated quietly.

When she realized everyone was looking at her, she continued, "With the establishment of a central Board of Health, I think towns will do what is right for the greater good to provide, at the least, clean drinking water."

Jane did not smile condescendingly, although she did shake her head slightly as if disagreeing.

"I pray you are right. Nevertheless, I think cholera outbreaks will continue and refuse will still run in the roads as long as landlords can get away with it."

"Refuse," exclaimed Jane's mother, as if she couldn't even bear the word.

"Or until some consequence touches those in power or their family," Grayson added. "If the greater good suits someone's private interest, then people may act."

"All right," Maggie conceded. "I agree. There are those who will do nothing for their fellow man unless it impacts either them personally or their bank account. However, that is precisely another reason I think this bill will make an impact. Mr. Chadwick has made a valid economic argument to that effect. The fewer sick poor people there are, the fewer poor seeking relief. Whatever is done to prevent sickness is money well spent, and even the most selfish and self-interested can see such a benefit."

"Bravo," cheered John, who'd been listening intently.

Maggie felt her cheeks warm. *You see*, she wanted to tell them, *I'm not merely a flighty female who likes fashionable gowns and dancing.* Although she did, of course.

"Margaret is correct," Jane agreed. "The economics will be the compulsion we need, even if the bill has no teeth, as they say."

"Economics," John agreed, "and people like you. What you did for London's orphans was a wonderful thing."

Back to Jane's accomplishments, Maggie thought unkindly, then sipped her wine. What a horrid person she was not to be pleased with Jane's success. And she *was* pleased for all the children who would end up with roofs over their heads. Why, though, couldn't Jane have organized her banquet with someone other than John Angsley? Clearly, his admiration for the earl's daughter had grown because they'd worked closely together.

Maggie couldn't think of anything she had done or would do that could equal Jane's charitable work. True, she'd tutored Simon Devere's young cousins in French before he'd married Jenny. But they were only half orphans and lived in the lap of luxury. Thus, most likely, they didn't count as evidence of her philanthropy.

What's more, Maggie had been well paid. Clearly, she didn't compare to the altruistic Lady Jane Chatley.

Sighing aloud, Maggie realized the room had become quiet at the same time.

"Are you unwell, Miss Blackwood?" Lady Cambrey asked.

Looking around the table, Maggie considered her answer. Her stomach was full and she'd definitely had enough wine. Moreover, she'd had enough of some people's company. With an intense desire to be away from Jane so she wouldn't have to compare her own useless existence and find herself lacking, Maggie did something she almost never did. She lied.

"Actually, I believe I had a little too much sun today. From riding, I suppose."

Mr. O'Connor cocked his head, looking puzzled. Only he knew they'd spent much of the time shaded by huge aged trees.

"I believe I have a headache coming on. Would you all excuse me if I retired for the evening?"

The men, except for John, stood as she rose.

"Will you be all right?" Simon asked.

Maggie wished she hadn't needlessly worried him.

"Fine. I think I'll go to bed early, and I'll be good as a shiny penny by morning."

Curtseying first to the three titled ladies and then to the three gentlemen, including Mr. O'Connor because to do otherwise seemed rude, Maggie made her escape through the door a servant now held open.

If she were living in one of the popular romantic novels, perhaps written by one of the Bronte sisters or that clever Jane Austen, then her heart's desire, John Angsley, would come after her. He'd find an excuse to leave the dining room and surreptitiously run into her in the hallway outside her room.

Unfortunately, Maggie couldn't recall any heroes in casts who needed assistance for a tryst. It would hardly be romantic if Simon or Grayson were carrying John around to meet her.

Climbing the stairs while feeling as if her satin slippers were made of stone, Maggie considered whether a bath would help. However, it seemed an unnecessary imposition to the housemaid. Instead, she let the maid who'd accompanied her from Belton Manor help her undress and take out the pins from her hair before braiding it. Then, much to the woman's surprise at having her duties end early, Maggie excused her for the night.

As soon as the maid left, Maggie realized she should have asked for some books from the library. Standing there in her shift, she considered. It had only been about half an hour. Surely, the guests would still be in the dining room. If not, they would be in the drawing room having an after-dinner drink. At least, the ladies would, and maybe eating some little fondant cakes, while the men had cigars and brandy elsewhere.

Drat! Now she wanted cake, too. Such was the price one paid for lying. She could ring for books. Yet, how ridiculous was that really. To bring some poor servant upstairs only to send her back down to the library.

Deciding to move swiftly, Maggie donned her wrap and slippers. Despite her hair being in a loose braid over her shoulder, she was presentable enough if anyone should glimpse her running about Turvey House.

And run, she did. Dashing and sprinting until she was in the Cambrey library. Smaller than the one at Belton, it was still far more than adequate, and she was confident there would be something with intrigue and excitement. Or even a novel filled with intense relations and aching romance.

Perusing the shelves, Maggie had just pulled out a thin book of the collected works of Edgar Allan Poe when she heard footsteps. Heart pounding, clasping her wrap together tightly over her chest, she tried to shrink against the wall behind the door.

It opened slowly, and a familiar head appeared. Simon peered around the room and spotted her.

"What on earth are you doing?"

Sheepishly, she held out the book. "Getting something to read."

"I went to check on you. Jenny would be furious with me if there was something really wrong and I didn't let her know."

"I'm fine," Maggie admitted with a wave of her hand.

"Why are you hiding behind the door?"

"I heard men's boots and thought it might be . . . *Oh*."

"It could only be me."

"Or Grayson, or the butler, or a footman."

"Unlikely. Why would Gray be haunting the library, or Cyril for that matter? Fess up, Cam's the person you didn't want to run into."

"Most certainly, not in my nightclothes. Not after this morning."

Simon grinned. "And you forgot he was in a pushchair, didn't you?"

"Stop it. It's not funny. If you could have seen the look on his mother's face when she found us."

"I should have let her force you two into marriage. I think it would have done you both some good."

Maggie felt her cheeks grow warm.

"Why would you say such a thing? Only think how happy he seems now Lady Chatley is here."

"Lady Chatley is old enough to be his mother."

Maggie made a face. "You're teasing me again. You know I mean the other Lady Chatley. The pretty one."

Simon shrugged. "I'm a fairly decent judge of women, and I think you're prettier than Jane."

Even if it was only her brother-in-law's opinion, his words gave her a boost of happiness, until he added, "Yet she does have a nice disposition. Somewhat reminds me of Jenny."

"Are you saying my disposition isn't as nice as Jane's?"

"I didn't say that. Though I don't think Jane would leave the middle of a dinner party, even if she'd been stabbed and shot, not if she thought it might offend the hostess. Especially if she merely wanted . . ." He tilted her book toward him until he could read the spine. "Not if she liked the man at the head of the table, who looked a little morose after she departed."

"Did he? How do you mean? Did John stop eating? Did he sigh and rest his head on his hand? How about his conversation? Did it drift off as if he were distracted?"

Simon's mouth fell open. "I think you need to befriend Jane and have this type of conversation with her, not me. Anyway, now I know you're well, I'll leave you to your evening. A word of advice though. Since people are now roaming about, mostly going upstairs, I suggest you stay here for a bit, given your state of undress."

As he turned to go, Maggie put her hand on his arm.

"Was there cake?"

Smiling as if recalling the most scrumptious piece of sponge, Simon nodded.

"Almost better than my cook's." With that, he left.

Scrunching up her face, Maggie considered. Simon was correct. She should settle in here and do her reading rather than risk running into one of the men, particularly if they were carrying John. Taking a wingchair next to the lamp, Maggie spent the next hour enjoying Poe's thrilling short stories.

Stretching, her stomach twinged slightly. *Hmm.* Go to bed thinking of glorious sponge cake, or seek it out and satisfy her craving?

Glancing at the book in her hand, she knew what good old Edgar would do. He would brave the somewhat dimly lit mansion, sneak into the kitchen, and raid the larder. For surely, there were plenty of leftovers somewhere.

Minutes later, she'd made her way through Turvey House's silent main living areas and stood at the door to the servants' wing, which not only housed the vast kitchen but also the pantry and larder. She assumed the staff's dining room was beyond that, and any sleeping quarters for servants who didn't sleep in the attic, such as the scullery maid.

At the swinging door between the hall and the kitchen, she hesitated. Perhaps this would be considered a terrible breach of domestic order and etiquette. What if they were all in their nightclothes as was she?

But sponge cake was on the other side. Gently and slowly, Maggie began to push the door inward. What harm could it do?

Jane would never barge into the Cambrey kitchens late at night.

With that sobering thought, Maggie stepped back, quietly letting the door swing closed. Sighing, she turned and ran smack into a tangle of arms and satin gown.

CHAPTER FIFTEEN

As if Maggie had conjured the devil herself, there was Jane. Except instead of looking demonic, Jane's only devilish trait was her slightly lopsided smile.

"I didn't expect to find anyone else roaming about," the young woman said, eyes filled with merriment. "I think I had a bit too much wine and not enough food to soak it up. Mother keeps an eye on what I eat. I thought another slice of sponge would do the trick." Jane actually giggled. "Do you see? Sponge to soak up the wine in my stomach."

"Yes," Maggie said. "I do see." But the idea of going into the Cambrey kitchen with a tipsy Jane gave her no joy.

"Why don't we go to the drawing room and ring the bell?" Maggie suggested.

"Oh, no. I don't want to do anything so rude this late at night, especially as a guest."

"I believe the kitchen staff would prefer it to us going into their domain at this hour. Don't you think?"

Jane frowned, swaying slightly where she stood. "No, I don't."

"That's fine," Maggie said, reaching for her arm. "I'll think for both of us right now."

Sighing but going along with Maggie's guidance, Jane let her lead the way to the drawing room. Turning up the lamps, relieved to find the fire still lit, Maggie held her breath and rang the bell, almost imagining she could hear it jangling back in the kitchen.

In a very few minutes, a maid entered, still tying on her apron.

"Yes, miss," she said, with a weary curtsey to Maggie, who stood in the middle of the room. Then the girl saw Jane, too, now lolling upon the sofa and added another curtsey.

As Jane began to hum, Maggie exchanged a pained look with the maid.

"My apology for bothering you this late," she began, and the girl's eyes widened in shock, most likely at being apologized to. "We were only wondering if we might have two slices of sponge cake, the one served with dinner. With custard poured over if you have it."

Then she recalled her mother's remedy for anything that ailed one.

"And a pot of tea, weak, but with plenty of milk. Actually, forget the tea, just two glasses of milk will do."

Keeping an entirely neutral face, the maid muttered, "Yes, miss." Bobbing another quick curtsey, she left. Maggie could only imagine the talk in the kitchen.

Jane started to rise. "Shall we go get some cake or at least a few biscuits?"

"Yes, it's coming," Maggie told her, breaking off as Jane held her hand to her mouth, a distinctly green tone overtaking her creamy cheeks.

Looking wildly about, Maggie located a crystal bowl filled with apples. Dumping the fruit onto the sideboard, she shoved the bowl toward Jane, who sat back down heavily, and leaned over the crystal. Luckily, her hair was still pinned up and only a few stray tendrils fell forward, which Maggie pushed back as Jane lost the contents of her stomach.

In a few moments, she had finished.

Removing the bowl from the other girl's lap, Maggie wondered what to do with it. It seemed a terrible thing to have it waiting for the maid bringing their snack, and the odor was starting to fill the room.

"Stay here," she told Jane who was leaning back, eyes closed. "I'll get rid of this and return shortly."

Heading for the water closet in the back hallway, Maggie truly hoped she didn't meet anyone now. Trying to keep the bowl as far away from her as possible, she wished she could hold her nose with one hand but needed both to steady the unwieldy crystal. Soon, she had dumped it in the toilet, thankful for the blessing of indoor plumbing. *What to do with the bowl?* With a shrug, she left it inside the water closet, tucked against the wall.

She had done her part. Sadly, some wretched housemaid would have to find this when she came to clean, most likely in the early morning. No doubt, it would be an unsolved mystery discussed by servants for years to come.

Hurrying back to the drawing room, she passed the maid leaving, nodding as the girl curtsied. In the lovely blue room was a tray with two pieces of delicate golden sponge smothered in warm custard, two glasses of milk, and no Jane.

"Can't let this go to waste," Maggie said aloud. Sitting down, she polished off the first piece and drank the milk.

"Tasty," she added, rather enjoying talking to the empty room. Simon had been right about the baking skills of the Cambrey cook.

Eying Jane's portion, Maggie decided she could likely devour hers as well but would eat it in the privacy of her own room.

Tucking Poe under her arm, she picked up the plate and glass and headed to bed.

CAM WAS ALREADY SEATED in the sunny breakfast room located on the east side of his home, awaiting his guests. It was the first time he'd been down to breakfast since his return to Turvey House. Still irked about the necessity of being carried and having his food cut for him, Cam had Cyril and his valet, Peter, bring him down exceptionally early so no one would witness his infirmities.

With his leg cast hidden discreetly under the table, propped up on a neighboring chair, he had chosen only soft eggs and toast, which he could easily eat with one hand. If only his stomach didn't hurt.

When half an hour later Margaret entered, he felt a flood of enjoyment course through him as swiftly as it had departed when she'd left the dining room the night before.

Simon was close behind, and Jane entered a minute later, looking what his father used to call *peaked*. However, since she'd had no complaints the evening prior, he directed his to Margaret.

"Are you feeling better?"

Strangely, she stared at him a long moment uncomprehendingly, even glancing at Jane as if the other would respond. Then her eyes widened.

"Oh, you *are* addressing me. Of course. Better. Yes, I'm feeling much better. Thank you. Nothing a good night's sleep couldn't cure."

He thought her good night's sleep had also made her hair look even more lustrous and her eyes shine brighter. Even her cheeks had a perfect creamy hue.

"You've transformed into the shiny penny you promised last night. I'm glad to hear it."

As they took their seats, he felt the need to excuse his behavior.

"Again, ladies, I apologize for not getting up."

Margaret told him he needn't offer an apology each time, and Jane, who remained silent, merely shrugged as she poured herself a cup of tea before staring silently down at the white cloth.

"Is everything all right?" Unlike Margaret, she looked more like a well-used shilling. "You're unusually quiet."

Not that he knew whether Jane normally chatted like a magpie in the mornings or not. Yet, come to think of it, she did seem to have an opinion or comment to make at most other hours of the day in which he'd been in her company.

Jane glanced at Margaret, and it seemed to Cam as if some unspoken secretive communication passed between them.

"I have a bit of a headache this morning," Jane said quietly.

"How odd! Isn't that how you felt last night, Miss Blackwood? Do you think some sort of illness is winding its way through Turvey House?"

"No," Margaret asserted at once. "I'm sure it is unrelated."

Jane nodded in agreement, then winced at the movement. If he didn't know better, he'd say she'd had too much to drink the night before.

Women! What strange animals.

Speaking of which, the elder ladies entered next. The conversation led by Lady Chatley turned quickly to babies and which couples had formed attachments during the Season, both topics seeming to make Jane shrink in her chair.

He should have warned his mother about Lady Emily Chatley's desire to make a marriage between him and Jane. At his bidding, she would not have invited them. He didn't like to see Jane unhappy.

"What plans do you have for today?" he asked to change the subject from the new romances of the *ton*. "Those of you lucky enough to be able to get about should seize the opportunity."

"I thought the four of us," Lady Cambrey began, nodding to the other females at the table, "could take a tour of All Saints. It's a lovely church. Right on the edge of our estate. You must have passed it when you arrived. And then we shall have a picnic on the banks of the Great Ouse. The weather looks fine."

Cam noticed the younger ladies looking not as pleased as the older ones, and could only imagine they were both missing the excitement of London's finer venues.

"Mother, I suggest Grayson go along as a guide, for he knows the area as well as I do. And, of course, Simon should go, too, to keep you all company."

Maybe with those two along with their good humor, the ladies wouldn't be bored.

"Simon came to keep *you* company," his mother pointed out, her face set in a mulish expression.

Hmm. "Fine, but take Gray—"

"Take me where?" asked the man himself, strolling in as if he owned the place, and Cam knew he was doing it to irk Lady Chatley, who'd thought it extremely odd Gray dined with them the night before. Unfortunately, she'd been vociferous in expressing her thoughts.

"I want you to escort these lovely ladies to the church and then to the river for a picnic."

Gray turned to stare at him so only Cam could see his face.

"A grand idea," his estate manager said, his expression professing the exact opposite of his words. "Although I do have work to do. Lord Lindsey knows the area only too well. Maybe he would like to accompany them."

Cam would not be out maneuvered. "Lord Lindsey is going to stay and chat with me since I hardly ever see him. Whereas with you, I am rather sick of your ugly face."

Lady Chatley, the elder, gasped, while Gray threw his head back and laughed heartily.

"Well said. I agree. I am fair sick of you as well."

Cam noticed Jane and Margaret were smiling, too. In truth, however, if there were a way to keep the latter with him, he would, but he couldn't think of any way to do it.

The butler had entered on his quiet servant feet, which Cam always found slightly astonishing. Suddenly, the man appeared next to him.

"Yes, Cyril?"

"Your chair has arrived, my lord."

Everyone hesitated and then understanding dawned.

"Bring it in," Gray said.

Cam shot him a look. Would everyone have to be witness to his humiliation?

"Yes," Simon agreed. Turning to Cam, he pointed out, "You've finished eating. Let's get you in it and try it out. In fact, I think this means we can all go on the outing today."

Cam felt his eyes grow wide. "Perhaps."

He was of two minds. He didn't want to appear as an invalid to Margaret. On the other hand, he truly wanted to be in her company, not to mention to be with her when she saw the sights near his home for the first time. In any case, he was probably going to use the damned chair for the next couple of months. Thus, he might as well begin. Particularly if it could get him beside her for the day.

In a moment, Cyril returned with the pushchair.

Gray whistled. "You spared no expense it seems."

"It is the fanciest one I've ever seen," Simon agreed, eyeing the contraption of rattan, mahogany, and brass-studded, tufted leather. "And look at the size of those wheels."

"That's so I can get about the estate," Cam pointed out. "Not merely for indoors."

"I think you could race my carriage with it," Simon joked.

Cam thought about it. "Let us see."

With as much grace as possible, he let Gray and Simon lift him onto the chair. Cam couldn't help smiling.

"It is superbly comfortable, precisely as I ordered."

Gray got behind it and gave it a tentative push. "And it moves very easily. Luckily, the church is close enough we don't even have to load this into a wagon. We can push you the entire way."

True. In a very few minutes, Gray was driving the ladies in Cam's open landau while Simon pushed him down the drive, toward All Saints Church.

"You know there's not really much here to see," Cam reminded his friend. "I don't know what my mother is thinking. It's not like it's St. Paul's." They both had a good laugh at the comparison.

"And why are they in a carriage?" Cam laughed even harder when he looked at it ahead of them. "One can walk there in five minutes."

He slapped his good thigh with merriment.

Simon joined in. "It took longer to harness the horses than the actual ride will take. I have to stop a moment."

He stood beside Cam, tears streaming from his eyes at the absurdity of all the ladies climbing into the landau for a two-minute trip. "I can barely breathe for laughing."

They were already halfway there, and in a moment, Simon started pushing him again. Then like a bolt out of the blue sky, Cam heard him ask, "Are you interested in Lady Chatley?"

Cam tried to turn in the chair in order to see his friend's face.

"Stop wriggling," Simon reprimanded as if he were a naughty child. "You'll tip yourself over. By the way, you know you'll be able to roll yourself around when the cast comes off your arm."

"Of course I know that, and I shall. Why, I'll have arm muscles like a gorilla by the time I'm out of the leg cast."

He said nothing more, hoping Simon would drop his line of inquiry.

"Well?"

"Well, what?"

Simon's sigh was loud and dramatic. "Do you have an interest in Lady Jane Chatley?"

"For God's sake, man, why do you care? Didn't we have a similar conversation the other day on the veranda?"

"Yes, however, that was *before* Lady Chatley arrived. I know I am behaving like an old gossip. But if you care for Jane and not for Maggie, then I need to know because I will have to report back to my wife. If you care for them both, then I might have to throttle you within an inch of your life. And if you care for Maggie and not for Jane, then we might end up as family."

Cam felt the smile spread upon his face. After a moment, he said, "I think I would like to end up as family."

Simon let out a whooping sound.

"Yet it is not," Cam added, drawing his laudanum bottle out of his pocket and taking a swig, "entirely up to me."

"True, although I think Maggie might be interested in you, too. I'll say no more, as it would be disrespectful to my sister-in-law. I think you should declare yourself sooner rather than later, since I plan on staying only a few more days. If I don't get to hold my wife and son again soon, I'm going to go raving mad."

"Understandable. You're lucky to have made yourself a family."

"I had the easy part compared to Jenny."

They laughed again.

"Are you in pain now?" Simon asked.

Cam thought about it. "No. I'm distracted by our conversation, so I'm not."

"Then why did you take a sip of laudanum just a moment ago?"

Cam almost hadn't realized he'd done it, but he could still taste it on his tongue. *Dammit*. And Simon sounded like Maggie when she'd started questioning him about the laudanum. He didn't like it one bit.

"In truth, the jerkiness of this pushchair has caused my leg to ache. I simply didn't want to worry you. It's strange having my leg straight out instead of elevated. Undoubtedly, it's swelling even as I sit here."

This was met by silence from Simon, and Cam wondered if he disapproved.

"You know, everyone takes laudanum for pain. It's as common as ale."

"True, but taking too much for too long is also common."

"Understood."

They spoke of it no more as they'd reached the entrance to All Saints.

"Why don't you go in and find the others. I'll sit here amongst the dead, or roll around in left-handed circles." He tested it by grabbing hold of the hand grip on the left wheel and pushing down until he began to spin.

Simon offered him a wry grin. "Perfect!"

After his friend disappeared inside the stone church, Cam considered his words. Perhaps he should declare for Margaret. After all, she'd seemed perfectly happy to receive his kisses each time he'd doled them out. If only she didn't seem happy to kiss everyone else, as well. What if she had kissed Gray while the two of them had been out riding the day before?

Luckily, he could find that out easily enough. It seemed like a perfectly reasonable question to ask his long-time friend, man to man. He knew his estate manager would be back outside soon since there could be nothing much fascinating in the interior of All Saints . . . except Margaret.

Unfortunately, when Gray did emerge, it was with the ladies Chatley and Cam's mother. They seemed to be in an animated conversation about the belfry and the date of the oldest bell, which Cam knew perfectly well was 1682. Still, he stayed silent while Lady Emily Chatley droned on for a few moments, reading from a leaflet she'd found in the church's nave.

Eventually, Jane looked over and waved to him, and then abandoned the others.

"You look better than you did at breakfast," he remarked.

"Do I? I feel better. I suppose I had too much to drink last night." Jane leaned close and whispered, "My mother has that effect on me. It really only takes a second glass of wine, and I feel as if I'm walking on board a ship."

"Only two?" Cam grinned. "You would do best to stick to sober-water, my girl."

"I know. And unfortunately, when I have wine, my stomach thinks I'm at sea as well."

Poor Jane.

"Miss Blackwood helped me last night when I was insisting on storming your kitchen for a treat."

"Did she?"

"Next thing I knew, I was ill. She took care of everything, and I confess to being cowardly and fleeing the scene."

Poor Jane, indeed. And Margaret, too.

Right then, Margaret came out of All Saints with Simon behind her. Glancing toward where he and Jane had their heads together, she got a decidedly strange look upon her face.

"I should apologize to her and thank her," Jane continued.

"Now's your chance," Cam said, but Margaret moved toward Gray as they began their tour of the church's exterior. The group stopped to look at the molded interior arch of the south porch before heading back to the small cemetery.

"Do you mind if I walk with you?" Jane asked him. "When I'm trapped with my mother and other people, she goes on embarrassingly about my 'accomplishments,' and then always manages to bring up engagements, weddings, and babies. In that order, of course."

Cam laughed. "Mothers treat their sons no differently. Anyway, what did you think of the wonders of our little church? Did you see the tower and the baptistery? The majestic nave? The brasses? The Mordaunt family monuments?"

"Yes, I saw it all. It is a positive gem to have. And handy, too, for when you marry."

Hmm. Jane was right. He could have Margaret from his house to the church in under five minutes. Taking a sip of laudanum, he set it back in his pocket, and realized he was stuck. He could get nowhere with one hand, and he couldn't ask Jane to push the heavy chair.

The others had all walked ahead and were examining the lichen-covered headstones.

When Margaret, whom he couldn't keep his eyes off, looked back, Cam gave her a little wave. Quickly, she said something to Gray, who came back at a trot.

"Didn't mean to leave you stranded, old boy." Pushing him swiftly over the trimmed grass and pavers, he added, "Margaret reminded me of your plight."

He called her Margaret now, did he?

"Nice of her since my two best friends forgot me."

Gray nodded at Jane who walked beside them.

"Luckily, you had this lovely lady's company. I think she got the wrong end of the sword, though."

"Ha! Now hurry up, let's make sure no one misses the mausoleum. You and I have only seen it a hundred times!"

MAGGIE COULD RELAX AND explore the churchyard as soon as Grayson pushed John into her sight. Jane remained by his side, like a devoted fiancée. Maybe she was. Possibly they'd already come to an understanding. Perhaps they would announce their engagement at the picnic, and everyone would celebrate. Jane could become tipsy again and sit on his lap in the pushchair for the ride home.

"Why are you scowling?" Simon asked her, and she tore her gaze away to look at her brother-in-law.

"Am I?"

"Yes. Anyway, you don't have to tell me. Some people feel that way in cemeteries."

It was as good an excuse as any so she said nothing more.

"By the way," Simon added. "I mentioned to Cam to be careful with the laudanum."

"Thank you."

"I'm not sure he took it well."

Glancing at John again, Maggie frowned.

"If they announce an engagement, I shall personally warn her of the danger. Then it will be up to her."

Simon's eyebrows rose. "Announce an . . . ? Is that why you're over here in the shadow of this sepulcher, scowling like a gargoyle?"

"Don't be ridiculous!" Picking up her skirts, she decided she'd been too familiar with her brother-in-law. It was time to rejoin the ladies.

After a few minutes of aimless browsing, Lady Cambrey declared it time for the jaunt to the River Great Ouse. As Maggie let Simon help her into the landau, she was pleased to see Jane leave John's side and board the carriage as well. Simon stayed with them this time to drive, and Grayson was elected to handle pushing John to the river.

For the entire short journey down the lane and to the water's edge, Jane seemed to have something she wanted to say. The other girl was glancing at her, saying something with her eyes. Maggie decided she would let Jane get her alone after they ate and speak her peace. No doubt it had something to do with asking Maggie to leave the field of honor, so to speak. Having two single ladies buzzing around the same bachelor was probably unsettling.

However, after the kiss she'd shared with John, and the exquisite sensation of her body atop his, Maggie had more than half a mind to fight for him. He might have chosen Jane for her placid nature, solid head on her shoulders, and all that, even for her sweet face and inheritance. Yet, the sparks Maggie felt with him were very real.

Could he possibly feel the same with Jane? It flummoxed her if such were the case, because her own experimental kisses with other men had been like a tepid flicker compared to a roaring flame.

Deciding to do the unthinkable, she would ask John outright. Was he willing to give up the exquisite burning sizzle they shared for a mere glimmer of warmth?

CHAPTER SIXTEEN

The Great Ouse was not exactly the Thames. Maggie knew the river was very long, but there, near Turvey House, it seemed hardly any different from the River Don near Simon and Jenny's Belton Park. Their carriage ride had taken slightly longer to get to the river than to the church since they'd driven practically back to the manor before taking a left onto a path leading down to the chosen picnic area. Mrs. Mackle, the Angsleys' extremely capable housekeeper, had sent servants to lay out a grand spread.

Where they alighted from the landau, there were multiple large cloths on which were already placed a stack of plates and silverware. Servants had carried down baskets of food and drink, which they now dished out as the ladies and gentlemen gathered around.

Grayson and John came last, and everyone turned away as the injured earl was helped from his chair to stretch out upon a blanket.

When he groaned, Maggie whipped her head around to see him rubbing his thigh before he pulled his laudanum bottle from his pocket. To her delight, he looked at it and then returned it to his coat without opening it. Maybe Simon's words had got through to him after all.

She was pleased to see the meal was light, merely individual cold pastry pies filled with meat and vegetables, easy to hold in one hand, along with fruits and cheeses. She drank only lemonade and noticed Jane did the same. The older ladies tipped back glasses of wine, and Maggie wondered if the ability to keep one's head came with age. All of a sudden, she missed her own mother and wondered what was happening back at Sheffield with Jenny, Eleanor, and the new baby.

Lost in thought, she nearly didn't notice when Jane gestured for her to walk to the water's edge. Brushing the crumbs from her hands, she stood up and followed. It seemed it was the time of reckoning. Or maybe Jane would simply try to be rid of any competition by shoving Maggie into the river.

"Don't go swimming, girls," Lady Cambrey called after them, as if knowing Maggie's musings. "Looks can be deceiving, and the current is rather swift."

"I haven't swum in a river or in the sea since I was a child," Jane mused. "I think it would be fun and most definitely refreshing."

Maggie looked out at the moving waters. "Perhaps deadly unless you're a strong swimmer. There are probably bends in the river where it is more placid."

Frankly, she was surprised at Jane's words, still thinking her more reserved than she'd proven herself to be either now or the night before. It seemed there was an adventurous, amusing Jane, one who had captured John's heart, and Maggie was only now seeing her.

Jane's glance went from the river to lock onto Maggie.

"I simply wanted to say thank you."

Oh, of course. Why hadn't that occurred to Maggie? She'd assumed it had to be about John. Offering her a reassuring smile, Maggie waved her hand, trivializing the moment.

"You're welcome. Besides, I ate your piece of cake, too."

Jane laughed. "You deserved it. You saved me from humiliating myself in the kitchen or utter mortification in the drawing room."

"We've all done something we wish we hadn't."

Jane sobered instantly, looking back at the group. Glancing over her shoulder, she saw John's gaze upon them.

"I suppose you're right," Jane murmured.

Maggie burned to know what Jane was recalling but asking her was out of the question. If she wanted to spill her secrets, she would.

"I like you," Jane told her abruptly. "I wish we'd been friends during the Season."

Feeling as if she'd been petty in some of her uncharitable thoughts regarding Lady Jane, Maggie could only agree and add, "There's always next year."

"Somehow, I doubt it," Jane said, sounding dour. "I don't think there will be another Season for me. At least, I hope not."

Feeling her heart clench, Maggie was certain Jane meant she would soon be off the marriage market, as it was called. Next year, Jane might be hosting parties for other debutantes at the Cambrey townhouse.

Maggie would prefer tossing herself into the Great Ouse than attending a party thrown by the Earl and Countess of Cambrey, especially if she were still a single lady enduring her third Season.

The others started to walk toward them, and their private moment passed.

"If you look farther along, you'll see our raspberry bushes are plentiful," Lady Cambrey said. "Not that I've ever picked them, of course, but our cook makes raspberry pie and sponge with fresh raspberries and cream. She makes preserves for morning toast, as well as raspberry wine and vinegar, too." She paused for a moment. "Then she starts putting raspberries over half the dishes we eat at lunch and dinner."

Staring at the bushes, Lady Cambrey frowned. "Come to think of it, maybe I should tear them all out."

Simon laughed. "It can't be that bad. Besides, I have fond memories of picking pails of them. I'm sure Cam, Gray, and I ate more than we gave to the cook."

Cam's mother smiled. "Soon, I hope there will be a new generation of Angsleys to pick berries."

Cam, who was back in his chair and being pushed by Gray, gave a loud mock groan. As Maggie watched, he shared an amused glance with Jane.

"Remember what I told you?" he called to her.

Jane nodded, giving a slight shrug.

A private joke between the couple, Maggie thought. They might have already discussed having children as soon as possible to please his mother or hers.

"Shall we walk farther?" asked Lady Cambrey. "There's a small bend a short way up. It's where John used to paddle as a boy."

"Mother," he admonished her.

Disregarding him, Lady Chatley cooed. "I would love to see it. Wouldn't you, Jane?"

Simon added in a loud voice, "Then we'll take a tour of where he had his first diaper changed."

Everyone laughed.

"Only you could get away with such irreverence," John told him. "As far as my mother is concerned anyway."

CAM NEVER THOUGHT HE would be glad to get back to bed and have his leg in the infernal sling, but he was. Even the modest outing of the day had been a painful, tiring ordeal.

Closing his eyes as soon as his head hit the pillow, he said to Gray, "Don't go yet."

The butler had already left, and Simon had decided to write a letter to Jenny. Thus, they were alone.

"Haven't you had enough of my company?"

"Just a quick question, but an important one."

Gray pulled a chair over to the bed. "All right."

Cam opened his eyes and looked at him. "You might not want to answer."

Gray nodded. "All right."

"When you went riding with Miss Blackwood, by any chance, did you kiss her?"

"What?" His long-time friend scrunched his face up into a curious expression, both disbelief and amusement.

Despite the shard of embarrassment cutting through him, Cam continued, "Actually, at any time you've been alone with her, not only on a ride. Or even not alone, I suppose." He rubbed a hand over his face. "Look, simply tell me if you've kissed her?"

However, Gray was already laughing, first merely a chuckle but then a loud guffaw escaped him.

"I fail to see what's funny?" Cam said, his tone clipped.

"Because I'm not the one asking you a ridiculous question. I've only just met the lady."

"That's neither here nor there. Upon first seeing her, you could have developed a great passion, which you then expressed to her while riding together. She should have had a companion, not been out alone with you."

"Because I'm such a randy beast?" Gray's satisfied smile never left his face.

"I don't know." Cam groaned. "My head feels muddled. All I know is I would certainly kiss her if I were alone with her. I have done, in fact, and upon numerous occasions."

Why had he felt the need to say that? It was disrespectful, he knew, but it did stake his claim.

"Oh, really?" Gray raised an eyebrow. "Besides here in your bedroom, do you mean?"

Cam scowled. "I'll not compromise the lady by discussing it with the likes of you. Answer the bloody question."

"I thought I had. The answer is a resounding no. I have not kissed her, nor do I want to."

That got Cam's undivided attention. "Whyever not? What's wrong with her?"

Gray laughed until he howled, holding his stomach and doubling over with mirth. All the while, Cam lay stock-still, arms crossed over his chest. *Damn the man for being amused.*

At last, in a calm voice, Gray asked him, "Do you want me to sing her praises or tell you what I don't like?"

"Neither," Cam told him. "I already know what's wonderful about her, and I don't care what you don't like. I'm glad there are things about her you don't like. She's mine, not yours."

"Good. I think you're well-suited. Why don't you tell her? I believe Miss Margaret and Simon are leaving soon."

Cam groaned. "Look at me. How do I approach a lady when I can't walk?"

"Pick a place," Gray said, suddenly in earnest, "and I'll get you set up first and then bring her to you."

"I'll think on it," Cam said, feeling grateful and irrationally emotional. This could be very important to the rest of his life. "Thank you."

"Am I dismissed, *my lord?*"

"Stop it, and yes, you are."

At the door, Gray turned. "Don't choose the spot where you had your diaper changed." He ducked out of the way as Cam threw a pillow at his head.

THE NEXT MORNING, HE didn't bother getting up early and racing everyone to the breakfast room. He didn't feel like eating anyway. His stomach pained him. Perhaps it was from lying awake most of the night pondering where he should declare his affections for Margaret. He didn't have the extraordinarily lovely gardens like Simon had at Belton

Manor, but Turvey House had some lovely views of the river. There was a stone bench which might do nicely.

At mid-morning, his mother appeared at the door with her newspapers.

"I didn't expect you to come today, not with a house full of guests."

She bent down and kissed his cheek. "Why didn't you come downstairs today?"

He shrugged "I felt tired when I awakened."

"And no wonder. You went from no exercise to quite a bit yesterday."

He didn't tell her he felt tired or groggy a lot of the time anyway. He only knew when he tried to skip a dose of laudanum, everything hurt more.

"Anyway, everyone is having a good time," she informed him. "Simon is out with the ladies riding, and he said he would come see you when they get back. Since Lady Chatley is by herself, I'll leave you the papers. I shall take her for a walk into the village."

Heading for the door, she turned back to him. "I hate to leave you alone."

"Mother, I'm a grown man."

Giving him a lopsided smile, she said, "You'll always be my little boy."

He couldn't help but smile back at her. Then she was gone.

Reading the papers was a good diversion and got the wool out of his brain. He rang for tea and then plunged into the next daily. He'd nearly forgotten how much he loved the maneuverings of the government, and got easily lost in an article on what Lord John Russell was up to.

Half an hour later, he was wrapped up in Ainsworth's *The Lancashire Witches*, which was being serialized in *The Sunday Times*.

"I might write a novel," he murmured aloud.

"You do need some company if you're talking to yourself," said a voice from the doorway.

Simon strolled in, looking as if he'd enjoyed a brisk ride and caught some sun and wind.

"Nothing wrong with talking to oneself when one is not only speaking sense but also a good listener." Cam chuckled at his own joke. "Actually, I have about a hundred thoughts in my head, and I believe some of them might even be original. At first, I was feeling muddled from inactivity and sleep. Now, I have an overabundance of creative notions. I should start writing some of them down."

Simon said nothing for a moment, then asked, "Shall we get you downstairs, maybe to the library? Probably do you good to get up once a day."

Cam considered. "Yes, let's. The library would be good for me. Get Cyril. Is there anyone else about?"

Simon shook his head. "If we hurry, then no. The ladies are changing out of their riding habits."

"Perfect."

In a very few minutes, he was downstairs and in his pushchair, which fit perfectly under the round oak table in the library. Fountain pen and paper before him, Cam started to write.

A few minutes later, a movement in the doorway snagged his attention. It was Jane, which was relieving. If he encountered Margaret before he was ready, Cam feared she would read upon his face he intended to ask her for her hand, and this wasn't the setting he wanted.

"Did you have a good ride?"

"Yes, lovely. Am I intruding?"

"No, not at all." He almost confessed she was interrupting a stream of thoughts, but her stay would be short, and he would have many weeks to write after the Chatleys' departure.

As if reading his mind, Jane said, "We're leaving tomorrow. I'm sorry you were surprised by us. I think our mothers had a bit of matchmaking in mind. Or at least, mine did."

"I know. And it's perfectly fine. I was glad for the company."

Jane arched an eyebrow. "Even when you already had such delightful company?"

Christ! His cheeks might actually be reddening. "Close the door, will you?"

Grinning, she did so and then came closer, to lean upon the edge of the table on the other side, facing him.

"I feel as if we've become friends with all the hours spent getting ready for the banquet. I hope you don't think I'm being too personal," she said.

"No, I don't, and I do feel as if you're a friend. Rather unusual during a Season, don't you think? To make a friend with a member of the opposite sex, instead of a romantic association."

She nodded in agreement. "It helps neither of us is the least bit bothered we don't have romantic feelings for each other. We couldn't have become friends if it were elsewise."

"True. A few times during the planning meetings, I was worried something more was being hinted at—"

"By my mother," Jane interrupted. "You can't blame her, can you? A daughter becoming wedged on the shelf and you, an eligible, titled man, right before her like low-hanging fruit."

Cam laughed. "Yes, that's me, formerly a juicy pear, now more like a dried sultana trussed up in plaster casts."

He was glad to see her laugh. "You mustn't let your mother get to you. You were in a terrible state after the cricket match. And then you let her drag you up here to Bedford. Glad as I am to see you, it puts too much of a burden on you, especially when you knew we weren't going to form an attachment."

She shrugged, dismissing his words and, in all likelihood, believing she ought to behave as a dutiful daughter.

"I mean it, Jane. Moreover, I don't think at your age, you should worry about being on the shelf, neither permanently wedged on it, nor precariously toppling off."

Jane sighed softly, and he wondered if he should put his brain to use thinking of which gentleman of his acquaintance deserved her.

"When the invitation came from your mother," Jane said, "it would have been rude to turn it down simply because I knew we weren't going to become engaged. Besides, coming to cheer you up was the least I could do after I'd cried all over you in that wretched tent."

"The tent was not wretched. It was perfectly lovely. And you have cheered me up. Our little outing yesterday was the first time I'd made it past the veranda. I wouldn't have done so if it had been only Simon and . . . ," he trailed off.

Jane grinned again. "*Ah* yes, that's why I came in here, remember? Because you didn't want me talking from the doorway about the delightful company I found already visiting you. And I don't mean the handsome Lord Lindsey."

Was he beaming like a fool?

"I don't know what you mean," he said foolishly.

"Ha! Ridiculous," she cried. "I've seen how you look at Miss Blackwood. She is a lovely girl, smart and kind, too, and I recall she wears a ballgown to perfection. Why, I'm positive you've danced with her during the past Season."

"Yes, yes, to all that. I know how she dances and how she looks in a ballgown."

"Does *she* know you know?"

Cam frowned. "What do you mean?"

Jane leaned toward him. "Are you going to tell her you admire her?"

"Yes, I believe I will. Soon."

She placed her hands upon the table in front of him and stared into his eyes.

"This is terribly romantic, John. The lady comes to visit with her brother-in-law because he is your good friend, and then you discover you are mad for her."

Caught up in her excitement, a hundred notions going through his brain about Margaret and romance—ignoring the fact they were opium-induced—he grabbed for Jane's hand, making her slip chest-first onto the table.

With her other hand supporting her chin, she giggled uncharacteristically.

"When you put it that way," Cam said, "the whole thing does sound marvelous."

He hadn't heard any footsteps. Yet, when the door opened, Cam saw the very lady herself, staring wide-eyed as if she'd caught him *en flagrante,* like in a French farce.

CHAPTER SEVENTEEN

Maggie literally could not believe her eyes. It was too impossible. There was John seated in the library, grabbing hold of a laughing Jane, who was sprawled upon the table within kissing distance, with her gown gaping open and her cleavage hanging before his face.

Letting the book fall from her fingers, she abandoned the stories of Poe, turning and fleeing the scene. Barely able to breathe, Maggie had to get out of the house. Was that what she had looked like to his mother and Grayson when they'd come upon her lying atop him?

It didn't seem to matter to John Angsley, as long as he had a woman, any woman. Or maybe when he'd given her his excuse about believing he was dreaming, he'd been dreaming of Jane all along.

Dammit! She would not cry. After all, she knew he had feelings for Jane.

At least she needn't bother asking him whether he could give up their fiery encounters for a tepid arrangement with Jane? They seemed to have plenty of heat between them.

"Stop," Maggie heard behind her. It was John's voice booming loudly through the open doorway. Then there was a lot of scuffling. Perhaps the lady was needing to rearrange her skirts.

"Please, wait." This time it was Jane who called after her, then suddenly, there the lady was, chasing Maggie down the hall.

Reaching the main door, she was intent on escaping outside. However, Jane was beside her a moment later.

"Oh, please, Margaret, won't you let me explain?"

"No, I think not. I have eyes, don't I? I saw the two of you."

Jane shook her head. "Oh dear."

"Precisely," Maggie told her, putting her hand on the door.

"No, I mean, oh dear, I can only imagine what it must have looked like. Please, come back to the library. John is most upset."

"This might seem like putting too fine a point on it," Maggie said, her voice shrill to her own ears, "but at this moment, Lady Chatley, I don't find myself caring whether the Earl of Cambrey is upset."

Jane had the gall to smile. "Yes, I can see why that might be. Except you mistook what you saw."

Maggie rolled her eyes, but Jane persisted.

"Come now, this type of silly misunderstanding only happens in a romantic novel by Miss Austen."

Maggie froze. "Are you saying you do not love our great Jane Austen?"

Jane sighed. "Well of course I love her books, but I wouldn't want to live in one, would you? With all the heartache and heartbreak, and the miscommunications and hidden *tendres*. Our lives are not like those, so please, won't you come back with me and speak to John?"

How ironic, Maggie thought, *to have been thinking just the other evening of life in a novel. What's more, Jane was correct. There was always heartbreak, drama, and even tragedy before there was a happy ending. Even then, sometimes, there wasn't one.*

Before Maggie could answer, Jane took her arm and half led, half dragged her back down the hallway. At the library doorway, Maggie could see one of John's feet protruding, the one sticking out of his cast.

"Damn and blast," John exclaimed, as he came into sight. "It took me all this time not to go in circles, and then I got myself hooked up on the casing."

Slightly sideways, he had one of the front wheels of his pushchair stuck on the door jamb. Maggie stared down at the floor, a little angry, a little scared, but then as she raised her gaze to his face, at the same time, he looked up into her eyes.

"Margaret," was all he said, but his tone resonated through her.

"If you don't mind my saying," Jane began, "I believe we should push you backward and not have whatever is to come next occur while you are in this doorway."

"By all means," John said, "get me unstuck, but then, if you ladies wouldn't mind, please push me onto the veranda. I'm confident we can make it."

Silently, they did as he instructed, and before long, Maggie, with Jane by her side, was pushing John down the hallway toward the back of the house.

"That's it, good going, girls," he cheered them on as if they were oxen at a plow.

When they reached the veranda, Jane excused herself quickly, with nothing but a muttered, "Good luck" before she disappeared without looking back.

"This is not what I intended," John began.

"No?" Maggie said, and nothing more. She was not going to help him with 'whatever came next,' as Jane had put it. In any case, she simply wasn't certain what he intended.

"No, this isn't. Gray was going to bring you to a romantic spot, probably by the river."

"Gray?" She knew her voice had an edge to it, but again, John had thrown her off balance. "Does *he* have feelings for me?"

John frowned, his face a study in confusion. Then he shook his head.

"No, not that I'm aware of. In fact, he has a list of what he doesn't like about you."

"I beg your pardon."

If John didn't look so very handsome and have such an attractive mouth at which she now found herself staring while waiting for him to make some sense, she might have been insulted.

"Let me begin again," he said, "and speak plainly. I hold you in great esteem and have for a long time."

Feeling her cheeks heat, she kept silent. This was one of those times when Jane Austen would write for the heroine to simply let the man speak.

"Even though I felt drawn to you, not merely for your looks but also for your nature, your good humor, your laughter, the way you see the world. Still, at first, I worried you were too young, and then, of course, I saw you kissing Burnley, which you later told me you were *happy* to do."

"Happy because that kiss demonstrated the vast difference between an ordinary kiss and an extraordinary one."

He blinked at her. "Oh, I see."

"However, it is difficult for me to credit this 'high esteem' in which you profess to hold me, after seeing you with Lady Chatley."

"Jane came into the library only to ask about my feelings for you. I was telling her when you walked in."

Maggie shook her head. "Not just now. I am referring to after the banquet. At that time, I thought we had an understanding, based again on another extraordinary kiss."

"As did I, but then I found you in Westing's embrace. Much as I adore you, Margaret, and I do, I won't live in question of whether my wife is devoted to me or equally interested in another man."

Maggie recalled the day. John with Jane and then . . .

"You came into the pavilion?"

He nodded.

"But Christopher was only comforting me because of what I heard and saw while standing in the tent opening. You and Jane. It left me shaken, and he ended up taking me home directly."

John rubbed a hand over his face. "I'm sorry. It was a misunderstanding."

"Exactly like in one of Miss Austen's novels."

Tilting his head questioningly, John waited for her to clarify.

"You know, as in *Emma*. You are Mr. Knightley, and I think you care for Harriet, but all the time—"

"All the time, I liked Emma, although she seemed very immature and not to know her mind. Moreover, she appeared to prefer Frank Churchill to Knightley."

At her surprised expression, he added, "I've read a few romantic novels in my day."

Maggie smiled. "Emma was young and inexperienced and didn't know whom she liked until she thought she'd nearly lost the man. I, on the other hand, grasped the nettle, leaping into the breach to kiss other men and draw my own conclusions."

John pinched the bridge of his nose, making a sound that might have been exasperation.

"I don't think you needed to kiss other men to determine your heart."

"It seemed more direct than, for example, going through everything Elizabeth Bennet and Mr. Darcy went through, don't you think?"

John took her hand in his. "I'm glad you're not wearing gloves." He caressed her palm.

Her breath caught.

"What you saw in the tent—and today, for that matter—was the strange circumstance of two people of the opposite sex who have become friends. And nothing more. I promise you. Jane appeared in the tent after the banquet when I thought I would meet you."

"I was on my way," Maggie explained.

"She got there first and was most upset because her mother was beginning to make it known she wanted Jane and I to come to an understanding. Lady Chatley hoped the banquet would be the day I was so enraptured by Jane's skills as a hostess, I would offer for her, even as the last wicket fell at the match. Also, Jane cannot drink worth a damn."

"I found that out myself. Apparently, she has an extremely low resistance to the effects of wine."

"Or champagne," John added.

They both chuckled slightly, then silence descended. They stared at one another.

"And you've never kissed her?" Maggie had to know.

"Not once. I didn't need to do any such thing to know how I feel about you. When I kiss you, I can't even think about kissing anyone else. Ever again."

Catching her bottom lip between her teeth, Maggie considered his words. He sounded very sure and very much as if they were going to have a future.

"In my defense, John, I hadn't kissed many men before you. And I believe you've done that and much more with other women."

His eyebrows rose and then he dropped his gaze.

"It's all right," she insisted. "Honestly, it would have been strange if it had been otherwise. If I were your age, even unmarried, I believe I would have experienced the act of a man and a woman together. As it is, I'm excited by the prospect of undertaking it. With you, I mean."

She watched his expression go from surprise at her bluntness to utter delight.

"As am I," he told her, bringing her hand to his lips to kiss her palm. "Let's get this done correctly, shall we?"

With the strength in his one arm, he tugged her onto his lap. Taking hold of her chin, he directed her to look at him. With their gazes locked, Maggie felt as if she were swimming in the hazel depths of his eyes.

"I offer you my hand in marriage and ask for yours in return. I offer you my name, my title, and all that goes with it. And I offer you my body," he broke off with a wry grimace, but she nodded encouragingly, "which will be whole again someday soon to provide the pleasure you deserve. And children, too, I hope. Most importantly, I give you my heart, and I promise I will never share it with another. Will you marry me?"

Feeling the tears coursing down her cheeks, Maggie sniffed and wiped them with her free hand.

"Sorry," he said and released her chin, delving in his pocket for a handkerchief, which he quickly used to dab at her eyes before giving it to her.

"I must look all red and moist and awful," she said, feeling ecstatic anyway.

"Miss Margaret Blackwood, you are infuriating. You must know you look lovely, even while crying. And you have not responded to my very romantic plea."

Maggie grinned at him through her tears.

"Yes, John Angsley, I will marry you. And I will take your title and your body, and all that. With great joy. Mostly, I feel extraordinarily fortunate to be given your heart. I give you mine, as well."

Instantly, his hand slipped through her hair to cradle the back of her head and draw her close. As his lips touched hers, she sighed against him. Opening her mouth to receive his skilled, probing tongue, she relished the thrilling sensations coursing through her.

After a few delightful moments, Maggie pulled back.

"I cannot wait until we are in bed for the first time. Kissing like that when one is completely naked and lying together must be utter heaven."

His cheeks seemed to color slightly, and she watched him swallow before he puffed out a breath of air. However, when she expected words of love and longing, instead, he groaned slightly.

"I'm afraid, darling, I need you to climb off my lap. You've awakened a part of me which needs to move and to have room. And unfortunately, your lovely rounded bottom is also starting to make my injured leg ache like the devil."

She jumped up as if burnt.

"You should have said something sooner." Then she stared at his lap to see the 'part' of him which needed to expand.

"I can *see* it," Maggie said, evoking a pained laugh from John, who put his hand to his ribs.

"Let's only hope no one else comes outside too soon. There are things I'd like to keep private between us."

"Agreed." Then she thought of his injury. "But your leg. Is it all right?"

"Throbbing a tad."

She watched him reach into his pocket, the same from which he'd pulled the handkerchief. This time he withdrew the familiar, dark glass bottle, opened it, and took a small sip.

"Only a few drops," he said when he saw her watching him.

She could hardly chastise him this time. Who would look after him, though, when she left? Then it dawned on her how much she didn't want to leave.

"Do you think I have to return to Belton now we are engaged?"

"It would be the proper thing to do. I won't marry you until I can stand by your side. And I want you to have a ring as lovely as your eyes, if such were possible. I need to get to London for that."

Then he groaned.

"What is wrong? Is it your leg?"

"No. I wanted to ask you to marry me somewhere singular and in some special way."

She crouched down beside his chair.

"I cannot imagine a more perfect place than being on your lap. It was extremely special."

A glimmer of a smile crossed his handsome face.

"Maybe we'll do the proposal again properly when I have the ring in hand."

Shrugging, she stroked the side of his cheek. "I don't mind if you wish to ask me again. My answer will be the same."

"Your answer?" Simon echoed, coming onto the veranda in time to hear her last words. "What are you two discussing?"

"Getting engaged," Maggie replied, standing up in time to catch her brother-in-law's delighted expression. "Which we just did."

"That's wonderful. I'm very happy for you both." Simon swept her into an embrace before reaching down to smack John on the shoulder in lieu of shaking his right hand. "Jenny will be pleased, too."

"I'm determined to be standing when I marry this lady," John insisted.

"Thus, we wait," Maggie agreed. "We'll have a decently long engagement, unlike some people." She shot an amused glance toward Simon.

"Are you saying your sister and I were indecent?"

Maggie shook her head. "Knowing my sister, your quick marriage was all done for very practical reasons."

"True," Simon agreed. "I couldn't keep my hands off of her, and so she decided we'd better be official."

Both the men laughed, but Maggie refused to find amusement at any remark that hinted at impropriety where her older sister was concerned.

Seeing her countenance, Simon coughed to cover his laughter.

"Tonight, we must have a celebration before the ladies Chatley depart tomorrow."

Maggie felt a little sorry Jane would be gone. She had proved to be a true friend and no threat at all.

"When the senior Lady Chatley hears our news, she might not be in a celebratory mood," John surmised. "And she might take it out on Jane."

"Nonsense. Jane's mother will have to realize there are as good fish in the sea as ever came out of it. Unquestionably, as good as one Bedfordshire earl." Simon considered. "Besides, we must know a few eligible men we can throw in her path."

"Into Jane's path or her mother's?" Maggie asked. "You two make it sound as if one earl is as good as another, or any man is the same to a woman. Which I assure you is not the case. If Jane had truly wanted John, then this would be a terrible evening all around. Only because her heart will not be injured, I am agreeing to our announcing this at all."

Simon stared at her.

"What is it?" She put her hand to her hair under his scrutiny, checking for stray tendrils.

"For a moment there, you sounded exactly like your sister."

The two men laughed again. This time, Maggie joined in. Suddenly, she couldn't wait to see her family, and that was the only consolation for leaving John and Turvey House behind.

JOHN HAD BEEN CORRECT about Lady Emily Chatley, whose mouth formed a thin line of disapproval as soon as he gave his announcement at the beginning of dinner. Then it seemed to Maggie the older woman was trying to decide whom to blame. Was it Maggie's fault for being in the right place at the right time, or was it some innate flaw in her own daughter which made Lord Cambrey choose one over the other?

Jane, for her part, expressed delight.

Maggie was glad, and more than a little relieved, John's mother also appeared happy. How awful if Lady Cambrey had had her heart set on Jane for a daughter-in-law!

Later, when Jane was playing the pianoforte, Lady Cambrey approached Maggie and took her hand in hers.

"We will be family, and I shall have a daughter at last."

Maggie felt tears prick her eyes. What a lovely way for John's mother to welcome her.

"You will probably have three daughters. Simon will want to visit his best friend, and thus, my sister Jenny will come. And Eleanor will want to visit Beryl, too, and most probably stay here with me some of the time."

"My little plan worked well."

Maggie wasn't sure she'd heard the older lady correctly.

"Your plan? I'm sorry, Lady Cambrey, I don't understand."

The woman clamped her lips together at the same time as she smiled, creating a droll, mischievous expression.

"I could see my son was taken with you from the beginning, and never wavered even all the weeks he worked with Jane. I thought I could help bring about this happy outcome. I wrote to Simon, hoping you would hear of John's accident. I knew you would be the best medicine for him. When you arrived, it was clear you cared for my son. And I invited the Chatleys because sometimes, nothing shows a man—or a woman—what they want as much as seeing what they don't want."

Maggie shook her head in admiration. "Lady Cambrey. I shall be honored to call you my mother-in-law."

The woman nodded. "I just realized we'll both be Lady Cambrey. I have never shared the title because my husband's mother passed away giving birth to John's father."

"Is my sharing it all right?"

"Of course. You will make an excellent countess, I have no doubt, which is why I sent you unaccompanied into his bedroom with the newspapers. I thought I would get a declaration of engagement out of him that very day."

Maggie was shocked.

"What are you two whispering about?"

John, who'd learned how to move the pushchair in a straight line with only one hand, was suddenly behind them.

His mother bent down and kissed his cheek.

"Women like to share secrets, dear boy, especially family." She winked at Maggie and walked away to sit by Lady Chatley senior.

John watched her go then, looking up at Maggie, crooked his finger so she would bend close.

"I wish I could pull you onto my lap again," he said quietly. "And I'm not even going to ask what my mother meant."

"I'm not going to tell you anyway. But I wish I could sit upon the part of you which likes to move."

They stared long at each other.

"I don't want you to leave."

"I don't want to. Except to see my family."

"Invite them all here."

Smiling, she shook her head. "As a newly engaged woman, I must grow up and act mature. I will go home and tell my own mother the good news."

"Please plan on returning after my arm cast is removed. You can bring your whole family with you if you like."

"Maybe Eleanor."

Jane had finished, and it was Maggie's turn to perform.

"Will you sing with me as we did before?"

"I'd be honored," he told her.

She kept thinking about the richness of his voice, and the sweetness of his last tender kiss when she climbed into the carriage for the long journey back to Belton a few days later.

Leaning out the window and waving to him until John and his mother were out of sight, Maggie reclined on the leather seat and stared at Simon.

"A successful visit," Simon remarked.

Maggie started to snicker at the neutral way he categorized what was the biggest event in her life so far. And then, her happiness spilled out of her as a hearty laugh, with which he joined in.

She never imagined when returning a few weeks later she would find such a changed, nearly unrecognizable man.

CHAPTER EIGHTEEN

Cam hadn't had a drop of opium tincture in two days, and his punishment was to writhe in agony all night, exactly as he had done all day and the night before. In fact, he was startled at how quickly he'd begun to feel wretched after deciding to stop sipping from the laudanum teat.

Within hours, he'd felt utter anguish.

Unable to sleep, he stared at the ceiling. His nose was running and his eyes were watering to add to everything else that was physically ailing him. Nausea was his nighttime companion despite having lost the meager contents of his stomach hours earlier. He'd already called for his valet twice, bringing Peter out of a deep slumber only to swear at him and send him away.

If Cam could crawl out of his own skin, he would. The only part of him which didn't hurt was low in his back, where for some reason, he felt inexplicably numb. Above anything else, he wanted to move in various positions, as it was sheer torture to lie still. What's more, he had not an ounce of sleepiness in his entire body despite yawning all day.

While no longer in the restricting sling, his leg cast hampered his movements. Regardless, he hauled it from side to side all night long as he tossed and turned.

At this point, he almost didn't care if he reinjured his leg. He simply had to move.

Tossing the bed clothes off his heated body as he had been doing all night, he knew in a very few minutes, the air would cool the sweat seeming to pour from him, and then he would feel chilled.

If he'd thought the stomach ache he'd been experiencing while taking opium was painful, he had been sorely mistaken. For now, the cramping in his belly was a hundred times worse, making him moan aloud.

"Aaaaahhhhh," he yelled for the hell of it.

Nothing happened in the silent house, and thus, he yelled again. His mother always slept soundly down the other end of the hall, and Gray had his own cottage on the estate. Cam could scream loudly enough to curdle blood without him ever knowing.

He wanted Margaret. He wanted to see her, to kiss her, to make love to her. A notion caught hold of his thoughts—if she were there, he would feel no pain. He was convinced of it.

What's more, he kept vividly imagining her luscious body lying bare beneath him, her rich honey-brown hair spread over the pillow, her lids heavy, her lips parted, her legs also parted. If he could plunge into her, there would be no pain for either of them.

"Margaret," he screamed into the darkness, not caring he sounded like a madman.

His valet returned again, bleary eyed and still dragging his coat sleeves on over his nightshirt.

"My lord?"

"I did not call for you," Cam yelled at him.

"I know, my lord, yet I am here nonetheless."

Cam beat his fists upon the mattress on either side of his body, glad at least the arm cast was gone and he had full use of his right arm again. It was a slender, pathetic companion to his other arm, but he would steadily work to make it stronger again. For Margaret.

If he couldn't have her, there was only one thing that could help him.

"Give me my laudanum."

"My lord?" Peter looked shocked and took a step back.

"Give me the laudanum," Cam repeated.

"You specifically ordered me not to, my lord."

"Now I am ordering you to. Give it to me."

"But, my lord, you said—"

"I don't care what I said. Either you find me a bottle now, or you are relieved from your position. I'll send you packing, as Shakespeare's Falstaff said. Do you understand? You will leave this estate this very instant without references, and I won't care if you fall in a ditch and starve to death. Am I clear?"

"Yes, my lord."

"Good. Now hand me a bottle, or I will hire someone who can take orders."

"Yes, my lord."

His valet looked as hot and sweaty as Cam felt, before disappearing into the dressing room for a moment. Peter returned with a bottle clutched in his hands.

As he approached the bed, the man dared to ask him, "Are you certain, my lord?"

Cam was not going to put up with this insubordination a moment longer. Holding out his hand, he remained silent. He had given his order and wouldn't repeat it. Maybe he would fire his valet anyway as soon as he felt better.

With a shaking hand, Peter gave Cam the opium. He snatched it with an equally shaking hand. How strange.

Holding it close, he unstopped it in a second and swiftly took a sip. He knew he must be careful. A few drops would be enough. Any more than that and he would be no good to anyone.

Letting the emotional relief and the blissful effect wash over him, Cam breathed calmly and waited, knowing all his anguish would soon be over. In a few moments, he felt euphoric. Everything was fine. Why had he ever believed not taking this miraculous liquid was a good idea?

Even as his mouth felt dry and his limbs became heavy, at least he no longer wanted to writhe and wriggle like a ridiculous worm.

"Water," Cam ordered his silent valet, who stood watching him with large eyes. "And ale," he added. "I think I shall want both."

The man departed, and Cam drifted off to sleep before he could have either.

"I CANNOT WAIT TO see my fiancé," Maggie practically sang the words as she and Eleanor approached Turvey House, with not two but four liveried Lindsey servants atop their carriage. It was the only way Simon would allow them to go alone.

"You keep saying that," her sister reminded her, not sounding as if she really minded too much.

"I know."

"I think you like to say the word 'fiancé' almost as much as you like to have one."

They both laughed.

"Just you wait, my girl. Another few years, and you'll have a Season and find a husband."

"That's not what happened for either you or Jenny. You both found your husbands in the country, not in Town."

"True. You're an observant girl." Maggie peered out the window for the hundredth time.

"We still have an hour to travel, didn't you say?" Eleanor pointed out.

"Didn't I say the same an hour ago?"

Eleanor giggled again. "No, more like five minutes."

"I wish Jenny could have come this time. Having a little one like Lionel certainly takes up all your time and energy. I don't remember Mummy being overwrought."

Eleanor shrugged. Having been the baby, she had no knowledge.

"Come to think of it," Maggie added, "Mummy had me and Jenny to help take care of you, which we adored doing. You were like a living doll with whom we could play."

This brought a smile to her sister's face, and Maggie saw for a moment the lovely lady who would emerge from the girl in the next few years.

"I can't believe it was sixteen years ago." Maggie might be sitting next to her own delightful daughter in a few years.

Eleanor fidgeted with her skirts before saying, "Jenny has Mummy and Simon."

They looked at each other a moment, then Eleanor gave a very unladylike snort at her little jest of having only those two for help. Their mother liked to bounce the baby on her knee, and that was about it, perhaps feeling she'd done her duty with three of her own. When Lionel cried, she gave him back immediately. When he was hungry, she returned him to Jenny's arms. And especially when his diaper was soiled, Anne Blackwood was extremely quick to hand him over.

As for the father, Maggie pondered her brother-in-law.

"Simon is earnest in his desire to help." Unfortunately, he seemed to be all thumbs around his son at present, and it was painful to watch him try to swaddle him.

"I think he will be more helpful when the baby is a grown boy, ready to learn to ride and hunt," Eleanor surmised.

"Agreed."

They lapsed into easy silence, watching the countryside go by under the late-afternoon sunshine, and occasionally munching on orange-flavored biscuits until finally, they turned onto the driveway leading up to Turvey House.

"Oh dear," Maggie exclaimed aloud.

"What is it?"

"I actually feel a little nervous."

Seeming wise beyond her years, Eleanor leaned forward and patted her sister's hand.

"I think it's to be expected. Last time you arrived here, you were not engaged, and you left quickly afterward. It must seem like starting over again."

Maggie stared at Eleanor. "You are right. I feel as though I'm meeting a stranger to whom I happen to have promised to wed. That's nonsense, of course. I know John, and I love him."

She watched her sister's eyes widen.

"I know," Maggie nodded. "I think it's the first time I've said it aloud. Believe it or not, I don't think we even said it to each other when he proposed."

The carriage came to a halt.

"I think you should rectify it at once," Eleanor advised as they heard the Lindsey driver jump down from his seat. "As soon as you see your fiancé, run into his arms and tell him how you feel."

That wasn't how things were done, was it? Still, it seemed like sound advice. However, when Cyril admitted them to the front hall of the house, which would someday soon become Maggie's home, John was not there to greet them. She and Eleanor stood under the splendid dome vaulting gracefully over the large staircase, and Maggie wondered a moment what to do next.

"I will inform Lord Cambrey you have arrived," Cyril intoned and disappeared upstairs.

Puzzled, Maggie bit her lower lip. Apparently, even after a few more weeks of convalescence and the removal of his arm cast as he'd mentioned in his last letter, John chose to remain upstairs during the day.

Solid, quick footsteps heralded the approach of Mrs. Markle from the back of the house. With her impressively calm demeanor and assured capability, she was the reason

Maggie didn't fear the role of Lady Cambrey. Of course, there was also John's mother who could run things for as long as she wanted as far as Maggie was concerned.

"Good to see you back again, Miss Blackwood," the housekeeper said, bobbing into a shallow curtsey.

Maggie and Eleanor both curtsied in return, causing Mrs. Markle to look aghast. Then Eleanor giggled and broke the awkward moment.

"This is my youngest sister, Eleanor. I'm sorry," Maggie explained, "we're not used to such deference at home. Neither of us have titles, you see."

"Of course, miss, but you mustn't show that type of courtesy to your staff regardless, if you don't mind my saying. You must have their respect or lose control of the household."

"Yes, Mrs. Markle," Maggie said. "I'm sure with your help, I'll muddle through. And with Lady Cambrey's, too, of course."

"Oh, Lady Cambrey!" Without elaborating on her exclamation, the housekeeper added, "And here I am keeping you in the hall. Come into the parlor, and I'll fetch you both some refreshments. Any preferences? Tea or coffee?"

When both the girls were in the parlor, Mrs. Markle added, "Or wine?" although the disapproving look on her face was enough to make Maggie shake her head emphatically.

Glancing at Eleanor, Maggie said, "Tea would be lovely."

"Of course, miss."

She was nearly at the door when Maggie stopped her.

"Is there something amiss with Lady Cambrey?"

"No, dear, but I think she has plans to travel with her sister after your marriage, and so, as you said, we shall muddle through together." She sped off, undoubtedly with a hundred things to do to run the house.

"I can't possibly sit again now," Eleanor said, stretching her arms overhead, "and I don't really want tea. Could we not take a walk first?"

Maggie hesitated. John might appear while she was traipsing about, and she very much wanted to see him.

"Why don't you explore a little, and I'll wait to see what the butler says."

Her sister needed no further invitation, dashing past Maggie, not even hesitating at the doorway. It was a good thing she'd already contacted Beryl's parents about getting the girls together. For she could imagine Eleanor none too happy after the newness had worn off in a few days. John's aunt and uncle would either send Beryl to Turvey House or invite Eleanor to go to their close-by estate.

Cyril appeared in the doorway. "His lordship will see you now, miss. Shall I take you up?"

"Thank you, no," Maggie said. "I know the way." What's more, now they were engaged, she could be alone with him in any room of the house without anyone judging her.

Feeling the butterflies in her stomach take flight, she climbed the stairs toward the man she would marry. The closer she got, however, the less nervous she felt. When she reached his door, which would become *their* door in a matter of months, she barely scraped her knuckles across it in a half-hearted knock before pushing it open.

Entering, she stopped in her tracks. The lamps were lit, but the room still seemed dim and smelled stale. Sitting in a chair with the curtains drawn behind him was John Angsley.

She knew that for certain, but only because she had studied his face for so many minutes, it surely added up to hours of her time over the past year. Otherwise, she might not have known him at first glance.

Gaunt was the word which came to mind. Below his eyes, dark smudges lay above hollowed cheeks covered in a scraggly beard that hung over his strong jawline. His sensuous mouth was no more! Instead, his lips seemed thinner and drawn. His hair had been left to grow long and hung in greasy tendrils around his face.

Taking all this in, she finally said, "I'm here."

"Sorry for not standing," he said in the same way as he had before she left. His voice was different, though.

She hated to declare it weaker, but it was.

"You don't have to keep saying that," she reminded him, offering him what she hoped was a cheerful smile.

"Come here, beautiful lady."

Running to him, she crouched beside his chair, resting her hands on his lap. He took her face in his hands.

"Let me simply look at you. My Margaret. I have missed you."

"I've missed you, too. Thank you for your letters. I read and reread every one."

At this nearness, Maggie could see how lusterless were his usually gorgeous hazel eyes.

"Initially, I dictated them to Gray," he confessed, "then I got the cast off my arm and found I could easily write again."

She'd known when he was writing privately by the more amorous tone of the later letters. Then they'd stopped.

Taking his right hand from her cheek, she held it before her, running her fingers up along his mended arm.

"I know," John said, "it's a bit scrawny, but until I have the use of my leg again, there's not much I can do about it. I can't show up at the pugilist's club in my pushchair."

Her brain instantly began to think of options. "I'm sure we can do something to help you work your muscles, even one arm. Perhaps lifting a sack of flour."

Instead of looking pleased at the suggestion, his face tensed. She thought she saw a flash of anger, but then his expression changed quickly to sadness.

"I need more time. I'm sorry I've changed."

The last thing she wanted to do was to make him feel badly.

"No, don't apologize. None of what's happened to you is your fault. I'm very happy to be back here with you. I've brought Eleanor to enliven the place."

He offered her a wan smile, then yawned.

"You look tired," she said without thinking, only to see his hurt expression again.

"I don't sleep well."

Nodding, she wondered how much he would let her help him. She knew she couldn't sit by idly while he seemed defeated. Later, she would speak with Lady Cambrey, finding it difficult to believe his loving mother had let him slip into this state.

Pasting on a cheerful smile, she asked, "Have you eaten dinner yet?"

John shook his head.

"Do you normally go downstairs?" she asked.

"When I feel like eating, I usually eat up here. Gray often eats with me, but he's not on the estate at present."

"I see. Well, I don't want you eating alone up here. Will you come downstairs tonight, and dine with me and my sister?"

His gaze slipped from hers to contemplate the air beside her, and then he shrugged.

"I'm not certain, Margaret. Most probably not."

She didn't like his apathetic response, having expected him to feel as excited as she did about their reunion.

"Do you want to come down now instead? I can get Cyril and your valet to help you downstairs—"

"No," he interrupted. "I don't think I will. My valet got me propped up here to visit with you, but I don't have any aspirations to go downstairs. It's an awful lot of bother, only so I can to sit in my pushchair like an old man."

"John, please," Maggie began, hearing a tone in her voice she didn't like. Desperation. Exasperation. How she wished Simon were there. What John needed was his best friend to knock some sense into him.

"Please, will you let me get you brought downstairs? I'm convinced you will feel better. When was the last time you went outside of this room?"

"I don't know. It's not important. I'll come downstairs tomorrow and see Eleanor and visit like a proper lord of the manor. You've come quite late today. We'll talk in the morning."

Shocked, she sat back upon her heels.

"Are you dismissing me after I've come all this way?"

Laughing, he sounded like the old John for a moment.

"No, of course not. You can stay with me for as long as you like. All night if you wish, although it might not set a good example for your sister. Besides, you've had a long journey, and I'm sure you don't want her to eat alone on her first night."

"You're right. When is Mr. O'Connor returning?"

"Why?"

She could hardly tell him she felt as though she needed assistance in dealing with him, her listless fiancé.

"Eleanor enjoys the outdoors. If he were here, he could show her the estate." God help her, she'd been in John's presence a mere few minutes and she was already lying to him.

This was not going how she'd hoped or dreamed. Could it be Eleanor's idea was correct?

"John, I love you."

His eyes opened wide. When his face broke out into a delighted smile, she felt her heart swell. He was hers, and she would help him to recover.

"I love you, too," he said softly.

"Good. Tomorrow, I shall get you all sorted out," she declared. "We'll get you into a hot bath and wash your hair, maybe get your valet to take the scissors to it, and you'll feel like a new man."

"What's wrong with the old one?" His tone was brusque.

Maggie started to smile, assuming he was making a jest. However, when his expression shuttered closed, she hurried to reassure him.

"Nothing at all. I only want to make you feel better."

"I see." He nodded. "And you think shearing me like a sheep and bathing me like a helpless babe will do that?" His tone had switched from morose to irritated.

"I don't know," she confessed.

"No, you can't conceivably know what this has been like. Rather like a trip to hell from which I haven't yet returned, and with no assurance I ever will."

He offered her a brittle smile, picking up her hands from where they rested in his lap to squeeze them gently.

"And to think it all happened because I came to *your* home to get some answers after seeing you with the infernally smug and perfect Westing."

Standing up, Maggie tried to pull her hands from his, but he only gripped them more tightly.

"Are you blaming me?" Her heartbeat pulsed loudly in her ears.

He stared at her in silence for a long moment.

"Of course not, my darling. Nonetheless, I don't think any of your ridiculous notions of my taking a bath or getting my hair cut will help in the slightest."

This was *not* her John Angsley. Not one bit. He was a gentleman, not someone who belittled others.

Swallowing, she stood there, refusing to be baited into saying something rash. Finally, he released her hands.

"There is unfortunately only one thing which makes me feel better."

He patted his pocket, and she knew to what he referred. Why, he was practically taunting her with his use of laudanum. If she hadn't spent many days traveling, if she weren't feeling heartsick, and if John seemed as if he were the smallest bit desirous of changing his situation, Maggie would take up the mantle of that terrible battle immediately.

However, she knew it wasn't the right time.

"I can tell you're out of sorts tonight. You're right, it is late, and I've had a long journey. I'm not myself, either. I'll eat downstairs with Eleanor and your mother."

Turning away, Maggie had to swallow the ball of sadness that was stuck in her throat. As she reached the door, she turned and added, "I'll make sure to get a tray of delicious food sent up to you. I hope you'll be able to eat it."

When he said nothing, simply nodding, she wanted to tell him he looked as if he'd missed more than one meal, far too many, in fact. Quite obviously, such a remark would not be received well. No more than any of her others had.

So much for running into his arms and declaring her love for him. Youthful Eleanor had been mistaken with her advice.

CHAPTER NINETEEN

Cam watched her go and a surge of anger raced through him. Margaret could walk out of his room easily and freely, while he needed to ring the bell and have help to get downstairs. With one man, Cam could do it, but it hurt his leg as he had to hop while holding the cast off the floor. Two men made it far easier, but then he felt like an infant.

He had noticed, too, how everyone handled him more easily as he'd lost weight. But, *dammit*, his appetite was almost nonexistent, and his stomach hurt most of the time. Not as badly as when he'd tried to stop taking the opium tincture, so he didn't complain. He simply chose not to eat until he felt absolutely light-headed with hunger.

As in the days following his accident, Cam never looked in a mirror anymore. He already knew he wouldn't like what he saw. Seeing the expression on Margaret's face confirmed it.

She'd arrived to find a sickly, skinny shell-of-the-man she used to know. On top of that, he'd been rude.

Taking a sip of laudanum, he relaxed. If she did send up a tray, he would try to eat the meal, every bite. For her sake.

BY THE TIME MRS. Mackle announced dinner, Maggie had regained her composure enough to venture into the dining room with a calm expression, eager to see Lady Cambrey. Having discovered Eleanor on the veranda beforehand, they entered the spacious room together, only to find it deserted.

A moment later, a maid hurried. She curtsied low. Glancing at Eleanor, who looked back at her, both sisters refrained from returning it.

"Pardon me, miss," the maid directed herself to Maggie, "but Lady Cambrey awaits you in the smaller dining room, where you ate your breakfast when you was 'ere before."

"Thank you. It's Polly, isn't it?"

"Yes, miss. Shall I lead you there?"

"I know the way. Thank you. We'll go directly. Will you take a tray of food up to his lordship immediately?"

"Yes, miss. We do every day and every night, miss." Another curtsey for each of them, and she disappeared.

"Imagine when you're a countess," Eleanor said. "My lady this and my lady that. What a nuisance!"

"Shh," Maggie warned her. "Make sure you 'my lady' and curtsey when you see John's mother again. Besides, Jenny has adjusted well."

They started down the hallway, then took a right to reach the dining room in the east wing.

"Jenny being Jenny seems to have everyone calling her by her given name. From the stable boy to the chambermaid. 'Far more pleasant for everyone' she told me, but you know it's her practical side," Eleanor added. "She said they're all simply speaking plainly to each other now."

"I don't think Lady Cambrey would appreciate if her servants started calling me Maggie or, God forbid, Mags."

As Eleanor laughed softly, they entered the room. Maggie noted her sister's laughter died even as her own smile fled her lips. The woman who stood before them looked nearly as changed as her son. For Eleanor, who hadn't seen Lady Cambrey since they'd been in London before Jenny's baby was born, the difference must be even more shocking.

Her normally good-natured expression had been replaced with a taut, unsmiling visage. If Maggie didn't know better, she'd say John's mother had aged years in the few weeks since she'd seen her. Now, the woman stood ringing her hands and frowning, even while trying to appear welcoming.

Deciding not to stand on ceremony, with only the briefest of curtsies, Maggie rushed forward to give her future mother-in-law a comforting embrace. For a moment, Lady Cambrey stiffened, then, as Maggie patted her back, the woman seemed to relax.

As they parted, Maggie stared into her eyes and saw such worry, undoubtedly mirroring her own.

"I hope you don't mind we're eating in here," Lady Cambrey said, still holding onto Maggie's hand, gripping it like a lifeline. "I don't like being in the formal dining room on my own and, thus, have got out of the habit. Tonight, Mrs. Mackle assumed we'd be in here."

"It's fine," Maggie stated. "You remember my sister Eleanor," she said, gesturing for her to come forward.

"Of course. Nice to see you again, dear girl."

Eleanor dropped into a deep curtsey, murmuring words of greeting.

"Shall we sit?" their hostess asked.

After they were settled, with a glass of wine before each of them, Lady Cambrey, despite her pinched appearance, began with the niceties. "Tell me all about your long journey."

Maggie took a deep breath. She hadn't told Eleanor much when they'd met upon the veranda—the very spot where she'd become engaged to John—but her younger sister had seen she was shaken to her core. At this moment, when both the Angsley family members seemed to be in such distress, Maggie couldn't pretend not to notice and chat about her trip like a woolly-headed ninny.

Deciding to be blunt, she said, "John is obviously in great discomfort and hasn't been eating. Do you think we should call for his physician?"

Lady Cambrey appeared to sag against the table, setting down the glass she had only just raised to her lips. Leaning over her plate, she closed her eyes. When she opened them, her abject misery was painfully clear.

"He won't let me." Her words came out as a whisper. Then she cleared her throat. "It is a terrible thing to witness someone you love deteriorate before your eyes. You will find it so, as well."

Maggie had slumped in her seat, matching Lady Cambrey, but at those words, she straightened. Glancing toward her sister who was taking it all in with wide eyes, she knew what she absolutely would not do—give up.

"No, I will not *find it so,* for I won't allow it."

Lady Cambrey produced a raw sigh, an expelling of pent-up air.

"Don't think badly of me, young lady. I have tried. After you and Simon left, it happened quickly. One day, he was still my John, although injured. And the next . . . ," she paused. "Very quickly, he started slipping away, refusing to eat or to come downstairs, uninterested in his appearance or his health."

She took a fortifying sip of wine, and Maggie reached over to cover her hand where it rested on the tablecloth. It was shaking.

"When the plaster cast came off his arm, I thought he would rally at the newfound freedom. He could use his pushchair by himself more easily, and he could write, including letters to you, which he did in copious volume."

"Yes, he did," Maggie agreed, trying to produce an encouraging smile. *At least, at first.*

"At the same time, he did nothing else except stay in his room. He argued with Grayson more than once, and he was cross with me when I expressed my worry regarding his condition."

"I think we should send for a physician, either the surgeon who mended him after the accident or someone who has knowledge of . . . ," Maggie trailed off.

"Of what? Do I look for someone who has a special interest in general malaise?" Lady Cambrey sounded at her wits' end.

"No, a doctor who treats those with a severely depressed spirit," she offered. Then she got to the heart of the matter. "And someone who knows how to help with opium addiction."

Lady Cambrey wrenched her hand free. "Opium addiction?"

"It's the root of all his trouble," Maggie began.

"No, dear girl, it's what helps him feel better and deal with the pain. Laudanum is a blessing."

"It's a curse," Maggie insisted.

"How can you say that? It's on every drugstore shelf. Mothers give it to their babies, for goodness sake. Why, I take it myself for headaches every now and again."

"I doubt you have ever taken it on a daily basis, multiple times per day for months."

Lady Cambrey considered Maggie's words. Then she shook her head.

"How humiliated John would be if it got out he couldn't handle a little laudanum."

Maggie felt like shouting but kept her voice calm. "Humiliation is better than the alternative. Certainly better than the current state of the man lying upstairs. And I don't think it's a *little* laudanum. He was dosing himself quite heavily weeks ago. I can only wonder how much he might now be taking if he's increased it."

Lady Cambrey stood up. "You are not his wife yet, nor mistress of this home. We shall say nothing to anyone about addiction."

Maggie rose slowly to her feet. "I hope to get the chance to become his wife, but John looks to me as though he's heading for death's door."

Lady Cambrey paled and shook her head.

"Maybe you have grown used to his appearance," Maggie reasoned, "but surely you can see he is in a bad way. You are aware of the recent demise of Branwell Bronte, are you not? We only know of him because he was somewhat famous. There are probably hundreds more like him, who are slowly dying from this drug. Including John."

"No," his mother shrieked, with uncharacteristically unbridled emotion. With that one word of denial, she turned and left.

Maggie heaved a sigh and sat again across from her sister.

"I'm sorry you had to witness that," she told Eleanor.

"You were magnificent," Eleanor insisted. "And you were right. You must send for the doctor at once. As with the natural world, you cannot do this rescue alone. Neither the bees nor the ants nor a pride of lions can succeed without their entire colony."

"I have *you*," Maggie said. "What's more, I think Lady Cambrey will come around and see reason. She is frightened for her child, like any mother. Let's not talk about it any further tonight. Tomorrow, I shall face this head on."

"Lord Cambrey couldn't ask for a better fiancée," Eleanor insisted as their first course was brought in.

Maggie hoped Eleanor was correct. For when she imagined a capable mate for John, a queen bee or even a lioness, it was Lady Jane Chatley who came to mind, not herself, ordinary Margaret Blackwood.

FOR THE BRIEFEST MOMENT when Maggie awakened, she forgot where she was. In the next instant, she recalled she was once again at Turvey House. John's condition came to the forefront of her thoughts, as well as his mother's denial, and the monumental task ahead of her.

"Dear God," she said aloud, "give me the strength and the wisdom to help the Angsleys. Oh, and the capability of Lady Jane Chatley, so I don't lose my sanity in the process."

After breaking her fast with Eleanor, without any sign of Lady Cambrey, Maggie rang for John's butler and his valet. The two men entered the drawing room, looking wary.

"Thank you both for coming."

They each bowed, mumbling a simultaneous chorus of "Yes, miss."

"I know your first loyalty is to Lord Cambrey and to his mother, of course, but I fear the former is too ill and the latter too overcome with sentiment to be making the wisest decisions."

The two men looked at each other, and then back at her, waiting.

"Cyril, please send to London for the earl's physician. I recall his name is Dr. Adams. Did he come to remove the cast?"

"No, miss, another doctor did. Dr. Brewster, a local man, who also unwrapped his lordship's ribs. The earl was told practically anyone could do it with a saw and some snips, but Lady Cambrey sent for the local doctor in any case."

"Then maybe I should speak with him first before we send for Dr. Adams. Please send him word that—" She could hardly say "Miss Blackwood requested his presence." Who was *she* to send for anyone?

"Please tell Dr. Brewster the earl's betrothed asks he come at his earliest convenience."

"Yes, miss."

Maggie turned to the valet. "I'm sorry," she told him, "I don't know your name."

"I'm Peter, miss." He bowed again.

"Peter, please draw a bath for your master, and sharpen your razor and scissors. We are going to get him cleaned up this morning."

She was well aware the man had paled while she spoke, and thus, she offered him an encouraging smile before adding, "I know the earl might not appreciate this—"

"Begging your pardon, miss," Peter said, showing his nervousness by the inexcusable act of interrupting her, "but his lordship will send me packing at once if I try to do what you ask. *Without* references!"

That would condemn the man to a hard life, indeed.

"No," Maggie said, "I won't allow it."

His hesitant expression reminded her once more of her precarious position.

"I promise you. What's more, we shall do this together. He can hardly send *me* packing, can he?"

On second thought, Maggie supposed John could break their engagement, but he'd declared his love only the night before so she doubted that would happen.

"Come along, then. Let's get to our tasks. Cyril, let me know when you hear a response from the good doctor. Peter, I'll be upstairs shortly. Even sooner if I hear any yelling."

"Yes, my lady." They both said at the same time.

All three of them froze at the error until she gave a nervous laugh and the men left. Perhaps she was going to do well at this countess position after all.

Maggie tried to hang onto such hope a quarter hour later when she pushed open John's door, only to have to duck as an object came hurtling in her direction.

"What on God's green earth?" she exclaimed, glancing down at the thrown book at her feet, then taking in the scene before her.

A copper bath had been dragged into the middle of the bedroom since the earl must have refused to go along the hall to the bathroom. The beleaguered valet was standing beside it, holding a towel in one hand and a soap cake in the other.

"I told you, miss, he wouldn't agree."

"You've been talking about me, have you?" John asked, sounding enraged. "Gossiping about your betters, eh, Peter?"

"No, he hasn't," Maggie said. "And you nearly hit me with a book."

John focused on her.

"Did I?" A chagrinned expression flickered across his face. "I was aiming for this creature." He gestured at his valet and then he looked angry again. "He's trying to get me into the tub. I've had a wash with a cloth nearly every other day, all the parts of me that matter, so this is unnecessary. Besides, I can't get my plaster wet. It will dissolve."

"I know you can't get your cast into the tub, but we can lower the rest of you into it, and keep your leg up in the splint if we rest it over the bath rim. It'll be unwieldy but not impossible."

She nearly uttered the unwelcome words of making him feel better, but bit her tongue at the last second.

"And either Peter or myself is going to wash that mat of hair, and then he's going to cut it. You don't have to do anything except to not impede our progress."

John crossed his arms over his chest, and she waited for his verdict. If he said no, what could she do? Threaten to leave, she supposed, but it might not work in her favor. She almost wanted to encourage him to take a sip of laudanum to make him more amiable. However, tackling that issue was going to be her next task, and she didn't want to even bring it up at present.

"Very well," John agreed, "but without Gray here, we'll need Cyril or a footman. Moreover, you must turn your back until I'm in the tub."

Nodding, Maggie immediately rang for Cyril. Inside, she was feeling elated. So far, he was much more cooperative than she'd feared he would be after last night.

"While you're bathing, we'll get your sheets changed," she added, deciding to keep pushing while John was obliging. "And directly after your haircut, I'm taking you downstairs to get some air and to visit with Eleanor."

He scowled at her. "It sounds like an exhausting morning when I'm perfectly happy resting in my bed."

"Resting from all your resting?" she asked.

Thankfully, instead of becoming annoyed, he grinned.

"Did you sleep well last night?" While they chatted, Peter began to set the sling up to rest on the edges of the bath tub.

"I did. I think it was knowing you were here."

"And did you eat the food I sent?"

Shrugging, he hesitated. "I ate some of it."

"Fair enough," she said, trying to sound encouraging.

Cyril arrived, and Maggie agreed to leave the room while they got the lord of the manor stripped and into the bath.

"The water better be nice and hot," she heard John grumble as she stepped into the hallway.

CAM DIDN'T MIND THE bath. Margaret had been right. It felt bloody good to submerge his body in hot water for the first time since the accident, even with his right leg up in the air. However, when she offered to be the one to wash his hair, he balked.

"Peter will do it," he told her. "I don't want you peering into the bathwater and seeing me."

She'd thought he was either joking or prudish. He was neither. He was vain. This was not the body he wanted her to see when she saw him naked for the first time. Luckily, she agreed to let him finish his grooming alone with his men, as long as he promised to come downstairs directly after.

Thus, bathed and with his hair cut and still damp, he let them carry him down the stairs and place him in his awaiting pushchair. When he rolled himself onto the veranda, he found Margaret looking beautiful in the midday sun and Eleanor chatting like a magpie beside her.

Margaret stood up immediately. He could see she was pleased by the results when she looked him over and gave him a spectacular smile, like a gift. In fact, Margaret, herself, was a gift of which he was not worthy, but for some reason, she was his.

And there was Eleanor, a fresh-faced debutante in the making.

He waved at her.

"He doesn't look appalling at all," she said, and Margaret blushed.

Out of the mouths of babes, he thought.

When he reached the table, Margaret leaned over, kissing him on his newly washed forehead.

Like he was her child or her grandfather! That would never do, but for now, with Eleanor seated nearby, he could hardly haul her onto his lap as he had done before.

"You were right," he began. "I do feel better." Reaching up to stroke his shaven chin, he added, "I'm sure I look better."

"You look very handsome," Margaret said, stroking his soft hair. "I hope it's all right for you to be outside with your hair not yet dry."

"I'm not an invalid," he said. Then hearing his own words and seeing the humor in them, he started to laugh. Both the sisters joined in.

Footsteps behind him and then a gasp heralded his mother.

"John!" she exclaimed and rushed to his side as Margaret returned to her chair. "I'm delighted to see you up and about. And looking very well, indeed, just like your former self."

He thought he saw his mother send a smug glance toward his fiancée.

"I knew all you needed was to get cleaned up and have a good night's sleep."

"All I needed," he added, taking hold of his mother's hand, "was my lovely Margaret to give me a swift kick in the backside and get me out of my room."

"Oh," his mother said. "Well, whatever it took, I'm glad you're feeling better. Tonight, we shall return to the dining room, and tomorrow, we shall invite your aunt and uncle. I can't wait to see them."

"As long as you're not throwing a ball and expecting me to dance," Cam joked, wondering at the frostiness between his mother and Margaret. That had not been there before.

"It will be lovely to see Beryl again," Eleanor spoke up.

"Yes," Lady Cambrey agreed, still staring hard at him as if she couldn't fathom the transformation.

He must have looked a terrible sight previously for his own mother to study him like a stranger.

"I suppose when all the womenfolk are here, you shall talk endlessly about the wedding," Cam said, trying to draw Margaret and his mother into a conversation. "Loads of plans to make for the breakfast reception and where we shall go for a honeymoon."

However, Margaret only nodded while his mother didn't look at her but kept her gaze on him, smiling tightly.

They had fought, he surmised. And probably over him. His mother had let him have his head and do what he wanted, whereas Margaret, in all likelihood, thought he should be taken to task. Exactly as she'd done. He could fix this.

"I'm sorry I've behaved badly," he told his mother. "I've been very hard on you. I'm glad you like how well I've tidied up."

His words brought a genuine smile to Lady Cambrey's face, and she visibly relaxed.

"My mother is very good with organizing large parties," he said, turning to Margaret. "If the *ton* escalates our wedding into the event of the year, she shall know exactly how to handle it. Without my mother, the cricket banquet would most likely have been a disaster. Or at least, the entire thing would have fallen onto Jane's shoulders."

"You did a fine job," Lady Cambrey said. Then she finally looked at his betrothed. "I do like to plan parties, though. We should discuss the location at least and the food and flowers. And maybe you have a particular liking to certain music."

"Yes, that would be wonderful. I'm glad you are here to give your advice," Margaret said graciously. "By the manner in which your homes are decorated, both this one and the London townhouse, I know you are a woman of great taste."

There, he thought, *they'd made up*.

"Shall we take a walk, or in my case a ride, around the property and show Eleanor the river?"

Eleanor clapped her hands.

"Perfect," Margaret agreed. "My sister will love to see your horses, too."

"Mother, will you come?"

"No, dear, I'm going to write to my brother-in-law at once and confirm their visit."

"Very well. Someone needs to call for Cyril to push me since Gray is away."

Margaret wore a surprised look upon her face.

"Whyever for? You wheeled yourself out here. We don't need to bother your butler, do we?"

"*Bother* my butler?" Cam tried to keep the irritation from his voice, thinking of the exertion it would take to roll himself. "I'm positive he will not find assisting me a *bother*, my darling."

"But it is unnecessary, isn't it? Only last evening, you said you needed to strengthen your weakened arm. Surely, this is a perfect way to work your muscles."

His mother made a humming sound, then said, "If John needs help, then he shall have it."

Margaret sighed. "John won't know if he needs help if he doesn't try to do it himself first."

"John is right here," he told them both. "And bugger it all, I will wheel myself if only to stop the two of you from behaving like fishwives."

He should have been ashamed of his language, but seeing both his mother and his fiancée close their mouths, he felt a sense of satisfaction.

"Very well, let's go." This from Eleanor, who was probably impatient with everyone's bickering.

In a short while, he was sweating like a ploughman as he pushed the rims of the wheels, round and round. So much for being clean and sweet-smelling from his bath. Now, he was hot and feeling out of sorts as they approached the river. The damn river he'd seen hundreds of times and, at this moment, didn't give a fig about unless he could throw off his clothes and swim in it to cool down.

"Bloody cast," he murmured.

"What was that?" Margaret asked.

"Nothing." They ended up at the water's edge. With his weak arm throbbing, he reached into his pocket. No bottle. A blade of panic sliced through him. Glancing back at the house, which now seemed a very long way away despite being merely a few hundred yards, Cam realized he hadn't grabbed the laudanum from beside the bed after Peter dressed him.

His countenance must have given away the alarm that was even then coursing through him, for when Margaret glanced his way, she gasped.

"John, is something wrong?"

CHAPTER TWENTY

Dammit all! Cam wasn't going to tell Margaret he wanted—no, he *needed*—his opium tincture. It would cause no end of questioning and delay.

How could he get her to want to return to the house, and quickly?

"Do either of you fish?" He had no idea why that question came out of his mouth, but it seemed to engender delight in the younger Blackwood sister.

Eleanor nodded enthusiastically. "I've caught many fish at home. My father taught me."

"What did you catch?" Cam asked, trying to keep his mind off his aching arm.

"Bream and perch," she said. "Do you fish here?"

"I used to when I was a boy. I caught some large zander, and we ate them for dinner." He looked at Margaret.

"I don't fish," she said, "but I'll happily eat it."

"Shall we go get poles?" Cam asked. "I'll return to the house and see if Cyril can find some poles, probably in the gardener's shed. If Gray were here, he'd know how to lay his hands on some. No matter, I'll find them. Perhaps in the stables. Though why would anyone keep fishing poles in their stables?"

He closed his mouth firmly on the babbling words flowing unbidden from it.

Beginning to turn his pushchair around, he heard Margaret laughing. A beautiful sound. So why, at that moment, did it grate on his nerves?

"We don't have to fish now," she said. "It's very kind of you, but for you to go all the way back is nonsense. We'll plan for it tomorrow."

"It's not nonsense." He hoped he sounded even-keeled while a cloud of unease was settling over him. He could see in his mind's eye the dark glass bottle. In it was everything he needed to feel good on this outing. If only Maggie hadn't forced him to have a bath and change his clothing.

"Look at Eleanor," he persisted. "She wants to fish."

"Do you, dear?" Margaret asked her sister.

Eleanor shrugged. "Tomorrow is fine."

"But we can fish now," he persisted, hearing a whine in his voice that made him seem younger than the girl whom he'd hoped would have been his ally. "Why wait? It might rain tomorrow."

"John, even I don't expect you to wheel yourself back and forth in one day. You'll be exhausted, and your arm will be terribly sore."

"True," he said calmly, despite the storm of jitters roiling around in his stomach. He could feel the sweat break out on his forehead and running down his back, as well.

"Perchance you ladies could help by pushing me back to the house, one at either handle. We would get there faster and then get back here more quickly, too."

"Really, we're happy simply to stroll along the river. I'm sure there are plenty of birds to keep us occupied."

Something inside him snapped. That was how he would best describe it to himself later when he lay upon his bed wondering at his rudeness.

"Fine! You two can look at the bloody birds if you like. I'm going back to the house."

As he wheeled away in the stunned silence, he heard Eleanor say, "Your fiancé must truly love to fish."

They did not come after him as he rolled away, his arm cramping in agony at the speed with which he moved his pushchair. As soon as he approached the veranda, he began to yell for help.

Mrs. Mackle was closest apparently, for she came rushing out of the back of the house, followed by his mother.

Should he ask them? He had no choice. He couldn't wait the length of time it would take to summon Cyril or Peter, nor to get help going upstairs to fetch the bottle himself.

"I need my laudanum at once," he said to the housekeeper. "There is a bottle beside my bed."

"Yes, my lord." She offered the barest of curtsies, befitting her age and station, and as she was unused to being sent on an errand, the housekeeper didn't seem to be moving quickly enough given the size of Turvey House.

"With haste, Mrs. Mackle," he called after her as she strolled to the back door.

Nevertheless, knowing the tincture was almost in his hand, he began to relax.

"You were yelling like a ruffian," his mother admonished him. "I thought you were injured or something was wrong with one of the Blackwoods. Where are they?"

Sighing, he knew she was going to be upset at his abandonment of their guests.

"Can't you see them from there?" Cam asked. "They are perfectly happy walking by the river and birdwatching."

"Birdwatching?"

"Yes, Eleanor is quite the naturalist. By the way, do we own any fishing poles?"

"Grayson would know," Lady Cambrey said. "But why did you go all the way there only to come back a minute later?"

"Wheeling the pushchair was too much for my right arm, I'm sorry to say. The pain is intense."

His mother paled. Just then, Mrs. Mackle reappeared and hurried toward him, clearly understanding the urgency after all. She thrust the bottle into his outstretched hands and he unstopped it, taking a small sip. He knew from experience it didn't take much to give powerful relief.

After a few moments, his mother asked, "Better, dear boy?"

"Yes." However, with the blissful end to his pain and the familiar euphoric sensation came a new feeling. Guilt, followed quickly by disappointment in himself. He'd behaved badly in front of Margaret and her sister, becoming impatient and yelling irrationally.

Determined to do better, Cam decided to do two things—to make certain he always had laudanum upon his person while at the same time being more discreet about drinking it. There was no reason for those around him to even know he was taking it anymore. In any case, it was his personal business.

As long as he remembered to have it regularly to take the edge off his agony, and at the same time, to keep pushing himself to strengthen his muscles, he would improve in all aspects.

"Are you going back to find them?" his mother asked.

Cam considered the task.

"I think not. They are most likely nearly as far down as All Saints by now. Unless they went up river. In any case, too far for me to wheel by myself."

"Why don't we play a game of cards, then? We haven't done that in ages. When the girls come back, they can join in."

BATTLING EMOTIONS OF ANGER and worry, as well as embarrassment at John's behavior, Maggie tried to enjoy her time with Eleanor before they headed back to the house. She was thankful her sister hadn't made further reference to John's strange behavior, which Maggie guessed was opium driven. In her bones, she knew it.

When he didn't return, she realized what a changed man he was from the one whom she'd met the year before. John had taken her whole family under his protection out of loyalty to his best friend, Simon, who had left the country and his wife, Jenny, behind in London. All the Blackwoods had experienced the Earl of Cambrey's kindness, and with every moment Maggie had spent in his company, either engaging in conversation or silently observing him, his character had impressed her greatly. And when they'd kissed the first time, she'd been overwhelmed with sentimental emotion. And desire.

Currently, he was short-tempered, sly—for she was sure he didn't care about fishing—and peevish. In fact, at the present moment, he was not the type of man whom she could envision herself marrying.

That thought, right as she reached the veranda, had her stopping in her tracks, causing Eleanor to bump into her from behind.

"Oomph. Are you all right?"

"Yes, sorry," she told Eleanor. "What are you going to do now?"

"Sketch. I'm heading to the stables as soon as I have my pencils and paper."

"Wonderful. I'll check on you later. Don't get—"

"I know, I know. Don't get hurt. For goodness sake, Mags, I'm not a child anymore."

Maggie chuckled.

"I was going to say don't get in anyone's way, but you're right. At your advanced age, you shall neither be in danger nor a nuisance."

Eleanor rolled her eyes before running into the house, exactly like a child would, to fetch her sketchbook.

Maggie knew what her next task was, and she didn't care for it one bit.

"Where is his lordship?" she asked the first servant she encountered, who turned out to be Polly.

"In the library, I believe, miss."

A moment later, she peered around the open doorway. John was seated in his pushchair, reading and making notes. Looking up at her entrance, he offered her a slightly sheepish smile.

"I hope I'm not disturbing you," Maggie began, remembering the last time she'd barged in there and had the nasty surprise of seeing him with Jane, seemingly in a loving moment. Shortly after, they'd agreed to marry, and her heart had bloomed with happiness.

"No, not at all," he said. "I've only just finished playing a round of écarte with Mother. I thought I'd make notes on investments I want to discuss with Gray if he ever comes back. Speaking to you is infinitely preferable, I promise."

How to begin? She wanted to explain again her reasons for being concerned because deep inside, he was still the man she wanted to share her life with. If only she could get that man to return.

"I'm sorry," John blurted before she could say anything. "I know I acted like a dunderhead."

It was a start, she thought. "You had a reason, I believe, for your behavior."

Frowning, he remained silent.

Was he going to be forthcoming or not?

She pressed the issue. "You didn't return to the house to seek fishing poles."

He had the grace to blush. "No, I was in some pain from using my pushchair."

Maggie felt a pang of guilt.

"I am sorry for your pain. I should have let Cyril push you down to the river."

"No, not at all," he said, shaking his head. "You were right. I need to strengthen my arm, and the only way to do so is to use it and suffer the consequences. I intend to continue wheeling myself around."

"I don't want you to ache," she made sure he understood. "However, I am extremely concerned."

"I'm going to stop taking laudanum," he interrupted, his voice sounding determined.

He had her attention. "Really?"

"Yes. I promise." He looked directly into her eyes as he spoke, and she saw earnestness flickering there.

"You don't know this, but I tried to stop already, and it was damnably difficult. However, I can see my taking opium bothers you, and thus, I am determined to persevere. Be prepared, though, for the discomfort makes me rather grumpy. Ask my valet in particular."

Her heart had lightened with each word he'd said.

"I didn't know you had tried before. I'm sorry it caused you pain, but this time I'll be right beside you," she promised.

"There is no one else I would want there."

He held out his hand to her. She took it, and in the next instant, with their hands clasped, he pulled her onto his lap and began kissing her to distraction.

With his lips on hers, all their problems fell away. Here, at last, was her John. When he kissed her, she could deny him nothing, or even remember why she'd felt uncertain about their future only a few minutes earlier.

Pulling back, he asked, "Is Eleanor going to walk in and interrupt us?"

"No," she said, her heartbeat racing. "She's sketching your horses."

"How very brilliant of her. Will it take her long?"

"At least half an hour. Maybe more."

"Wonderful!" And he brushed his knuckles across each of her breasts, exactly as he'd done in his bedroom when he thought her a dream.

With her nipples tingling and tightening, she threaded her fingers in his clean hair, relishing the silky feel of it. Then to her astonishment and delight, he cupped her fullness with his palms, holding each of her breasts gently, rubbing his thumbs over her now-sensitive peaks.

Oddly, and she could hardly credit the sensation, it seemed as if he were stroking her elsewhere. Indeed, with each caress of her nipples, she felt it between her legs.

Her core heated, and she began to wriggle against him, wanting more.

"John," she moaned against his lips as they kissed again.

She felt him trying to gain better access, but her high-necked blouse and tight, figure-hugging jacket made it impossible. Moreover, when he reached under her skirts, he was impeded by the awkward angle of her sitting on his lap.

Hearing him groan, she took his face in her hands and kissed him fervently, her lips parting and her tongue darting out to seek his.

The rest of him froze at her boldness, but as he opened his mouth and drew her tongue inside, sucking on it, she knew he was enjoying their encounter as much as she was.

After a time, Maggie realized he'd altered the kiss to thrust his tongue between her lips. Therefore, precisely as he had done, she sucked gently. Meanwhile, his hands, which had momentarily stilled, came back to life, roaming over her back and then across her breasts to finally settle at her waist.

When the kiss ended, they were both breathing heavily.

Grasping the front of his waistcoat, she said, "I think it is a good thing you are in a cast, or I question whether we would make it chastely to the wedding night."

He gave a frustrated laugh. "Chastity is highly overrated, my darling. If I weren't in this cast, I can promise you I would be attempting to breach your innocence long before the wedding night. And you would thank me for it, too. Right before you yelled my name."

Blushing, Maggie had no doubt he was correct, for everywhere John touched her, she seemed to awaken with exquisite new sensations. Her breasts were literally aching to be uncovered and held.

"Not *all* of you is in a cast," Maggie pointed out and wriggled her bottom once more.

He groaned again. "And *none* of you is. Perhaps we should go upstairs and see what we can accomplish."

Biting her lower lip, she considered his proposal. They were to be married anyway. She was safely engaged with no blemish upon her reputation, and she no longer needed to fiercely guard it.

"We shall make a plan," she whispered against his ear. "Stay downstairs with me the rest of the day. Tonight, I'll come to you."

She watched him swallow.

"Do you know what you're saying?" he asked.

"I think so."

Feeling his sigh, she let him take her chin in his hand.

"You think so, do you? I want to claim you for my own in a way that is utterly irrevocable. You only have one chance to give your body for your first time."

Excitement raced through her. Could they really join in the way of a man and woman while he was impeded by plaster and bandages? Despite her earlier fears, John Angsley was firmly in her heart, and that wouldn't change. For her part, she saw no need to wait until their wedding night. After all, this wasn't the middle ages, and she was an enlightened woman!

"I decided to give my body to you when I agreed to marry you. What does it matter if we wait until we're actually wed? Should I worry after you've taken my maidenhead, you'll renege?"

"Of all the things you may worry about, that is not one of them. I don't want you only with my body—although I desire you so much, it almost scares me. But I truly want you with my head and heart, too."

As she smiled, he laughed.

"There it is. Your gorgeous smile. I used to think it was a weapon you unleashed upon unsuspecting bachelors whom you hoped to ensnare. And it was extremely successful, by the way. Now I know, however, it is simply your natural expression of joy. I hope I can always conjure it."

Thinking of a rejoinder, Maggie wasn't aware the door had been pushed open or notice her future mother-in-law had entered the room. By the time Lady Cambrey offered a delicate cough, it was too late for Maggie to jump off her fiancé's lap and appear presentable.

In any case, John encircled her with his arms, imprisoning her in the compromising position.

"Yes, Mother?" His voice was dripping with innocence, daring her to comment, while Maggie felt her face inflame with embarrassment.

"I am glad to see you two happy." Lady Cambrey said. "It makes my maternal heart very glad."

She turned on her heel and left, closing the door behind her.

Into the silence that followed, Maggie stared at John, eyes wide, before they both burst into laughter.

From then onward, with her anticipation raging high, Maggie thought the day dragged on endlessly. All the while, through meals and conversation, through games of whist and charades, she would steal a glance at John to find he was staring at her. He would raise a devilish eyebrow or wink, causing her heartbeat to race.

One time, he even licked his lips, and she felt her womanly parts start to pulse.

Good God, would it ever be bedtime?

Retiring early, she took a long bath, refraining from washing her hair since she had no intention of going to John dripping like a cat left out in the rain. Instead, she brushed it, leaving her hair to hang around her, knowing it would entice her man to touch it and her. A simple pale-pink cotton nightdress of the softest, finely woven lawn and her blue dressing gown were all she needed as she slid her feet into her favorite soft house slippers.

Heart pounding in her throat, Maggie wondered at her own daring. Shouldn't she be afraid instead of excited? Was she dreadfully wanton for wishing to experience this joining?

Tiptoeing along the corridor, past her sister's room, she reached John's door. For the first time, she hesitated but only long enough to take a deep breath, glance down at herself for reassurance, and then push the door open.

CHAPTER TWENTY-ONE

Cam watched Margaret enter, and the mere sight of her caused his loins to tighten. How was he going to do this without embarrassing himself by spending before they even got started? It had been a long time since he'd enjoyed a woman. At that moment though, he couldn't even recall the last one he'd been with. There could be no other in his thoughts except Margaret Blackwood. And no wonder.

Entering quietly, after locking the door, she padded across the carpet, a sensual vision in a sapphire-blue robe with her hair hanging loose around her shoulders.

"Am I dreaming again?" he asked when she reached his bedside.

"Don't tease me," she said, "or I might come to my senses and retreat."

"I am definitely going to tease you," he promised.

Patting the bed, he held her hand as she climbed upon the mattress. Settling on his left side, opposite to his cast-bound leg, Cam propped himself upon his good arm and looked down at her. To his delight, a thin, braided belt was the only closure for her robe, and he swiftly untied it.

Underneath, she wore only a sheer nightdress of the palest pink. He could see the darker shade of her nipples beneath, and he thanked God his vision hadn't been impaired in the accident. Not wanting to hurry, he bent low to claim her warm lips in a long, languid kiss, which she returned with equal ardor.

"I want to kiss more of you," he told her, before nibbling a trail down the soft skin of her neck and lower.

Hearing her swift intake of breath, feeling her hands clasp in his hair, he pressed his mouth to one of her nipples through the soft fabric, then tugged ever so gently at it with his teeth until she arched toward him.

When he pulled away, she gazed at him, her lips slightly parted. "I liked that," she confessed.

"Good." Leaning farther, he gave her other pearled nipple the same attention, and then he desperately needed to see her bare skin.

"Will you sit up and slip your arms from your robe?"

Wordlessly, she did as he asked. The nightdress had long sleeves and no buttons or ribbons he could see.

"I think this might have been the time to wear a nightshirt which opened in the front."

"Oh, yes," she said, her voice breathy and soft. "My error."

"We can easily fix it if you'll let me raise it from the bottom or . . ."

"Or what?"

"I could simply render it down the front, tearing it in two," he told her matter-of-factly. "With my teeth!"

Her eyes widened. "Like a pirate?"

She stroked his healing facial scars, and he found he didn't mind at all.

"Exactly. I feel like I could be a raiding corsair when I look at you."

"I rather like this nightgown," she told him. "That's why I wore it. If you don't mind—"

Reaching for the hem, Cam began to raise it, exposing her bare legs inch by inch.

"I wish I'd left more lamps lit," he said ruefully.

"I'm glad you didn't."

"Don't be shy, Miss Blackwood. You are so lovely, you should never be clothed."

He said it to relax her, and by her answering giggle, he had succeeded.

"I decree when we are married, you shall never wear a nightgown to bed. It's a crime to hide this beautiful body."

She laughed again.

Distracting her with his words, he had lifted her gown to her waist and was raising it even more to expose her most intimate places to his hungry gaze.

However, when she felt the cool air on her skin, she instinctively reached to cover herself. Before she could, he bent low again and blew on the soft curls between her thighs.

"Ohh," she murmured.

He wanted to put his lips there, to kiss her where she would feel it most intimately, but he restrained himself.

Start slowly, he cautioned.

Raising her gown higher, he revealed a flat stomach, which he softly kissed, first below and then above her navel. Her skin was like satin. Kissing his way higher as he lifted the hem, eventually, he revealed her gorgeous breasts, full and firm.

"Touch me," her shaky voice commanded, surprising him.

He palmed them, stroking, circling, kneading, and then ever so slightly pinched each nipple. Her hips bucked.

"Raise your arms," he instructed, "and I'll pull your gown over your head."

She did. As he tossed the offending garment over his shoulder, she crossed her arms over her breasts.

"Don't hide yourself, sweet lady. I wish to worship every inch of you."

It was more than Margaret's physical appearance that captivated him. His heart was entirely engaged, and because of this, he wanted to make love to her but also to cherish her, to protect her, to bring her a world of delight.

In that instant, he decided they would pleasure each other without the final act. Perhaps he was old fashioned after all, but he wanted to enjoy the honor of claiming her body on their wedding night. He hoped he wouldn't come to regret this newfound reverence.

Gently tugging at her arms until she uncovered herself, Cam lowered his mouth to her breasts again and latched onto the closest peak. A lick evoked her sigh, suckling made her moan, and a gentle bite caused her to whisper his name. He did all three and then trailed his hand down her stomach to the heart of her passion.

Damp curls met his touch. She was already taut with desire. He slipped a finger between her folds, feeling her body tense.

"Easy, darling. You'll enjoy this." Speaking with his mouth against her breast, he felt her relax again before lifting his head to watch her face as he stroked her for the first time.

Margaret's head tilted back, her white, slender neck arched. She wouldn't last long, he could tell. Careful not to apply too much pressure to her nub, when she seemed near to spending, he inserted a second finger inside her. She peaked, lifting her hips from the bed while gripping the bed clothes with fisted fingers.

OPENING HER EYES AS she settled back onto John's bed, Maggie felt too exhilarated and languid at the same time to be embarrassed. Gazing at the face of the man she loved, a man wearing a slightly smug but tender expression, she shook her head.

"*Gracious!* I had no idea. I mean I've . . . well . . . by myself, but when you do it to me, it's magical. I lost track of where I was."

"As long as you didn't forget whom you were with."

She wrapped her arms around his neck and pulled him down to kiss her. After a moment, however, he reared back.

"Sorry, my darling, I have to untwist and lie flat a moment. Keeping my right leg down on the bed while leaning over you has caused a cramp, I think."

As he lay staring at the ceiling, she sat up. Was he going to take a sip of laudanum to ease the pain? And what of *his* enjoyment? It seemed as if he had given to her without taking. Could she give the same back to him?

"John." Grabbing the edge of the counterpane, she held it against her naked body. Where *was* her nightgown?

"Yes."

Gazing her fill of his broad chest and the brown hair sprinkled across it, she suddenly wanted to touch all of him. Reaching out, she gently smoothed her fingertips over first one nipple, then the other. To her amazement, they hardened. His body was similar to hers, she realized. Undoubtedly, he would enjoy similar sensations.

"May I do for you what you did for me?"

A slow grin spread upon his face.

"Not necessary. I think you will need some instruction, and I feel encumbered with this plaster cast."

"Nonsense," she told him, and yanked at the counterpane, which covered his waist and legs.

"Oh!" she exclaimed, seeing his midriff was entirely bare. What's more, his male member was stiff and, since she'd moved the blanket, was protruding at an angle toward the ceiling.

He groaned.

"Are you well?" *Was he in terrible pain?*

"Having you look at me is exciting, but I need you to touch me, or I may have to touch myself."

She understood at once. When her body was exposed, if he had simply stared at her, making her feel heated and prickly, she would have needed to touch herself to ease the wanting.

Clearing her throat, she bit her lower lip and grasped him halfway down his shaft. He groaned again.

Nervous laughter over what she was doing bubbled up, but she fought to tamp it down. Instinctively, she understood laughter would be the incorrect response at an intimate moment such as this.

The skin over his shaft was softer than she'd anticipated, certainly smoother than an arm or a leg. Thinking of how he'd pleasured her, keeping her fingers curled around him, she stroked him up to the oddly shaped tip, hooded like a mushroom with a slit in the top, and crowned with a bead of liquid. Then she stroked down to the base.

When she looked more closely, Maggie saw his sacks, which she knew contained the seed necessary to make a baby.

Steering clear of those, she began to rhythmically pump her hand up and down, lightly, unsure of the pressure she should use.

After a few moments, his large, strong hand closed around hers, helping her to stroke him more forcefully and quicker. A glance at his face showed his eyes to be closed and his jaw clenched. Clearly, he was enjoying himself.

Maggie saw the moment he arched his head and opened his mouth to let loose a short, guttural cry. At the same time, his fingers squeezed hers harder, his member stiffened, and pearly liquid shot from the slit in an arc he aimed away from her.

Good Lord! His release was quite a display, far more impressive than her silent spending. Imagining full relations, she knew his warm seed would have gone straight into her womb to create a child. Baby Angsley!

"Why are you smiling so serenely?" he asked her, his voice husky and his eyes open once more.

"I was thinking of the child we will make some day."

"When that day comes, I will be the happiest of men. You can let go now."

"Pardon?"

"My yard. You can release it."

Looking down, she realized he had removed his hand and now only her fingers remained, fisted around a softening shaft.

She let go. "You were splendid."

"I am the one who is supposed to say that, not you, silly woman. And thank you," he added.

Feeling her cheeks heat, she shook her head.

"No, I thank you. It was all truly wonderful, and you made it not at all awkward."

"It will be even better when I can sink myself inside you. Imagine the same pleasure but expanded."

"I cannot imagine it any better," she confessed.

On the other hand, she knew he didn't need to merely imagine it. He had done this and far more with other women. Previously, she hadn't begrudged him his prior associations. Moreover, she was benefiting from his experience. However, now she knew what this was all about, knowing he'd already shared such intimacy saddened her.

"You wear every emotion upon your face. What is wrong, my love?"

My love. She liked the sound of that. Then another vexing thought crossed her mind. Perhaps he had said the same term of endearment to every woman he'd bedded.

Drat! She would drive herself mad if she let jealousy over his past consume her.

"I am new at this, and I know you have had similar interactions with women who knew what they were doing and with whom you experienced the *expanded pleasure* you mentioned."

Sighing, he pulled her down until her cheek rested upon his chest.

"Margaret, I will tell you something with absolute honesty. You must believe me and then never let my past trouble you again. Will you promise?"

She nodded.

"Very well. No one I've ever known compares with you, not in any capacity. How can I put this delicately?" He paused a moment.

"Other women were necessary because a man has particularly strong urges at my age. About the time I needed to shave, likewise, my physical cravings needed particular attention. Do you follow me?"

Maggie rolled her eyes at his explanation. "You are saying the women you lay with were only for utilitarian purposes."

He laughed heartily, jiggling her head where it rested on his chest.

"When you put it that way, no. Obviously, pleasure was involved, but in comparison to being with you, it was like a practical transaction as opposed to an act of love. It was never that."

"You never loved before?" She held her breath.

"No, I promise you. I have felt infatuation, attraction, even admiration, but not what I feel for you. I have never experienced love until I came to know one Margaret Blackwood."

Smiling to herself, she was satisfied by his explanation. Still, she had another question.

"And you don't use the term lightly?"

"Which term?" he asked, then yawned broadly.

"*My love.*"

"No, I don't say anything to do with love lightly."

She was utterly content. "Very well."

He pressed her close with his arms tightly around her.

"You are my love and, soon, my wife. How did I get to be this fortunate?"

"I am told I can be demanding and even sharp-tongued. However, I think I am only exacting and forthright."

Chuckling, he kissed the top of her head.

"Either way, I accept you as you are."

"As I do you." *Except for the laudanum,* she reminded herself, but she wouldn't bring it up right then, not when everything seemed idyllic.

John's yawn brought on one of her own. Easily, she could drift asleep in his arms, but it would be dangerous. True, they were engaged, yet if her sister went to Maggie's room and found her gone, she would set a bad example.

Moreover, Lady Cambrey might consider it a pattern of indecent behavior if Maggie were once again discovered in the earl's bed. This time, bare as her day of birth.

"I should return to my room."

Immediately, his grip tightened on her, and she laughed.

"It's only down the hall, not across the world."

Relaxing his hold, he stroked her shoulder. "I know. That was my honest reaction to your leaving my arms empty. The bed will feel cold the instant you have left it."

"Kiss me again to warm us," she said, climbing on top of him, relishing the sensation of her skin against his. "And then I will go."

Immediately, his hands were in her hair, threading through her tresses as he pulled her down and claimed her mouth. For a long, intimate and silent time, they simply kissed. Her body was tingling everywhere as if she hadn't felt satisfied only minutes ago. Was it immoral of her to think of doing it again, right then? Feeling his swelling shaft under her indicated he was of the same mind.

Raising her head, she knew she had better climb off John or risk getting with child before the wedding. The promise of experiencing everything sensual with him, she held close in her heart. Sometime soon, they would enjoy the full coital relations, and it would be beyond anything. This taste of intimacy had shown her that.

Dropping another kiss upon his lips, receiving another in return, she climbed off him and slipped from his bed.

Goodness, she was standing entirely naked in the lamplight in a man's bedroom. *Where were her clothes?*

"I tossed your nightgown over there," he said helpfully. "I'm going to watch while you bend to pick it up."

She couldn't help laughing at his lascivious remark. Instead of being embarrassed, she felt like a beautiful goddess because of the way he'd made love to her and the things he had said.

"I give you leave to watch." She found her gown on the carpet. Bending slowly, her rear end facing him, she heard him groan.

"You have become a temptress in an evening."

"You have made me one." She slid her nightdress over her head before returning to the bed for her robe. It lay crumpled in the spot where he'd slid it from her. She'd been a different person then, an innocent.

"I very much like the new, experienced me."

Reaching for her robe, she was startled when he grabbed her arm.

"There is much more to learn. You're hardly a skilled lover yet, my darling, but I intend to teach you and take great pleasure while doing so."

"I am a willing pupil."

"Only with me," he reminded her.

Had the throaty, sensual laugh really come from her?

"Of course, my lord. Only with you."

"Go now, or we shall have to have another lesson at once." He released her arm.

Sighing at the wonder of it all, Maggie left him to what she hoped was a good night's rest. For her part, with her body and mind both equally pleased, she would sleep exceedingly well.

AS SOON AS THE door closed behind Margaret, Cam opened his bedside table and extracted the bottle of medicine, as he thought of it. For that was what laudanum truly was—pure and helpful medicine. Nothing more.

Taking a small sip, he put it back, covering it with clean, pressed handkerchiefs.

Then he relaxed back onto the bed, waited for relief from any lingering pain, and contemplated his life.

Margaret was perfect, and perfect for him. Their marriage would be supremely successful. He was confident of that. For he liked her mind and humor. Moreover, they were going to have passionate, fulfilling relations, and he couldn't wait to touch her again.

His cast would come off in a matter of months, and he would work like the devil to get his strength back.

Yes, everything was in order. Except he had to lie to his fiancée because she didn't understand how necessary it was to keep the pain at bay. When he was no longer in pain, of course he would once again go through the agony of ceasing to take the opium tincture. Until then, he would do what he knew was best.

Regrettably, even in the remedy for pain, there was more pain. His stomach bothered him nearly as soon as the laudanum went down his throat, or so it seemed. On the other hand, if he took a little more of the tincture, he would drift off to sleep easily despite his stomach, although he risked the possibility of nightmares.

Never mind. He would bear the stomach cramps. Enraptured with the memory of pleasuring Margaret and of how she enthusiastically touched him in return, he was sure he would sleep well.

Unfortunately, when he awakened, sweating and breathing hard a few hours later, it was from a terrible dream with carriages racing too quickly toward treacherously high cliffs, like those he'd visited in Dover a few years back with Beryl and her family.

What he wouldn't give if Margaret were beside him! Barring that, he wished he could jump out of bed and take a walk instead of lying there, feeling trapped, with no choice but to drift back off to another troubled slumber.

Irritation sliced through him again. If the man who'd been driving the other carriage hadn't been killed, Cam could easily have hunted him down and wrung his sorry neck.

CHAPTER TWENTY-TWO

Beryl, her five siblings, and parents, Cam's Uncle and his wife, arrived early the next day, after a breakfast during which every time Margaret glanced at him, her cheeks erupted in a rosy blush.

If her sister or his mother didn't guess something had happened between them, Cam would eat his hat. Or perhaps Eleanor was too young to think of what might have occurred, and his mother . . . Well, she wasn't too old. No, that was certain. Luckily, she was preoccupied with her in-laws' arrival.

"I have a grand time planned," Lady Cambrey told the visitors as soon as they'd arrived, but before she could say anything else, Eleanor grabbed Beryl's hand and they disappeared amongst a cloud of giggles and whispers.

Both Margaret and Eleanor's mother, Catherine Angsley, apologized for the girls' behavior.

Cam's mother began again. "Much later, we shall play parlor games, and I'm sure those young misses will enjoy them. Meanwhile, my son gave me a good idea the other day. We have found some fishing poles, and we shall take my nieces and nephews to the river to see what they can catch."

Three boys and two girls of various ages squealed in delight.

Cam noticed Margaret looked at him with concern. And no wonder. She didn't want a repeat of the previous outing's events. To reassure her, he smiled.

"Let's get everything prepared," Lady Cambrey suggested, "and then we'll see if Beryl and Eleanor wish to join us. I believe the youngest Blackwood sister likes to fish."

Not too many hours later, Cam found himself once more at the River Great Ouse, this time surrounded by children. It seemed as if there were sixty, not six, of his cousins.

How strange, he considered. At his age, he could have fathered the younger ones.

Watching Margaret as she chatted with the other women, looking youthful, with her hair in a long braid down her back, he knew she would bear him beautiful and strong children of their own. Moreover, the previous night indicated they would enjoy making each and every one of them.

Watching his own relations next, he found himself looking forward to stopping what now seemed to have been an endless bachelorhood.

Yes, he was eager to take up the mantle of husband and father. A life that had grown a tad dull seemed exciting again. It would expand past duties of Parliament and idle pleasures of the *ton*. As soon as the dratted cast came off!

With the sun shining, they'd gathered at the bend in the river where there was a little sandy deposit, which they had loosely called "a beach" all his life. Here, the water slowed and the fish pooled nearby. It was idyllic.

Margaret seemed a natural with the wee ones, yet he noted she did not put bait on a hook. Eleanor, who had very much wanted to come and dragged Beryl with her, was a crack at baiting hooks and showing the children how to toss the line and to angle. Margaret, it seemed, was better with adjusting bonnets, wiping grubby hands, and generally encouraging everyone toward happiness.

Even he could take a turn at the rod. Letting Eleanor cast his line for him, he sat near the water's edge and fished as he hadn't in years. It was pleasant, especially with Margaret standing close and chatting amiably. Then he felt the familiar tug on his line. *Wonderful!*

When he drew a large perch from the river, lauded by everyone around him, his own happiness would have been complete if he weren't trapped in his pushchair and wondering how long it would be until he could be alone for his next sip of laudanum. Only if he needed it, of course.

Having let his Uncle Harold push him to the river's edge, at that moment, Cam was in no pain except the constant ache of his body being in the same position.

However, he was determined to wheel himself back to the house to work his arm muscles. By the time he did, he knew he would need a little opium tincture to get him through the evening until bedtime.

"Time to eat," his mother called out, calling them all to a picnic already laid out, this time on wooden tables she made the staff carry to the river's edge. He had to smile. As hostess, she was in her element. And to his surprise, he'd worked up a little appetite.

When everyone had eaten their fill, it was time to return to Turvey House for his mother's next entertainment. Having two aging ponies in their stables, Lady Cambrey thought the children who were old enough would be delighted to ride them around the paddock.

Cam thought it would be more fun for them to ride a properly trained mount with a child seated in front of an adult. Of course, no one had asked him since he couldn't ride anyway. Even more frustration in his day! For there wasn't much more pleasurable a thing to do in the country than have a good ride and give a horse its head.

Looking at Margaret, who happened to capture his glance and return it with quizzically raised eyebrows, he smiled thinking of one or two more pleasurable things.

With everything packed up, suddenly, Lady Angsley screamed.

"George is in the river! Help!"

Everyone began scrambling, running to the water's edge. With his heart pounding, Cam was half out of his chair before he realized he could neither stand, nor swim. It was torture to sit there powerlessly, barely able to see past the gaggle of his relations, whilst his uncle, the boys' father, jumped in the river after the toddler.

Luckily, his aunt had seen the incident as it happened, standing mere feet from her child, who'd taken a step too many and been sucked in by the slope and then the current. Neither the boy's mother nor the other women could safely go in the water to save the tot, knowing their dresses would weigh them down to a quick drowning if they lost their footing.

However, Cam's Uncle Harold, only in his forties, was a strong swimmer. As the boy was only a few yards from the shore, in a brief amount of time, the father had his son in his arms.

Back upon the bank, Harold held the boy upside down by his feet and whacked his back to get out any water he might have inhaled or swallowed. Thankfully, it had happened so quickly, young George was declared perfectly fine, except for being wet, scared, and wrong side up.

"Stop it, Harold. Let him down," ordered Lady Angsley, reaching her hands out, obviously desperate to hold her son in her arms.

As Harold righted him, Margaret moved quickly to wrap up the boy in the picnic blanket and hand him to the grateful mother.

Like a flash of oil on flames, Cam's anger flared as he watched the scene unfold, surprised to see smiles already returning to his family's faces and how calm everyone seemed. The whole event, in fact, set off his irritable temper, which seemed always close at hand lately. Infuriated, he gripped the handles of his chair.

"Someone should have been watching the child more carefully," he stated. "The boy could have died, drowned right next to you, and the blame would have been easy to place."

Catherine Angsley, who had seemed relatively calm, started to cry, and Harold Angsley looked daggers at his nephew before snatching his son back from his wife. Hoisting him high upon his wet shoulders to carry him back to Turvey House, he set off without another word.

Lady Cambrey pursed her lips at her own son, while Eleanor and Beryl gathered up the rest of the children to begin the short trek back.

However, it was Margaret to whom Cam looked. Her reaction was to shake her head, as if disappointed in him, cutting him to the quick. Unable to get his plaster cast wet and help rescue the boy, or even stand for that matter, he had done nothing but sit like an old man and fish, and when faced with an emergency, he could do naught but sit some more.

No wonder she wore an expression of disappointment.

He ought to go into solitary convalescence until the cast could be removed. Perhaps he would begin writing that book he'd considered before, or take up painting. Or maybe he would sit staring out a window and go stark, raving mad. It seemed the most likely of the scenarios. This long lesson of patience and humility had worn extremely thin. And he was displeased with how easily irritated he became.

A melancholy group, except for the youngest, they returned to the manor with Cam breathing hard to keep up. By the time the veranda rolled under his wheels, he felt no qualms in asking Cyril to help him upstairs to rest until dinner.

And he was well within the bounds of reason for needing some tincture of opium to ease the agony in his arm muscles. He didn't see how anyone could blame him for that.

SITTING IN THE LIBRARY, penning a letter to her mother while the Angsley family visited in the drawing room, Maggie tapped the pen to her lower lip and considered her words.

She intended to write to Anne Blackwood how happy she was to be back with her betrothed, and for the most part, it was true. The previous night had been beyond what she'd expected from relations with a man. She truly had not understood how awkwardness and fear would fall away when faced with love and desire.

Nevertheless, she was wary of John's occasional strange behavior. Nor had Maggie forgotten how greatly changed he had seemed when first she arrived. True, after a bath, haircut, and shave, he was more like his old self. Combined with how quickly she'd come to accept the small differences, such as his pallor and his thinness, she was indeed happy to still call him her fiancé.

However, only the day before, he had sworn a rude oath and left her and Eleanor without a backward glance. When she'd confronted him later, he'd seemed a completely different individual, contrite and calm. What's more, he'd instantly promised to stop taking opium.

Then today, out of the blue, he said something unnecessarily harsh, greatly disturbing Lord and Lady Angsley.

Neither incident would seem strange if John were not the Earl of Cambrey, a man who had been in society for a decade and bred to the title, which he had now held for four years since his father's untimely passing. He knew better in both instances than to behave like a brute.

Sighing, she wrote to her mother John's arm was well-mended except for its slightness. She added the story of fishing and of Eleanor's great pleasure in visiting with Beryl. Naturally, Maggie left out the near-disaster that befell George, as well as any doubts she felt about marrying a man who was showing a new and unpleasant side of himself.

Sealing her letter, she went to find Cyril or Mrs. Mackle to ask about getting it sent with the early morning post. As she crossed the domed hallway, she heard the front door open.

"The lovely Miss Blackwood, soon to be the Countess of Cambrey."

Grayson had entered the front hall, still wearing a long traveling coat.

"Are you recently back from London?"

"I am." Ambling toward her, he took her free hand and offered her a polite bow over it. "I dropped my trunk at my own dwelling and came directly here to see how his lordship is faring."

Frowning, Maggie asked, "Why? Were you worried about him?"

Tilting his head, he gave her a wry smile. "How long have you been here?"

"A few days."

"Then you have seen him?"

"Of course!" Maggie recalled the prior evening. She'd done a great deal more than *see* John Angsley. Then Grayson's meaning dawned on her.

"You refer to his appearance. I think you will find him greatly changed for the better."

His eyebrows rose. "Really?"

"Yes, but I'll let you see him for yourself. Was there anything besides his hair and beard that worried you?"

"I don't like to tell tales out of school, Miss Blackwood. If he has improved as you say, then I shall be extremely pleased."

"Won't you call me Maggie, or at least Margaret?"

"Yes, I will, if you'll call me Grayson."

"All right, I will." With enough worries of her own, she decided not to press him on the matter of his concerns regarding John. "If you'll excuse me, I will let you go visit with John while I find the butler."

He bowed again. "Good day, Margaret."

"And to you, Grayson."

She had to admit she was relieved the estate manager was back. She couldn't speak to any of the staff about her apprehensions over their master, nor could she express her fears to Lady Cambrey. She'd certainly learned that lesson. While Grayson was also in John's employ, like Cyril or Peter, they were friends before anything else. If the man was concerned, she hoped he would speak up.

By seven at night, except for the five youngest children, everyone was gathered in the main dining room, including Grayson. John appeared relaxed again, and his relatives had seemingly forgiven him for his unfortunate statement, causing his aunt to cry.

Maggie knew, in all likelihood, a long evening of charades and whist or loo was in their future. She hoped John would keep an even temper throughout, and she planned on visiting him again in his room. If not for a repeat of the previous evening's pleasure, then at least to ask him in private how he felt since stopping the opium.

WITHOUT A MOMENT'S PRIVACY, Cam hadn't been able to invite Margaret to another late-night tryst except with his eyes. Still, he knew she would come, and he was ready for her when she slipped into his room after everyone else had gone to bed.

"Are you asleep?" she whispered.

"No," he whispered back, "are you?"

Laughing, she ran across his thick Persian carpet and launched herself onto the bed beside him.

"Oof!" He expelled a breath.

"Did I hurt you?" she asked.

"No." Although somehow her elbow had ended up in his stomach as she'd settled beside him. He didn't care. She could batter him blue and black and he would still love her.

Realizing she had put herself in the same position as the night before, as if entirely ready for lovemaking, he bent low to kiss her. Unexpectedly, she placed her delicate hands on his chest and held him at bay.

"I didn't come here for this. Or even expecting it. You understand? We may converse, if you like."

Grinning, he untied her belt to find her entirely bare. At once, his body reacted, and his brain seemed to empty itself of any intelligent thought.

"Oof," he said again, making her giggle. "It seems to me, my lady, you came here ready for me to do precisely this." And he claimed her mouth before trailing kisses down her neck and over each of her breasts.

When he slid his hand into her feather-soft curls and started to stroke her as had done the night before, they spoke no more except for sighs and moans and guttural groaning.

It was a long-time later, after much teasing and kissing, more caresses and stroking, and some perfectly learned handiwork on Margaret's part, when he spent upon the counterpane. It was easy to imagine a time when he might do the same inside her.

Cuddling together, he wondered if tonight they might drift off to sleep and let the consequences happen, until he recalled he hadn't had the necessary last dose of laudanum. Perhaps if she fell asleep quickly, he could reach over her. Or maybe, he should tell her it was time to return to her own room.

However, he needn't have worried, for instead of closing her lovely, gold-flecked eyes, she fixed her gaze upon him.

"How are you feeling?"

Smiling, he squeezed her closer. "Need you ask after what we just did?"

"No, my love, I meant since you stopped taking any opium tincture. You said before it made you grumpy. Undoubtedly why you snapped at your aunt and uncle this afternoon. By dinner, though, after you came upstairs to rest, you seemed your normal, amiable self. And what about now? Are you in any pain?"

Lying to her was the absolute last thing Cam wanted to do, but he couldn't put the burden of worry upon her, not when he knew he was doing the right thing. Eventually, he *would* stop taking laudanum, and then his words would no longer be a lie.

"I feel at times a little irritable as you witnessed at the river, but then I feel better, especially when you are with me. At this moment," he paused to brush his hand along her bare arm, "I feel no pain."

Goosebumps rose upon her skin, and he thought they could most likely pleasure each other again before she left.

"And are you pleased Grayson is back?"

He blinked.

"*Grayson* is it now? Not Mr. O'Connor? Should I be jealous?"

She made a fist and punched him softly in the stomach.

"I'm lying naked in your arms after we have touched each other in the most intimate fashion. Do you *feel* jealous?"

"Not at present. But I could easily tear a man limb for limb if he ever touches you. And I will scowl fiercely at anyone who so much as lets his gaze linger upon you too long."

"It could end up being rather a scowl-filled marriage then."

He rolled her atop him. "I think it will be a marriage of laughter and love."

"As do I," she agreed.

"As soon as the damnable cast comes off, I will stand before God and before witnesses and make you my wife. I cannot wait."

"Until then," Margaret said, her voice fairly purring, "we can still have plenty of love and laughter." Lowering her head, she kissed him, then scooted down to kiss each of his nipples as he had done to hers. "And passion," she added before continuing to pleasure him.

She stayed even longer than she had the night before, and when she did leave, he felt the weight of guilt settle heavily upon him as he scrabbled in the drawer for the bottle.

Uncorking it, he sipped and then returned it to its place before considering one problem.

Gray had returned and exclaimed favorably over his improvement. No longer listless and sitting in the darkened room unable to give a fig about anything, Cam had been revived by Margaret and her loving ministrations.

Unfortunately, his friend knew Cam was still taking laudanum. Gray hadn't asked him or even mentioned it. Yet Gray, who had witnessed his previous attempt at stopping, well knew if Cam weren't still enjoying the benefits of opium, he would be a shell of a man, writhing on his bed. He would have been unable to attend dinner as a gracious host, nor, he suspected, could he have made such exquisite love to his fiancée.

His whole focus would be on crawling out of his own skin, moving his cramping muscles, and wondering how to get a drop of opium tincture without anyone noticing.

What if Margaret mentioned to Gray how Cam had supposedly stopped?

If Gray realized Margaret believed it, would he gainsay her? Would he go out of his way to disabuse her of her incorrect notion? Cam sincerely hoped not. He had a feeling she would take it hard, indeed, to discover he had been dishonest, no matter his good intentions.

In any case, if they loved him, they wouldn't discuss his personal business amongst themselves. Which was what he would count on—that they loved him.

CHAPTER TWENTY-THREE

With his worrisome thoughts of the night before still in his head the next morning, Cam was determined to be downstairs early. As host, he would be congenial and attentive, and his estate manager need never have reason to spend time alone with Margaret.

Within minutes of Cyril seating him in the east dining room, Cam was startled as the Angsley children came squealing in, halting in their footsteps when they saw him. They were followed a moment later by the fifth one and their nanny, who held his leading strings in one hand. The woman hesitated. She had not gone to the river with them the day prior as Lord and Lady Angsley considered themselves broadminded parents who liked to look after their own as much as possible, or so his mother had told him.

And see where that had got them? Cam thought. *Nearly with a drowned boy.*

Regaining her composure at seeing the earl of the manor already awake and at the table, the middle-aged woman curtsied.

"Apologies, my lord. The wee ones do rise early. I usually get them away from the lord and lady so they can finish their sleep undisturbed. Which room shall I take them to? I noticed you don't have a nursery."

Not yet.

"If you help oversee them, they may stay here. Food will be brought in shortly, and if there's anything they don't like, we shall ask for something else."

The nanny bobbed another curtsey. "Very well, my lord."

Meanwhile, the little ones, except the very youngest who was still firmly tethered, were trotting around the table, full of energy. Around and around, like horses in a paddock, only far noisier and apt to bump his chair.

Instead of feeling annoyed, Cam, who'd recently had a dose of laudanum upon awakening, laughed.

"Delightful," he said. "And there's George, looking hale and hearty."

Indeed, the boy seemed to have completely recovered from his soggy ordeal. Shyly, George smiled.

When two maids came in carrying trays of food, both hot and cold, for the sideboard, the nanny cautioned the children to stand still. To the woman's credit and Cam's admiration, they obeyed.

After the staff had served him and left, Cam invited them all to sit, although usually, of course, they would dine in a nursery or, as they had the day before, in the kitchen. The nanny shuttled back and forth with plates of food for each one.

For his part, it had done Cam no good to tell his staff he had only the barest of appetites. They carried on as they always had. Thus, his plate was weighed down with his favorite breakfast of kippers, back bacon, grilled tomatoes, fried mushrooms, a poached egg on top of buttered toast, two bangers, and a grilled oatcake. The children, however, seemed to be extremely picky eaters.

Fascinated, Cam looked on as the nanny gave them each a single slice of buttered toast heaped with sweet preserves and a couple rashers of bacon."

"Is that all they're having?" he asked, spearing his poached egg so the yoke ran over his toast.

The nanny paused as she poured milk for each child.

"If they finish that and want more, then they shall have it, and not before. I don't like to waste food on those who don't eat it." She sent a meaningful glance around the table.

Cam was impressed. Nonetheless, he hoped she didn't notice how little of his own breakfast he ate. He feared she might start shoveling it into his mouth or give him a reprimand.

"I do think that's very sensible of you, Mrs. . . . ?"

"Mrs. Wendall, my lord."

He would consider poaching the woman off his uncle and aunt when the time came for Margaret and him to need a nanny. Stealing other people's well-trained servants by offering a little extra in their wages was the tried and true method of getting good help.

As if thinking of her had conjured the very lady herself, Margaret entered with Eleanor close behind. He'd learned she was often an early riser from her first visit.

"Good morning, ladies. We are already dining, as you can see."

The beaming smile of amusement on his betrothed's face warmed him. Conceivably, she approved of his paternal display, surrounded by behaved youngsters.

"You seem to have everything well in hand," she remarked, going to the sideboard with her sister where they would help themselves.

"Honestly, no. Not without Mrs. Wendall."

The girls looked around to see the nanny, who'd taken a corner chair and now offered a little wave.

"Good morning," both the Blackwood sisters said.

"Have you eaten?" Margaret asked her, and Cam felt a twinge of shame. There he was, stuffing his face as were the little Angsleys while the nanny sat with nothing.

What a potato root he was!

"Yes, I have, miss. Don't you worry."

"A cup of tea, perhaps?" Margaret persisted. "I don't suppose you get a minute to yourself except when these little ones are eating or sleeping."

The nanny shrugged in good-natured agreement.

"I wouldn't say no to a cuppa, miss, but I can help myself if no one minds."

"Absolutely," Cam told her, wishing he'd had the thoughtfulness of these sisters from a different class. When one grew up with nearly invisible servants, one assumed they neither ate nor drank. Nor slept for that matter.

As Mrs. Wendall poured herself some tea, sopped up a milk spill, and gave two children a sausage, Margaret and Eleanor took the remaining seats.

"What is on our program for today?" Margaret asked.

"Will you take us fishing again?" the oldest boy asked, and to Cam's surprise, he was speaking to Eleanor.

"If I did, it would have to be only you and your older sister, or we will need more adults to watch over your siblings. We'll see, shall we?"

Cam nearly laughed at how grown up Eleanor sounded. But then, like Beryl, she could be coming out to London society in a year if Lady Blackwood deemed her daughter ready.

"Lady Cambrey may have something in mind for today," Margaret put in, then looked to Cam, her cheeks pinkening beautifully as their gazes locked.

"I'm not sure. There isn't much to do in Bedfordshire unless one journeys by carriage. But, of course, the children have been everywhere local. Their home is only a few miles down the road. I believe all except Beryl are going home later this afternoon."

There were groans all around.

And then in walked Gray, who normally came for meals. His cottage was roomy, big enough for a family, but he kept no staff.

"There you are, ol' chap," Cam said, as the man glanced around at so many in the small dining room. "You've come to the right place for happy children clearing their plates."

"I see that I have." Gray addressed the youngest Angsleys. "As your pony rides were postponed yesterday by Master George's unplanned swim, we'll do them after you've finished eating."

The children cheered.

"And then maybe we can take a wagon ride to my best orchard. I'll let you pick some juicy apples if you stay clear of the tree fairies."

The children squealed this time, possibly a little alarmed.

Cam laughed. "All of our tree fairies are Angsley fairies and will do you no harm since you are family."

Gray shrugged and rolled his eyes. "Merely trying to create a little excitement."

"I, for one, will be thrilled to see the fairies," Eleanor said, without a hint of irony.

Cam nearly believed she thought them real. Then he saw her wink at Gray. Yes, she was nearly ready for her first Season.

"Where's Beryl?" Gray asked. Since the man's parents were from Lord and Lady Angsley's estate, he had grown up with Beryl under foot as much as Cam had, like a little sister.

"Still abed," Eleanor offered. "We stayed up quite late talking in her room."

Cam shot Margaret a glance, and she raised her finely sculpted eyebrows. Hopefully, the girls had heard nothing of Eleanor's older sister creeping back into her own room after a night of pleasure with him.

"Will you ladies come out and see the ponies?" Gray asked.

Eleanor readily agreed. Cam had been told she had a love of nature, especially animals. However, before Margaret could decide to go along, too, Cam spoke up.

"As for Margaret, would you like to spend some time discussing the wedding plans?"

Gray's head swiveled toward him, and then he made a face only Cam could see, which entailed puckering his lips and closing his eyes. Cam grinned, holding back a laugh.

Luckily, Margaret seemed not to care about ponies. "Yes, I would."

And soon everyone left the room, allowing the servants to clean the table and reset it for the rest of the visitors.

When the nanny and her charges along with Eleanor and Gray had left for the stables, Cam wheeled himself out to the veranda with Margaret leading the way.

"I like it out here with you," he said. "It will always remind me of your agreeing to marry me."

"We don't truly have wedding plans to go over, do we?"

He shrugged. "Not unless you care whether we have mutton or beef at the meal, or what color flowers decorate the church. I care only about standing beside you and having us declared man and wife."

"Besides, no matter which decisions I try to make, I believe your mother and mine will have the final say." Margaret said it with a smile, as if she didn't mind in the least. "What shall we talk about then?"

"A million details of our upcoming life, I suppose. For instance, do you like my bedroom or shall we choose another one?"

She dipped her head. "I like the one you have and will be pleased to keep it as is." Then she frowned. "That is, unless . . ."

"Unless?"

"John, you haven't invited other women into your room, have you?"

If he'd been drinking, he would have spluttered. What on earth did she think of his previous life as a bachelor?

"Certainly not! My mother would never allow it."

He laughed at his joke, but Margaret wasn't smiling.

"I'm only fooling, my love. The answer is no."

"Good," she said. "Next question."

"Will you mind spending the Parliamentary session with me in London, or will you prefer to remain here at Turvey?"

"Not only shall I go with you, but I expect us to attend social events and to dance. You may recall, I do like to waltz. As I will be a married lady, I can enjoy myself without wondering who will be on my dance card."

"I shall be the one worrying who is on your dance card."

"Foolish man. You know I won't have one."

"True enough. What about when we have children? Will you stay in Town?"

She paled slightly, and he remarked again how guileless her expressions were.

"I would like to be by your side regardless," she said. "Parliament is in session a long time, and I would miss you dreadfully. Do you not want me there?"

"Of course I do. But I wouldn't force you to be in Town. I know many women wish to lead separate lives from their husbands."

"And take lovers," Margaret said off-handedly.

What on earth?

"That is entirely forbidden," Cam insisted, trying to keep his tone light, although a needle of jealousy lanced him at the thought of her with any other man. "Do I need to order a chastity girdle along with your wedding gown?"

Laughing, she shook her head. "I meant the husbands, you dunce. It is common knowledge men go to their clubs and then afterward directly to their mistresses."

Tilting her head, she asked, "Do I need to request a . . . is there a man's equivalent for a chastity girdle?"

"Yes," Cam told her, taking her hand and bringing it to his lips. "It's called love and devotion. Those will keep me true to you for the rest of our lives."

She unleashed her spectacular smile upon him.

"Perfect."

Except for when her sister asked her to sit for a sketch, which Eleanor wished to gift to her soon-to-be brother-in-law, Maggie let the other visitors enjoy any events Lady Cambrey or even Grayson had planned. For her part, she was satisfied remaining by John's side, playing cards and chess, and finding out neither of them cared for losing. Fortunately, they were well enough matched they took turns winning.

"Will this be a normal day at Turvey House for us?" Maggie asked after he'd taken her queen.

Cam took his gaze from the board.

"I enjoy spending time with you whatever we're doing. Yet, when my cast comes off and my leg is strong, I think it would be enjoyable to ride together. There are many beautiful areas better seen from atop a horse than in a carriage. What's more, if you're willing, I would like us to journey to the Continent. Do you have an interest?"

"Oh, I do."

"I recall you speak French exceedingly well."

"*Oui, monsieur.*"

He chuckled. "I will let you speak for us both then, for my accent is atrocious, I've been told."

"So, we shall journey to France, and where else? Have you been to Italy?"

"No, I haven't. I was waiting to take the most beautiful woman I've ever known to one of the most romantic places."

They smiled at each for a long moment.

"I should very much like to go to Greece, also. If it's safe," Maggie added.

"Let's take in Lord Elgin's statuary in London first and then we'll see about a trip to Greece," he said. "I will want to go on ample walking tours after this experience."

"Maybe closer to home, too. The Yorkshire moors," she suggested.

"We'll climb Ben Nevis, too."

"What are you two plotting?" It was Grayson. He tossed himself into a chair.

Margaret knew her smile was huge. "All the places we shall go after John is completely healed."

"I'm happy for you both. However, after a day with that lot," Grayson gestured to the children who were now running in circles around their nanny in the far field, "I think a sedentary holiday is the one for me."

Her fiancé shook his head. "When I'm out of this blasted chair, I don't think I shall ever sit again."

"Understandable. Speaking of the pushchair, while I was in London, I inquired as you asked me about the identity of the driver."

"Oh dear," Maggie said, hating to think of the needless loss of life.

John patted her hand. "Anyone we knew?"

Grayson shook his head. "I don't believe so. A man named Robert Carruthers. Old enough at three and twenty to have known better, but young enough one can almost forgive him."

"Any family?" John asked. "No wife, I hope."

"No wife. Son of a well-to-do businessman, something to do with wool. Victoria has gone and made the father a baronet over his fine fiber. If it's any consolation to the parents, the dead man had a twin brother and a couple other siblings."

Maggie considered if the unthinkable had happened, and John had perished instead.

"It may sound terrible to say as each person is an individual and as important as any other. Still, in my limited experience with death and losing loved ones, I believe it must be a small consolation, indeed, to the rest of his family. When we lost my father, had my mother also died, it would have destroyed us. Despite all us sisters being nearly adults, we would have felt like orphans. And think of Lady Cambrey. If John had died without any siblings, I'm sure she would have been utterly inconsolable. It would have been the loss of a family's entire generation in one fell swoop."

Placing her other hand on top of John's, they stared at each other a moment. His mother aside, Maggie couldn't conceive of facing life without this man.

"I have never thought of myself as a family's entire generation. I don't think I like it. Far too much pressure."

Grayson laughed. "To think it's come down to you, old boy. Lord Anguish."

Silence descended as John looked at him, his jaw tightening.

"What did you call me?"

John's childhood friend never seemed bothered one bit by his moods, or whether he was going to cause one. For Maggie, it felt like an unfamiliar and definitely unpleasant new worry.

Grayson merely smiled. "It's what I heard a few people calling you when I started making my inquiries. Some members of the *ton* think they are witty."

"They think wrong," John's tone was flat, obviously annoyed at the notion people were talking about him. He withdrew his hands from hers and sat straighter in the pushchair.

"I assure you, they're not making fun. In fact, I think they're somewhat in awe. Most can't believe you lived, what with the increasingly gory versions of your many broken bones and all the blood loss."

After another long moment, in which Maggie wondered what he was thinking, John offered a wry smile.

"*Awe*, indeed. They haven't a clue."

With the mood lightened, Maggie looked at the chessboard once again. To her delight, she saw the pieces anew and realized her opening.

"Goodness," she declared, moving her bishop into place. "It's checkmate."

"What?" John exclaimed, raising his voice slightly.

Maggie felt a frisson of nerves rustle through her. Was he going to become upset? Would he lash out in irritation? Biting her lip, she waited.

Then he burst out laughing. "My fiancée is one of the best chess players I've ever encountered. How is that possible?"

"Because she is a woman," Grayson said off-handedly. "No doubt she's been distracting you with her beauty and feminine wiles." His wry smile softened the effect of his words.

"Nothing of the sort," Maggie told him. "I know you're half-joking, but I'll play you later if you like. No feminine wiles will be used upon you, good sir."

Grayson opened his mouth, but John cut him off. "He's probably too busy for such frivolity."

"I just gave pony rides and picked apples while searching for fairies!"

"Exactly," John said. "I assume you are still my estate manager and will be working this afternoon in your office. Plus, I have some investments to discuss with you."

"Slave driver," Grayson said. Then he turned to Maggie. "Our game will have to wait for some other day." He was nearly at the door to the house when he turned.

"Cam, do you need anything? What about laudanum?"

Maggie saw John's face pale. Perhaps he hadn't told Grayson he had stopped dosing himself.

"No, I'm fine," her fiancé said evenly, turning away to end the conversation, fixing his glance on the children in the field.

Most probably it was still uncomfortable for him to think about opium, knowing the relief it would give him, particularly if he were in any pain at that moment. Maggie decided to speak with Grayson privately to let him know not to bring it up while John was still weaning himself from the substance.

After dinner she found an opportunity. They were already down to six with most of the Angsley family having returned home after the midday meal, leaving only Beryl with them. Having excused herself to go to the water closet, before returning to the drawing room in which everyone was playing cards, Maggie encountered Grayson in the hallway. In his hand, he held a bottle of apple brandy.

Holding it up for her inspection, he quipped, "His lordship had a thirst for this."

Nodding, she thought how best to approach the subject.

"I know you and John have been friends for many years, and I would not tell you how to behave around him except in this one important issue."

Grayson tilted his head, staring at her with interest.

"Go on."

"He has ceased taking laudanum, and I would ask you not bring it to his mind, nor tempt him with it at present. I know doing without it is extremely difficult for him."

The man stared at her, and she hoped she hadn't offended him.

Then he sighed. "Margaret, I understand your concern. However, I must tell you you're acting under a misapprehension."

"I beg your pardon?"

Grayson frowned. "John hasn't stopped dosing himself with laudanum."

His words fell on her like bricks. "Why do you say that?"

"Because it's the truth." His gentle voice somehow made it worse.

Her ire flashed like dry leaves touched by a torch. "You're wrong. John promised me he would stop taking it after I found him in a terrible state. Why, in the past few days alone, the hollowed look under his eyes has all but vanished, and he's eating more. Stopping the tincture has done him a world of good already."

Gray shook his head, dashing her hopes, yet her brain still fought against what she was hearing.

"Having you here is what has done him some good. He definitely wouldn't bathe for my benefit or let us cut his hair. Not even for his mother."

"Why do you believe he is still taking opium?"

"Because I was here the last time he tried to stop. It was a terrible sight to see. When he is fighting the effects of wanting opium, he doesn't look calm as he does now, nor act civilly. When he needs a dose and doesn't have it, he is impatient and irritable, downright rude, and sometimes, he lashes out with irrational full-blown anger."

"A few times I have witnessed such behavior over the past few days."

"It would be consistent, Margaret. What you may have witnessed was him needing his next dose. If he behaved better soon after, then he took it. I'm sorry, but I am confident in my assertion."

"He looks better," she protested.

"There's the proof. When he stopped taking it before, he looked terrible. He had uncontrollable sweating and shaking of his limbs. His body will have to go through some very unpleasant sensations again when, or if, he stops. I believe it happens while one's personal chemistry, if you understand me, is releasing all remains of the opium. Like those who cannot handle their alcohol and must give it up or die. I've been around my share of men 'drying' out, as they say. It is not agreeable to watch and worse to experience, and I think the effects of opium are far more severe."

Her heart sank. All sense of relief she had previously felt vanished.

"He promised me."

Grayson touched her shoulder. "I'm sorry. Please don't hold it against him. He is a good man, one of the finest I've ever known. This accident has thrown him off-kilter. I know him, though. Cam will persevere."

"What should I do?"

He dropped his hand from her arm. "Confront him, I suppose."

"What if he lies to me again?" *Dammit.* She couldn't keep the tears from her eyes.

"I believe you hold the key, Margaret. Nothing and no one else will make him give it up. It is too difficult a thing to ask a man. In fact, maybe until he has his cast off and can be distracted by walking or riding, it isn't fair to ask it of him anyway. When I arrived yesterday, I thought that was the arrangement you had made with him—to let him take laudanum until he had an entirely healed body with which he could fight the terrible symptoms of not taking it."

"I don't know what's right. I fear the longer he waits, the harder it will be."

"You may be correct. You will be his wife soon. I leave it up to you to decide."

With an encouraging nod, he walked past her to reenter the drawing room. As he opened the door, she could hear John's happy laughter alongside Eleanor and Beryl's. How different from the man she'd encountered upon her return!

What should she do? She wished she could ask Jenny or Simon. Perhaps she should write a letter, confessing her dilemma, and asking for their advice. One thing she did know with certainty. Whether she thought it acceptable for him to continue taking laudanum until his cast came off or persisted in her request for him to stop, Maggie could not allow him to lie to her any longer.

If he could show her such disrespect as to make a promise and lie to her face before marriage, what would stop him from betraying her afterward? He must tell her the truth, or she feared it would be the end of their engagement.

With such a dire thought in her head, she followed Grayson into the drawing room.

CHAPTER TWENTY-FOUR

Cam relaxed in his chair when he saw Gray return alone, and he let his friend pour a round of apple brandy for all of them. At his mother's permission, even Eleanor and Beryl received a few mouthfuls in small sherry glasses.

However, when Margaret entered the drawing room a few moments later, with her readable countenance plainly distraught, his heart sank. He had a suspicion she knew.

Sipping his brandy and trying to catch her eye, he allowed for a small feeling of outrage to seep into his heart when she wouldn't look directly at him.

How dare they discuss him as if he were a child!

No one had the right to dictate what he should do, a grown man who'd been through hell, and he mightily resented Margaret's judgmental attitude. When every man jack used laudanum for each and every tiny ache, not to mention the women dosing themselves for their natural monthly flow, which was probably utterly painless, why shouldn't he, who had suffered broken bones, be allowed to ease his anguish?

At that moment, he knew he was only a couple hours from turning in for the night and enjoying his last dose of the evening. The anticipation of relief gave him a sense of peace. She had no right to wish to take it from him. None at all.

Tossing back the brandy, he held out his glass toward Gray who, with raised eyebrows, refilled it.

Nodding his thanks, Cam settled into his chair for the next round of whist.

Nevertheless, his enjoyment of the evening was dimmed by Margaret's cool reserve, so noticeable, Eleanor asked her sister if she felt well.

"A slight headache is all," Margaret said, and Cam could only hope it were true. In his gut, though, he knew it to be otherwise.

Gone was the lively, loving fiancée, and he sorely missed her. Glancing at Gray, Cam considered whether he should question him on what was said. It was damnably difficult to arrange to catch someone where and when he wanted while stuck in the pushchair.

Before he could think of a way, the night was over, and Gray had left for his own home across the field. There was always tomorrow. In any case, if he couldn't speak to his estate manager that evening, he could at least hope to speak to Margaret.

In his bedroom, watching the glowing of the coals in his fireplace, Cam yawned and punched his pillow, occupying the wait with thinking how much he loved her. Should he confess to still taking laudanum drops knowing it would upset her?

Waking with a start, Cam realized he had dozed off. Glancing at the clock on his mantle, he frowned. It was far later than any of the other nights Margaret had visited.

Finally, it occurred to him she was not coming.

What should he make of that?

He could ring for Peter and ... and what? Ask him to knock on his betrothed's door and summon her to his room? *Hardly.*

Another thought struck him. Could he possibly get to her room unassisted? He'd had a cast on his leg for two months, or thereabouts. Surely, he could stand upright, hop on his good leg, and touch the injured one down on the floor, when he needed to, without doing it any harm. If only he had crutches, which he had soundly eschewed.

Cursing his pride, he recalled how he'd forbidden the doctors from bringing any into the house, either his London home or to Turvey House when the doctor who removed his arm cast had offered one.

"I will not look like an invalid," he had railed. "Nor a beggar!"

In his mind's eye, he'd seen those unfortunate men and women from Covent Garden or Whitechapel.

Stupid vanity! Who cared what he looked like if a crutch helped him to reach Margaret?

Swinging his good leg off the bed, he eased the other one down until his foot touched the floor. There were those toes which had never heralded gangrene, thank goodness, and which he could now wiggle if not effortlessly, at least stiffly.

Easing to a standing position, Cam hopped. Then he hopped again. So far, so good. Hopping once more, he realized he was bloody exhausted already. Breathing hard and feeling sweat trickling down his back, he would need another bath in the morning.

Lowering his right leg to the carpet, he winced at the strangeness of it. He dared not put any weight on it, at the risk of re-injuring bones that weren't yet set. Thinking of what could happen if the large thigh bone shifted, he felt the blood drain from his head.

"The Devil!" he swore, and then he toppled over.

Lying upon his thick, soft carpet, he considered his options. He could attempt to crawl to Margaret's room. Most probably, she would think it a good arm strengthening exercise.

Alternately, he could creep toward the bell pull by his bed and pull the damn cord to summon Peter. Such a course of action seemed preferable since he was utterly naked. In hindsight, he would have been prudent to grab his robe before he got out of bed. Regrettably, his mind simply wasn't thinking clearly, perhaps due to the lateness of the hour.

In any case, there was no doubt had he attempted to hop or crawl to Margaret's room, he would have been caught somewhere in the middle between his room and hers, with his bare arse and his yard on display for all to see.

Sighing, he dragged himself the short way back to his bedside, finding it nearly impossible to crawl with only one knee and with the other leg out straight behind him. Rising up on his good knee, which took him a few long minutes, at last, he was leaning on the side of his bed at an awkward angle.

Reaching for the bell pull, brushing it once, twice, three times with his outstretched fingers, at last, he grasped it and yanked hard.

Then he waited. He had never taken a really long look at his bed with its solid walnut headboard and footboard, elaborately carved. He traced the elegant arched moldings and leaves with his gaze, finding it satisfactory.

In a few minutes, the door opened behind him. Craning his neck, Cam saw Peter in his robe, staring at him, eyes popping from his head at his bare-assed lord.

"Don't stand there like a ninny-panny. Help me back into bed. And in the morning, first thing, I should like a hot bath."

MAGGIE AWAKENED FEELING EXHAUSTED as she'd spent the better part of the night battling with herself about whether to visit with John in his room. A couple times, she'd even made it as far as his door before turning back.

Lying awake, she'd stared at the ceiling considering what would happen if she went to him. He would overwhelm her senses with a kiss and then they would become intimate again. If that happened, it wouldn't be appropriate to bring up her concerns or to accuse him. Finally, she'd fallen asleep, still in her dressing gown.

Bleary eyed, she arose the next morning, still pondering her best course of action. She must hold onto the fact she loved him and his assurance he loved her.

Unable to get him alone until after breakfast, when Beryl and Eleanor went gamboling off like colts to do who knew what and Lady Cambrey went to the drawing room to read the dailies, Maggie stared at him. *How to start?*

"I missed you last night," John said.

"I missed you, too." She might as well be honest since truth was the issue at hand. It had been difficult to forsake having his mouth and hands upon her. Even more difficult, though, to think he was lying to her.

"I didn't want to come to you again until I spoke with you, and last night didn't seem the right time."

"I wish you had come to me. I will discuss anything with you. Any time."

Very well. Taking a deep breath, she asked, "Are you still taking laudanum?"

Frowning, his glance slid away from her, and she knew it to be true. Instead of answering, he asked, "Did Gray tell you that?"

"Why does it matter? I only want to know if you lied to me."

"It matters if my good friend and my lovely intended are speaking about me behind my back."

The importance of this discussion was not lost on her. Standing up, Maggie found she needed to pace the room.

"Two people who care about you happened to believe opposite things. Which of us is correct? If Grayson is correct, then you lied to me and broke a promise."

John was silent for a long moment.

"I need the opium tincture at this time," he said at last, his voice soft.

"I see."

"Do you, Margaret? For I am not certain you do."

Maggie felt tears prick her eyes but worked hard to tamp down her emotions.

"You offered to stop taking laudanum. I didn't ask. You offered."

"I knew you wanted me to. Despite the fact I need it for the pain, you wanted me to stop taking it." His tone was accusatory.

Nodding, she felt a cold chill run up her spine. "And then you promised me."

"I shouldn't have."

"No, I suppose you shouldn't." He didn't look contrite, not one bit. "You've made other promises, and now I must wonder about all of them."

"Don't," he said at once. "Except for this one instance, I have never lied to you. I had no choice. Why can't you allow me the benefit of opium for as long as I need it? You shouldn't want to take this small relief from me, and I shouldn't have had to lie about stopping."

Was he blaming his lie upon her?

"How long do you think you will need it?"

"I don't know for sure. How can I? And will you please stop pacing?"

Frustrated, Maggie came to a halt before him.

"Don't look sad." John reached out and took her hand. "Nothing else has changed."

Staring at their entwined fingers, Maggie disagreed.

"Nothing except I know you can easily stare into my eyes and lie to me. Nothing except I am engaged to an opium addict."

Dropping her hand like it was a hot iron, he worked his mouth into a thin, angry line. "An addict! That's absurd."

"If you weren't, you could stop when you wish."

"I don't want to stop because I'm in pain," he insisted.

"Are you? Even now?"

"Not now," he muttered, "because I take a dose every morning when I awaken." Then with a louder voice, he asked, "You don't feel the least to blame for my accident, do you?"

She felt her mouth drop, and then closed it. "You blame me? Because you misinterpreted what you saw at the pavilion and chose to come to my home? What of the reckless driver? Am I more to blame than he is?"

Silence for a moment as John considered. She hoped he realized how absurd it was for him to lay the responsibility at her feet, despite the moments of severe guilt she'd already experienced over the entire event.

"Of course, I don't," he said at last, his voice tight. "My apologies for implying anything of the sort."

"Your apology is accepted," Maggie answered, mirroring his formal tone. However, she didn't feel any better.

From now on, there would be this issue between them. Moreover, she didn't want to be intimate with him while he was addicted to opium. She wasn't even certain she could explain why. Perhaps because he had once mistaken her for a dream. At any time, how would she know if he were lucid or in an opium-induced state, like Coleridge when he wrote his strange *Kubla Khan?*

When they were touching each other, had John even known she was real?

"Margaret, what are you thinking?"

"We are at an impasse because I will not—cannot—stand by while you are addicted."

He made a face of disgust. "Are we back to that again? I told you I am not addicted."

"No, you simply cannot stop taking it."

He crossed his arms, his expression mutinous. "Again, you shouldn't ask it of me."

Nodding, she realized an awful truth. "As I said, an impasse. I shall leave at once."

The words were out of her mouth, and she could not call them back.

"What?" John uncrossed his arm. "How can you do such a thing?"

How could she? Yet, how could she not?

"Margaret, I ask you to reconsider. You think I am weak, but I'm not."

Was that what she thought? Every time she mentioned his addiction, he turned it around as her fault for suggesting he should stop. Had he spent a moment considering he couldn't?

"When I was a youth," he began, "I fell from my horse and dislocated my shoulder. It hurt like the devil, but I was far from home and alone. Do you know what I did?"

She shook her head.

"Fortunately, there was a fence nearby. I had to use my good arm to lift my useless arm over the fence. My fingers still worked and I grabbed a hold of the lowest rail I could, and then I hung there, using my own weight and a good deal of yanking until the pressure from the top of the fence rail forced my arm back into the socket. Rather with a nasty snap, it went, too. When it was over, I wretched violently from the entire experience."

During the recounting of his tale, Maggie had felt the blood drain from her head.

"That must have been extremely frightening and painful."

"It was both." Running a hand through his hair, he looked up at her with soulful eyes. "I faced the pain, and I handled the situation. I am not weak."

"I know you're not. But, John, you didn't go home and begin a months-long course of opium."

"I will stop today," he said abruptly. Then frowned. "Or first thing tomorrow morning, after I've had a good night's sleep."

Maggie simply did not believe him. Tomorrow, she feared he would say he would stop the following day and then the next. Eventually, she would probably give up asking. Moreover, even if he vowed he had ceased to dose himself, she would not trust his word.

"How do you feel at present?" she asked him.

"I am fine."

"Then you should be determined to stop at once."

"In a few hours," he reminded her, "I will be in pain."

"From the injuries or the effects of the opium?"

She watched his jaw work, until he clenched it in silence.

"Does your stomach hurt?" she asked.

Still, he didn't answer.

"Is your mind as sharp as it was? And what of your temperament? You used to be an even-tempered man. Do you not feel at this moment as if you could lash out at me?"

He shook his head.

"No? Because your face is reddening, as if flushed with anger. What of this sleep you keep mentioning? So precious to you. Truthfully, do you sleep peacefully, or are your nights filled with vivid disturbing dreams, like De Quincey mentioned?"

"Damn it all!" he swore. "Again, with wretched De Quincey. I wish to God he'd never written his ridiculous memoir. If he was such an addict, how can anyone believe his words? I'd like to give him a good throttling."

"And what about me?" she asked.

"I wish you would simply drop this infernal nagging. If this is any indication of what you will be like as a wife—a tedious scold—then maybe it is I who must reconsider."

Gasping aloud before she could stop herself, Maggie fisted her hands by her side and took a deep breath.

"Do not bother reconsidering, Lord Angsley. This engagement is over."

With that, she turned and stormed from the room. By the time she'd run up the stairs and reached her bedroom, some of her anger had dissipated, as well as the silly notion if she'd had a ring, she would have gladly removed it and tossed it onto his lap.

Closing the door behind her, she considered what had occurred, acknowledging a feeling of utter disbelief. If she had left the room a few minutes earlier, then they would still be engaged.

She was no longer the fiancée of John Angsley! *What had she done?*

Crossing the room, she dropped onto the chair by the window, which overlooked the back of Turvey House. Maggie Blackwood, middle daughter of deceased Baron Blackwood, examined her emotions. A wall of sadness swiftly built itself around her. Tears welled up in her eyes and then spilled over.

What about his humor, his intelligence, and his beloved hazel eyes? What of his kissable, sensual, talented mouth? He understood her and suited her perfectly. He said he loved her and, thus, she'd let him touch her intimately.

Was she really going to walk away from all that? What's more, she'd come to care for his family, both his mother and his cousin Beryl.

Eleanor! In all the high drama, she'd forgotten about Eleanor. Standing, Maggie went to the bell pull by the bed and tugged it. Glancing around the room, she considered how quickly the maid could get both their trunks packed. Her sister would be unhappy to leave her friend, but she wasn't a child anymore. Eleanor would understand the need for a hasty departure once she knew the situation.

First, Maggie had to find her. Yet, she didn't want to go traipsing around the house or the property and risk encountering John. How mortifying! And if he'd already told the formidable Lady Cambrey and she ran into her, oh, the humiliation!

A knock at the door heralded the maid. Or did it?

"Yes?" she asked softly.

"It's Polly, miss."

Relieved, Maggie invited her in, instructing her to begin packing in haste, and for her sister, too.

"By any chance have you seen my sister?"

"Yes, miss. I believe she recently came in from a ride with Lady Angsley. They were each going to their rooms."

"Wonderful, thank you."

With her hand on the door, Maggie halted at Polly's words, "Miss, a moment."

"Yes?"

"I shall be sorry to see you go. I hope you'll be back soon and not wait until after the wedding."

Nodding past the lump in her throat, Maggie murmured her thanks and left.

Luckily, Eleanor was in her room, alone, changing out of her riding habit. After a brief, painful explanation, Maggie found herself in her sister's tight embrace, and the tears began to flow again.

"I'm sorry," Maggie managed between sniffles. "I know you are having a wonderful time with Beryl. You see why I cannot stay, though, don't you?"

"Of course. We must get you back to Mummy and Jenny."

"I know this seems cowardly, but I don't want to see the Angsleys, not any of them. I just want to leave."

"Perfectly understandable, yet it may be impossible. I'll go tell Beryl."

"Oh," Maggie moaned.

"As little as possible. Only that we must leave and that whatever has occurred is between you and the earl. May I say as much?"

Again, Maggie was impressed by her sister's maturity.

"Yes, thank you."

"Then I'll speak with the butler about readying our carriage and horses and gathering Simon's staff. We came with four, didn't we?"

Maggie watched her sister leave to prepare for their long journey home. Returning to her own room while Polly continued to pack, Maggie penned a letter to Lady Cambrey, one of gratitude for their stay and apology for her abrupt departure, hoping against hope John's mother would forgive her.

Somehow, fortune smiled upon her. Half an hour later, she made it down the stairs and out the front door to the awaiting carriage packed with their trunks, without seeing anyone except staff.

And then, it seemed, her luck ran out.

"Miss Blackwood!"

Grayson O'Connor was hot on her heels like a dog at the hunt.

Nodding to Eleanor to climb aboard and settle in with the many baskets of food and drink Mrs. Mackle had packed for them, Maggie turned to face him.

He hesitated as if unsure what to say or merely reluctant to speak. At last, he said, "You're giving up on him?"

A flash of anger raced through her. "How unfair of you! You said it was my choice to confront him, to learn the truth. You also said he might not be able to relinquish laudanum while still in the cast. You may be correct, but I am not staying to watch what it's doing to him."

"I didn't think you would leave like this."

She wondered what he already knew. "We exchanged unpleasant words."

"You know he loves you," Grayson insisted. "Anything he said was not really from him."

"Of course not! It was opium talking. That's the problem, isn't it? You, his mother, everyone allows him to behave uncivilly because of his injuries and the influence of that cursed drug. What's more, I am expected to remain devotedly by his side and let opium be his excuse for every bad behavior? I think not."

Pausing, she stopped herself from apologizing in the face of this man's apparent disapproval.

"You said I hold the key. But you forgot to take John into account. He said he no longer wishes to take me for his wife."

Grayson's face expressed his shock. "Did he?"

"Yes, or words to that effect. So, you see, I have no choice but to leave. I am not giving up on *him*, not on my John Angsley, but . . ." She gestured toward the house. "The addict he has become is not the man I want to marry."

She let him help her into the carriage and close the door.

At the last moment, Maggie leaned out the open window.

"Please, Grayson, take care of him."

He raised a hand in farewell as the carriage rolled away.

CHAPTER TWENTY-FIVE

Cam couldn't believe she'd left. Just like that!

He'd been absolutely, positively correct in his first impression of her as she was an immature, fickle miss. And stupidly, he'd given her his heart. And then he'd even offered her his hand!

Fool, dunce, dullard! He deserved every ounce of misery he was now experiencing. Every bloody ounce!

Gray returned from the front drive.

"She's gone," he intoned.

"Naturally," was all Cam said. Margaret had said she would go, and she had. Except she'd also said she loved him and would marry him.

Reaching into his pocket, he pulled out the laudanum. It was a new bottle as of last night.

Gray eyed him, eyebrows raised, as he unstopped it. Feeling defiant, daring his estate manager to say a word, Cam took a small sip.

Suddenly, a commotion in the front hall snagged his attention. As Gray had left the door open, they could hear someone had arrived.

With his heart instantly pounding, Cam dared to hope Margaret had returned. He would crawl out of the pushchair and throw himself at her feet to beg her forgiveness and declare his undying love.

Cyril entered.

"Dr. Brewster has arrived, my lord."

"The doctor? Whatever for?" He looked at Gray. "Is it possible he's here to remove my cast?"

Gray shrugged.

"Show him in, by all means," Cam ordered.

A moment later, the doctor strode through the door and made his greeting.

"To what do I owe this visit?" Cam asked. If Brewster removed his cast, perhaps he could manage to get on a horse and ride after Margaret.

The doctor looked around expectantly, for what or whom, Cam couldn't guess.

"I'm not entirely sure, my lord. By any chance, is your fiancée available to speak with me?"

Stunned at the timing, Cam could only shake his head.

"You do have one, don't you?" the doctor persisted.

What an odd question, particularly at that moment. Cam looked at Gray who shrugged again. It was becoming a nasty habit, and he'd have to mention it to his friend in private. In any case, he knew the correct answer.

"No, I don't believe I do."

The doctor was clearly flummoxed. "Then who summoned me? One of your servants came to my practice and said your betrothed wished to meet with me. Unfortunately, that day, I was called away nearly the same hour and have been treating a terrible case of—"

"Please," Cam held up his hand. "You needn't go into details.

"What his lordship means," Gray said, and Cam heard the sardonic tinge, "is he *had* a fiancée, as recently as an hour ago. Sadly, though, he has lost her. If I may be rather forward, I believe I know what she wished to discuss with you, and I think it's best if you do so with the earl, himself. What say you, *my lord?*"

Cam didn't appreciate Gray taking over, nor the tone of mockery, nor did he wish to have any conversation with the doctor now he realized the topic.

"No is what I say."

Dr. Brewster looked from one man to the other.

"Then I am not needed here?"

"No," Cam repeated.

"Not if you think there aren't any ill effects from copious and continuous use of opium," Gray said.

The doctor wrinkled his brow. "It is an extremely safe drug."

"*Ah ha!*" Cam couldn't resist a small triumphant crowing.

"Nonetheless," Brewster continued, "I cannot recommend one taking it, as you said, in *copious* amounts or on a *continuous* basis."

"*Ah ha!*" Gray exalted.

Dr. Brewster looked back and forth between the men.

Gray pressed the issue. "Why wouldn't you recommend it, Doctor?"

"Because it is highly addictive, which is why it is best used to treat an acute pain. Something that is not ongoing, if you take my meaning. If one has a headache, even a migraine, I tell my patients by all means have a little laudanum. However, if one has a chronic issue, gout, for instance, or insomnia or—"

"Or overall physical aches and pains from healing injuries and too much inactivity," Gray interrupted, staring at Cam.

"Why, yes." Perhaps realizing precisely what the issue was, Dr. Brewster set his leather bag down and approached Cam in his pushchair. Crouching before him, the man stared him right in the eye.

"My lord, you must be very careful if you're still taking laudanum this long after the accident. Your body will start to need more and more, and to crave it fiercely. Moreover, the more you take, I tell you, the worse it is for your health. It can severely damage your organs."

Cam didn't like the sound of that. He was quite fond of his innards working well.

"I assume a strapping man such as yourself wants to live a long, full life. The sooner you stop taking opium, the better. Mark me, it won't be easy. It will take a number of days for the last traces of the drug to leave your body, and a few more for your mind to stop craving it."

Then he flashed what Cam imagined passed for an encouraging smile.

"In comparison to the many years ahead of you," Brewster added, "especially if you find your lost fiancée or get yourself a new one, then the suffering of withdrawal is really only the blink of an eye."

A new one? He didn't want a new one. He wanted Margaret, who had been right all along. He'd been fooling himself, or the opium had.

Standing, Dr. Brewster retrieved his bag. "Is there anything else, gentlemen?"

Cam was lost in thought over the words he had exchanged with Margaret and the terrible task ahead of him. He didn't mind when Gray answered for them both.

"His lordship would be ever so pleased if you removed his cast today."

Dr. Brewster shook his head. "That's weeks away. I've told you that," he said, staring hard at Cam. "If I took it off now, you might be crippled for life, and, if the bones shifted . . . ," he trailed off, shaking his head again.

Cam couldn't help shuddering at the notion. "Then I suppose that is all, Doctor. Thank you for coming."

Heading for the door, Dr. Brewster turned before he left.

"I recommend you don't try to stop the opium all at once. It could be agony. Best if you wean like a baby from the teat when it's ready for solid food. If you take it twice a day, then only have it once. If you have a large sip, then make it a small one. You understand me well, yes?"

"Yes," Cam said. He understood all too well.

The doctor bowed to the earl. "Good day, gentlemen."

When the echo of the doctor's footsteps had faded, Cam still stared at Gray.

"I'm frightened, old chap."

Gray nodded. "With good reason."

"When I lied and told Margaret I had stopped, I also said how hard it was. She said she would be with me."

"You have me," Gray said. "It's probably best if she doesn't see what it does to you."

Cam chuckled. "Frankly, *I* would rather not see what it does to me."

Reaching into his pocket, he withdrew the dark glass bottle. With a quick flick of his wrist, he tossed it to Gray, who snatched it out of the air.

"Best start now, I suppose."

Gray nodded. "Mind what the doctor told you. We should ease you off of it."

Cam considered. *Wouldn't it take longer?* He wanted to be free of opium and its effects as soon as he could, especially if he was going to try to get Margaret back.

"You cannot leave laudanum in a place where I can get it, nor where any of my servants have access. I will order them to get it for me. What's more, I'll threaten to remove them from their positions if they don't. Most likely, I will threaten you, too, but you are the only one who can stand up to me. Certainly, poor Peter cannot."

His expression serious, Gray agreed.

Cam didn't like to think of the days and nights ahead of him.

"I will do nothing about Margaret until I'm myself again."

"Perhaps a letter telling her your course of action?"

Cam shook his head. "She won't believe me. *I* wouldn't believe me. Besides, I want to walk up to the lady I love with a gorgeous ring in my hand and ask her to marry me again. Properly this time."

"Understandable."

Cam smiled. "I like how you are often a man of few words. I'm going outside to enjoy the weather. Unseasonably sunny and warm, don't you think?"

"It is."

"And tonight," Cam continued, as he started to roll himself out of the room, "I plan to drink heavily, so make sure we have my favorite brandy at hand."

"We do."

"As well as madeira," he added, picking up speed as he traversed the long hall to the back of the house.

"Yes."

"And sherry."

"Of course."

"Port, too."

"I'll make certain of it," Gray told him.

Cam wheeled out onto the veranda.

"And whiskey. Better make sure we have plenty of whiskey."

Finally, Gray laughed. "I don't think you're going to miss the opium at all."

NEARLY TWO MONTHS LATER, Maggie stepped out of her brother-in-law's carriage followed by her mother and younger sister. From the carriage ahead of them, Simon was assisting Jenny, who carried baby Lionel. The entire family—the Deveres and the Blackwoods—were taking up residence in Lord Lindsey's townhouse as Parliament came into an early session.

As they approached the front door, Maggie couldn't help but think of John on these very steps finding out she'd left

London, and then moments later, being in the accident that changed his life. And hers.

"You're blocking the entrance," Eleanor said churlishly, before stepping around her. They were all a little out of sorts after a particularly long trip, made longer by Simon and Jenny's carriage breaking a wheel the day before.

"It is lovely to be back on solid ground," her mother said, also going around her.

Maggie followed them inside before she obstructed anyone else.

Everything looked the same, of course. But nothing felt the same.

Making her way up the stairs to the room she knew would be hers, her feet felt as if they were trudging through mud. The last time she'd been in London, it held the promise of the Season and the excitement of gentlemen callers. There was the extraordinary experience of John's first kiss and then the silly misunderstanding resulting in what she had thought was heartache at the pavilion.

Until she'd experienced the real thing.

Until she'd left behind the man she loved, not knowing if he would survive or perish.

Simon had written to his good friend as soon as Maggie and Eleanor had returned to Belton Manor. Distraught, Maggie had expressed her worry over John's laudanum intake and told Simon of his thin, hollow-eyed appearance when she'd first arrived at Turvey, and of his conduct before she'd left.

Of course, she kept all mention of their evening trysts to herself, although the exciting memories haunted her when she was alone.

At first, Simon received no reply to his missive, and then, a few weeks afterward, a letter arrived addressed only to him. Maggie had paced outside the library while he read it. Then, he'd invited her in, her heart pounding.

With an odd look upon his face, Simon offered her a seat.

"Cam says he is grateful you summoned the doctor."

Her mouth had dropped open, as she'd forgotten entirely about having asked Dr. Brewster to meet with her. What's more, it was hardly what she expected to hear from her former beloved.

"Is that all?" Naturally, given how she loved John even then, Maggie assumed he would have something more personal to tell her. Did he not feel longing or regret?

"He apologizes for his behavior while you were residing at Turvey House, and he says his mother misses you greatly."

Frowning, staring down at her hands, she shook them briefly to stop from clasping her fingers tightly. His *mother* missed her!

What could she say? It was humiliating.

"He wrote very briefly, as you can see." Simon held up a single sheet. Indeed, there were only a few lines on it.

"I'm sorry," he added. "He does say he hopes he will see you when next we are all in London."

At her questioning look, he explained, "I told him we would all be going to Town when the summer heat has dissipated."

"I understand." John knew they were going to London, and he planned to go as well, most likely as soon as his cast was off. He *hoped* to run into her. It sounded vague, not like a man who was desperate to win back his beloved.

"Thank you." Turning, she knew she had better flee before either her sadness or her ire got the better of her, the latter being used to shore herself up against the former.

"Maggie," Simon began, but she held her hand up. If her brother-in-law offered her pity and became too gentle with her, then she would definitely shatter.

In a moment, she'd slipped out of the library.

Now, she was back in London with the threat of running into a man who'd told her he didn't really want to marry her after all. He considered her a nag, a scold. Like the proverbial fishwife or Shakespeare's shrew, Katherina.

Maybe John had turned her into one. Wasn't she too young to have such weighty concerns of a grown man's vices draped around her shoulders?

Considering her situation, Maggie took a deep breath and released it, then began to change out of her traveling garb. She was once more in Town, an unattached woman with her whole future ahead of her. As long as she didn't remain unattached too long. In which case, she might live with her mother and then eventually with her sister.

Shaking her head at the notion of not having her own husband, home, or children, she decided to jump back into the social events, whatever they were at this time of year.

The first thing to do was write a brief note to her good friend Ada asking if she could visit her in the morning. When she did, she would discover if Ada had any upcoming society plans in which Maggie could join.

She might still be in love and nursing a broken heart, but she'd be damned if she'd put herself off the marriage market and miss out on a lifetime of experiences.

Rushing downstairs, she gave her note to Simon's faithful butler, Mr. Binkley, who had come a few days earlier to make everything ready for their arrival.

Within days, Maggie was dressing for a Thursday evening soiree at the Royal Society for the Encouragement of Arts, Manufactures, and Commerce to be held in their Elizabeth Rooms. Ada's father was a member and friend of the esteemed inventor, Henry Cole. Why, the man had even invented greeting cards. Such a clever idea and so much fun!

Rather thrilled to begin her new London life at such an event, Maggie dressed with care and didn't neglect to have a pleasant smile upon her face when Ada and her parents picked her up.

There was a line of polished carriages pulled by well-groomed horses waiting outside the event. From inside the vehicles came elegantly dressed members of the RSA and their guests, all clamoring to enter the Adam brothers-designed building. Eventually, Maggie and her companions handed their tickets to a smartly dressed employee of the society. Entering, she surveyed the scene of twinkling lights, fruity punch in fluted glasses on trays, and an absolute crush of people.

Why did she instantly feel alone?

"If you don't wipe the sour expression from your lovely face, then we shall be avoided like plague carriers."

Nodding at Ada who was probably correct in her assessment, Maggie fixed her smile, batted her eyelashes for good measure, and took her friend by the arm.

"Let us go forth and conquer."

And conquer they did. They danced every dance they wanted to, sat out those they didn't, had no unacceptable partners, and proclaimed the food to be delicious. It seemed the musicians never hit a wrong note. What's more, Ada's family didn't drop her home until two in the morning.

Still, Maggie found it difficult to be enthusiastic as she reported the evening's highlights to Jenny the following day when she finally arose from her comfy bed by mid-morning.

"What was the best part of the whole night?" Jenny asked, trying to coax some tidbits from her sister.

Maggie wanted to say taking off her dancing slippers and going to sleep. Instead, she said, "I suppose it was the dancing."

"Did you have any partners whom you particularly liked?"

Shrugging, she considered. "I didn't know anyone and didn't dance with the same man twice. It wasn't the same group as I knew during last Season."

Maggie had hoped to see a familiar face, Lord Westing or Lord Burnley, perchance. However, the RSA was an exclusive group, certainly not the usual crowd of debutantes and wife-seeking bachelors she was used to. What's more, she'd found pretending to be interested in each new man a dreary effort.

Starting over it seemed was going to be tedious.

"What are your plans for this evening?" Jenny asked.

"A ball somewhere. I've forgotten where," Ada said.

"Not a public one?" Her sister sat back, looking alarmed.

"No, of course not. Mummy would have a fit if I went from being an earl's betrothed to attending a public dance."

"It's a good thing only our family knew of the engagement."

"Why?" Maggie asked, spearing a thick piece of bacon and considering whether it looked too fatty to bother eating.

"If Cam had posted the banns early and then you suddenly showed up in London *sans* fiancé, there would have been no end of speculation. The whispers would be heard from Tower Bridge to Regent's Park. I remember how dreadful it was as a married woman coming to Town without my husband." Jenny shuddered slightly.

"I suppose people would want to know who called it off and why."

"Precisely. It is no one's business but yours and John's." Jenny had a sad sigh to her voice.

"Stop it, please," Maggie ordered. "There's no reason to lament. We rushed into an engagement without knowing each other's foibles sufficiently. I based our relationship on the silly romantic reason of how I felt when he kissed me."

Jenny shook her head. "Mags, don't you dare sound so practical. If you ever base a relationship on anything other than that feeling, then you're a fool."

Maggie couldn't help but smile wryly. "Then I suppose I had best get to kissing a few more bachelors until I discover the feeling again."

Her older sister chuckled, yet Maggie knew Jenny and Simon were remaining firmly behind the hope she and John would still make a good match.

That night, she wore one of her favorite gowns in a becoming shade of lilac, trimmed with cream ribbon and lace. Looking like a true debutante, she was confident no one could guess she'd spent more than one night feeling a man's intimate touch while lying naked in his bed.

Thank God she hadn't lost her virginity. Truthfully, she ought to thank John for not taking it, since she would have given it to him willingly. Then she would be utterly ruined for good society and unable to hold her head up when introduced to a prospective suitor. No man should be deceived into thinking he was getting an innocent bride if he wasn't. At least, Maggie would be able to offer her innocence to whomever became her husband.

A tap on her arm and she turned to see Lord Westing.

"There you are, Miss Blackwood, every inch of you the belle of the ball."

Foolishly, she wanted to hug him for looking the same and behaving the same as if the past few months had never happened.

"Thank you. It is good to see you, too."

"I hear congratulations are in order."

Her heart skipped a beat. *Dear God!*

"You hear?" she repeated, feeling the blood rush from her head.

"Margaret? Are you all right? You look pale. I'm sorry if I spoke out of turn."

She had to know the extent of the damage.

"What have you heard?"

"That you and the Earl of Cambrey are blissfully engaged. However, by the look on your face, I would say I'm off the mark."

"Not so much off the mark as late to the start. We *were* engaged. Briefly. It is over now."

He winced. "I thought . . . that is, I am sorry." And the marquess did look sorry for ever having mentioned it.

"From whom did you hear of it?" She glanced around as if expecting to see all of *the ton* staring back at her. "Does everyone know?"

"I don't believe many people know. Yet. And I thought I was being clever, perhaps even the first to congratulate you. I heard it from my mother, who is friends with Lady Chatley. They returned only recently."

The Chatleys were back in London! Jane's mother was in all likelihood decrying the loss of the eligible earl, snatched out from under her daughter's nose by a veritable nobody. What's more, now Maggie was a nobody who had broken it off. Except no one knew that.

"I must stop Lady Chatley from telling anyone else. Do you think it's possible?"

He looked as doubtful as she felt about containing such juicy gossip.

"I will tell my mother Lady Chatley was in error and ask her to speak with the woman."

Maggie bit her lower lip. *How bad could it get?* she wondered. Jenny seemed to think it would make for an awkward time.

"Forget about it for now." Christopher gave her an encouraging smile. "You are a single, beautiful lady at a ball. Is your card full?"

She held up her empty wrist. "No cards this evening, my lord. Rather a free for all, and I, for one, welcome the change." Or she had, until he'd put a damper on her spirits.

Apparently, though, he was not going to let her wallow.

"A free for all, is it? Then let us get in on the fun and dance, shall we?"

What else could she do? She certainly couldn't stop tongues wagging. Even then, Lady Emily Chatley might be having a glass of sherry somewhere and discussing her stay at Turvey House. Or Christopher's mother might be entertaining a dining room full of guests and sharing the Earl of Cambrey's new status as an engaged man.

Gritting her teeth, Maggie decided to do what her friend said, join the fun and dance. What did it matter if she danced too many times with Christopher or with Lord Burnley or even the pointy-nosed Lord Whitely?

However, she didn't want to kiss any of them. In her heart, she would trade every dance for merely one of John Angsley's heated looks or an enticing lift of his scarred eyebrow. She'd trade an entire social Season for the feel of his lips brushing hers.

Instead of being content with how everything was the same in London, Maggie felt positively hollow. She'd believed herself lonely at the Royal Society event because she hadn't known anyone. But somehow, being with people she knew, and knowing John was not among them, was even worse. Another Season like this, at the same events with the same gentlemen when she'd already made her choice—what made her believe she would prickle with desire over any of them?

Eventually, she would have to settle for the warm, friendly feeling she had with a man like Christopher. Not the worst thing in the world. Having experienced the sizzle of desire, though, she knew she would keenly miss the exciting flutter of butterflies in her stomach every time she was kissed.

"You are sighing," said another partner whose name she'd forgotten. "Do you wish to stop dancing?"

And be known as the girl who walked off the floor in the middle of a polka? An unpredictable, unreliable partner? *Never!* Flicking her glossy curls over her shoulder, she flashed him her best smile.

"Positively not, my lord. I was sighing with happiness."

Not the first lie she had told at a ball, nor likely to be the last.

Toward the end of the evening, sometime after midnight, Maggie saw an unfamiliar face. What's more, the face was staring directly at her. A man about her own age, his fashion perfectly *à la mode*, stood a few yards away, sipping champagne.

If she'd had any doubt he was watching her, it vanished when he nodded in acknowledgment. However, he didn't come closer or try to engage in conversation for the rest of the night.

In fact, Maggie would have forgotten about the incident altogether if she hadn't seen him again a few nights later at another dance.

As she twirled in the capable arms of Lord Burnley, who had never again mentioned their kiss or seemed interested in repeating it, she again saw the stranger, standing on the edge of the dance floor, a grim expression upon his face.

And most assuredly, he was looking at her!

CHAPTER TWENTY-SIX

When the dance was over, Maggie waited with Ada for refreshments. At the same time, she scanned their corner of the ballroom.

There he was. Quite noticeably, he stood apart, neither dancing nor seeming to know anyone.

"Who is that man?" she asked Lord Burnley when he returned with their glasses of lemonade.

Studying the stranger a moment, Burnley shrugged.

"No idea. I'm sure I've never seen him before."

Then he smiled at her. "Are you interested, Miss Blackwood? Even if I don't know him, I can still make an introduction."

Lord Burnley was an affable fellow, who changed his mind weekly about which lady currently had captured his heart. Since he admitted openly to needing one with a vast fortune, Maggie was safe to count him among her platonic acquaintances.

"No," she told him with no uncertainty. "I am not interested. At least, not in that way. Simply curious, I suppose. Aren't you?"

Burnley laughed and signaled for Westing to come over.

"Miss Blackwood, Miss Ellis, and I are wondering who the newcomer might be. Any ideas, Christopher?"

Westing glanced toward the man. "The son of a baron, I hear. First time in society. Keeping to himself. Perhaps he's trying to be a man of mystery to capture the ladies' attention. Apparently, it's working," he finished, looking at Maggie.

"No, it's not. Not on me, anyway. He merely seems a little rude. Maybe he doesn't know any better."

She thought no more of it. Especially when two other people offered her congratulations on her engagement to the Earl of Cambrey, and she didn't gainsay them. Glad the gossip was still at a trickle, she simply accepted their felicitations with what she hoped was a smile rather than a grimace.

By the time she and Ada had danced their slippers nearly to shreds hours later and were ready to leave, Maggie was surprised to find the stranger suddenly near her again.

Deciding to grasp the nettle, she was about to wave him over when he approached of his own accord.

"Miss Blackwood," he greeted her, his accent betraying him as hailing from the north. "You know who I am?" she asked, realizing it was a ridiculous question even as she asked it.

"Obviously."

He spoke as rudely as he behaved.

"May I know how?" she asked.

An unreadable expression crossed his face, which she would consider handsome if he didn't look so serious. His was the demeanor for a funeral or an execution. Hardly suitable for a London ball.

"Doesn't everyone know you?" he asked.

For a moment she thought he was going to add, "as the Earl of Cambrey's fiancée." What other notoriety might she have?

"No, I don't believe they do," she pressed.

He laughed softly, although she knew it was not from good humor.

"You are mistaken, Miss Blackwood. You are known as the Earl of Lindsey's stunning sister-in-law, who had, until recently, taken the Season by storm and then faded for a few months from the social scene. Congratulations to your sister and her husband on their child."

"Thank you." Maggie thought this the oddest conversation, with him having such intimate knowledge of her family and her knowing nothing about him.

Suddenly, Ada was at her side. "Papa said the carriage is waiting. Are you ready?"

"Yes," Maggie said, despite the evening having become more interesting in the last few minutes. "I would introduce you, however, I don't know this gentleman's name."

Ada glanced at her friend's tall companion who bowed slightly.

"My name is Philip Carruthers. I won't keep you ladies from your departure."

With another bow, he disappeared into the throng.

"A little unusual," Ada said, standing on tiptoe to peer after him. "Rather dashing, though."

The next morning as Maggie sipped tea while her mother read the papers, she remembered where she'd heard the name before. At least part of it.

Robert Carruthers was the man in the other carriage, the one who was killed. Maggie was certain of it. Moreover, Grayson had mentioned a twin brother. She shivered. An unlikely coincidence, yet it explained the man's melancholy manner, which she had mistaken for rudeness. What did the brother want with her?

Not one to pussyfoot around, she would ask him at her very next opportunity.

Cam realized this wasn't going to be easy, not the standing or the walking. Definitely not the dancing, although he was determined to do all three when he next encountered Margaret.

He had dreamt of her face and could imagine the look upon it when she saw him stride into one of London's ballrooms, bow to her, and sweep her into a waltz.

He only hoped his weak leg didn't slide out from under him on the parquet and leave him sprawled at her feet. Not the worst place in the world, he supposed. Plus, the view!

No, the worst place for Cam was riding in a carriage from Bedfordshire to Town. They had to stop every few hours to let him walk around. The cramping was terrible. After months of sedentary behavior, now he'd started walking again, his muscles demanded activity. Over the previous weeks, he'd walked every foot of Turvey House, including going up and down the stairs a hundred times a day, and then he'd walked around its grounds, too. He'd progressed to skipping like a child to work his muscles even harder, and then put on the clothes he used to wear for an afternoon at one of London's pugilist clubs, and he'd run around the acreage, looking more than half a fool.

He didn't care. He was free to move at last.

Doctor Adams, who'd made the trip to Bedfordshire to remove the cast, had proclaimed his bones to be healed. His leg muscles, of course, had succumbed to mild atrophy, which Cam had worked like the devil to remedy.

Before the cast had come off, Cam spent hours lifting flour sacks while sitting on the veranda, exactly as Margaret had suggested. He'd even prepared for his freedom by exercising his good leg as much as possible.

After weeks of strengthening his limbs, Cam and his mother sped toward London. Thank God he hadn't wasted time going north to Sheffield seeking Margaret at Belton Manor. After a letter to Simon addressed to the manor had been routed by Lord Lindsey's staff to Town, Cam had received a reply from his best friend—all the Deveres and the Blackwoods were once again in England's fair capital.

Cam was ready—and now able—to go down on bended knee to the woman he loved. However, since it was after dinner when they reached London, the proposal would have to wait. Besides, he planned to have a ring this time. He'd had plenty of opportunity to think about it, and he envisioned presenting her with something dazzling enough to match her beauty.

"I don't know why you can't give her my mother's ring," Lady Cambrey said the next morning when they were on their way to Hatton Garden, where the best jewelers plied their trade.

"Because Grandmother's ring is ugly," Cam said. And that was that. He wanted to see Margaret's face light up with pleasure, not polite acceptance.

An hour later, after strolling the street filled with goldsmiths and diamond merchants, Cam found what he was looking for at Mayer and Sons. In the well-lit store, where everything glittered to the point of nearly giving him a headache, he didn't go for a snake ring such as Victoria and Albert had made popular. Too trite for his Margaret.

Then he saw it, a cobalt-blue sapphire encircled with tiny pearls and sparkling diamonds. It was magnificent. As they were leaving, he spied a serpentine bracelet with sapphire eyes and purchased it as well, knowing how the ladies of his acquaintance admired this symbol of eternal love. If all went well, he would have many other occasions on which to present it to Margaret.

Pleased with his choice, he simply had to plan the big event, glad he had his mother with whom to discuss ideas. They'd already decided not to rush over to Portman Square and surprise the love of his life. He wanted something grander.

"Do you think she will like my second proposal taking place in public?"

Lady Cambrey smiled. "I think there is not a woman alive who doesn't wish to have her gentleman declare openly for her and make her the center of attention. Especially tonight at the Duchess of Sutherland's ball. Everyone will be there. Everyone!"

His mother seemed almost as excited as he felt. Thank goodness she held no grudge against Margaret for breaking the engagement the first time. He wanted the two ladies in his life to get along well.

MAGGIE LET THE MAID work on her for hours as soon as the sun went down. For this night was not a humdrum event. This was a ball at Stafford House, the premiere townhouse in London, situated next to St. James Palace. Even Simon and Jenny were deigning to go out in society and leave little Lionel at home with Anne Blackwood. For the first time, she would see the grand, bifurcated staircase and the three-story ceiling in the foyer, the magnificent Corinthian columns, and more marble than she might ever see again.

Moreover, the queen, who was special friends with the Duchess of Sutherland, might make an appearance. Everyone loved to see Victoria, and any ball she attended became instantly successful and, of course, utterly majestic.

Maggie wore a blue gown, all satin and lace and seed pearls, thanking the heavens for having a wealthy brother-in-law, allowing her to own such a creation. More pearls and a single blue feather adorned her hair, which was up in a braided, swirling bun, with enough ringlets to soften her appearance.

"I am escorting two exquisite jewels," Simon announced as they entered the Sutherland mansion and looked up to the grand, double staircase that funneled the multitude upward both to the left and to the right. "An emerald and a sapphire."

Jenny, dressed in a rich shade of green, responded by smacking his shoulder with her fan. "We are not objects for men to admire."

"Speak for yourself, dear sister," Maggie said. "You are a countess while I am in danger of being shelved. If men wish to admire me and call me a jewel, they are welcome to do so."

Along with Jenny, she dispensed with her cloak and street shoes. Adorned in her satin dancing slippers, she was ready to enjoy the evening.

Climbing the enormous staircase to the second-floor ballroom, Maggie wondered how she would ever find her friend in the mass of hundreds. Grabbing a glass of champagne from a passing waiter, she gave up skirting the throng and dove into the middle.

Familiar friendly faces, acquaintances, and strangers, all blended. At one end of the cavernous ballroom, musicians were already playing, and Maggie knew there was a clear space for dancing, if she could only reach it. Also, somewhere, there would be a dais where the Duchess of Sutherland and her handsome husband, Duke George as his wife called him, would be in all their finery.

It was also where Queen Victoria would sit when she arrived, with or without Prince Albert. One never knew if the prince consort would make an appearance, but it didn't matter. People wanted to see their queen.

An hour later, Maggie was breathless, having danced three dances with strangers, and still no sign of—

"Ada," she called out as her blonde friend appeared for a moment and then disappeared again between two couples.

"Drat!" Maggie exclaimed and set off after her at an unladylike trot. However, as she pushed between the wall of well-dressed partygoers and scanned the people before her, she sighed. *Where had Ada got to?*

"Miss Blackwood," said a voice at her elbow.

It was him. In all of these people, Philip Carruthers was beside her.

"What a coincidence!" she intoned.

"Hardly that." His expression was a little less severe this evening. Once again, he was dressed impeccably.

Yes, she noted, he was a dashing man, exactly as Ada had remarked.

Taking her hand, he bent over it as any gentleman would, but then he brushed his lips over her gloved knuckles, and she could feel his warm breath through the satin.

Staring, Maggie slowly drew her hand back.

"How so, not a coincidence? I've been searching for my friend for ages and have not yet managed to find her. In fact, I was on her trail when you appeared."

"I did not intend to spend the evening looking for you. I waited by the front door until you arrived and have kept my eyes on you ever since."

"Oh." How expedient of him. Jenny would approve of such a practical method. Absolutely more effective than what she had accomplished.

"Why have you been keeping watch over me?"

"Besides the obvious reason of you being the most beautiful lady here?"

"I don't take kindly to empty flattery, sir." Maggie tried to sound stern. Then she gave him her practiced smile, adding a dash of coyness. "Indisputably, there is at least one here who might best me."

To her amazement, she managed to wipe away his stern countenance. He laughed, and when he did, he looked a different man altogether. In that instant, he reminded her of John.

John! Was he even then languishing in Bedfordshire? Would he still think her a terrible nag if he could see her dancing and chatting with ... *oh dear*, the brother of the dead man! She must focus, despite the champagne, the glowing lights, and everyone's contagious gaiety.

"Are you titled? I'm sorry, but I don't know how to address you."

Rather than telling her his status, he said, "You may call me Philip."

"Fine, but you may not call me Margaret."

"Understood. I suppose you are curious as to why I keep popping up."

She must be frank with him. "I know who you are."

Instead of appearing surprised, he simply nodded, although she noticed his jaw had clenched.

"And yes, I am curious," Maggie admitted. "What can you possibly want from me?"

Snagging two glasses off a passing tray, he handed one to her, tapped the rim with his own, and drank down the champagne in two gulps. Then he looked at her, a slight frown on his face.

"Honestly?"

Sipping from her own glass, she looked him directly in the eyes, startled to realize they were practically black. "Of course."

"You know who I am, meaning you know who my brother was. Correct?"

"Yes."

"After Robert died so carelessly, and out of character for him, if I may say, I wanted to find out everything about the accident. It wasn't hard to learn what happened to the Earl of Cambrey. I thought to write to him, I suppose to apologize, but words failed me. Besides, I found I couldn't apologize when my brother lost his life."

"I know Lord Cambrey was most unhappy to learn of your family's dreadful loss. Moreover, I don't believe he expected an apology. His injuries are temporary, after all."

Or at least some were. For all she knew, John was even then taking more opium, suffering from a painful stomach and worse maladies because of it.

"Be that as it may," Philip said, "I considered whether to approach you when I realized who you are—"

"Who am I? To you, I mean?" For he couldn't know of her love for John or their brief engagement.

"By chance, I discovered your family and his family were very close through the Lindsey side. I saw you arrive with the Earl and Countess of Lindsey, and I know he is Lord Cambrey's closest friend. However, you left London at the time of the accident."

"Quite by chance," Maggie told him, thinking of the long and hurried carriage ride to reach Jenny before the baby was born. "I still don't understand what you want from me."

"As it turns out," he began, then paused. His dark eyes took her in from the blue feather in her coiffure down to the hem of her dress, then back to her face, piercing her with his gaze.

"As it turns out, Miss Blackwood, I want nothing from you. I was in a bad state at first. Robert was not only my brother, he was my twin. You have siblings and undeniably understand the bond. But he and I were even closer. His death was like losing my arm, or some would say, more like half my brain."

"My condolences again." She wouldn't mention his brother was ostensibly driving like a madman.

He nodded, but it was a dismissive gesture. Undoubtedly, her sympathetic words could mean nothing to him, nor touch the pain he felt.

"I wondered for a while whether some reparation was due."

She puzzled at his words. "You mean toward Lord Cambrey for his injuries?"

"No. Toward me and my family for our loss. As I said, I was in a bad state." He leaned closer, until she could see her own reflection in his obsidian eyes. "I meant vengeance, Miss Blackwood, for the irrational rage I felt toward the earl."

She raised her eyebrows in alarm. "Oh!"

Then it dawned on her. "You sought your revenge through me?"

"An eye for an eye, or in this case, for the pain of losing someone."

Her hand fluttered toward her throat, and looking around, she made sure she was still surrounded by hundreds who could help her.

"You thought to kill me?" *Was he insane?*

His own brows rose. "Dear God, no! My ill-conceived plan was to ruin you after having learned you and the earl had a special friendship."

Is that what people had concluded? That she and John had a close friendship, such as the one he had with Jane Chatley?

"How monstrous!" she proclaimed. "Lord Cambrey has suffered enough, I can assure you."

"Understood. Besides, I didn't really have the heart for it," Philip admitted. "Even less so after meeting you the other night."

Falling silent, he too glanced around at their impressive surroundings.

"Despite mourning still, I find I would prefer to dance with you than ruin you. Flattery or not, you are truly a beautiful woman, and we are at what might prove to be the event of the Season."

Maggie's head was spinning. He'd had nefarious plans for her, yet confessed them. Now he merely wanted to dance. Could she believe him?

Would a dance with him be any more satisfying than any of the others she'd had since returning to London? The only partner she desired on or off the dance floor was John, and his were the only hands she wanted touching her.

John was miles and days away, though, and she was there with a man who was hurting.

"All right, let us dance." And Maggie allowed the tall, dark-eyed stranger to lead her onto the polished floor.

CHAPTER TWENTY-SEVEN

Cam had spent an hour searching when he finally found Simon and Jenny. Both ahead of him and in his wake, the buzz of his return was on everyone's lips. As people parted before him and he reached the Deveres' table at last, his best friend's eyes bulged from his head.

Simon rose to his feet, and Jenny smiled with delight.

However, dear as these two people were to him, they were not the one he had come there to see.

"Where is Margaret?" Cam asked without preamble.

"Good evening to you, too." Simon, recovering from his surprise, wore a boyish grin on his face and draped an arm around his lovely wife. Jenny also stared at him as if he had appeared out of the ether.

Cam sighed. "Sorry. Good evening," he returned to Simon, then to Jenny, he said, "You are a vision in green, a veritable goddess."

"Sit," Simon invited him.

Cam shook his head. "I've been here for ages and—"

"Good to see you, ol' boy," came a voice from behind, right before he felt the now-familiar, hard slap on his back. "So, you're all mended, are you?"

Turning, he greeted yet another acquaintance, this time a fellow member of Parliament.

"Yes, thank you, David. Much better."

Satisfied, the man walked away.

"And *that* keeps happening. I swear, I've been struck more tonight than ever in my life."

"Lord Anguish! You're alive," exclaimed another well-wisher before he, too, slapped his shoulder with hearty cheer before disappearing into the crowd.

"What did he call you?" Simon asked, his eyes dancing with merriment.

"Never mind. Where is *she*?"

It was Jenny who spoke. "She is dancing, as far as we know. We haven't seen her in ages."

Sighing, Cam surveyed the crush of people once again. "I may never find her. What a ridiculous place for a ball!"

Simon laughed. "Most would disagree. You're grumpy for a man who looks to be completely healed."

Cam shrugged. "If you see Margaret before I do, tell her I'll come back to your table each half hour. That way, I'm sure to run into her eventually."

"She's clad in blue," Jenny called after him as he dove back into the crowd.

Blue! Of course, her favorite color, and his when it was on her. However, the information barely helped, since it was apparently a popular color with the *ton* this year.

And then the murmuring which had followed him all night became a distinctly louder chatter, and he knew it was not *his* appearance anymore spurring it, but someone far more important.

"The queen, the queen," he heard from every quarter. Victoria had arrived.

Would Margaret head toward the dais he'd already seen twice on his hunt for the woman he loved? There, the regal Duchess of Sutherland was holding her own small court.

Letting the surge push him forward, he got as close to the dais as he could, near enough to see their diminutive queen with her brown hair piled on her head and her round cheeks slightly rouged for the occasion.

"God protect her," he whispered under his breath, and then began his search once more in earnest.

MAGGIE HADN'T LAUGHED SO much in months. Despite Philip being in mourning, he managed a steady stream of witty remarks, which, as if he were a skilled bowman, hit their targets perfectly. Whether he spoke regarding an older lady with a startling amount of face powder—*"She ought to apply to the plasterer's guild"*—or a dandified gentleman with an hourglass figure—*"He's got the tightest corset at Stafford House tonight"*—Philip had a cutting quip.

Suddenly, the babbling of conversation swelled until she could hardly hear her witty dance partner. From his higher vantage point, Philip scanned the room. Then leaning down, his mouth close to her ear, he told her the reason.

"The queen has arrived."

Maggie's heart thumped. "Do you think there's any way to see her? I know it sounds terribly plebian of me, but I don't remember a thing about meeting her when presented at the palace during my first Season. I think I had my eyes closed. I swear, I was shaking so badly, I could hardly walk, and I believe I slobbered over her hand."

Her words brought a slight smile to her companion's otherwise austere face.

"We can head in that direction if you wish."

To Maggie's delight, she did see Victoria in all her regality, complete with a glittering tiara and a royal blue sash over her dove-grey silk gown. It was enough simply to catch a glimpse of Her Majesty looking happy, standing on the dais beside the pretty duchess.

"Are you content?" Philip asked.

Maggie grinned and took his arm as they stepped aside, making way for others who were eagerly pushing forward to see the queen.

"I am. Do you think she noticed me when I curtsied?"

"If you drooled upon her hand once, in all likelihood, she remembered you. In truth, I think she said to the duchess, 'We are happy to see young Miss Blackwood with the overly active spittle.'"

Maggie dissolved in laughter, then saw an expression cross Philip's face that made her insides tighten.

She wasn't ready to begin again. Was she? Her heart was still full of John and aching for him. But Jenny had reminded her not to settle for less than a man who made her tingle with a special sensation. And it all started with a kiss.

As if she'd conjured her sister with her thoughts, Maggie suddenly saw Simon and Jenny mere yards away. Unfortunately, with the crowd surging between them, they were impossible to reach.

"Jenny," she called, and was rewarded when her sister turned. With an excited look, Jenny grabbed Simon's arm before waving and gesturing at Maggie.

"There's my sister," she told Philip, whose arm she still held. Looking again, she realized Jenny appeared to be mouthing some words.

"Whatever is she trying to tell me?"

Philip peered in the same direction. "It looks to me as if she said someone is here."

"Oh," Maggie said. "Of course, the queen. They must be going to see her."

"Shall I escort you back to your table?" He hesitated, catching her gaze with his. "Or perhaps you'd care to leave this crush a moment and take a stroll in the gallery."

She pondered a moment. This was most certainly *not* her first ball. A stroll meant one thing, as far as she had experienced. Back to the safety of the Devere table or . . . a stroll?

"It will take my sister and brother-in-law a good half hour to see the queen and get back to our table." She blinked up into the face of this stranger. "Yes, let's go see the gallery."

Turning back, she waved again to her sister and then let Philip lead her to the closest door.

As soon as she set foot upon the thick, red-carpet runner, which stretched endlessly along the main upper hall of Stafford House, Maggie knew she was doing the wrong thing.

This man was grieving, as was she, although for different reasons. *What good could come of this?* For all she knew, he had confessed his plan to ruin her so she would drop her guard. She might be playing into his wicked plans at that very moment.

Sighing, her step didn't falter. When had knowing the right path ever stopped her from taking the wrong one? Wasn't she supposed to find sizzle with another man? Or should she pine for John the rest of her life?

As expected, they walked only as far as an arched and shadowy alcove with columns standing on either side as sentinels. Philip stopped and turned to face her.

Taking both her hands, he backed her nearly into the vase perched on a pedestal, the only object in the deeply recessed nook. As he did, she felt the porcelain wobble and tap her back before it settled back into place.

Gracious! Any vase on display and owned by the Duke and Duchess of Sutherland must be worth more than her family's entire cottage in Sheffield.

"Take care," she murmured as her new acquaintance stepped closer.

His actions, both predictable and expected, didn't cause her even a tremor of fear. Rather, she worried at her own blasé acceptance of what would occur. Philip would kiss her, and she would feel nothing more than mild curiosity.

"You just sighed," he told her.

"My apologies. Proceed." Maggie closed her eyes and tilted her head.

She waited. Nothing. Peering through one raised lid, she saw his surprised expression.

"Well?" she demanded.

Releasing her hands, he ran one of his own through his hair, messing it up terribly, and then raised the other to the wall to lean upon it.

"You definitely make it tough on a man."

"Whatever can you mean? I'm making it easy."

"Too easy. You seem about as interested as if I were about to shine your shoes."

Smiling, she reminded him her satin slippers needed no polish.

Suddenly, they heard voices and footsteps. A small group of partygoers had left the ballroom and were traversing the hallway.

How could they hide?

To her surprise, Philip leaned closer, one arm snaking around her to press her against his body and shield her from their sight.

Betraying their high spirits and probably too much champagne, a few passers-by whistled. One said, *"Huzzah, huzzah!"* And then, they were gone.

Philip looked down into her face, his eyes wide with alarm.

Against all decorum, Maggie giggled. After all, he had threatened the ruin of her reputation. Instead, he had protected it.

"We're not going to kiss, are we?" Philip asked.

"No, you're bloody well not," came a familiar voice.

Impossible. It couldn't be!

Pushing Philip aside, Maggie faced John Angsley in high dudgeon by the look of his thunderous expression.

"In fact," John added, his tone like ice, "you won't even be standing in a minute."

With one arm, John tried to sweep her out of the way, while he drew his other back, ready to deliver a five-fingered missive to Philip's face.

Oh dear!

"No, don't," Maggie cried, struggling against the strength in her former fiancé's arm as she tried to get between them.

With Margaret's hands wrapped tightly around his left arm and her warm breasts pushed against him as she struggled, Cam could hardly keep his attention on the knave who had tried for an ill-timed tryst. With *his* woman!

Who was this audacious stranger, standing with legs slightly apart, his arms at his sides, braced and apparently willing to take the blow?

It was the other man's stance and attitude more than Margaret's entreaty which caused Cam to hesitate.

"Are you going to defend yourself?" he demanded.

"No," the blighter responded. "Are you going to harm the woman?"

"What? Of course not! How dare you?"

For that remark, Cam felt the urge to hit him rise up again.

"John, you are here, in London!" Maggie exclaimed. "You're standing and walking!"

She sounded pleased, but it didn't take the sting out of catching her with another man.

Particularly when the man chuckled. "I've noticed a tendency in Miss Blackwood to state the obvious."

Cam saw red. Had this smug toad truly spent enough time with *his* Margaret to offer an opinion on her behavior one way or the other? His hand fisted once more.

"I have never noticed any such inclination. Possibly you are so extremely dull, sir, there is nothing else for her to comment upon except your apparent tediousness."

Margaret had succeeded in stepping entirely in front of him. Standing extremely close, radiating warmth, her spectacular smile in place despite their situation, her sparkling eyes gazed up at him.

"How did you find me?" Her soft voice threaded through his anger.

"I encountered Simon and Jenny near the queen's dais, where I thought you might be. Your sister said she'd seen you leave the ballroom with this mutton-headed blackguard."

"Rather harsh," the stranger said.

At last, taking her eyes off him, Margaret turned to the man who still stood too close behind her.

"Perhaps you'd best leave us alone."

The man's gaze went from her to Cam and back again. "Don't you want to introduce me to his lordship?"

Margaret seemed hesitant. That worried Cam. *Were they a couple? Was he too late?*

"What's going on?" he ground out, keeping his eyes on her. Her answer might mean his happiness or his abject misery.

Watching her worry her lower lip with her teeth, Cam felt a spike of desire. He had almost forgotten how her nearness affected him, but it was hardly the time. What if this man was her new paramour? What if Cam had incited her passions with all their nighttime encounters, only to have her seek relief at the hands of another?

At last, she shrugged. "John, this is Philip *Carruthers*. You may remember his brother—"

"His brother died on Oxford Street," Cam finished for her, all his attention now on the stranger. This unexpected turn evoked the terrible day clearly, particularly the moment when he'd seen the driver's panicked expression.

Despite the months of agony this man's twin, Robert, had caused him, Cam felt all the fight instantly drain away. Except . . . why was he bothering Margaret?

"How do you know each other?" His voice sounded too loud to his own ears.

"We don't," Margaret said quickly. "I only met him the other night, and then he, well . . . ," she trailed off and looked over her shoulder again.

"I approached her tonight to tell her who I was. Beyond that, there is nothing between us. I understand you were gravely injured. I offer my apology on behalf of my family."

Cam swallowed the last vestiges of anger.

"You lost your brother. I am sure it is difficult to tender an apology to me, but I assure you, it is accepted. I am sorry for your loss. Senseless, as it was."

The man stiffened.

"On that we agree, Lord Cambrey. Utterly senseless."

Carruthers turned to Margaret. "It was a pleasure meeting you, Miss Blackwood, and I thank you for the dance and for lifting my humor somewhat these past few hours."

She nodded.

Then he addressed Cam. "I'm glad we met. It makes it easier somehow."

Then, with nary a backward glance, the man strode away.

"Poor man," Margaret murmured, drawing Cam's focus.

"Were you really going to let him kiss you?"

She sighed. "Is it important?"

Was it? Yes. No. He didn't know.

"How many men have you kissed since we parted?"

"Since the day you called me a nag whom you had no wish to marry?"

Had he really? That wasn't how he remembered it, but he had been under the influence of more than a little opium.

"I apologize. I wasn't myself, as you know. I am now, by the way."

He was rewarded with her smile.

"I can see it," she said, her gaze locked on his. "Yes, I can see it in your eyes."

Reaching up, she traced her fingers along the thin white scars at his temple. "You look very fine, indeed. And how is your leg?"

In answer, he took her in his arms and proceeded to waltz her down the corridor, enjoying her lilting laugh as her skirts swished around his legs, once again strong and stable.

Feeling her warmth beneath his hands, Cam's heart swelled. Pausing, he bent low and swiftly claimed her lips, but when he straightened and looked down at her, her eyes were still closed and—*what the hell?*—a few tears leaked out to trail down her face.

"Margaret?" he asked, unsure of her thoughts.

Her beautiful gold-flecked eyes flew open. Dashing her tears away with the back of her hand, she stared up at him.

"Kiss me again!"

Relief flooded him, and he obeyed her. Slowly this time, Cam lowered his mouth to join with hers.

Almost at once, it wasn't enough, and, with a groan, he backed her against the wall for anyone who happened upon them to see. With a hand pressed on either side of her head, he continued the kiss, slanting his head, pressing his tongue to her lips until she welcomed him inside with a sigh. Bowing his tall body, he couldn't help but push his hips to hers, relishing the way she arched against him.

She made a soft sound which drove him wild. The queen of the British Empire was a mere few yards away, the most powerful woman in the world. Yet, it was Miss Margaret Blackwood who was the queen of all Cam was and would ever be. With a small sound, she could bring him to his knees.

When they broke apart, both taking lungfuls of air, she reached up and held his face.

"Yes, in truth, I would have let him kiss me," she began, her words cutting him like a sword. "Only because I was going to start searching for our sizzle."

"Our sizzle is ours alone," he reminded her. "I've never felt anything like it before."

"I know. And, no, I haven't kissed another since you made me yours at Turvey House." She blushed at her own words, offering him the vivid memory of her sprawled beside him, completely naked and looking sated.

He wanted the very same again, and soon.

"You can kiss a hundred men," he said, making her eyes widen, "and you will never find one who loves you as I do."

Now was the time to confess. "You were right about opium. It *was* killing me, I think. For I can't believe anything that put me in such agony of mind and body could have been good for me. It was the devil's own work to stop taking it, but I did. I'm glad you weren't there to see me."

Margaret nodded before standing on tiptoe and planting her own brand of kiss upon his lips.

Afterward, reaching for her hand, he tucked it in his and escorted her along the hallway. Just before they passed through the large double doors back into the ballroom, she held his arm, halting him.

"Are we a couple again? Are we engaged?"

"No," he told her in no uncertain terms. "We are most definitely not."

CHAPTER TWENTY-EIGHT

Maggie felt as if the floor had fallen out from under her. What could John mean? They had kissed as passionately as ever. *The sizzle!* It was there in obvious abundance, practically making her melt.

Trying to speak with him in the loud, echoing room, she couldn't, not while he continued to drag her along, her gloved hand firmly clasped in his own.

Pushing through couples and groups, he finally halted on the shiny parquet and brought her around to face him.

"What are you doing?" she hissed, embarrassed at the rude way he'd been shoving dancers aside.

"Hear ye, hear ye," John said in a loud voice, causing people around them to quiet, and then those beyond also to fall silent, which rippled outward until the entire room seemed to hush.

Maggie opened her mouth, mortified. *What was he up to?*

The musicians, perhaps startled by finally being able to hear themselves play after so many hours in the noisy room, hit a few loud notes and stopped.

The only sound was the duchess on the dais speaking animatedly to Queen Victoria. Or at least, Maggie assumed it was Her Grace's voice she could hear over the loud beating of her heart.

And then, to her astonishment, the unmistakable voice of the queen.

"Lord Cambrey! What do you think you are doing, interrupting our lovely gathering?"

Gasps were heard throughout the room, and dancers moved aside until Maggie found herself in direct view of those on the dais.

Since Queen Victoria was looking in her direction, Maggie dropped into a low curtsey, and head bowed, she remained that way, gaze fixed upon the floor.

"Your Majesty," she heard John say, "I apologize for the interruption. And to you, as well, Your Grace," he added to the Duchess. "However, there was a time when noblemen could not marry without permission of the crown. Since you are here, Your Majesty, and since I love this woman you see before you, I thought it the perfect time to ask her to marry me and to gain your blessing."

Don't faint! Maggie counseled herself. *Do not!*

"Who is this lucky woman?" the queen asked. "Is she the one? That girl in blue?"

"This is Miss Margaret Blackwood," John said loudly. "The middle daughter of the late Baron Lucien Blackwood and Lady Anne Blackwood."

"Rise, Miss Blackwood," Queen Victoria commanded, and Maggie thought she would be ill from nerves and disgrace herself.

Breathing deeply, she slowly raised her gaze to their queen and stood straight. At thirty-one years, Victoria had already mothered six children, but to Maggie, she still looked like a young lady.

In her mind, she recalled Philip Carruthers ridiculous words that the queen might remember her for slobbering upon her glove, and the notion relaxed her.

For a long, few moments, the queen took Maggie's measure in the silence of the ballroom. Somewhere, Maggie knew her sister was watching this spectacle.

Lord, but they would have something to tell their mother tonight.

"Do you love Lord Cambrey?" the queen's voice rang out clearly.

Maggie glanced once at John, who stood beside her not looking at all nervous. His bemused expression gave her courage.

"Yes," she began, but it came out in the mildest of whispers. Swallowing, she coughed lightly and then found her voice.

"Yes, Your Majesty. I do."

"And why not?" Victoria said, causing a few to chuckle. "Fine gentleman that he is. We heard of your accident and are relieved to see you looking well."

"Thank you, Your Majesty. I am quite mended."

"Then ask her," the queen prompted. "We are waiting. And mind you, do it properly."

"Yes, Your Majesty."

Turning toward her, John took her hands, and at the same time, went down on bended knee.

Those close enough to see gave another collective gasp.

"I will not make this long so as not to further inconvenience either Her Majesty or Her Grace's other guests. In any case, to tell you how greatly I admire you would last at least until dawn. Tonight, I will merely say, I love you."

With his beloved hazel eyes, he gazed up at her. "And ask if you will do me the honor of marrying me and letting me give you my name."

"Here, here," some gentleman called out.

"Hush," said Queen Victoria. "Let the lady answer."

Maggie fought the tears and won. Time later to weep with happiness when it wouldn't make her appear ugly and hysterical in front of the queen and half the *ton*.

"Yes, my lord," was all she could manage.

"Huzzah!" called out another. "Bravo!"

"Wait," John said as the crowd started to murmur and move.

Releasing her hands, he stood up and began digging in his pockets. After a moment, he pulled out a small black velvet bag, which was closed with a satin drawstring. Opening it, he turned it upside down, letting the contents fall onto his palm.

It was Maggie's turn to gasp as she saw what he held.

"Remove your glove, please," he asked her.

Never taking her gaze from his, she stripped the glove from her left hand, even while feeling as if she were undressing in public.

Holding the ring up a moment to catch the light, causing another wave of murmurs from the onlookers, John took her hand again and slipped the ring upon her finger.

There was a moment of silence.

"*Now*, you may cheer," he told the crowd, and they did.

"Well done," Maggie thought she heard Queen Victoria say, and then suddenly, Jenny was crashing into her. They hugged. Simon shook John's hand, and then they made their way back to the table.

It took over an hour, what with people congratulating them and others exclaiming over John's triumphant reappearance.

"Champagne is in order." Simon said as he snagged an entire tray from a passing servant and placed it on their table.

"Champagne is always in order," John said, "but I suppose especially tonight." He winked at her, such a small gesture, but it filled her with joy.

"It was an excellent display," Jenny said, raising her glass. "You did yourself proud, and you certainly did my wonderful sister justice. I am overjoyed for you both."

Maggie still felt dazed at the rapid turn of events. Holding champagne in one hand, she glanced down at the ring on her other.

LORD ANGUISH

"Isn't it the most beautiful thing you've ever seen?"

John was staring at her. "Not even close, my love."

NO ONE MINDED WHEN the Earl of Cambrey decided to hold a small, intimate wedding at the chapel adjacent to his property. After all, how could a London wedding, no matter how grand, top the very public and celebrated engagement attended by hundreds including Her Majesty?

With his bride's family staying at his house, Cam hoped Margaret wouldn't feel embarrassed when he whisked her upstairs early on their wedding night. Actually, he found he didn't care much what his new in-laws thought. He'd waited long enough to claim his countess.

Her eyes were sparkling with the excitement of the day.

"Everything was perfect," she said, as he started to undress her before the fireplace, which he'd ordered duly stoked to make the room warm enough for being naked.

"Yes," he agreed, working on the pearl buttons down her back.

"The ceremony, the weather. My sisters were beautiful. Your mother made me cry with happiness with her toast. And the food. What a glorious meal."

As she rambled on, he managed to divest her of her cream-colored gown, laced with blue ribbon, and started in on her corset.

"Oh, thank you," she said as he loosened her stays and then dropped it on the ground. "I think Tilda tightened it a wee bit too much for the occasion. I could hardly breathe."

"You seem to be breathing just fine."

"What?" Then she laughed. "Oh, because I'm talking too much, is that it?"

"No. I love the sound of your voice." He thought of how he'd called her a nag, a scold. *Never again.* "Your voice is lilting, like beautiful music. I never want a day to go by without hearing you speak."

She turned in his arms, standing now in only her shift.

"I'm very glad to be back here in your room."

"*Our* room," he reminded her.

"Yes!"

As he reached for her, she danced out of his reach and, to his amazement, she hurled herself into the center of the bed. Like a child. And yet, not at all like one.

True, she was eight-and-a-half-years younger than he, as he had learned, but she was all grown up. She had been wiser than him with her understanding of the addiction that had such a firm hold of him. If not for her . . .

"It is a most comfortable mattress," she declared, sitting in the center of it. Her shift had fallen askew, baring one of her pale shoulders, and the sight alone inflamed him. Thank God he already knew her to be a passionate creature, or this night would go very differently.

He'd already removed his jacket. Hastily unfastening his collar, cuffs, and shirt, he tossed them all onto a nearby chair. When he looked at her again, she'd grown silent, staring at him, but her expression was one of anticipation, not fear.

Truly, her undone hair hanging wantonly across her shoulders, her nearly transparent shift, and her slightly parted lips caused a feeling of reverence to course through him, nearly as strong as his passion.

Radiating desire, she held her hands out to him, and he finished undressing swiftly.

"I've seen you bare before, Lord Cambrey, but never like this."

"You mean standing?" he joked, enjoying her gaze wandering over his body and imagining her fingers doing the same.

She smiled. "You are magnificent, my husband. Whether lying or standing. Right now, I would like you to join me in our bed."

Needing no further invitation, he walked toward her, knowing his yard was at full attention because even his sacks felt tight. It would be difficult to last long for their first time. But if he didn't, he would make it up to her with many more times after that.

Crawling onto the bed, he took her face in his hands and kissed her, a long and thorough kiss which had him throbbing and her breathing heavily.

"May I remove your shift?"

In answer, she raised her arms and let him pull it over her head. When he chucked it behind him, she laughed.

"You're not afraid." Gently, he cupped her breasts, playing her nipples with his thumbs, watching with fascination as they hardened.

"Not even a little," she vowed.

He looked her in the eyes while continuing to caress her. "It might hurt for a moment," he told her.

Shrugging, she mimicked his movements, her fingers running over his chest, playing with his nipples in such a way as to drive him wild.

"A moment's physical discomfort is nothing really," she said.

She was right, and he would make sure she felt much more pleasure than pain.

To that end, he lowered her to the mattress, taking time to spread her hair out around her so it didn't get caught under her back.

"How thoughtful of you," she told him, taking hold of his erect staff.

"And now there isn't a thought in my head," he said, groaning as she clasped him tightly.

"Shall I stop?" She was grinning at him.

"God, no!"

While she stroked him, he traced his fingers across her smooth skin, marveling at the woman before him. He caressed the line of her collarbone, so elegant, then up and over the swell of each breast, then down her stomach and across her hip bones, causing her to shiver.

Through it all, they remained silent, simply looking at each other.

Finally, he stroked between her womanly folds, where she was sweetly damp and plainly ready for him.

She froze. "I can't seem to focus on what I'm doing when you—"

He stroked her again.

"Yes, that."

She said nothing else, and he didn't even mind when her hand fell away from his shaft to grasp the sheets, her other hand doing the same.

Splayed before him, her eyes closed, head already arched back, legs spread, Margaret was the epitome of everything sensual. And by some miracle, she was his.

Fitting the head of his shaft to her opening, he leaned down to kiss her breasts, sucking a nipple as he inched inside her.

Before he even penetrated her barrier, she lifted her hips to take in more of him and breached it herself. "Oh," she exclaimed.

He froze, feeling a slight sheen of perspiration break out on his skin.

"Margaret?"

"Yes?"

"I'm dying to thrust into you. Are you ready?"

"Yes." Her arms locked around him and her fingers pressed into his back.

Needing no further invitation, he drove himself slowly inside her. Then he drew back, and she made a noise of pure pleasure, which he could feel in his loins.

He could climax at any time, but looking down at her, vulnerable and utterly trusting, he controlled himself.

While fully seated inside her, feeling her body clamping around his, he paused. Resting on one elbow, he reached between them, twisting his hand until he had the angle he wanted, and then he proceeded to caress the bud of her desire.

Gasping, her eyes flew open. "John," she said on a breath of wonder before closing her eyes again as he touched her.

Continuing his ministrations, he was determined their first time would be equally enjoyable for them both. Barely moving his hips, he continued to stroke her with his fingers before lightly brushing her nub with his thumb.

Cam felt her climax as it started. Arching higher, all Margaret's muscles tightened under him and around him, sending him nearly into delirium.

"Ohh," she moaned, and the sensual sound caused sweat to break out on his forehead.

When her own release seemed to peak and crest, he pulled back and surged into her, pumping with all the pent-up passion of having wanted this woman for an eternity. His body tightened, released, and he felt his seed spend inside her.

In the next moment, Cam desperately wanted to collapse. Instead, he rolled to the side, taking his wife with him.

They lay in silence for many minutes.

At last, she stirred, opening her eyes, brushing her fingers over the hairs of his chest as she sighed.

"Happy?" he asked.

"Very. John, I'm glad we waited until after being wed." She stretched and made a soft humming sound of satisfaction. "If we'd done what just occurred," she added, "and *then* had broken up . . . actually, I probably could not have left you at all."

He chuckled, stroking the smooth skin of her back. "In which case, I rather wish we *had* done it earlier."

"No," she protested. "You know I'm right. If I hadn't left, I fear you wouldn't have stopped taking the laudanum."

She was right. *Damnit! Was she always going to be right?*

Then he smiled with his mouth against her hair and realized he didn't mind at all.

"You were exactly right to leave me. And you were equally right to come back to me."

She laughed softly, and the sound filled him with peace, far more than opium ever had.

EPILOGUE

They sat upon the veranda early the next morning before anyone was awake. Maggie knew this would be their special place, one where they had intimate conversations, possibly even arguments, where they would make up, too, before going upstairs to make up properly. Here, they would play chess, entertain friends, and watch their children run on the grass. Maybe John had already planted a child in her womb.

"I hope you're smiling because of me." He held her hand while they sipped tea.

"I am." She was glad to be home. And it absolutely felt like her home. Having him drive her away with his unkind words had been among the worst moments of her life, along with finding out he'd been injured. Coming back had been the sweetest.

"I made it easy on you," she told him, thinking of the hallway at Stafford House and how quickly she'd acquiesced.

Grinning, he nodded. "Because you love me as I love you."

"Obviously. But if I had not been won over, what would you have said? I mean, if I had wished for you to grovel a little for being such a cad?"

"Cad?"

She nodded.

"*Hmm.* I suppose I would have complimented you on your appearance. Yes, I would have said, 'Margaret, you're a diamond of the first water.'"

She twisted her mouth in disgust. "Then I am glad you didn't. That phrase is so hackneyed as to be almost an insult."

"Really?" He stroked his chin thoughtfully, where his overnight shadow of growth made him look terribly dashing and sensual. She might not let his valet remove it later.

"Then I suppose I would have told you how I admire your thoughts and your skill at chess?" His tone sounded as if he was asking a question.

She giggled. "Better, I suppose. It is a good thing the queen was there for you to make your grand gesture."

"What queen?" he asked.

"Oh, that is good." She loved how he teased her.

"I could see no woman there except you."

"Even better, my lord."

"If you hadn't been won over by my surprise arrival and the return of my dashing good looks," he grinned, then grew serious, "then I might have confessed to how bloody awful it was after you left."

"I'm sorry," she said. "It would have killed me to see you suffering that way."

"I never knew one could want to live and die at the same time, but I did. Every time I reached over to the drawer where I had kept the bottle, I encountered Eleanor's drawing of you. I put it right there to remind me why the hell I was in such agony."

She put her hand to her mouth, shaking her head.

"It worked, you know. I must remember to thank your sister." He sipped his tea and looked into the distance. His next words were so quiet, she almost missed them. "I still crave it sometimes."

Fear, like a bolt of lightning, passed through her. Before she could say anything, Cam turned to her, holding her gaze with his.

"Don't worry. I am telling you because I'll never lie to you again. And I'll never give into the craving, either."

She entirely believed him. After all, he was the most fearless man she knew.

Leaning over, he kissed her. First her lips, which tingled delightfully, then he trailed warm kisses down her neck, causing her to arch into him.

"Mm."

"I love that sound," he confessed. "I intend to be the cause of it for the rest of my life."

"Good!" Sinking her fingers into his thick hair, she raised his head and kissed him in return. Her happiness bubbled over.

"Enough sitting, don't you think, my lord? Let's pretend we're at a particularly boring ball and go for a stroll."

She waggled her eyebrows at him, and he laughed with a husky tone that made her quiver.

"Perhaps to the river," she suggested, glancing at the house with its many windows, "away from prying eyes."

He was on his feet practically before she finished speaking.

"To the fishing hole," he proclaimed, "where I shall give you a lesson."

They ambled down across the brick and onto the grass.

"I don't need to be schooled by you in how to fish." She swept her curls over her shoulder and walked faster, thinking of other things they could do at the water's edge.

Catching up with her, John grasped her hand, matching his stride to her shorter one.

Maggie couldn't imagine being any happier. Then her husband stroked the soft skin on her wrist, and she shivered.

"I shall think of some other lesson," he promised. "Because I am a generous teacher, and I have a most willing pupil. What would you like me to teach you?"

Stopping, she stood upon her tiptoes and whispered in his ear, delighted when his eyes widened and a slight blush appeared on his handsome face.

Flashing her smile, she broke away, running toward the Great Ouse, with laughter upon her lips and her heart filled with love. Hearing his solid, steady footfalls behind her—her earl, now healthy and strong—she thought it the best sound in the world.

ABOUT THE AUTHOR

USA Today bestselling author Sydney Jane Baily writes historical romance set in Victorian England, late 19th-century America, the Middle Ages, the Georgian era, and the Regency period. She believes in happily-ever-after stories for an already-challenging world with engaging characters and attention to period detail.

Born and raised in California, she has traveled the world, spending a lot of exceedingly happy time in the U.K. where her extended family resides, eating fish and chips, drinking shandies, and snacking on Maltesers and Cadbury bars. Sydney currently lives in New England with her family—human, canine, and feline.

You can learn more about her books and contact her via her website at SydneyJaneBaily.com.

Lightning Source UK Ltd.
Milton Keynes UK
UKHW010336281220
375792UK00002B/609